The Adventures of Monsieur de Mailly

BOOKSHIP

THE ADVENTURES OF MONSIEUR DE MAILLY

(a.k.a. *A Blade for Sale*)

by

David Lindsay

Published by Bookship, 2019.
First published by Melrose, 1926 in the UK.
Published as *A Blade for Sale* by Robert M McBride & Co., 1927 in the US.

ISBN 978-1-9996269-2-1

Contents

I

The Nephew of the Sieur de Jambac

Towards the close of a dismal afternoon in March, 1700, the Sieur de Jambac, having completed the ascent of the fourth flight of stairs in one of the oldest and most ramshackle houses of the Rue du Mail, Paris, paused for a moment on the top landing to recover his breath, adjust his wig, and put his attire to rights. He next proceeded to examine the card, yellow with age, which was pinned to the door immediately facing him, and found it to bear the superscription: "Monsieur Jean Fleurus, Notary Public." This being the individual he had come to seek, he set his hand on the latch, and entered without ceremony.

The lawyer, whose face was shaped somewhat like that of a horse, looked sharply up from his desk by the window, to behold a gentleman of sixty or thereabouts, stately, tranquil in manner, and even fashionably dressed, but still obviously from the provinces. To the length and leanness of his body was joined a certain self-conscious stiffness which could only arise from an existence passed in a small and friendly society, outside which the world was full of pitfalls to be guarded against. However, since country purses were as good as town ones, Fleurus promptly descended from his stool, bowed respectfully to the stranger, and stepped across the room.

"You are the notary Fleurus?" asked the gentleman.

"At your service, monsieur."

"I am the Sieur de Jambac. . . . Is that person asleep?"

He pointed a finger to a young man lying at full length on a wooden bench for callers near the door. His eyes were closed, his breathing was heavy and regular, but as he was not actually snoring, the question was legitimate. Hat, wig, and sword, in a heap on the floor beneath him, seemed to establish his gentility, yet why a gentleman should elect to sleep in daytime in a lawyer's office, Jambac could not fathom. Whatever his reasons might be, he was a remarkably ugly fellow, though of a good-humoured type of ugliness—short, broad-chested, a pale face, pitted by the ravages of smallpox, with black hair, a wide mouth, excellent teeth, and eyebrows arching outwards, the sign of an imaginative mind. A countenance full of character.

Fleurus followed his prospective client's gaze with a shrug of vexation.

"Yes, he is asleep. It is a customer."

"The law is very fatiguing!" said Jambac dryly.

Recognising a *mot*, the notary hastened to complete his resemblance to a horse by neighing loudly.

"That is to say, he has patience, monsieur; and patience is the main thing."

"I have no doubt. But do you always laugh in that way?"

Fleurus made all speed to restore to his face its professional gravity. "I do not often laugh at all, monsieur. In my trade there is not much to laugh at. It was that your remark appeared to me droll."

"H'm. . . ." The visitor stared around him critically. "However! I have heard of you, and I have come here with a case. You will see what you can make of it. Bring me a chair, and send your sleepy gentleman packing!"

"He is better so, monsieur. He is really asleep, but when he wakes he will start to be troublesome again, and I shall not easily get rid of him."

"Then set the chair as far from him as may be, and I will speak softly."

Fleurus brought, not one chair, but two, to the desk by the window.

"Do you mean to sit also?" demanded Jambac bluntly.

"So I shall listen more at ease. Also my legs are weak."

"Since, however, my case does not concern itself with your legs, but with your head only, I shall beg you to treat me with the customary respect."

"Monsieur . . ."

"A gentleman, because he entrusts his affairs to you, is not thereby constituted a tavern companion, I hope."

The notary bowed angrily, and withdrew the second chair.

"It seems you are not very well up in these civilities," pursued Jambac, staring hard at him. He seated himself. "Let us have confidence that you are better versed in the interpretation of the law. You claim to know your profession?"

Not trusting himself to speak, Fleurus bowed again.

"We shall see! Your manners do not reassure me, and it may yet be that I shall have to take my case elsewhere. It is not straightforward, to begin with. It is not a quarrel over a bone. No one has stolen my property, and no one has run off with my wife—even if I had one, which I have not. My affair is not any of these. If you handle the simpler sort of cases only, you will say so at once."

"I undertake all sorts, monsieur; and, for example, I do not violate any confidence when I inform you that I have at this very moment some half-dozen of a complicated interest which I think will challenge comparison with that of an equal number on the list of any other lawyer in Paris; in other words, in France."

Jambac produced a snuff-box, and fed his nostrils with composure.

"Yes, but there are cases which do not come within the purview of the law at all, and I do not know that mine is not such. Certainly, equity must pronounce for me, but that is another matter. . . . However, since I am here, I shall tell you. I find myself, then, in an intolerable *impasse*. I am persecuted."

"There will be no difficulty in bringing an action for a real persecution, monsieur, but if it be imagined only, it will largely depend."

"I do not want an action. I desire the persecution to cease."

"Describe its nature, if you please!"

Jambac made an airy, yet dignified gesture.

"It is a woman."

"That does not make your affair better, but worse, monsieur. A case in which a woman appears already promises to be vexatious. Proceed, however! you would say that this woman persecutes you. Then we shall see if there is no statute to fit her malpractices.”

“It is a lady, a country neighbour, who is set upon joining herself to me in matrimony, against my inclination.”

Fleurus smiled. “That she cannot do, save by persuasion.”

“However, you had better wait to hear the particulars. I say it is my nearest neighbour, where I live, at a place not fifty leagues from Paris. Also, I will not go so far as to affirm that the match is in itself unsuitable. Her birth is good, her connections are great and influential, she has not always been unknown at Court, her estate is vast; if she is fifty, I am still older; if she has the stature of a grenadier and the manners of one, it cannot be denied that she possesses a high degree of *esprit* and character. It simply is, then, that I do not wish at my age to become entangled in a petticoat, having had the good fortune hitherto to view the sex from a prudent distance. In respect of marriage, I am quite of Montaigne’s opinion. A marriage is an unequal contract. If women gain by the state—and unless they gain, why have they made it the principal affair in life?—then men must lose to an equivalent extent. The argument has a mathematical exactness which cannot be gainsaid, and until someone can clearly demonstrate to me its fallacy, I shall not, by the free exercise of my will, marry. . . . In any case, I do not think that I have, during my sixty-two years of life, steeled my resolution against a score of youthful beauties, only to sink upon the withered bosom of a dowager at last!”

“That might at another time form the ground of a very agreeable debate, monsieur. As it happens, I myself am married, and extremely happily; my sympathies, therefore, are not with your logic. However, the point is, you do not want to marry. Continue, I pray!”

Jambac stared him to silence.

“If you are to interrupt me so persistently, I shall not know where I am.”

“Having described the lady, monsieur, you were about to come to her misconduct.”

"Then her misconduct is this. She wearies me with her attentions, she makes me a laughing-stock, and the thing rapidly approaches a scandal. That is everything in brief. I could furnish twenty instances, but refrain from doing so. If you cannot, from the bare summary, comprehend the sort of persecution that I mean, there is little use in going forward. Either you are acquainted with women, or you are not."

"Nevertheless, the mere infatuation of a woman for a man, however publicly expressed, is not in itself an offence against law," said Fleurus sharply. "You do not pretend that she has assaulted you, monsieur?—and in this sense, a kiss or an embrace, for example, might be construed, technically, as an assault."

"*Pardieu!*[1] she has not yet forgotten herself to that extent, though who can say what is germinating within her?"

"Until the seed has become an individual, the law cannot recognise it. You will have to say what she really has done, monsieur. Has she trespassed on your estate? That might be used against her."

Jambac moved impatiently. "Pshaw! we cannot avoid our neighbours in the country. You would not have me shut myself up a prisoner in my house, I hope? There are constantly visits of ceremony, parties of pleasure, the chase, and what not. I suppose that we encounter each other thrice or four times a week, in the ordinary course, without premeditation. It cannot be avoided. In the country we are a happy family, living in a residence the apartments of which, it may be, are separated by leagues of field and forest. What the devil would it effect to have my fellows keep her out? The scandal would suddenly explode, that is all."

"Then I can only see slander. Slander is a reasonably elastic plaint, and if you can bring witnesses to prove that she has put sentiments into your breast which do not properly belong there— if she is disseminating injurious reports concerning an affection for her on your part which has no existence in fact . . ."

"Yes, but I keep telling you that I do not want an action. The affair has gone quite far enough, I fancy, without dragging it into the courts. Because twenty now snigger at me behind their hands, is that a reason why I should procure all France to roar aloud? The absurdity is not that she slanders me, but that she forgets her sex to court me. It is humiliating that the Sieur de Jambac must blush and stammer in society because of the mad fancies of a witch without beauty to recommend her; but assuredly it will not improve matters to have each one of her sighs, glancings and oglings neatly set forth for the edification of a crowd of grinning judges and lawyers, thence to be circulated to the whole world! You must think of something better than that!"

Fleurus scratched his head in perplexity.

"Well, then, monsieur, we must frighten her. We must threaten her with this action, without actually bringing it to the push. We must make a show of suborning witnesses, and so forth. She will see that you are in earnest in detesting her, and, being after all mature and wealthy, she will think twice before sending good money after a failed passion. I shall write her a preliminary letter. In the majority of cases, a preliminary letter is all that is required."

"The scheme is admirable!" said Jambac dryly, again helping himself to snuff. "The only objection to it is that a suit, I suppose, will take six months at the least to come before the court. . . ?"

"It will depend."

"Whereas, if things go on as at present, she will have married me in as many weeks! Judge if she will be exceedingly alarmed at a lawsuit of which the plaintiff will be her own husband, and the disputed matter, her right to annoy him with attentions! You must still think better."

The notary smiled. "There is always one more way with the law, monsieur! Provided that I am able to satisfy the court officers that the case is not intended to come on, I have no doubt that I can procure the announcement of its coming on immediately; but it will cost money. It is for you to decide."

"I do not know. How much will it cost?"

"I shall make some circumspect inquiries. Monsieur stays in Paris awhile?"

"For a few days. I am here with my nephew, M. de Fargues. We lodge at a tavern in the Rue des Capucines. You had better send to me there; and in the meantime I shall have thought whether this contrivance of yours is the best. I may tell you at once that I am not a fool; consequently I am quite agreeable to parting with gold, but only on condition that I am the principal one to be benefited. Because I am a provincial gentleman, while you are a Paris lawyer, that is not to say that I am to be pumped by you. So we shall investigate what your notion is worth. You may wait upon me in person if you prefer it, but I am never visible till after noon."

"I shall appear to-morrow, then, monsieur. But what is the name of your tavern?"

"My memory grows worse; it has escaped me. . . . I fancy it is some animal. I am nearly sure that it is the *Cheval Blanc*."

"Then I am very sorry for you, monsieur!" A pleasant voice sounded from the bench by the door.

Jambac and the notary turned quickly, to perceive the gentleman with the pitted face in the act of stooping to pick up his wig. He retrieved it, to clap it carelessly on his head; then, after assuming his hat and sword, he sat upright on the bench, facing the pair with a good-humoured smile.

"They say, monsieur," he continued, "and my experience tends to confirm it, that the wine sold there is so vile that an apothecary is permanently resident on the premises for the purpose of treating sick customers. 'Tis also affirmed that the beds are not exactly as peaceful as the tomb; but on that point I cannot personally pronounce."

Fleurus strode towards him furiously.

"The *Cheval Blanc* is known to everyone in Paris as an establishment of the first class, regularly patronised by the most distinguished persons. Do not heed this gentleman, monsieur! He is a wit."

Jambac brushed a trace of dust from his coat nonchalantly.

"I do not object to wit, but I dislike people who fall asleep in the wrong place, in order to awake at the wrong time!"

The young man rose to his feet, stretched his limbs, with fists clenched, and stifled a yawn.

"Monsieur, you do not speak at all rationally. When my eyes closed, you were not here; they open themselves, and you are here. Was I to know that you intended this visit? You should have waked me at the beginning. The complaint is silly."

"M. de Mailly," said the notary, "I beg you to go away quietly at once. I discuss business with a client. You have no right in my office, and I insist upon your immediate departure, without another word!"

Mailly smiled provokingly. "Thus it turns out well that I have an appointment for this hour. Yet how am I to fulfil it? 'Tis at the *Trois Fontaines*, these fountains spout wine only, which must be paid for, and my purse . . ."

"In a word, monsieur, you want money, as usual! Very well, I shall give you some, but on one condition only; that you do not babble over your cups of what you may perhaps have dreamt during your slumber here. There are five pistoles![2] 'Tis more than you deserve, seeing that you deserve none at all, and I cordially hope that you will not show your face again for many weeks."

Mailly pocketed the coins carelessly.

"*Peste!* you compel your money to work hard for you, Fleurus! And have not I told you over and over again that I do not accept bribes? It is not five miserable pistoles which will prevent my relating a ridiculous dream, if I choose to do so. Fortunately for you, I am a gentleman. You have my word for it that I shall not publish the intelligence that Monsieur stays with his nephew at the *Cheval Blanc*, perhaps to study the grape in its most curious forms."

Fleurus flung the door wide.

"I cannot tell whether you have overheard everything or not," he said in a quick, low voice, intended only for Mailly's ear, "but do not be in haste to spoil this case for me, for I promise you that will finally close our acquaintance. Prudently handled, it will bring me something substantial; and you shall participate. Do not come to me till next week. The situation is very delicate. Do not speak a word to anybody. I confide in your honour and good sense."

Mailly went downstairs laughing, and, upon reaching the bottom, gave an additional cock to his hat, before passing into the street.

In the gathering dusk lights were being lit in the tall houses, the upper storeys of which nearly met overhead, across the narrow thoroughfare. A melancholy drizzle descended, and the gutter swam with liquid mud. Whether it were due to abstraction or whether he had another and more urgent appointment at the *Cheval Blanc*, it was to that hostelry, in the first place, and not to the *Trois Fontaines* that he directed his steps. In so doing, he utilised his intimacy with the geography of Paris especially to avoid those streets which permitted wheeled traffic; for there, on such an evening as this, the flying splashes of undesirable black paste would amount to a veritable cannonade.

The windows of the *Cheval Blanc* were brightly illuminated, while throngs passed in and out of its doors. Mailly entered with the rest. Ambert, the short, bow-legged, red-faced, truculent-eyed host, was standing in the centre of a group of gentlemen who obviously were from the country, such was the deferential awe with which they received his conversational pronouncements. Mailly took his salute coldly.

"Good evening, Ambert! Thus you are still coining gold from wine?"

"Fortune smiles on you too, M. de Mailly, since we see you here again!"

"Faith! you have a queer notion of smiling! However, this time I have not come to drink your liquors, but to visit a gentleman who lodges with you—one M. de Fargues."

The landlord detached himself from his circle.

"He is on the premises, I think, M. de Mailly, but I do not know where. An hour ago he was on his way to drinking himself insensible. As he will certainly not last out the evening, it is lucky you have called so early."

"Be so good as to have him found for me!"

Ambert beckoned to a server.

"Conduct M. de Mailly to M. de Fargues, wheresoever he may be! It is probable that he has descended to the cellar."

"In case the house is dark, here is something to light the way!" said Mailly, selecting from the coins which he drew from his pocket a half-pistole, and flicking it to the man, who caught it with a dexterity born of long practice.

At the end of the passage, a wooden ladder went down to the vaults. They lowered themselves. A tallow dip set on the stone floor showed Mailly a tall young gentleman, sitting insecurely astride an empty cask, a glass in one hand, while the other emphasised the points of a discourse he delivered to Charles, the cellarman, who stood before him, in baize apron and turned-up shirt-sleeves, a sheepish grin on his face. The gentleman's countenance was wooden, impassive, big-featured, and very pimpled. Suddenly aware of newcomers, he broke off his harangue, threw a cold, unseeing glance in their direction, finished his wine at a gulp, and silently passed the glass to Charles to be replenished.

The server smiled. "M. de Fargues, here is one to see you!"

Fargues looked round again.

"'Tis well, and you may go. . . . What can I do for you, monsieur?"

Mailly advanced politely. "I have come to drink with you a little, monsieur."

"That is good news! But I think I do not know you?"

The server returned upstairs.

"*Peste!* every acquaintance has to begin," remarked Mailly lightly. "At least, if you do not know me, your uncle, the Sieur de Jambac, does so. 'Tis a sort of introduction. I hope you are not to be unsociable!"

"My uncle is one person, and I am another," said Fargues, in a tone of solemnity. "Nevertheless, since you have set your heart upon drinking with me, I am not proud, and I will drink with any gentleman. Therefore, fresh glasses, Charles!"

Mailly grimaced.

"But not here, monsieur! I have just awoke from sleep, and my throat is like a furnace. Do not require me to desecrate a virgin thirst by absorbing Ambert's vinegar."

"That is a true word. I have felt it from the beginning, but I have put it off and off. Well, then, we will patronise another house. Charles, be obliging enough to assist me to disencumber my legs of this miserable barrel. I am to leave you. Whither do you take me, monsieur?"

"There is a charmingly quiet little place, not a pistol-shot from here. . . . Charles, here is a half-pistole for you! M. de Fargues seeks the Sieur de Jambac. I accompany him to the top of the stairs only. You cannot now be beautiful, so be discreet instead!"

Charles accepted the coin with a cheerful wink.

"I think that he will be discommoded as soon as he feels the fresh air, M. de Mailly."

"But if so, we shall attribute it to the atmosphere, and not to your cask-wash."

"And if so, beast," added Fargues, "the proof will be that I shall return here to cut your ears off! Monsieur—what the devil is your name, again?"

"De Mailly."

"Then pray precede me up this accursed ladder, while Charles plants my feet from behind. 'Tis a veritable death-trap, and all holes! I have never yet understood why the best part of a house should be approached with so little regard to convenience."

At the top, Mailly waited for him, laughing.

"Let us link arms," he suggested. "I have a light dizziness, brought about by the rainy weather."

"I have noticed that you were unsteady," replied Fargues gravely. "Do you suffer much in this way?"

"It will pass with the first glass. Therein I flatter myself that I differ from others, who are most certain in their movement when entirely sober. There has been one historical exception—Socrates. It is possible, however, that you are another."

"I am delighted to make your acquaintance, monsieur. I have always admired Socrates stupendously on that very account. For his philosophy, not so greatly. In my opinion, virtue is very much overrated. It is more for shopkeepers."

They joined arms, and, passing out by the back way and through the stable-yard, presently entered the street. Fargues's conversation began to take bold leaps. From shopkeepers he travelled to milliners, from milliners to ladies' maids, from ladies' maids to husbands, and from husbands to the last joke of M. de Lausun. By the time that he had reached this point, they were already arrived outside the *Trois Fontaines*.

At The "Trois Fontaines"—And After

The establishment was modest, and situated in a dark, silent and unfrequented court. Lights were in the windows, but nobody passed in or out. Fargues took from his pocket his purse, to hold it in his hand.

"You are to drink with me, monsieur," said Mailly with a certain nobility.

"I thank you," replied the other simply. "If I take my purse in my hand, it is because I have been told that your Paris thieves are enterprising, and I do not know what place we are coming to."

"*Parbleu!* that is different. Retain it there by all means, in that case. I do not know that the sight of your purse will keep off thieves, but it will assuredly keep off disrespect."

The public room of the tavern was deserted save for the host, Midard, who came forward, with sallow, smiling face and sleepy eyes, to meet them.

"Midard," said Mailly, returning his salute, "can you give us a private apartment, with a fire, for an hour or so?"

"In fact, I have two good rooms at your disposal M. de Mailly. In the wainscoted chamber a fire of oak logs is ready to be ignited, while in the little blue salon one of peat actually burns. The fumes of peat are declared to be exceedingly beneficial."

"I am very fond of peat," said Fargues.

"You hear Midard! We prefer the *salon*. And for wine. . . ."

"If you drink white wine this evening, monsieur, a very magnificent Xeres has just come to me from Bayonne."

"Six bottles, by way of commencement! Then we go upstairs at once."

"I will light you up, messieurs." Midard took a lighted candle. "You will inspect the room, and if everything is not exactly to your disposition you will tell me."

Fargues still held Mailly's arm. "They are politer here than at the *Cheval Blanc*," he whispered in a tone as loud as another man's conversational voice. "On future visits to Paris, I shall use this house."

The host halted to turn and bow, before continuing his progress along the passage and up the winding stairs. Arrived at the *salon*, he ignited with his one candle a branch of six others, stirred the peat fire, and drew a heavy velvet curtain across the window. The room was warm and cosy, while the shadows danced fantastically on the walls. Fargues sat down and yawned, but Mailly remained warming the back of his breeches at the fire.

Midard returned a few minutes afterwards with the basket of wine, glasses and a corkscrew. His guests having expressed themselves fully content, he finally took his departure.

Fargues emptied half a bottle before speaking again.

"'Tis fair, but I have tasted better!" he pronounced at last.

"In Paris?"

"I do not say in Paris, but at Montjeu."

"And where the deuce is Montjeu?"

"It is near Bar, which is not far from Troyes. It is my uncle's *château*, where he lives, and where I live with him, since neither of us is married."

"Drink, M. de Fargues! . . . You refer to the Sieur de Jambac, I think?"

"Yes. 'Tis all the uncles I have."

"And all you require, *pardieu!*—provided that this one is rich, and you his heir. You said that?"

"Yes, I am his sole heir, and the estate is superb."

"Then you are devilish lucky! Besides, he must be getting on in years. There cannot be any more fear of marriage for him, bringing with it new heirs and new successions."

Fargues scowled, and emptied another glass.

"You would think so. But *mordieu!* it seems women do not reckon by age, but by other considerations. There is a damnable conspiracy afoot, monsieur. Let us say no more about it!"

"So that your natural inheritance is not so assured, after all?"

"Bah! nothing is assured in this beast of a world, except

ingratitude. The woman I speak of—her name is Ruvigny—I ask you, has she sacrificed all her life to my uncle? Has she borne with his humours and caprices? Has she stinted herself for years on an insufficient allowance, in order merely to remain on polite terms with him? A thousand thanks, no! But she has watched another do all this, and when that other believes to reap his reward at last—for the leaf turns yellow—then *corbleu!* she snaps her fan together, rises to her feet, and holds forth her paw to my uncle with a smile.—'Take me, monsieur! I shall add my half-hour of life to your ten minutes, and together we will pace a minuet towards the grave!'" The parenthesis Fargues uttered in a high falsetto. "*Peste!* when these ancients start to imitate the loves of the young, 'tis but one step further to the cradle again."

Mailly laughed loudly.

"But does she pursue his estate or his person?"

"Her own estate is finer than Montjeu, and she wants nothing of him except kisses. 'Tis the most absolute moon-madness. I do not know whether one could not complain to the King."

"*Prutsch!* that would be a clever scheme!"

"At least, it is one."

"Come! Louis XIV is in years himself, and still addicted to the worship of Venus, 'tis said. Tell him that the old must not love, if you wish to, but do not ask me to stand beside you while you are saying it!"

"I know not what to do," said Fargues, "but I am very unhappy."

"Address yourself boldly and briskly to the lady, and make clear to her the unkindness of her conduct."

"I have done so, on set occasions—to say nothing of missives, innuendoes, and the like. 'Tis but three days since she has struck me, calling me *puppy*, and bidding me travel for my education's sake. I was minded to strike her back. My stomach was upset for all that day."

"Positively, she is an Amazon. But what replies the Sieur de Jambac to all this? Does he capitulate?"

"I assure you he is as terrified as myself, or more so. In pacing our chambers at night, the one hears the other. I affirm that it is the devil himself in petticoats, and she has him by the throat. What is to be done? He trembles, he weeps, the next day the assault is carried twenty feet further. She will marry him at last. Imagine that I do not abandon him, but things spin beneath my feet. I storm at him, I rave, I insist, I threaten desperate measures, I plaster this foul enchantress with calumnies; all is to no purpose, he is wax, and she will get her way!"

"And so you have drawn him to Paris for safety?"

Fargues tossed off a glass.

"He is here to see what the lawyers are able to do for him. As it is to remove him from Montjeu, I have not dissuaded him, but I have no such faith in law, I."

"Nor I, for I have seen too much of its working. I do not care what the suit may be, I will engage that the suitor will emerge from it altered in three respects; before it is over, he will be a poorer, an older, and a wiser man."

While Mailly, pleased with his aphorism, flung himself back in the recesses of his chair with a smile, Fargues, in deep dejection, rose unsteadily to uncork the second bottle.

He drank, and reseated himself.

"My dear monsieur," he said, in a melancholy voice, "through meditating this affair too profoundly, my soul has become of the consistence of treacle, and all my thoughts run together. What must I do to preserve my inheritance?"

"Bah! there is one thing that you might do; neither does it require a great deal of looking at."

"There are no males of her family to be challenged."

"But if there are no males, there is a female."

"In fact, I would fight her with pleasure, but it cannot be."

"I do not say fight her," replied Mailly carelessly, "but I say marry her."

"Ha!" exclaimed Fargues, after a moment's stupefaction. He set down his glass violently. "*Certes*, that is a scheme! I myself am to marry the witch. Yet where is the profit?"

"*Peste!* I rather fancy that two inheritances are better than none at all!”

“And where are two inheritances?”

“Your uncle’s and this other. Both must come to you. You will throw the two estates together, procure for yourself a title, and blossom forth a great *seigneur*. I do not understand why you continue to hesitate.”

“’Tis too simple, that is why. I shall think of reasons against it in a minute. Meanwhile, she is so old, and so infernally ugly!”

“Your wings will always be stronger than hers, and the world is wide.”

“That is very true. Then I will marry her. But I believe she will not have me.”

“Take her, monsieur, and thus make sure!”

“Ah, bah!” said Fargues, stumbling to his feet, in growing agitation, and holding on to a chair-back, apparently for no purpose whatever. “It is plain you do not know her. We do not marry this sort of woman at the point of the pistol. She would first knock out your teeth with the butt.”

“Shall we try, however? I do not talk of pistols. We are French gentlemen, not brigands. Leave it to me, and I will arrange everything. ’Tis practically settled in my head already. Listen, monsieur! We separate at Bar. . . .”

“But, my dear monsieur, we are drinking wine in Paris, and Paris is I do not know what number of leagues from Bar! First of all, let us be reasonable!”

“We shall take horses to-night, so as to arrive there to-morrow.”

“*Diable!* we lose no time. I think I cannot sit a horse to-night.”

“Then we shall hire a light conveyance. . . . Thus to-morrow we separate at Bar, in order to reunite later on. You, monsieur, will return to Montjeu, where you will have out your flimsiest closed carriage, your freshest pair of horses, and some half-dozen of your cleverest and most unscrupulous fellows, by way of escort. In the meantime I shall have hunted up a priest, and if I cannot get to hear of a secluded spot for our ceremony, *peste!* we will celebrate it by the side of the road. . . . Can you conceive a more straightforward elopement?"

"But what is the closed carriage to do?"

"Decidedly the wine has mounted to your brain! It is to fetch the lady."

"She will not come, however."

"It may be true that she will not come for you, but she will very assuredly come for the Sieur de Jambac. *En route* to Bar, I shall contrive some probable story. Your uncle is ill, or the like. It is a minor point, which is of no importance now. Having, then, coaxed your Ruvigny woman into your coach, your fellow will whirl you like the devil to our *rendezvous*, and pff—the thing is accomplished, before we have time to cool again. You will be man and wife, and on the way back to her house she will thank you for it. In civil life, as in warfare, I have noticed twenty times that it is always the plan without complications that does not fail."

"The King will punish me for this."

"And if so, 'tis worth a year in the Bastille to be heir to two great properties. But why should he punish you? Who will complain to him? Not Madame your wife, who must, after all, prefer a young husband to an old one, and who, besides, will be flattered to her bones by your compliment in abducting her. 'Tis the equivalent of affirming to her face that she is a second Helen of Troy for beauty, and for ever hereafter she will swear that her mirror lies. You will ascend in her vision as a paragon of taste for having been so civil."

Fargues applied himself to the bottle.

"And so we are to do—what?"

"*Pardieu!* monsieur, we are to stop drinking and make our way to the first stables. You have money?"

"It is a good scheme, and, for my part, I am with you. I have forgotten your name."

"My name is of no consequence, monsieur, but money is. I therefore repeat my question: have you any?"

"I shall give you five hundred pistoles."

"For my service?"

"Yes, for the scheme is excellent. Five hundred pistoles. It is not too much. On the other hand, it is not a sum you will find growing on every bush."

"Bah! five hundred, a thousand, two thousand—what signifies it! I shall rely on your gratitude when you shall come into your own. However, there will be expenses after I shall part from you to-morrow, and I have no time to return to my lodging. . . ."

Fargues opened his purse, and counted out ten pistoles.

"This is but my drinking-purse, so that I cannot give you more now. My money is at my inn. When I return there to acquaint my uncle with my departure, I shall bring it away."

"But the devil! my dear monsieur, your uncle must know nothing at all about it!"

"I must fetch my money, however, for I cannot leave it in Paris unguarded. Moreover, we cannot travel without any."

"But you will not see your uncle?"

"No, for after all, I have seen enough of him for one day, and he will only bore me with his tale of the lawyer. Should he catch sight of me in passing through the house, I shall merely nod my head affably and say 'Good evening!' He will thereby comprehend that I am in a morose humour, and he will leave me alone."

"Then I will accompany you to the *Cheval Blanc*, to make sure."

He rose, and set his hat on.

"What is the hurry?" asked Fargues, still holding on to the back of the chair, and swaying. "There is plenty of time, and she will not marry him to-night. We have three bottles to drink yet. 'Tis a subtle wine; one gets to like it."

"Midard shall reserve them for our return to Paris, monsieur. I will tell you why. My head cannot stand much more. If we do not depart at once, we shall perhaps not start for Bar this evening, and if not this evening, perhaps not at all. *Morbleu!* I should never forgive myself if I drank away your double-inheritance for the sake of another hour in a warm room. We shall drink in the dawn together, in more settled times."

"I have frequently noticed that it is only in the country that one meets with good drinking constitutions," responded Fargues. "For me, beyond a certain point, I never get much drunker; still, if you are delicate, you are delicate, and there is an end of it! All the same, it is a piece of rudeness to return good wine to the cellar, and I do not regard it as a favourable omen for our affair."

$$* \quad * \quad * \quad * \quad * \quad *$$

The music of seven o'clock played from a church belfry in the vicinity as, arm-in-arm, they re-entered the *Cheval Blanc*.

"Is it my imagination, or have we a large congregation here?" demanded Fargues.

"No, it is the fact," replied Mailly. "There is some commotion on foot."

The hostelry, in effect, was thronged. Men stood clustered, talking and laughing, in little groups. The host, remarking the entrance of the pair, waddled up to them, with his self-sufficient countenance and bold eyes.

"What is wrong, Ambert?" asked Mailly, where another would have inquired merely, What has happened?

"A gentleman has been carried off, M. de Mailly, that is all."

"*Peste!* you take it very easily! What gentleman?—and by whom?"

"I do not believe that you know him, monsieur, but M. de Fargues is sufficiently intimate with him. M. de Fargues, it is your uncle, the Sieur de Jambac."

"What!" cried Mailly.

"You are a liar!" said Fargues stolidly.

"Monsieur! . . . Here are plenty of eye-witnesses. Ask them. It occurred in this very room, and not twenty minutes since."

"But you permitted it?" demanded Mailly, cocking a stern eye at the landlord.

"M. de Mailly," was the firm reply, "I endeavour to obey the law, but it is not my duty to dispense it. I have no force here to resist armed parties. If I had, I could not command my tapsters to lay hands upon a lady of quality."

"What says this animal?" asked Fargues. "What lady of quality has encountered my uncle?"

"As to her name M. de Fargues, I do not know it. As to her person—tall, full-formed, purple-visaged, attired in the habit of a man, and looking like a man. . . ."

"*Mordieu!* it is she! She has arrived for him, and he is a lost soul!"

Ambert smiled maliciously. "With her were four tough fellows in livery. A closed carriage waited without. M. de Jambac was bundled in without ceremony."

"Wretch! do you speak of gentlemen in this way?" exclaimed Mailly, shooting glances of fire at the circle which had closed around them.

"I describe what happened, monsieur. It cannot be pretended that he entered willingly. Some recall that he was struck, but I did not see that."

"Yes, he was struck!" offered a voice from the crowd. "I witnessed it distinctly. His struggles angered her, and she caught his ear soundly with her open palm."

"'Tis she," repeated Fargues mournfully. "I had the fellow to that blow but three days since. She takes him back to Montjeu, and we behold the last act of the tragedy."

"Do not give up so soon," whispered Mailly in his ear. "We may still pursue them."

Ambert, whose ears were wide, caught the word "pursue."

"Better sup the porridge which is set before you, M. de Mailly," he said comfortably. "They are five, without the lady, and you are two."

"Unmitigated scoundrel! do you compare grooms with gentlemen?"

"Yes, monsieur, if the grooms are armed, as these are. And I shall tell you another thing besides. You will come up with them too late."

"Too late for what?"

"At least a priest was in the carriage, if that foretokens

anything!"

"A priest!"

"So that, unless Madame is one who cannot travel without her confessor, we must suppose that they are by this time nearly man and wife."

Mailly glared at the floor, hammered it impatiently with his toe, and repeatedly shrugged his shoulders. He could think of nothing more.

"Your uncle, then, is truly married, de Fargues!" he said, in a tone of defeat.

"Yes, and I shall go to bed," replied Fargues.

"Has the Sieur de Jambac left no message for his nephew, Ambert?"

"No, monsieur; he had no reasonable leisure. Madame, on the other hand, addressed to me from the window of her carriage some parting words, which she desired conveyed to M. de Fargues; but, since manifestly they were spoken in heat, I have forgotten them."

"Nevertheless, they may give us the clue to what we seek."

"M. de Mailly, they were insulting, this gentleman patronises my house, and I shall beg to be excused."

"I am able to repeat those words," said the same voice as before.

"Do so, monsieur, and we shall be grateful."

"She spoke thus, looking very flushed and triumphant, and I heard her: 'Bid M. de Fargues,' she said, 'absent himself from Montjeu until his uncle shall have communicated with him. Being in Paris, let him look for employment, as the allowance which he will henceforward receive from his uncle will no longer maintain him in a luxurious idleness. But should he,' she added, 'have the impertinence after this to show his face again at Montjeu, in spite of all, then will I cause him to be horsewhipped in the stables by the stable-lads, and his allowance to be entirely ceased!' After she had said so much, monsieur, the driver of the carriage prevented more, by whipping up his horses."

A great burst of laughter went up from the assembly. Ambert

discreetly retired. The heated air, the dazzling lights, and the uproar affected Fargues so disagreeably that he lurched against Mailly.

The latter lent him his arm out of the public room. Before finally leading him away, however, he stopped at the door to address the hilarious throng.

"Messieurs," he said, in a high, ringing tenor, sharp as a blade, "I, too, am very fond of laughter, and your joke appears to be a good one. My friend, who is indisposed, doubtless through drinking bad liquor, as I warned him, is to go to bed. Upon descending from accompanying him to his chamber, I shall request to be shown your jest. But, since I am a critic, if I find it to be not good, I shall take the liberty to indicate to the most argumentative among you its vices. And, messieurs, I caution you beforehand that my logic is very *acute!*"

Understanding that no one was to reply to him, and unable to meet the eye of any, he considered that he had sufficiently asserted his honour, and forthwith, while the room was still in a hushed and embarrassed silence, proceeded to escort Fargues through the doorway.

III

Breakfast With Mimizan

The ten pistoles of Fargues, together with the remnant of the five of Fleurus, disappeared with the first days of April. On a fair, sweet-smelling, mild, but heavily overcast morning Mailly, breakfastless at last and without the money requisite to purchase a breakfast, descended the dark and narrow staircase between his apartment and the house door opening to the Rue Michon, and passed outside. He stood for a minute looking down the street, rubbing his newly-shaven chin and screwing his eyes, in doubt as to which one of his acquaintances he should first consult on the all-important topic of his exchequer. He did not know that Fortune smiled at his elbow.

A friendly palm smote him heartily on the shoulder from behind. Starting round he found himself to be held by a well-dressed gentleman, of his own age, or but slightly older, whose tall, martial form, swarthy countenance, bold black, flashing eyes, and exquisitely crimson lips, proclaimed the identity of Pierre de Mimizan, his brother-in-arms of former days.

"Good morning, Gaston!" uttered the familiar, clear, nasal bass. "And in what hole, pray, have you hidden yourself during these five hundred years?"

They embraced warmly.

"I have not been abroad much," said Mailly, turning away to avoid the unflinching gaze of his old comrade. "I have been unfortunate."

"What! you do not mean an affair of justice?"

"Faith! no—I have not come to that. It is simply that I have been, and am, devilishly hard up."

"Bah!"

"Yes, yes—I too say bah! when I have money, but at present it is as I say; I have none. 'Tis very absurd, but true."

"You astound me, my dear fellow! You are actually without

funds?"

"*Peste!* it is plain that we regard things differently. It is the possession of funds which amazes me. I have forgotten how money is come by in these days."

Mimizan laughed. "Come to Court, Gaston! That is where money is made."

"I thank you. I am not sufficiently political."

"Political is good! Have not you a headpiece?—nothing else is necessary. Regard me! I have not done so ill, yet no one has yet accused me of having a special talent. I am brave, I go with my eyes open, the women favour me—that is all my catalogue. And I have fallen on my feet."

"I see it well, and I rejoice at your good fortune. For me, however, I have lost confidence; I am a man without luck."

Mimizan stared at the broad, pitted, sad, yet good-humoured face of his friend with something as nearly akin to compassion as his exuberant egotism would permit.

"Come, my dear fellow! what I have done, you can do—that is all I mean. But shall we discuss your case over breakfast, or have you already eaten?"

"At least, I will eat again, for the pleasure of your company."

"I have ordered some provender at the *Grand Gaspard*. The food there used to be passable. Of late, I do not come to Paris much. I follow the Court."

They began to walk.

"For my part, I live in a cave," said Mailly. "It was even unknown to me that you had quitted the Service."

Mimizan yawned. "There was no war, and I was bored. They say confidently that when the King of Spain dies there will be one with the Empire, backed by England[3]—I do not pretend to know. If so, perhaps I shall buy a regiment."

"*Diable!* Then you are very wealthy?"

"So-so, and moderately! I do not affirm that I am a power in France. I climb, and I shall continue to climb."

These few words had the effect of making Mailly very thoughtful, during the remainder of their brief journey to the tavern. When, soon afterwards, they had sat down to the meal which awaited them, in the quaint little first-floor apartment, overlooking the street, he believed that the time had arrived to solve the mystery of his old companion's advancement in life.

"Enlighten me, Pierre, for I am confoundedly ignorant—how is money made at Court? At play, for instance?"

"That is a source, but not the only one."

"Offices, appointments, sinecures, you mean?"

"They are very nice, if you can get them!" replied Mimizan, winking jovially.

The conversation was interrupted by the appearance of the serving-man.

"What liquor will messieurs drink?"

"For me, Burgundy," said Mailly.

"And for me," added Mimizan, "a tankard of small ale, sufficiently watered with schnapps. And when I say 'sufficiently,' Jacques, I mean let the proportions be equal. And let this great tankard be accompanied by another. . . . Yes, my dear fellow," he went on, after the man had departed, "there are still other ways, which come under no category, and which you must see for yourself to understand. And apropos, I think I may have something good to set before you, if positively you stand in need of employment. But before we talk of all that, let us investigate this famous pie, which, I freely confess, has for several minutes past excited my curiosity."

With geometrical accuracy, he sliced the magnificent confection into four equal parts, and, allowing two to remain in the dish for later service, proceeded deftly to transfer the other quarters to his own plate and Mailly's. The beverages having appeared, the two friends were left to their own society, and for a short time no sound was heard but the pleasant symphony of knives, forks and palates.

"Well, then, let us hear!" said Mailly at last, throwing himself back in his chair. "What is it that you have to put in my way? I am willing to undertake anything within reason, and am even prepared to turn courtier for it, though that is a sea I have not yet learnt to swim in. I cannot resist the belief, however, that it will be a little difficult for a novice to compete with that crowd of assassins, who have reduced to such delicacy the art of mounting to heaven on other people's shoulders."

Mimizan, whose mouth was full, held up his hand for silence.

"Listen! . . . All that is abracadabra. I know, for at one time I held the same superstition. Let us take any six men at Court. One is an assassin, perhaps. The other five are tailors' gentlemen, who do nothing, and congregate there as so many sheep. A soldier— that is to say, one who has had to exercise his wits, if only to keep out of fire—will go through those fops like a knife through cheese. 'Tis so, my dear Gaston, for I have seen it too often myself."

"Since you say so! But how does one gain a footing? Is it not essential that one should attach oneself to some personage of importance?"

"As to that, yes! 'Tis advisable, for people do not come running with open arms to greet one, on one's *début*. That is what we shall now arrange. Do you know the Marquis de Puy?"

"No. I know no one, Pierre. Let us start on that basis."

"'Tis a young sprig of the nobility, but recently come into his own. Affairs fatigue him, so I help him with his; and you, in turn, shall help me. Let us take a step forward. The Court, as you know, is still at Versailles."[4]

"Where I am to go?"

"You are acquainted with Versailles, however?"

Mailly coloured. "Let it pass as acquaintance."

Mimizan, having finished the last crumbs of the pie, and drained the second tankard, permitted his eye to roam meditatively across to the Burgundy.

"Has that wine body, Gaston?"

"'Tis a fair Beaune. Sample it!"

Mimizan drew the bottle across the table between two fingers, and, filling a glass, re-emptied it at a gulp.

"On the thin side! . . . So it is arranged we go to Versailles. What is the time—ten, eleven. . . ?"

"Nearer eleven, I think."

"Then I must hurry away. Puy's carriage starts at noon punctually for Versailles, and I have body-linen to buy. Be outside his Hôtel at that hour, my dear fellow. We shall travel in party."

"*Peste!* give me a little light on affairs."

"Afterwards!" Mimizan got up.

"But where is his Hôtel?"

"Rue Joigny. That is not your best coat, Gaston?"

"No, I have a better. But tell me, Pierre—how long must I stay at Versailles? I ask, because I hire my abode by the week, and it would be cursedly awkward were they to let it over my head during my absence."

"All going well, you should get back to-night. The business will not take an hour. It is but a conversation. . . . Let us have that waiter up, to pay for our devil of a pie, which already I begin to regret!"

"But do wait a moment!—the hour cannot be as late as we think. With whom is this conversation, and what is it to effect?"

"Poh!" replied Mimizan. "Can you ask, on an April morning? 'Tis an amour—a spring rash!"

"Our little marquis has seen his first violet of the season, doubtless?"

"Yes, nature has him by the ears. It is quite orthodox."

"And the fair *inamorata*, who is she?"

"A tall girl, my dear fellow; new to Court. A Milanese *signorina*, with yellow hair, a skin of marble, a voice running up and down the scale like the notes of a flute. Those who admire statues might even call her pretty. The name is Papiria Molfetti. Her birth is fair, her fortune indifferent. I have found out all about her. You have but to step up, and say 'good afternoon!'"

"But you, Pierre—why cannot you say this 'good afternoon!'?"

"As a last resource I shall do so, but Puy is known, I am known, we have modest dispositions, we do not wish to awake the unholy chorus. You, tumbled from the moon, my dear fellow, can effect what would be deuced awkward for us."

"There are no complications, however?"

"Bah! there never has been a simpler affair. 'Tis a classic model." And Mimizan crossed the room, to tug violently at the bell-rope.

"Then are they acquainted?" persisted Mailly, following him about.

"'Tis precisely this acquaintance that you are to arrange. Try to fix some little meeting. If she be coy, at least see if you cannot extract a few smiles for Puy, that he may at all events know that he is not walking on the wrong road."

The man appeared, to present the bill.

"Permit me to pay!" said Mimizan, producing a full purse.

"Very willingly," assented Mailly, and he added in a whisper, "I shall even take the opportunity, while your purse is out, to borrow a few pistoles."

"Whatever you think sufficient," said his friend, holding out the purse to him, and turning away.

"Thanks, Pierre!" Mailly took some coins. . . . "Then we shall meet later."

"Come better dressed, however, since you are to act as ambassador. And if I can serve you in any other way, my dear fellow, you have but to command me."

They separated in the street, Mimizan to go about his business, Mailly to return to his lodging, to change into that blessed other suit which he reserved for extraordinary occasions, and which, though no longer quite fashionable, was still rich and handsome.

At a few minutes before noon he made his way to the Rue Joigny. A carriage was drawn up, in the pale sunshine which had tardily appeared, before a large house at the far end of the street, and Mimizan was on the pavement beside it, yawning and stretching his arms, as though weary of a prolonged waiting.

"Am I late?" called out Mailly, as soon as he was within a conversational distance.

"No, but you have run it fine. Puy is just coming out, and we should have been off without you. . . . Come, get in, my dear fellow!"

The carriage was a closed one. Mailly entered, and at the same moment there emerged from the house a short, slight, insignificant, thick-lipped, bilious-faced young gentleman, supported by a footman in livery. He looked sleepy and stupid with recent dissipation. Following Mailly into the carriage, he sank down rather sulkily on the opposite seat, facing the horses. Mimizan then got in, and the footman closed the door.

They started off at a walking pace, over the cobbles.

"Whom the devil have we here?" demanded Puy, after having blinked at Mailly for half a minute. Mimizan yawned.

"If you do not know him by sight, marquis, you undoubtedly know him by repute. 'Tis M. de Mailly."

Puy bowed in a somewhat puzzled way, obviously having no recollection whatever of the name.

"I am delighted! Do you play *lansquenet*, monsieur?"

"Sometimes, monsieur," replied Mailly.

"I, too. I played till five this morning, and they skinned me to the tune of eight hundred livres and more. What with that and the bottle, I feel like a boiled scrag of mutton! I shall sleep all the way to Versailles. They can skin me of money, but they cannot skin me of sleep. Do you know the Duc de Coislin?"

"Not intimately."

"Do you know the Duc de Sully?"

"Come, marquis, he knows everyone," intervened Mimizan, still gaping. "He has not arrived from the Equator!"

"Is that coat in the newest mode?" inquired Puy of Mailly.

"It will be universal to-morrow, I am told. One likes to keep a little ahead."

"If you assure me of that, I shall order one like it. 'Tis *dégagé*,[5] yet dignified. Do remind me, Mimizan—my memory is all holes."

"Bah!" said Mimizan.

"Well, I shall close my eyes."

"Mailly is here to put a shoulder to our little affair, marquis. He is to see the *signorina* for us."

"The devil he is! We are gathering an army, it seems!"

"You must understand that he is very good at that sort of thing," pursued Mimizan carelessly. "What he does not know about women may be put upon the point of a cat's whisker. He is to procure a *rendezvous* for us."

"Do try what you can effect, my dear monsieur," said Puy. "She is enchanting—a lily, standing out amongst daisies and marigolds! Her voice comes from heaven. I shall never love another woman after this one." His eyes shut, and his head began to nod.

"But as to this meeting, monsieur," Mailly started to say. "Where and when . . ."

His words were interrupted by a heavy breathing, such as precedes the first gentle snore. Mimizan threw his hat and wig on to the opposite seat, and laughed heartily.

"*Peste!* leave her something, my dear fellow! If she is to capitulate, at least let her march out with the honours of war. Puy will be sufficiently accommodating. Let us fix, for example, six o'clock in the morning, on the Terrace of the Orangery—'tis all one to him, he will be there, I will bet a hundred pistoles!" And he went on laughing.

Not knowing the least in the world where the Terrace of the Orangery might be, Mailly thought it politic to look wise, and say nothing. Shortly afterwards Mimizan, too, closed his eyes.

Versailles was reached at half-past one.

IV

The Terrace Of The Orangery

The slumberers awoke, and the three gentlemen alighted in the Great Courtyard. Many idlers were there, on the watch for new arrivals. Scarcely had they completed the ascent of the staircase when the Marquis was separated from his companions by the throng of intimates who pressed upon him from all sides.

Mimizan hurriedly wrung Mailly's hand. "Here we part, my dear fellow. Puy and I have other fish to fry. Our little Italian is to be found in one of the attics of the New Wing. Go there and work your miracle! In two hours I shall stretch my legs a little in the Gallery."

Without pausing for a response, he hastened after his patron, who was in the act of disappearing from sight, escorted by a knot of familiars, all eager to impart their quota of fashionable scandal.

"But how the deuce am I to inquire for this same New Wing, without disclosing my ignorance of geography to these court crawlers?" reflected Mailly, standing fast, and pushing back his wig to scratch his head.

An elegant gentleman advanced upon him, with a mocking bow.

"You appear lost, monsieur!"

"On the contrary, monsieur, I am trying to find, something," returned Mailly good-naturedly. "It is the New Wing. . . ."

"And what are the present prospects for the crops this summer, monsieur?"

"Monsieur, I have the honour to request to be directed to the New Wing!"

"Hay, for example, does that shape well?" proceeded the gentleman calmly.

"*Pardieu!*" thought Mailly, "if I am from the country, I am from the country!" And he said aloud:

"Monsieur, I am somewhat hard of hearing, which prevents

me from catching all that you say, but I understand that you are one of the attendants so thoughtfully provided by His Majesty, to conduct strangers and newcomers at Court. Be so good, therefore, as to bring me to the New Wing. I shall fee you well. And since I fear we may become separated in such a crowd, I shall take your arm. Although I am a gentleman, you comprehend, I possess no false pride of that sort."

Before the other could realise his intention, Mailly had linked arms, and was drawing him forward.

His victim feared to struggle, lest he should provoke a scene. He expostulated, indeed, with some vigour, but it appeared that Mailly's deafness prohibited his perfect understanding of what was said. It was thus not until they had arrived at the foot of the staircase ascending to the upper apartments in the New Wing that the two parted. Mailly pressed a pistole into the gentleman's hand, in sight of all, and with a loud courtesy thanked him for his service.

On the first landing above, he stood aside to allow passage for two ladies who descended. One was a thin, handsome, quizzical creature, of twenty-eight or so, with charming limbs and laughing eyes. The other—a mere child, of perhaps nineteen—was tall, cream-faced, and demure; her violet eyes resembled pools, while her simply-dressed, unpowdered hair was of the colour of pale gold.

"If this does not prove to be the signorina herself, I will never listen to another programme of charms!" thought Mailly, and he saluted the pair respectfully.

The ladies returned each a slight acknowledgment, but were about to proceed downstairs. He bowed again, still more politely.

"Pardon the presumption, mesdames, but I believe that I have the honour to address Mdlle. Molfetti, and if so, 'tis very fortunate!"

They stopped. The senior lady smiled, the girl pouted her lips, fastening her eyes upon the floor at her feet. She had straight eyebrows.

"I am Mdlle. Molfetti," she replied, in a voice like a fountain.

"Speak, monsieur, if you really have business with me, but be brief, I beg."

"I shall even be terse, mademoiselle. My name—which, however, does not concern you—is de Mailly. I am the bearer of a message to you, but it is private." And he bowed once more to the companion.

"No matter for my friend, monsieur!" responded the girl, without in the least departing from her composure. "I have no secrets from her. Deliver your errand, if you please."

They moved further along the corridor, to be out of the way of people ascending and descending.

"From whom do you come?" demanded the elder lady.

"Madame, from M. le Marquis de Puy. Do you know him?"

The girl stole a long glance at Mailly, believing herself to be unperceived.

"It is that one who is unfortunate in his person, I think?" counter-questioned the companion, with a twinkle.

"No, madame, you have confused him with another. He is young, handsome, and fashionable."

"It is of no consequence. What wants he of us?"

"Of you, madame, nothing. Of Mdlle. Molfetti, a better acquaintance."

While the girl coloured, the other laughed.

"You are as good as your word, monsieur, and it is a veritable Lacedaemonian[6] that the Marquis has sent us for a messenger! But then, he is in love?"

"I shall not conceal it. He has been hit at long range."

The ladies began to talk together hurriedly, in Italian. The girl's eyes flashed fire, but her friend was merrier than ever. They ceased abruptly, and Mdlle. Molfetti now took it upon herself to address Mailly:

"You have no Italian, it is to be hoped, monsieur?"

"No, mademoiselle."

"Or you would have heard words not the most polite in the world! Now declare to me your proposition!"

Mailly bowed.

"Mademoiselle, we desire a meeting."

She was on the point of bursting into an ungoverned reply, when her friend forestalled her by saying, with a whimsical smile:

"But we are at Versailles, not in a desert, monsieur. Where, for instance, is it possible to meet?"

"The deuce! madame, that is very easily answered. M. de Puy, who loves nature and solitude, will take a turn on the Terrace of the Orangery to-morrow morning, at six o'clock."

"What!" exclaimed both ladies in chorus.

"That is to say, if they are to spy on us, we will at least have them out of bed for it."

"But do I hear you aright?" demanded the older lady. "The Terrace of the Orangery?"

"Your ears do not deceive you, madame, and in fact, speaking for myself, I think it would be difficult to hit upon a more admirable *rendezvous*. It is at once select and convenient."

"Do not go on insulting us, monsieur!" said Mdlle. Molfetti, in a low, but vehement voice. "I very well see what it is. It is a bet! I am a foreigner, and so it is permissible to make game of me!"

"Do not believe so, mademoiselle! I convey to you a genuine passion, and M. le Marquis de Puy really covets this meeting."

"No, it is a bet—it is a bet!" She tapped the ground rapidly with the toe of her little shoe. "I am alien, and on that account it is imagined that I shall not understand. I am to fall into your trap, *plomp*! But no!—every girl is not so simple. Return to your employer, monsieur. Let him offer his basket to some other innocent."

Once more the ladies turned their backs on Mailly, to pour forth twin torrents of Italian. The companion, holding her side mirthfully, appeared to be persuading to something. Presently the *signorina's* anger collapsed of a sudden, and she too began to laugh.

"*Peste!* they are to accept, but they do not appear to take it very seriously!" reflected Mailly uneasily. "Under the circumstances, I shall do wisely to levy toll on Puy's gratitude this afternoon, instead of deferring it until after the event."

The companion turned round to address him.

"Come then, monsieur! it is a settled thing, and we shall be there."

"It is very civil of you, madame! But not both of you, I hope?"

"Yes, for although M. le Marquis may possess excellent virtues, we still know nothing of him."

"Oh, fie, madame! what you propose is against every law. We might just as well arrange nothing at all. You give with the right hand, to take back with the left. Remember the needs of youth!"

"My memory is not of the strongest!"

"Madame, you are the youngest of all! But on that account you should be very tolerant."

The lady blushed and laughed.

"Would not a solution be that a fourth should be procured?"

"For to-morrow morning?"

"I am sufficiently rebuked!"

"Madame, there is an individual at Versailles who does not yet know of the great good fortune awaiting him. I shall accept the arrangement on behalf of my principal. Permit me, then, to be your envoy to this lucky cavalier, and we will settle everything out of hand. His name, if you please?"

"I may rely upon your discretion?"

"Certainly, madame."

"Well, then, I am of opinion that M. le Comte de Luxelles will be sufficiently gallant to bear me company at an unusual hour as soon as he is informed that I shall otherwise stand in grave danger of a personal assault at the hands of M. de Puy." She cast down her eyes.

"Ah, that good Comte!" said Mailly, who had never heard of him. "I go to him at once. But where is he to be found at this hour?"

"If not in attendance, he perhaps promenades the Gallery."

"I bet that he will not rack his wits for excuses, madame! But alas! I have to confess it—although your name is undoubtedly familiar to me, I am at a loss. . . ."

"But surely!"

"The admission humiliates me, nevertheless I must . . ."

"The mortification is mine, monsieur! I had imagined my face to be as well known as another's. However, I am Princesse de Coo."

Mdlle. Molfetti turned suddenly away.

"Where the devil is Coo?" asked Mailly of himself. "Bah! 'tis some little foreign principality. We shall not depart backwards from the presence of this one!"

He made a moderately humble bow. "So I shall hasten downstairs before you, madame, in order to get the affair arranged without delay."

She inclined her head graciously.

"Then where must I see you again, with my intelligence, madame?"

"We, too, go to walk in the Gallery, monsieur; but you are not being very polite!"

"In fact, if I find the Comte, there can be no necessary answer to bring back; but it is still possible that I shall fail to find him."

The Princesse smiled sweetly in condescension. Both ladies then returned very slight courtesies to Mailly's parting flourish of his hat. He proceeded down the staircase, and, as he did so, a faint feminine tittering caught his ear, coming from behind.

"*Diable!* 'tis a romance that transforms itself into a comedy," he meditated. "Let us see what they intend! I think that they well keep this tryst, for otherwise they will lose the cream of the joke; but on the other hand, I fancy that Puy will not be greatly forwarded by attending on his part. That is not my affair. I am to arrange the meeting, and I have arranged it. It is decidedly to-day, therefore, that I must receive my fee, and slip away. Moreover, Mimizan is no fool. By this hour to-morrow the jest will be circulated throughout Versailles, and all concerned will have the gauntlet to run. Hence, perhaps, the breakfast and the purse! Already I start to feel not quite so grateful to this good friend. Bah! 'tis some poison in the air here. A fortnight in such a warren, and my left eye would begin to suspect my right of winking unperceived. I shall hasten to effect my escape while I have still a portion of innocence remaining to me.”

A few minutes later, as he stepped thoughtfully along the Gallery, wondering how to set about discovering his Comte, two youths passed by, laughing and turning their heads to review a group which followed not far behind.

“Behold Luxelles, with his Academy!” said one to the other.

Mailly halted, so as to half-face the advancing group.

“*Peste!* this luck of mine savours of diabolism!” he reflected. “I have but to want someone, and I am instantly obliged. I shall play to-night.”

The little knot of noisy gentlemen came up. The only one who maintained a decent reserve was Luxelles himself, whom Mailly was able to identify from the circumstance that all the rest turned to him as to their chief. He was perhaps fifty years of age. His sallow face was heavy, fleshy, and large-featured, while his big chin wagged slowly in silence from side to side, as though he were masticating. His eyes resembled those of an elephant.

Removing his hat, Mailly stepped forward, fastening a steady regard upon the Comte.

“Do you wish to speak to me?” asked the latter in a drawl. The whole group stopped, and became quiet.

“Yes, monsieur—provided you are M. le Comte de Luxelles?”

“I am he.” He calmly signed to his bodyguard to wait, and drew Mailly into a retired alcove.

“Well, monsieur?”

“M. le Comte, I shall be very brief, since I see that you are in company. My name is de Mailly, and I represent Mme. la Princesse de Coo.”

The Comte’s eye wandered over Mailly’s person, but he went on chewing, without comment.

“The Princesse desires to notify to you, M. le Comte, that she will take a turn upon the Terrace of the Orangery to-morrow morning, at six o’clock. I have the honour to await your commands!”

After a moment of reflection, Luxelles looked towards his friends, and raised his voice to speak to them, without, however, permitting it to become either loud or hurried.

"Messieurs, attend, if you please! This gentleman is M. de Mailly. Mme. la Princesse de Coo will promenade the Terrace of the Orangery to-morrow morning, at six o'clock precisely."

A roar of laughter greeted the announcement. The Comte continued to masticate gravely.

"Leave me, messieurs!" he added. "I desire to arrange things, and I shall rejoin you after. Do not speak more of this business than you feel compelled to!" He set a finger against the side of his nose.

There was a second outburst of unseemly mirth, and the Academy passed along. Mailly, pale with indignation, and shrugging his shoulders, watched its members disperse, some going this way, others that. The Comte turned to him with a polite bow.

"I thank you for an excellent joke! Those gentlemen require to be fed constantly."

"M. le Comte, I do not know the procedure here for the punishing of insults, but had this happened elsewhere, I promise you I would first of all have pulled your ears!"

"Thus you are new to Court?"

"Whether I am so or not, is not in question. I affirm that you have fastened a public ignominy upon Mme. la Princesse, and through Mme. la Princesse upon me, her envoy."

"Not the least in the world!" replied Luxelles composedly. "There is no such person, and if a lady jokes with me, I shall joke with her, that is all. If you take such ready offence at innocent jests, my dear fellow, you will get yourself into bad odour here."

"The devil—a pseudonym, then?"

"Very much so! However, I shall not pretend that this fair mask is altogether strange to me. It is she who affects Italy, I fancy?"

"It does not import, for you have spoilt all now. The Terrace of the Orangery will be impossible for everybody after this. You should rule your tongue better, M. le Comte."

"Not at all, and if I demolish the Terrace of the Orangery, it is because I wish it to be demolished. Know, my dear fellow, that I already have an assignation there with another lady, for a somewhat later time to-morrow. I prefer the one you bring me, and so I have chosen this means to render the other impossible. You have just admitted it. But will you complete your kindness?"

"Speak!"

"Be my ambassador to the disappointed. Explain to her my grief at the notoriety which will to-morrow morning be given to the Terrace of the Orangery, bid her have patience, say that I shall think of something else, but be careful to do all this less in words than by winks and nods, and, above everything, do not name my name. If you cannot be delicate, do not go at all. She will probably profess not to understand what you are talking about. I shall await your return here, and meanwhile some other *rendezvous* will have occurred to me for our Princesse de Coo."

"*Pardieu!* I shall go from one to the other until there are no more left!" thought Mailly. He inquired without enthusiasm:

"Then who is it?"

"'Tis that little Noircamp woman. Do you know her?"

"No."

"So you must positively undertake the mission if only to make her acquaintance. You will be delighted; she is all soul. Go at once, my dear fellow. It is the Governess of the Maids of Honour to the Duchess of Burgundy. Her apartments are on the second floor, looking out on to the Court of Princes."

"Well, I will go, if it is only to say that."

"You need not add another word. But I repeat, do not mention my name, even should she pretend anger. That is important. Her office demands that she shall set an example in her conduct; and, between ourselves, 'tis the only affair that she has, as far as I know."

Mailly departed.

Madame de Noircamp, by good fortune, remained in her apartments, and he was admitted quickly.

Upon entering the room, he involuntarily staggered backwards, for the sole occupant did not in the least conform to the anticipation planted in his mind by Luxelles's eulogy, though it was true that the Comte had referred only to her spiritual qualities. If the lady who bridled at his entrance were still under sixty-five, she aged badly. Her mouth was of the shape of an O, what little chin she possessed was sparsely sprinkled with black bristles, while her skin resembled cork. To make amends to Venus, her attire continued very gay and youthful.

"Madame," said Mailly, intending a speedy retreat, "I heartily beg your forgiveness for my intrusion! They have shown me to the wrong place. I seek Mme. de Noircamp."

"I am she, monsieur."

"I mean that one who is Governess of the Maids of Honour to the Duchess of Burgundy."

"I am she."

"*Peste!* we must go cautiously to work," he thought. "This is perhaps another of Luxelles's jokes; while, on the other hand, he may really have appointed a place of meeting for so withered a branch, with an eye to one of her charges." And, bowing again, he said:

"Well then, madame, I shall build upon the identity, since you assure me. I have the honour to bear a message from one who shall be nameless, but whom you will be able easily to recognise from the circumstance that it has been arranged between you to meet no later than to-morrow morning, at an early hour. Need I speak more plainly, madame?"

"You are impertinent, monsieur!" The words were sucked in, as though she were imbibing lemon-juice from a spoon. "I do not arrange meetings at all, and I have certainly arranged none for to-morrow."

Mailly admired her discretion, but proceeded:

"However, I shall assist your memory by remarking that it is that one for the Terrace of the Orangery."

Mme. de Noircamp emitted a strange, weak laugh. "That would indeed be pleasant! Come! what is this joke, monsieur? To whom am I indebted for these kind attentions?"

"Madame, I will conclude my commission, if you please. It

appears that the Terrace of the Orangery will be disagreeably crowded to-morrow morning; he from whom I come begs, therefore, to be permitted to consider other arrangements."

"What is your name, monsieur?"

"It is de Mailly."

"I think that one sees your face at Court but seldom?"

He bowed.

"Confess, now, that you do not know Versailles!"

"Madame . . ."

"Believe me, it will do you no harm to admit it. You are, then, ignorant that the Terrace of the Orangery lies immediately before the windows of the Royal apartments, that it is reserved to His Majesty himself, the Sons and Daughters of France, and the Princes of the Blood, and that consequently people do not meet there?"

"O the devil!" muttered Mailly, turning pale.

"Your ignorance of the circumstance is manifest, monsieur, and therefore I shall not complain to those who would have it within their power to punish such an insolence. You have been used. Some wit has practised upon your innocence. I shall not demand his name, for I do not wish to know it, but depart quickly from the *Château*, and, if you will take my advice, breathe not a word of this affair to any. It reflects very little credit on your intelligence. . . . Adieu, monsieur!"

Angry, nervous, and humiliated, he bowed himself out.

A few minutes later, as he re-entered the Gallery, to seek Mimizan and report to him the lamentable failure of the negotiation, a pair of elegantly-dressed young courtiers approached him, simpering and bowing with an excessive politeness.

"Pardon, monsieur," said the spokesman of the two, staring insultingly straight into his eyes. "Is it you who distribute tickets for the Terrace of the Orangery? If so, my friend and I would beg for two apiece!"

Mailly forced a smile. "Monsieur, it is a bet. I have bet that fifty silly gentlemen shall make application to me this afternoon for these tickets. You are the first two, you head the list, and I am extremely obliged to you. Add to your kindness by not interfering with the progress of the wager."

All within hearing laughed, the mockers retreated in confusion, but Mailly was not destined to get off so cheaply. In his course down the Gallery, one gentleman after another accosted him, individually or on the behalf of parties, with the civilly expressed request for tickets for the Terrace of the Orangery. The throng gathered around him, until his passage became triumphal. Jeering laughter, stifled titters, caustic words uttered in clearly-audible undertones, smote upon his ear from all sides. Even his dress and person furnished a rich guard for the agreeable quizzes of the Court. The Gallery had no end, Mimizan was nowhere to be seen, and, short of positive flight, he could not discover a means to disengage himself. All Versailles appeared to have assembled for the purpose of witnessing his shame and mortification.

A hand lightly held his sleeve, and turning about with a sharpness engendered by his situation, he distinguished a person of the valet type, who seemed desirous of addressing him.

"What do you want?"

"Monsieur," whispered the man, "you will be pleased to accompany me at once to M. Bontems."

"And who the devil is M. Bontems?"

A smile of contempt preceded the reply. "He is First *Valet-de-chambre* to His Majesty the King, and Governor of Versailles and Marly."[7]

V

Great Monarchs Do Not Love To Be Laughed At

"*Mordieu!* you don't say so," exclaimed Mailly, thunderstruck. "But what does he want with me?"

The messenger wasted no time on explanations, but led Mailly through the ranks of the ever-increasing mob. The courtiers exchanged malicious smiles.

A richly-equipped officer stood on duty in an otherwise empty ante-chamber, having an interior door.

"M. Bontems will be here immediately," Mailly was informed by the attendant. "Be so good as to wait."

He went out.

"What place is this, monsieur?" inquired Mailly politely of the officer.

"It is the entrance to His Majesty's Council Chamber."

The inner door opened softly, and an elderly gentleman squeezed himself through, closing the door again behind him. Although obviously in his last natural decade, he remained tall, erect, portly, ruddy-faced and handsome. Catching sight of Mailly he regarded him with some surprise.

"What do you here, monsieur?" he demanded in a rough and strong, but not unkindly voice.

"I have been sent for, monsieur, but I do not know why."

"What is your name?"

"De Mailly."

"Ah, you are that one! You are the hero of the latest joke? You are going about to invite people to the Terrace of the Orangery?"

Mailly shrugged his shoulders. "It is a transaction which can be explained, monsieur."

"It is fortunate for you, since His Majesty has taken up the impertinence in person. Perhaps he will see you at once. Wait!"

He scratched upon the inner door, re-opened it by inches, and passed through. The door closed.

The officer winked one eye good-humouredly.

"Now you are in for it! Luckily, he is in first-class spirits to-day. That little Duchess of Burgundy[8] has just left him. Speak up boldly, do not spare the jam, and I dare say your head will remain on your shoulders!"

Bontems came out again, to beckon to Mailly.

"Take off your sword!"

Mailly did so, then followed the First Valet into the interior chamber. The latter at once returned outside, shutting the door after him.

The King was sitting lightly on the end of the council-table. He was a small man in a snuff-coloured suit, a richly-embroidered green satin waistcoat, and high heels. His poise was upright and extremely dignified, but, for the moment, his face appeared relaxed, gracious and pensive. In his sixty-second year Louis XIV could afford these affabilities. If foreign nations no longer trembled at his name, those of his subjects who were brought into daily contact with him took excellent care not to contradict his will in the smallest particular; he was thus able to be amiable and paternal without thereby encouraging an improper familiarity on the part of inferior persons. Since, in addition, he was still one of the handsomest men of his kingdom, and his manners could be of the most charming, in descending to a nominal equality he provided himself with opportunities to establish his princeliness in a double sense. Between two humble bows, one from the door, one from half the distance to the table, Mailly stole a daring glance at the physiognomy of this puissant monarch, whom hitherto he had beheld only at reviews and public ceremonies. What he saw did not appear to him very terrible, and, while waiting tranquilly at three paces from the royal person to be addressed, he began to cogitate how so favourable an occasion might be improved.

The King viewed him with a good-natured, indifferent yet penetrating regard.

"Well, monsieur, and what is all this affair?" he asked.

"Sire," replied Mailly politely, "it seems that I have had the misfortune to start a joke, of which I have been the very last to see the humour.”

“But you have been inviting people to the Terrace of the Orangery, they tell me!”

“That is to say, Sire, certain of my friends begin to feel the influence of the Spring, and I have tried to oblige them.”

“At the expense of my privacy, I think!”

“Sire, I was about to add—it is within the last fifteen minutes that I have been shocked to learn that the Terrace of the Orangery does in fact constitute a part of Your Majesty’s reserved apartments.”

“Thus you have not known what all the world knows!”

“For a very good reason, Sire. It is absolutely my first visit to Versailles.”

“So that is it! Yet you bear a good name, and should be a gentleman. How comes it that at your age you have never yet appeared at Court?”

“Sire, during six campaigns, in which I have had the honour to receive three wounds in the service of Your Majesty, my time has not been my own. Since the Peace, I have been otherwise employed.”

“In what fashion, monsieur?”

“In combating a sordid and disgraceful poverty, Sire, and if I have not paid my respects to Your Majesty, it is because I have not possessed the means to do so.”

The King began to study him with a greater interest.

“But still, you have been very rash to arrange meetings for a place of which you have no knowledge. You see the consequence. Everyone is laughing at you.”

“If that were all, Sire, seeing that I should have deserved it, I should endeavour to endure my misfortune with equanimity.”

“So that you are principally concerned for my displeasure?”

“Yes, Sire, your displeasure—and something else besides.”

Louis frowned.

“Speak, monsieur!”

“Sire, that I am laughed at is bad enough, that I have

ignorantly taken a liberty is far worse, but the worst of all, in my opinion, is that, through my folly, the Terrace of the Orangery itself has in a manner become ridiculous, inasmuch as I think that for a very long time to come people will scarcely be able to name it without general hilarity; and, as it is Your Majesty's private walk, I freely confess that the circumstance seriously oppresses me."

"So you see! One cannot be too careful with one's tongue at Court."

"I see it very well, Sire, and I shall not offend a second time. Moreover, although perhaps this impertinence might still be avoided, I perfectly understand that it would be highly unbecoming in me to presume to offer suggestions to Your Majesty."

"Let me hear, however!"

"'Tis a thought which has occurred to me a moment ago, Sire. I do not know if I am being absurd, but it seems to me that, were the Terrace of the Orangery really to be opened—I do not say to all the Court, but to ten, twenty, fifty, or whatever number Your Majesty might fix upon—at that hour to-morrow which I have been silly enough to name, that is to say, at six o'clock in the morning, the jests would certainly cease, and it would be universally credited that I had, in some unauthorised manner, received intimation of Your Majesty's actual intention. For the leak itself you would very properly punish me, Sire, and thus all would end in the best conceivable way."

The King continued to view Mailly with a mild graciousness, as though he found pleasure in the sound of his voice.

"That is very clever, monsieur. But why should the Terrace be thrown open?"

"For example, to hear a concert of music."

Louis laughed. "At six in the morning! That would indeed be a novelty."

"Yes, Sire, a novelty; and one which would delight the younger ladies of your suite, if few besides."

"Yes, but still, we cannot do outrageous things without a

reason. If it were an anniversary, or to celebrate a betrothal, I would not say, but there is absolutely no excuse for it at all.”

“At the risk of your resentment, Sire, is there no lady to whom you could wish to pay so unique a compliment? I will engage that it would be worth to her many gifts of greater value.”

The King’s face expressed at the same time amusement and reflection.

“But it appears to me that you are a very bold fellow!” he said.

“If the thing mystify the ladies and gentlemen of your Court a little, Sire, that also will do no great harm. It will at least teach them to be less ready to make discourteous jokes in a house not their own. In effect, I have no doubt that the announcement by Your Majesty of this opening of the Terrace of the Orangery will be understood generally as your Majesty’s method of rebuking an insolence, the direct notice of which would perhaps be more difficult.”

“That argument is the best of all yet, monsieur. For a man of your years, you have a high degree of tact and intelligence, and I am quite astonished that you have hitherto not done better for yourself. Well then, be good enough to step to the door, and request M. Bontems to come to me.”

Bowing low, Mailly turned exultingly to obey. Bontems came in.

“Bontems,” said the King in the cool tone of a master, and flicking his shoe, as he sat on the table, with the riding-switch he held in his hand, “the Court Musicians will play a concert of music to-morrow morning at six o’clock, to last for half an hour, on the Terrace of the Orangery, before the windows of my grand-daughter, Madame the Duchess of Burgundy. A list of pieces will be submitted to me this afternoon. Places, without seats, will be reserved on the Terrace, for ten ladies and the gentlemen of the general Court. A lottery will be held this evening in the great guardroom to decide to whom these places are to go. The price of a lottery-ticket will be ten crowns, and you will make known my desire that as many as possible shall apply for such tickets. The concert will be in honour of Madame the Duchess of Burgundy.

You will circulate it at once."

Bontems bowed.

"And the profit derived from this lottery, Sire?"

"You will have the whole amount delivered to-morrow to M. de Mailly, at the address which he will give you. That, also, you will circulate, but privately."

Mailly bent profoundly.

"It is the best I can do for you, monsieur," said the King, with a smile. He added gravely, "It is not right that harmless gentlemen, new to my Court, should be ridiculed for mistakes committed in ignorance. We are not barbarians here, I hope. Especially, it is not right that officers who have sustained wounds in my service should be insulted by people who perhaps have never stood fire. I regard your annoyance as my own, monsieur, being very well assured that you could not have conceived the Terrace of the Orangery as a general *rendezvous* without a malicious prompting; and I am only sorry that I cannot help you in a better way. Nevertheless, I hold no sovereignty over courtiers' tongues. You had better keep away from Versailles for a few months, until all this has died down. Afterwards, we shall see."

Mailly thanked him with simple dignity, bowed twice, and departed from the Council Chamber, conducted by Bontems.

The officer in the ante-chamber scrutinised his face with a smile which was prepared to broaden upon encouragement, but, regarding his presence only so far as to draw the First Valet to a retired corner, Mailly made haste to put the inquiry uppermost in his head.

"How much is this worth to me?" he murmured.

"It should be worth to you anything between five thousand and ten thousand crowns," replied Bontems, with a shrug.

"Honour me by accepting one crown for every ticket sold, for your trouble and kindness. I am very well aware to whom I owe so favourable a reception. The balance be obliging enough to send me at Rue Michon, 23, Paris."

The other responded only by a dark smile of patronage. He

took from his pocket a note-book, and pencilled in it Mailly's address. The latter made ready to go out.

"Wait here for me a minute, monsieur!" said Bontems. "I shall send some of my people to whisper His Majesty's arrangements into the ears of a dozen, and then, if you will take your time up the Gallery, I have no doubt that before you reach the end you will find the weather amazingly cleared."

He disappeared.

The eyes of Mailly and the officer on duty met.

"Are you well up in the politics of Versailles, monsieur?" asked the former.

"Moderately so, monsieur. What is in the wind?"

"Do you know the Marquis de Puy?"

"Very well."

"Do you also know a Mdlle. Molfetti?"

"Yes."

"Then perhaps you can tell me—what hope is there for Puy in that quarter?"

The officer laughed only.

"The devil! is there none?" demanded Mailly.

"She is very pretty, but he is too late. Marsin has just had his audience of the King."

"What Marsin?—and what audience?"

"*Peste!* I know only one Marsin—the Prince de Marsin. He is to marry the Italian girl. She is lucky, and there will be female heartburnings. The King has just given his consent. It is queer you should have raised the case at this moment."

Mailly grew very thoughtful.

"It is still more queer, monsieur, to reflect that, had this Prince de Marsin obtained his audience of the King yesterday, instead of to-day, I should not have procured mine at all!"

"And yet, as I prophesied, your head remains on your shoulders," suggested the officer, gnawing his nails.

At the same moment Bontems came back.

"You may now come with me, monsieur," he said to Mailly.

The latter bowed to the officer, and followed the other out. It was the hour for promenading, and the Gallery was thronged. Every group they encountered made way for the First *Valet-de-chambre* with the utmost respect, so that it became increasingly evident to his companion that he was in the society of a very great personage. Twenty paces further along, Bontems halted, to rest an arm in the most condescending and amiable fashion upon Mailly's off shoulder, while grasping his nearer hand in his own.

"Here we part, then, my dear M. de Mailly!" he exclaimed loudly, for the benefit of those in the vicinity. "A pleasant journey to Paris—and I shall not fail to notify to you the result of His Majesty's negotiation. Good day to you!"

There was total silence within a radius of five yards as Mailly returned his bow.

With a parting smile across his shoulder, Bontems went back, and Mailly proceeded on his way. He found it interesting and novel to watch, as through an optical glass, the very act of percolation of the news of his reception by the King, and its result. A few, having heard nothing of a change of circumstances, continued to regard him as fair game for wit: by far the most of all eyed him curiously as he passed, whispering among themselves and shaking their heads; but there were also those, the ferrets and the weasels of Versailles, who, within five minutes, had already received and digested the intelligence of the concert of music to be given upon the Terrace of the Orangery next morning, and were prepared to take advantage of their superior knowledge by conciliating, while the field was still open, the mysterious unknown who had so strangely forestalled the King's announcement, following it up by a prolonged audience of His Majesty. A round half-dozen such advanced upon Mailly, one after another, with smiles and ingratiating bows, as he walked forward alone. He allowed his eyes to wander past their faces, and they concluded their smirkings to the empty air.

A hand gripped his arm from behind. He beheld Mimizan.

"What in the name of all the furies have you been up to, my dear fellow!" he demanded grimly, his countenance being very red. "Come over here into the corner, and tell me what has happened. The entire *Château* is laughing at you!"

"It is you who say so!" replied Mailly coldly.

They moved apart.

"But what have you been doing? What is all this nonsense about the Terrace of the Orangery?"

"There is to be given there a concert of music to-morrow morning early, and a limited number of places are to be balloted for, but I know of no other nonsense."

"Bah! they have fed you from the bottle, my dear fellow! You had better run off home at the double. My ears have been positively burning with shame for half-an-hour at what they are saying about the affair. I suppose there never has been such a joke! How the devil have you been living to fall into a trap like that?"

"So you assure me that the Terrace is not to be opened to the Court to-morrow?

"You are perfectly and completely mad!"

"Then the King has lied to me, that is all."

"Wretch! then the jest is deliberate?"

Luxelles passed by, with three or four attendant gentlemen. Seeing Mailly, he started, hesitated, then came up, unaccompanied.

"Ah, Mimizan—you are in the fashion, then. M. de Mailly—my very humble apologies! How was I to know that you were not joking? Forgive me, my dear monsieur, and do me a favour, to clinch the forgiveness."

"What do you want, monsieur?" asked Mailly coldly.

"Procure for me from Bontems two of those little tickets for the Terrace to-morrow, and I shall be everlastingly your grateful servant! He will easily do it for you. We know on what terms you are together."

Mimizan's face fell. "What is all this affair, Luxelles?"

"*Mordieu!* you are ignorant, then? The Terrace of the Orangery is to be invaded at six o'clock tomorrow morning, and this monsieur is the Grand Master of the Ceremonies. He has just arranged everything with the King."

"Come, you joke!"

"On my soul, no!—and the proof is that the news is official. The royal valets have just been up and down the Gallery with it. You are infernally behind the times, Mimizan! But these tickets, monsieur?"

Mailly moved forward somewhat from the pair, in order to address the Comte's companions, who stood waiting for him, talking amongst themselves.

"Gentlemen, attention, if you please! The Academy of M. le Comte de Luxelles is dismissed. He grows old, and his shots begin to bring down the wrong persons!"

Luxelles turned green, Mimizan fiery-red. The gentlemen addressed looked embarrassed. Mailly made the Comte a very low bow.

"I am always in Paris, monsieur. The address is Rue Michon, 23. I have the honour to wish you a good afternoon!" And, seizing Mimizan's arm, he walked away.

For a minute there was silence between the two friends.

"Well then, this business is beyond me," said Mimizan at last. "But what of Puy?"

"As to that, I have nothing to say, Pierre, except that you have brought me here to-day under false pretences."

"What the devil do you mean?"

"Mdlle. Molfetti is betrothed, you must have known that she was about to be so, therefore you have wasted my time, though for what purpose I cannot imagine."

"She is betrothed?"

"Yes, to Marsin."

"To Marsin!" repeated Mimizan, in a tone of stupefaction. "But are you positive?"

"At least I have it from an excellent source."

"Then it is all up with Puy! That is a man who goes back to Clovis, and has the wealth of a tax-farmer, besides being devilish handsome into the bargain, which Puy is not. He will easily console himself, I have no doubt. I am very grieved about you, however. What can we do for you?"

But Mailly was unable longer to maintain his offended gravity. After having relieved his feelings by a prolonged and hearty roar of laughter, to the enormous sensation of all those who still lingered near to remark his further doings, he proceeded to deliver such a thwack on Mimizan's back that even that robust individual was momentarily discomposed.

"What can you do for me, Pierre?" he brought out in a suffocating voice. "You can lend me a few pistoles to take me home, if you like. 'Tis only till to-morrow. Bontems is to send me five or ten thousand crowns to-morrow, I do not know the exact sum."

Mimizan stared at him.

"I begin to believe all that you say. But what has really happened?"

"Let us walk towards the entrance. I have been scrupulous to follow your advice, that is all. It has turned out well, and I am exceedingly obliged to you."

"What advice?"

"You recommended to me to attach myself to some person of influence, and I have lost no time in doing so."

"Who has taken you up, then?"

"*Pardieu!* the King himself! If one is to aim, why not aim high?"

"But what is that money for?"

"It is my reward for being the one sensible man in the whole of His Majesty's Court. I have seen what no one else could see, and his gratitude has taken the shape of coin."

"And what have you seen?"

"I have seen, my dear Pierre, that great monarchs do not love to be laughed at!"

They arrived at the staircase descending to the Great Courtyard. Mimizan, with a sigh, drew forth his purse.

"Take what you will, Gaston! At least, I am very glad to have been of service to you."

Mailly transferred ten pistoles to his own pocket. He set his hat more firmly on his head, and prepared to go downstairs.

"I am your eternal debtor. When next in Paris you will call upon me? I shall hope within a few days to have some decent rooms."

Mimizan gazed downwards at his diminishing form with eyes which became bigger and bigger. Then, with a prophetic shake of his head, he turned away.

VI

A Proposition To Fleurus

Mailly rose from his first breakfast in the pleasant first-floor corner apartment, with double windows facing the Rue Carcassone and the Rue Martel, which he had so often coveted during his long months of tribulation, and which at last, as happens in the world to patient spirits, his triumphant stroke at Versailles had enabled him to acquire. The witty courtiers had been compelled to beat the *chamade*[9] to him to the tune of nine thousand crowns. Scarcely a week had passed since his return. He had duly paid and insulted his old landlord, who had plagued him so often in the past, he had moved his belongings to these new quarters, so superior, he had settled his debts, he had renovated his wardrobe, and he had shown his face once more in society. Eight thousand crowns still remained to him, health, youth and leisure, that blessed trinity, were all his, he had no feminine entanglement to retain him to one spot, or to one mode of life; nevertheless, he was already bored.

It was a superb April morning. The summer seemed to stretch her fair limbs, nearly for the first time, and although she would presently turn over to sleep again, the deception was very agreeable. The light breezes floating through the open windows were both delicious and stimulating; but stimulation, when it is uncoupled to a definite activity, may be tormenting, and Mailly was tormented. He paced the chamber uneasily, seeking acquaintance with his elusive desires now in the busy street ten feet below, now on the blackened ceiling decorated with fat Cupids, but finding nothing within to illuminate his soul, save that he remarked it at the end of ten minutes as a circumstance, that those in the thoroughfare upon whom his eyes chiefly rested were belonging to the long-haired gender. He snapped his fingers wearily, ceased promenading, and sat down.

"Bah! what is the matter with me is that the season has me by the throat, and I am sickening for an intrigue. If we do not go carefully to work, some pink-and-white phantom will suddenly appear, to warn us of the quick dissolution of our new-born wealth! 'Tis what women are for. Were I to sit in the very heart of a desert of sand, clasping a bag of gold between my knees, before evening females would begin to arrive; before next morning I should be alone again, but this time without treasure. . . .

"I need occupation to drive these rosy devils out of my head! I will go to exhibit myself to Fleurus in my new rôle of proprietor. 'Tis three weeks or more since I was there—perhaps he has an interesting case which I may buy of him. Nowadays, when none fights save through the law, 'tis among litigants that one must look for breathing exercise. Then, too, eight thousand crowns are very well, but what divine commandment has been laid upon me that I am not to increase them? Versailles has taught me that money is not so difficult to come by, there is abundance of it in the world, only it demands a certain acuteness of vision to detect the door into an affair; but, once detected, it is sufficiently easy to enter by it. 'Tis not to be conceited to admit to myself that I have a talent for negotiation. I shall see if he possesses a political case to offer me. Could I once get a footing among those who have taken it upon themselves to misgovern France for its own good, I engage that I would learn the customs of the tribe very quickly, and would do as well as any. In politics, as elsewhere, there are nine pedants to one man of resource. My successes will come to be spoken of, I shall be summoned from branch to branch of the tree of fortune; and one fine morning they will take me behind the screen to offer me a minor embassy! It is my manifest destiny. I do not know how I have failed to understand it earlier."

He seized his hat, made his way out of doors, and started towards the familiar office on the fourth floor of the decayed house in the Rue du Mail.

Fleurus was alone, writing diligently at the desk on the further side of the room, before the dust-grimed window. He shot one glance over his shoulder, identified the visitor, threw down his quill angrily, and leapt from the high stool on which he sat. His long features of a horse were distorted with rage, while his teeth projected fearfully. Mailly, laughing, held a warding hand before his face. He feigned a retreat.

"Hold there, Fleurus! This time I have not come to eat you, but neither have I come to be eaten! *Diable!* what a reception for the bearer of good tidings! Come, you see before you a man of substance, a capitalist, a financier—do you understand? I have come into my own. My pockets burst. I no longer say: 'Give to me!'—I say: 'Go to the devil!' I am a metamorphosed person."

The notary's face composed itself, though it remained guarded.

"You have found your way to some money at last?"

"So it seems! A trifling gift from Heaven. Some nine thousand, ten thousand crowns, there is no need to go into the exact sum."

"You have this money?"

"*Peste!* I hope so, seeing that I received it but a week ago, and that it is still as dear to me as a new wife. We do not quit each other's sight, this treasure and I."

"Well, I must believe you, monsieur, since it cannot profit you to tell me that sort of lie. So, then, you have come here to repay your loans in the past? Be seated, and I will make up your account."

"Tut! we do not need paper for such a trifle. A few pistoles will cover all that. Moreover, 'tis too fine a day to discuss fly-debts. I am here about something else."

Fleurus looked up sharply.

"You desire to consult me on a point of law?"

"Not the least in the world!" replied Mailly, flinging himself in a chair, a good-humoured smile upon his pale, pockmarked face. "My errand is quite different, and more advantageous for both of us. Know, Fleurus, that I have had a thought since breakfast!"

"There are thoughts and thoughts, monsieur."

"You do not wish, then, that I shall put money into your pocket?"

"And how will you do that?"

"I come to propose a partnership to you."

The notary laughed aloud. "A partnership! Since when have you become educated in the law, M. de Mailly?"

"'Tis well put, but do not interrupt. My department will not be to interpret the law. That I shall leave to you. Now attend, however! It must sometimes happen that you receive inquiries which are of the wrong size and shape for your pigeon-holes. . . . But is it so, or not?"

"Persons come to me who have no case, if you mean that."

"You speak like an angel! I mean that, and nothing else. Then what do you do with these persons who are foolish enough to believe that the law is for their benefit? Do you still squeeze them?"

"If I cannot see a good result, I do not take money, monsieur. I am honest."

"It does you credit. Nevertheless, Fleurus, I affirm that the holes of your sieve may be too great. I propose, therefore, that I shall assist you to collect the grains of gold which slip through. The cases which hitherto you have turned away as hopeless, we shall henceforth save for a closer examination. *Peste!* the law, at best, is but a clumsy instrument, and where one has not legal right, one may still have moral. Much may be accomplished by private treaty, much may be achieved locally, a mutual accommodation will sometimes advantage even the stronger party, since he will gain his claim with good will, and without extravagant costs. Well then, this sort of finer transactions you shall pass to me, I will see what can be done with them, and we will divide the profits according to a fixed proportion, though you will also observe that I am presenting you with this money for nothing at all."

"And what is your notion of a fair division, M. de Mailly?"

"You shall receive fifteen per cent of all moneys after payment of my expenses."

"The cases which I abandon are not worth much, you may be sure, and I do not see a gold-mine in all this. 'Tis but an hour since I have sent a lady packing. I deliver her to you with pleasure, but it is not fifteen per cent I shall demand, it is equal shares, and even so I see not how to secure my receipt of whatever proceeds there may be accruing to me."

"For you are a lawyer, Fleurus; which is to say, an animal trained out of noble sentiments. But listen! I shall give you fifty per cent in the smaller cases, twenty-five per cent in the greater. *Peste!* let us not enlarge so much on the sordid aspect. In a word, we shall get what we can, and divide it somehow. You know me. I shall not run away."

"However, since you are in funds at present, I shall ask a deposit."

"Beast! . . . Well, you shall have your deposit, too." He took from his pocket a packet of bills. "Write me a receipt for ten-thousand livres, repayable at thirty days' notice, with interest to be reckoned at five per cent annually. Here is the money. Take up your pen!"

"Let me see the money, if you please, monsieur."

"You are a veritable monster of suspicion! Here then, take them! You do not lift your nose at Hôtel de Ville stock?"

Fleurus counted and recounted the vouchers, then moved with them to his desk. He took quill and paper, and began to write.

"But how is one to find your lady? since you have dismissed her," asked Mailly.

"She is from the country, she is staying in Paris, and I have the address, but I do not know whether she is to return home to-day or to-morrow." The notary wrote on while replying.

Mailly allowed the quill to creak for a minute longer before opening his mouth again.

"But is she of quality, or but a courtesy-lady? For instance, I do not greatly care to have to do with citizens' wives, or such-like."

"Here is your receipt, monsieur!"

The young man read it through with all the loving attention which a novelty engenders. He bestowed it in his pocket.

"I repeat my question: this Atalanta, whose turn it is to let drop golden apples for us—has she birth, or is she of the *bourgeoisie*?"

"'Tis a lady of fashion, though but a provincial one," replied Fleurus, again counting Mailly's notes, before finally putting them away.

"Then let us come to the case."

"I will tell you all I know of her, and you shall judge for yourself the possibilities of a favourable negotiation. She is of good family on both sides; and handsome. Her age she gives as twenty-five, to which we shall add the few years usual with women. She is one of twin sisters. Although of legal maturity, both appear to remain under semi-tutelage of an aunt, but the precise relation is vague. The parents are dead. I have said that she is handsome; she is also clever. It seems, however, that cleverness may co-exist with a deficiency of understanding, for she demands an unconscionable thing, sanctioned neither by law, nor by custom, nor by religion. . . . Conceive well, that, in my profession, I am not ignorant that ladies may possess queer fancies; and yet to the present I have encountered very few who have not known more about the ordinances of marriage than I myself, for example. 'Tis their study. 'Tis the last extension of personal adornment, coquetry, and love, and she who is unacquainted with whom she may marry, and whom she may not marry, is, in my judgment, little else than a prodigy. Well then, monsieur, this one appears to possess no comprehension whatever of such matters. For all her elegance of bearing and dignity of speech, one would imagine that her education has hitherto been among the Tatars of Asia."

"Let us hear!" said Mailly judicially. "It may be that your eyes have failed to stretch to the horizon of the case, Fleurus. Where women are concerned, everything does not present itself at once, there are vistas beyond vistas. To me the affair smells well already, and I am very glad I have come to see you this morning. Proceed! We shall endeavour to penetrate the mystery underlying this strange ignorance of civilised customs."

"It is possible that you have a head teeming with expedients, M. de Mailly, nevertheless I will stake ten thousand livres of my own money against the ten thousand you have deposited with me, that you will nowhere find it set down in the statute books of France that a woman shall be permitted to wed a man who already enjoys a wife! That is what this one desires to do. She desires to marry a man already married. She insists that the business of the law is to help her to such a happiness. She is entirely persuaded that if we do not assist her, 'tis because she is an unbefriended lady, who has not inspired the requisite confidence." Fleurus smiled maliciously. "So that is the case which I shall have the honour to pass to you as a commencement, monsieur. I wish you joy of it!"

"Bah! you joke. There must be more in it. A woman of fashion of that age is not an innocent. *Peste!* if she is mad, her friends would have confined her."

"Every madness begins, and it appears she has recently experienced a grief, which perhaps has disordered her wits. I think she is mad."

"You see! You now talk of a grief. I am convinced that you have listened to this poor creature's story pedantically, and, as it were, in your robe. It is just such an extraneous case as I have imagined. So what has been her grief?"

"There has been a misadventure. A double-marriage, it seems, was arranged between these two sisters and two gentlemen of their acquaintance, one of whom greatly outshines the other by reason of his rank, being no less than a Peer of France, allied to very important families. Well, monsieur, it is our mademoiselle who was to have married the Peer. All was contracted to that effect; but a few hours more were to pass before she would be marquise. Satan, however, was at the wedding, for mademoiselle, doubtless owing to a natural heat set up by the prospect of her elevation in standing, must take it into her head to fall sick at the eleventh hour; while the simple gentleman—he who has no rank—was foolish enough to be some minutes late in arriving at the place of ceremony. The other sister is of an obliging disposition, her beauty is the same as this one's; she found it uncivil that so great a *seigneur* should be made to look absurd before those assembled. She put a constraint upon her private feelings, the contract was revised, the priest was contented, and so it has come about that it is this other who, after all, is marquise.

"She who visited me an hour ago has thus lost husband and title at a blow. 'Tis understandable she should be exasperated. I do not complain of that, but it is an inexcusable stupidity to further imagine that the law can interfere in such a case, which may have something of criminal in it, but not for us. The contract was signed before a notary, the names set down have corresponded with the parties of the ceremony, the marriage is binding, and there is no more to be said. There are crimes of heaven, monsieur, and crimes of earth. The law has only to do with the last."

"And that is to admit that there is still need for gentlemen to carry a blade! Not only do I accept your line of distinction, but I think it admirable. Honour is too delicate a quality to be judged by long-ears. However, one sees that your little mademoiselle has no champion, or that rascal of a marquis would before this have received a lesson in honesty from someone!"

"I keep telling you that it is a reinstatement she demands. You may deal the marquis fifty great wounds, but he will none the more on that account be her husband."

"Then she cannot be helped. But tell me: is it the man she is infatuated with, or what he carries on his back?"

"Without having it from her own lips, there can be little doubt that she grieves for the departed rank."

"So her fall at least has not been from Paradise. I do not see what can be done. It seems that she must be content to wait until some other nobleman declares his passion. *Peste!* I will bet she will not be late at church on the next occasion! . . . You have no other cases, then, Fleurus?"

"None that I can spare to you, monsieur."

Mailly sighed, and became pensive. He wandered aimlessly about the room, gazing down at the brim of the hat in his hand, with which he toyed.

"Who is your marquis?" he demanded at last.

"His seat is in the vicinity of Auxerre. A Court command confines him there. In receiving the King's permission to marry one sister, it appears that he did not receive it for the other. 'Twas thoughtless not to apply for both together, but I learn that thoughtlessness is his character, and that his estate, to take a single example, is already much impaired on this account."

"How do they name it?"

"Jussault."

Mailly knit his brows.

"Do I know it? I seem to. Jussault is familiar. . . . Bah! don't say you have been speaking of the Marquis de Ventailles all the time? He that was Vidame de Cléry?"

"The same, monsieur. Do you know him, then?"

"Faith! he was Colonel of the regiment of which I commanded a troop, in, I think, my third campaign, in Flanders,[10] if you call that knowing him! We had much time on our hands that summer, play ran high, and this same Ventailles won such sums of me that I have been embarrassed ever since. He had money at his back, money engenders audacity, without audacity one is but a cripple at cards, and so I was a beaten man before ever I sat down at table with him. . . . Come! all this occurs together; 'tis like feathers flying in the wind. Fate offers me my revenge at the precise moment that wealth is in my pocket. I am to visit Jussault. We shall see which of us has advanced the more since six years ago. The deuce! he was already past thirty then; what fiend has whispered in his ear to get married on his way downhill!"

"And our affair, M. de Mailly?"

"Poh! if the bottle is uncorked for us, we will drink; not otherwise. You have said that it is desperate. Complete your descriptions in five words, merely that I shall not need to begin at the beginning with this dear friend. Acquaint me with Mademoiselle's name—she who was here to-day; she who perseveres to make herself a third where two are enough."

"Her name is Mdlle. Aglaé de Dampierre, the name of the marquise in fact is Claire, but the aunt's name I do not know."

"*Pardieu!* the aunt is very well in her box, we shall not trouble her to dance her *pas seul* on this occasion. The other gentleman, however, he who picks his teeth over breakfast while others are carrying off his bride, what is this one named? Where is he established?"

"It is a M. de Villary-Loguette. He also is seated near Auxerre. You have a scheme, then, monsieur?"

"*Ma foi!* no. I see no way into this dumpling. An ignorance of affairs causes us to be lightly regarded, that is why I have questioned you. If I really make the journey, it will be to visit an old comrade and chief. I do not know this road as well as others. Does a good mount get there in a day?"

"No, but in two days. It is forty leagues. The way lies through Fontainebleau, which is fifteen leagues."

"You speak as Caesar wrote, Fleurus! So it is understood— always assuming that I go—that I sleep to-night at Fontainebleau, to-morrow at Auxerre, and the next night where Heaven wills, for to-day is Monday, and I shall defer my visit to Ventailles until the Wednesday morning, in order to present myself entire. *Parbleu!* a wet shirt is nothing to that good soldier, but he has a lady."

"You will not visit Mdlle. Aglaé before leaving Paris, then, M. de Mailly?"

Mailly, who had approached the door by degrees backwards, put his hand behind him to draw it open.

"No, for it is disloyal to condemn a friend unheard. 'Tis not in Mademoiselle's tent that I have slept and eaten. 'Tis not in her company that I have stood enemy fire some score of times. I do not know her, but Ventailles I know, and I have ever found him a true and honourable gentleman. I do not doubt that he will have at least as much to say as she. *Peste!* because a disappointed lady summons tears of spite to her eyes, must we all howl in unison? . . . Adieu, Fleurus!"

"I do not understand your intentions, monsieur. Is the case abandoned?"

"It is not abandoned, for there is nothing to abandon—you yourself have said it. I do not believe, with you, that she is mad, but I think that it is a greedy virgin, who hopes by noise and slander to procure gold from her sister's husband. Ventailles will tell me what it is all about; but in the meantime that is my faith. Upon my return, you will have other cases to put before me of a more promising cast, and then we shall see what we can do together, Fleurus. Farewell!"

"But, M. de Mailly . . ."

The door, however, had closed behind Mailly, and the notary returned slowly and ruefully to his desk, once more to contemplate the stock receipts which the other had left behind. After inspecting these sharply, at varying distances from his eyes, and at different angles, he laid them down again with a sigh.

"If he has made ten thousand crowns," he reflected, "it has been by the exercise of his wits, so that he is a clever rogue, which I have always known; and will perhaps make other sums by the same method. I ought not to have discouraged him. He will carry his brains to another shop, and I shall lose him. A proof of his ability is that he has an admirable insinuation. Where his foot is once set inside the door, his whole person presently enters. When he returns, therefore, I shall find him a case somewhat less decayed, offering it to him affably, as it were a casket of gems, though it will not be that. By this means I shall set him upon his honour, and he will perhaps throw into the common pot cases of his own. My nose still has an excellent scent for an advantage, but age creeps upon me, and I sink too much into spiritless routine. I am fifty-seven, which is a stage of life at which one begins to sweep together what one has already acquired. To-night, in bed, I shall make some new rules for my conduct."

VII

Monsieur Le Marquis De Ventailles

At eleven o'clock on Wednesday morning, Mailly walked his iron-grey gelding slowly up the avenue of chestnuts which constituted the approach of honour to the Château of Jussault. Although so early in the year, the day was brilliant, the air was filled with song and perfume, while the trees almost visibly unfolded their emerald leaves. The sky was all of blue and white.

"Faith! Ventailles should be a happy man, to enjoy a fair wife amidst such surroundings," meditated the rider, who was in ceremonial attire, having taken pains with his wardrobe at the inn, in the thought that he was to meet a marquise new to her quality. "I do not call it a punishment to be exiled from Court upon these conditions. *Diable!* he hunts, he drinks, he sees his neighbours, he philanders with his bride, who must be almost strange to him, seeing that it is the wrong one; then, of course, there are parties of pleasure, feasts, balls, music, and what not. 'Tis an ideal way of life, which no man of sense would exchange for that other which consists of spitting venom in the galleries of Versailles and Marly, in the company of the cats, foxes, weasels and snakes of both sexes, who congregate there as in the devil's temple. Louis has been very obliging to him, and if he is not grateful, it must be because his Eve has started to press against his teeth the apple of ambition, an apple whose only novelty consists in the fact that it is offered this time by beloved fingers. . . .

"Nevertheless, the estate has the first beginnings of decrepitude, and if I remember to mention it, I shall advise this old comrade to change his steward. The present, it may be, comes from a part where wildness is in vogue, but *corbleu!* everything around a young wife should be neat, bright, and glittering as a dress just arrived from the milliner. This drive threatens to become a grass-track, I would not ride along it on a windy day, the trees are as precarious as ninepins. There is an air of desolation over all which does not speak of married bliss; but perhaps it is that they have too much otherwise to occupy them, they have not yet had time to visit the suburbs, they will spend a blessed summer in altering and improving the grounds."

Amid these contemplations, he came within view of the *château* itself, an imposing erection of stone, outstanding against a half-circle of tall, dark trees. Twin flights of stone steps, ascending from the drive before the house-front, faced each other at their respective heads from the opposite ends of a stone landing, from which a further single flight of steps mounted to the Italian gallery in front of the main apartments. In the centre of this gallery appeared the seigneurial entrance to the interior of the house. Sitting stolidly upon a chair with arms flanking the door outside, was a man in livery. The door was open.

Mailly, having fastened the reins of his horse to a stone pillar of the lower staircase, lightly ran up the steps, whistling between his teeth as he did so. The fellow in livery rose without haste to his feet, and stood smoothing down the coloured waistcoat where it protruded over the inflated part of his person. His face was purple, loose with fat, elderly, and dignified; and apparently the spectacle of a young gentleman on horseback failed to impress his imagination, since it was with scarcely lifted eyelids that he murmured hoarsely the interrogation:

"Monsieur?"

"Bah! if they do not go for ceremony here so much the better," thought Mailly. "The *ménage* doubtless is one of rustic simplicity, it will save much fuss, and Ventailles will introduce me to his lady as to a charming friend." Aloud he said:

"I desire to be announced to M. le Marquis. The name is M. de Mailly. In case it is not his time for receiving, be pleased to add that it is the M. de Mailly who was in the Service."

"M. le Marquis is at home, monsieur, and he will receive you or anyone else with pleasure, for he is extremely bored."

Mailly raised his brows.

"Eh, we are a happy family here! . . . However, 'tis understandable that she should avoid wearying him with her constant presence." He muttered the remarks. The porter turned aside to stifle a yawn behind a hand which for one instant Mailly mistook for a great stuffed glove of crimson cloth.

"Then how does one proceed in the matter of being announced, my friend?"

"M. le Marquis amuses himself with his poodles, monsieur. I will bring you to him, if you will do me the honour to follow me."

"Forward, then. But where is Mme. la Marquise?"

"She is not yet in residence."

"*Peste!* Why not?"

"She is not yet arrived to take up her establishment."

"But are not they married, then?"

The porter shut his eyes contemptuously.

"The marriage was a week ago," he brought out.

"And still she is not here!"

"She is not here, monsieur."

As Mailly walked with shortened steps behind the man up the great central hall, which was painted, both as to walls and ceiling, with love-passages of the classical age, represented with a taste perhaps already too robust and jocular for a generation which pursued the sex with a more delicate ardour, he bit his lip in perplexity.

"So here is a mystery at once," he reflected. "The estate falls to ruins, the lackeys are impudent, he has been married a week and still does not embrace his wife, he welcomes any sort of society, he plays with hounds, and he is bored! I will bet, to begin with, that he is hard up; in which case my journey has been for nothing, it is of no use to sit down to cards. . . . Bah! I can play with anyone, at any time. I have not come for that. I must have scented in Fleurus's shop that this good comrade and gallant gentleman has fallen upon evil days. In journeying down, I have lost the scent, and have fancied him happy. Now again, my inner voice justifies itself. I see why it has been necessary for me to come down, and what I am to do here. A cool head is needed to introduce order to his affairs.

"He is disgraced with the King, he is tumbled into the devil of a scrape with a brace of women, he has perhaps exhausted his supply of ready money, and no one visits him any more. I shall offer my services. In the first place, friend must ever stand by friend; and in the second, he is too good a man to be lost to the world; knowing his qualities as I do, were he a very stranger I would lend him my wits. But since a proud soul detests to be compassionated, I must go about it gently. I have business in Auxerre, I have come a few leagues out of my way to visit an old commander, and the recital of his griefs will amaze me. Between us, we will find a door out. So it shall be!"

The porter paused abruptly before a closed door at the upper end of the hall, turned the handle to throw it open, and drawing himself up, with closed eyes, croaked out to the invisible occupant of the chamber:

"M. de Mailly, to see M. le Marquis de Ventailles!"

The closing syllables diminished into a hollow wail, reverberating through the empty galleries. Without waiting to mark the reception of his announcement, he re-opened his eyes, favoured Mailly with a slighting bow, and at once turned his back to retrace his way down the hall.

Mailly entered. A tallish gentleman, not yet forty, clad in a blue hunting-coat with gilded buttons, fastened to the throat, without cravat, and in black satin knee-breeches, above white stockings and shoes with enormous silver buckles, was sitting perched upon the edge of a polished table in the middle of the room, holding a small wand in his hand. Around the table three disconsolate-looking elongated black puppies were marching in file upon their hind legs, to the word of command. The apartment was all in dazzling sunlight and violet shade.

The gentleman, who wore his own hair, gazed towards the door expectantly to discover who came in, and Mailly identified with some emotion the long, strong, tranquil, handsome features of his chief of former days, little changed since Flanders, save that the pallor of Court life had descended upon cheeks which six years ago the elements had ruddied.

"My dear Mailly!" he exclaimed, after a long pause of

imperfect recognition, accompanying the words by jumping down from the table, and advancing.

"Eh, he knows me!"

They embraced, then held each other at arm's-length, to read the writing which time had left upon their respective countenances.

"Faith! you have altered little," said Mailly, releasing himself at last. "They pretend that you have been in trouble, Ventailles, but you will not make me believe that this eternal youthfulness springs from philosophy. . . . Come! I have left the Service, I have money in my pocket, and I think you will not have to send to Paris for a pack of cards. I can give you till evening, but have my horse taken round."

"*Diable!* you go fast, my dear fellow! Let us talk first. . . . Hold—it occurs to me that I still have the remains of a cellar." He touched a bell. "What is it that you drink in the morning?"

"What you will! But do tell me, Ventailles—does this procession of animals continue all the time that we are together? I feel as in a dream!"

"I am trying to instil morality into their heads by means of discipline, my dear Mailly. I am not yet satisfied, however, whether they resemble human beings more nearly when marching on two legs or when in the act of descending to four. I read at present Diogenes Laertius,[11] who gives such an excellent account of the Cynic Antisthenes. Well, Antisthenes has not taught me to laugh at mankind, but he has taught me that I am not the first to do so, and therefore that I am not mad." He threw his wand at the head of the nearest poodle, and all immediately dropped to the horizontal. At the same moment, a footman entered.

"Wine!" commanded Ventailles. "The '82 Bordeaux. And remove these quadrupeds. Let M. de Mailly's horse be stabled."

The servant bowed, gathered the puppies together in his arms, and retired with the confusion rendered indispensable by such an operation.

"Are you well served here?" asked Mailly, preferring to toy with insignificant topics until the wine should have arrived and they should be alone.

"No man in the kingdom is worse served, I fancy! I have collected all the eminent blockheads within twenty leagues. I do not know how other noblemen get on, but my fellows think that I should be always following the Court. When I come home, they sulk. I shall take service with the Grand Turk!"

Mailly gaped, and looked about him.

"But you—how do you amuse yourself in these days?" proceeded Ventailles nonchalantly. "Are you coupled yet?"

"Eh, no, I have escaped catastrophe so far!"

"For I think you have no inclination that way?"

"That is as it may be, but one with neither rank nor estate does not get exactly the pick of the basket, and because I am nothing much in my own person is no reason why I should resign myself to choose a wife from among the witches. I shall find myself before the altar one day, perhaps, but at least nature will have dragged me there."

"Nevertheless, you are not getting younger, my dear fellow."

"Bah! there is always time for follies," replied Mailly, sucking his teeth.

The footman returned, bearing a basket of wine, with glasses. The basket contained six bottles.

"Uncork all, and retire!" directed Ventailles.

As soon as they were alone once more, he set the glasses on the table, and filled them from the first bottle.

"Bring up a seat for yourself, Mailly. I shall stay where I am, for I am unquiet. Things go wrong!"

Mailly pulled forward a chair, into which he sank, with legs outstretched. Tasting his wine, he gazed up at his host.

"You are in disgrace in high quarters, they say!"

"Tut! that is nothing, and I do not allude to that. Exile from Court is what may happen to any. Between ourselves, 'tis better to be master at home than to be lost amongst a herd of *nouveaux* and nobodies at Versailles and such places. I refer to more tangible evils, my dear fellow. They have told you of my marriage?"

"*Ma foi!* yes."

"It seems I have done something new, for I am fast wed, yet I have no wife! 'Tis my old impetuosity again. There is, after all, something to be said for that *bourgeois* virtue of thinking six times before acting. This weakness of mine has become common property, and it has been taken advantage of perhaps fifty times in my life. Well, this is once more, that is all! . . . Let us pass to a more amusing subject."

"But is it not your affair in which two sisters appear upon the scene? Or am I confounding it with another?"

The Marquis laughed.

"Rest assured there are very undoubtedly two sisters, *pardieu!* That is the hole into which I have slipped. The Dampierre heiresses, daughters of—devil knows whom. The lineage will pass, they have a sort of gentility. Do you know them?"

"No."

"They are twins, my dear fellow. As like as the two halves of a face. He who falls in love with the one, by the same process, and with the same shot, sinks to the other. In effect, but for the accident that they possess two bodies and different names, they are one person. It is to be doubted if five people exist who could distinguish between them."

"But of these five you are one!" And Mailly yawned.

"Do fill your glass! Don't wait for me; I cannot conjure up a thirst in these days. 'Tis an ironic arrangement that when we most stand in need of wine, we have a repugnance to it. . . . Well then, yes! I do not wish you to imagine that it is the money I am after. I have a strong enough eyesight to enable me to enjoy a preference. No two women are alike in temper, however it may be with their pretty flesh, and though I do not affirm that either of these is a saint, yet, for all her fire and storms, 'tis Mdlle. Aglaé, after all, who has it with me. Her sister, Claire, is more civil and obliging, I admit it at once, but she is also more cold, more calculating, and more avaricious. If it were not that her beauty is something supernatural, she would make an admirable notary's wife, that one. How two such dissimilar souls have come to be enclosed in identical vases, I do not know, but so it is."

"Come! which have you married?" demanded Mailly impatiently.

"Alas! my dear fellow, I was contracted to marry her I prefer, whereas I have actually married the other."

"Bah!"

"I assure you that it is so. They have put a trick on me."

Mailly, making a gesture of incredulity, helped himself to a third glass of the Bordeaux, which he found excellent.

"I could sketch the story for you on a thumbnail," added the Marquis, "but you would not be interested, so we will talk of something else instead. Or what is better still, we will play!"

"But where is your wife at this moment?"

"She is at her own home."

"And why not here?"

"That belongs to the story, my dear fellow."

"Then let us have the story," said Mailly.

Ventailles shrugged his shoulders, and drank off a glass of wine.

VIII

The Double Wedding

"The wedding ceremony was a week ago," began the Marquis, swaying a long leg to and fro on the edge of the table. "Before that was a prolonged period of gales, rain, thunder and lightning, and I do not refer to the weather, my dear Mailly. There is an aunt, no longer young, with whom these demoiselles live, a few leagues beyond Auxerre, nearer Paris. Represent to yourself a face like a gipsy's, having eyes which squint, a moustache, and upper teeth which descend upon her chin in the manner of a cascade. I think she is a kind of sorceress.

"Well then, this charming personage appears to be entirely under the thumb of Mdlle. Claire—for so we shall call her, although my wife in name. She is the favourite niece of this aunt, they feel easy together, they peer out at the world through the same eyes. Conceive, Mailly, that for months past these two have been engaged in working upon the mind of Mdlle. Aglaé, in order to spoil a marriage which has not agreed with their desires. *Peste!* she is just the one to be worked upon. My temper is indolent, but, when all is said, I know what is due to my station of life, while, on the other hand, Mdlle. Aglaé pays scant respect to ancestors when she is enraged. You understand, therefore. There were lovers' quarrels, and lovers' quarrels may settle into a habit. However, the day approached, and we put all that behind us. . . Ah, the devil! I had forgotten. Mdlle. Claire, you are to know, also had her affianced. A gentleman of the neighbourhood, a M. de Villary-Loguette, a man of fair estate, but no birth to speak of, a farmer sort of individual, who spends his time between his fields and his counting-house. Heaven knows what or why these persons are, I simply narrate the fact. Again, how she came to be betrothed to this bear we are not to inquire, but doubtless she believed that something in hand would be useful to her in the event of other negotiations."

Mailly, with an air of weariness, emptied the remainder of the first bottle into his glass.

"Come, Ventailles, you are speaking of your wife!"

"You have said it! I am speaking of the creature whom the lawyers and the priests declare to be my wife, I am speaking of her ill, and I have a perfect right to do so. You will see. To proceed. It appears that we were all to have been married at a blow, a thing very absurd, but our demoiselles would have it so, and I chose not to risk a last storm for a bagatelle."

"We are come to the wedding-day?"

"The rest will nearly conclude itself, my dear fellow. Yes, the day is here. Nieces and aunt are to drive across to Jussault early, to sign the contracts, before proceeding to the church. Villary-Loguette will come, to play his part. 'Tis an honour paid to my nobility, the necessity for which I have made clear to all concerned, since these are days when a single concession by a single *seigneur* is forthwith snatched as a right from our whole body. . . . Thus the contracts are to be signed before notaries and witnesses, after which the whole train will move off in carriages to Auxerre, where the religious ceremony is to be celebrated at the church of S. Pierre. Everything is settled, to the very rosettes of the coachmen. Figure to yourself, then, the scene! Ten o'clock in the morning arrives, the doors are flung wide open, it is brilliant sunshine. I post twenty lackeys in new liveries to line the entrance to the hall. I myself am not too far away, be sure. . . ."

"I will finish it for you! Mdlle. Aglaé was persuaded to stay at home, the gentleman was delayed on a pretext, and Mdlle. Claire took advantage of your ill-humour to offer herself in the place of her sister. 'Tis a nimble lady, and you have gained a wife who will advance you, that is all. I do not know what you would have!"

"*Mordieu!* nor I, my dear Mailly. They have shattered my honour for me, and I still stand looking at the fragments, but what I would have I know no more than yourself. Be silent, listen, and judge!

"Those two—Mdlle. Claire and the aunt—step forth from the

carriage alone. 'Where, then, is Mdlle. Aglaé?'—They exchange regards. Will M. le Marquis favour them with six words in private? I draw them into an apartment. 'What is the matter? what has happened?'—My betrothed cannot attend this day.—'Is she indisposed, then?'—They do not speak, and I lose my temper. 'In the devil's name, what is amiss?'—Mdlle. Claire hangs her head and looks away; the old witch brings herself together with a snap, so that one hears in fancy the bones creak. 'Aglaé is afflicted with a vicious spirit, she has said things impossible to repeat, the ceremony must be postponed.'—My face by this is of the colour of chalk, and I am terrible. I twist her wrist to make her speak. She is frightened, the truth at last comes gushing forth as from a decayed fountain.

"'Aglaé is insistent that you have but entered upon this marriage to patch your estate, and she will still make you wait awhile. 'Tis a female revenge for all your affronts of late. If the wedding must go forward, she bids me counsel you to step before the house and whistle shrilly, a hundred marriageable demoiselles will come running up from all four quarters! She bids me say that, for her part, her need of a husband is not so pressing, she is in no haste, she will look about her a little, prudence at first is better than sorrow at last!'

"All this and more the old beldam spits out swiftly and surely, as a toad shoots its tongue. She seems to mock my misery, and I am minded to slit her yellow, desiccated throat; yet she has borrowed the accents of my betrothed, by some diabolic art 'tis she whom I hear speaking these endearments! I turn upon the other. 'Come, Mdlle. Claire, is all this truth that I listen to?'—She is as pale as I. 'My sister is mad, I think! I assure, you, monsieur, I have wetted her feet with the tears from my eyes, yet she is stubborn in fixing this cruel dishonour upon you. Would that I could expiate our disgrace in my own person! Gladly would I relinquish happiness!' Her tears flow in reality.

"In the midst of my anger I stop to mark her distress. 'Come, come, mademoiselle!—it is no fault of yours, you must not shed tears on your wedding-day, your bliss at least is assured. But where is Villary-Loguette?'—They do not answer.—'Where is he, then?' My voice is brisker. Mdlle. Claire brings out in a breath no louder than a leaf falling: 'He is with Aglaé!' . . . At this, a skin drops from before my eyes, and I think I see all. I say nothing, I oblige my face to preserve its calm, I pace up and down the chamber in rapid meditation. Thus he is her lover, and all those storms have resulted from her antipathy to my person! . . . Enough, my dear fellow! I am skewered as neatly as a partridge! I cannot wait for vengeance, I must have it upon the spot. Mdlle. Aglaé must be taught that she is not so indispensable. Villary-Loguette must be made to understand that my plans are not so easily upset, and that he has but succeeded in robbing his new beloved of a title, for which she will presently not thank him.

"After six more turns up and down, I propose the thing. 'Come, mademoiselle! it seems we have no alternative, they compel us to it!'—She is admirable. Conceive that Villary-Loguette is but round the corner, as it were. She has, perhaps, not ten minutes in which to yield to my persuasions, and to sign new contracts before he will appear. Yet she contrives her gradations in the most natural way in the world, she stints nothing of sighs and hesitations, and still she does not use all the time at her disposal. She is still weeping gently when I leave the room in search of the notaries and witnesses. Smiles, raised brows, whispers, head-shakings, are ignored. The signing is accomplished. That part is done. We set our carriages towards Auxerre at the gallop, for such feats must be carried with a rush, and enthusiastically. At the church, the priest, who is a good fellow, rattles through our business for us at top speed. We find ourselves beneath the porch again, man and wife together! My feelings have liquefied into a paste. I do not know if I am of the blessed elect, or a raging demon!"

Mailly set down his glass again.

"'Pon honour! you describe things admirably, Ventailles! The first trick is hers, then!"

"Listen, however! We are still beneath the portico of S. Pierre, prepared to re-enter our carriage, that is, Madame my wife and I, for the aunt is not to return with us, I am imbecile only on one point—when suddenly there is great clatter of hoofs under the gateway, and a man comes pricking up like the devil in chase of a lost soul. He throws himself off his roan. 'Tis Villary-Loguette! At first I fancy him in liquor, but it is but the excitement under which he labours.—'*Ah, mon Dieu! mon Dieu!*—what has taken place here? What is all this that I see?'—I am calm for everybody, though already hideous doubts begin to oppress me. I refrain from reprehending this person in the presence of my wife; that will come afterwards. Politely and coldly I satisfy his curiosity. His countenance becomes green. 'Thus I was sent to Ballieu in order that I might arrive at Jussault too late!'—Ballieu is the residence of nieces and aunt—'You have been very cunning, mademoiselle or madame, whichever we are to call you, and I congratulate you heartily! M. le Marquis has perhaps gained a cleverer wife than he is aware of!'—It is for me to defend my spouse against brutalities, and I do so. 'Have the goodness to address your insolences to me, monsieur! I shall know what to do with them.' 'I shall address what I please to you, monsieur, at my own time, and where I shall choose! At the moment I content myself with addressing information to you, supposing that you have been deceived equally with myself. Learn, then, that I was bidden this morning to Ballieu by Mdlle. Claire, to escort all those three ladies to your *château*. On arriving at Ballieu, however, in obedience to my summons, I found Mdlle. Claire and Madame already departed to Jussault; but Mdlle. Aglaé had not departed with them, owing to the circumstance that she was confined to her chamber, by a fever. Thus it appears to have been thought that my escort was unnecessary for two only, since I was not waited for!'—As Villary-Loguette says all this, more brokenly perhaps than I repeat it, my hand releases the arm of my wife, and I regard her sternly. 'Come, madame! we have not previously heard of this fever, I fancy!'—She smiles loftily. 'Fever is a name covering many conditions, monsieur! That she is confined to her chamber, I admit. Would you prefer that she should go about her duties on such a day?'——'Why did you send for this gentleman?'—'Was not it my privilege?'—'Then why did you not wait for him?'—'He was late in coming.'—Villary-Loguette changes from green to scarlet—or, rather, I do not know of what colour he is. 'Madame, I was before my appointed time. Moreover, your sister's fever is genuine, since I have spoken to the physician in attendance. He departed as I entered, and it seems that he imagined me to be her affianced, come to seek her. "She will not get out of bed to-day, monsieur. I do not wish to have to discuss it all over again!"—"I have not seen you before, monsieur, whoever you may be!"—"I am the physician, and I tell you at once that if I have not succumbed to mademoiselle's pleadings, I shall not succumb to yours. A marriage which is to be succeeded by a funeral is no marriage at all, and if she rises from her bed to-day, I will not answer for the sequel. Come to me tomorrow, and I shall then tell you whether she is to be better or worse."—Greatly perturbed, both on account of this poor lady and myself, I hastened forward to Jussault, only to find the birds still flown on. I have sped hither. I behold you issue from the church, so doubtless some sort of ceremony has taken place. I do not know what it is, or whether you are indeed man and wife, and I shall not even inquire. You have behaved very ill, M. le Marquis, to cast off from you your betrothed so frivolously, even supposing that these ladies have ensnared you and that the thing has been resolved upon suddenly, which I do not know. I have not the right to debate that with you, but you have also robbed me of my contracted wife, and we shall discuss this further between ourselves. For you, madame, I have but one word of counsel. You cannot undo your sin, but, as you value your immortal soul, proceed no further; do not carry it to the extent of happiness; do not bring down upon your head the just vengeance of Heaven! Retire to some convent while there is yet time, there to expiate your wickedness with mortifications and midnight prayers. You are young, with perhaps many years before you, and it may be that it will be forgiven you before the end!'—Upon concluding the harangue, he springs on his horse again, and rides off. We stare after him."

Mailly took up the third bottle.

"He seems a very good sort of fellow, however, this one!"

"I turn upon the aged beldam, who avoids my eye, and titters nervously. 'Well, madame, what am I to understand from all this?'—'Monsieur, you are starting very early to be suspicious, that is all I have to say!'—'I have been fairly tricked, is it not?'—She looks abashed and shakes her feathers and metal ornaments like a frightened hen. My wife speaks for both. Her eyes gleam. 'Monsieur, we will continue this conversation at Jussault, if you please! 'Tis too public here.'—My choler is by this at its height. 'Madame, if you so much as show your face at Jussault to-day or at any other time I swear to you that I will have you put out by the lackeys! You will return to your home. I shall consider what is to be done, and I shall communicate with you. Come, madame! don't compel me to push you away, for I promise you that is what will happen should you attempt to enter my carriage with me!' . . . Enough, my dear fellow! She swoons, or pretends to do so, and while her people are gathered around her, I step, like one conducted to the gallows, into my vehicle, and am driven off. The sun goes in; the landscape becomes obscured. I will give ten thousand *louis* to be in the place of the gentleman who, next after me, is the most wretched in the world! We see each other no more."

"We then consult the oracle of the law, I think?"

"Yes, we visit the lawyers, who tell us that a marriage differs from all other contracts in this, that it cannot be terminated by a mutual consent; who tell us that wedded life follows the marriage ceremony as an effect follows its cause, and that Mme. la Marquise de Ventailles, be the circumstances what they may, can no more return to be Mdlle. Claire de Dampierre than a chicken can re-enter its shell! . . . Bah! I have taken a fine revenge! To punish her for her treachery, I have sent her away; I have given her all France for a *château*, and every Frenchman for a lover! Imagine if she is exceedingly distressed to exchange Jussault for Paris, for example. However, there is still a notable check in store for her, there is still a last ditch to cross before she is high and dry, and I fancy she will find it a difficult one. Learn, my dear Mailly, that I am no longer Marquis de Ventailles!"

Mailly arrested the upward motion of his glass, to stare at his host.

"I sink back to Vidame de Cléry. Villary-Loguette has won my marquisate of me at play."

"At play—after what has happened! *Diable!* that goes a little beyond me, I confess!"

"Come, my dear fellow! Can't you see? It was my marquisate against a half-million livres of his. *Peste!* I could not well refuse him satisfaction, while a duel with swords has been made too difficult an affair in these days. It was a gallant proposal, for that half-million would have crippled his estate, and he has had small experience with cards. . . . In short, he won. We played in this very apartment, but two days ago. Within an hour he had piqued, repiqued, and capoted me,[12] and had walked off with this parchment in his pocket, as coolly as though it had been a pound of raisins! I assure you that he made less of it than I myself, and I was yawning. He who has a bad wife is dipped in the Styx against all other calamities."

"Bah! he may plaster the interior of his house with scrolls of nobility, but he will be none the more a *seigneur!* The King's consent must be procured, and he will straightway refuse it. You might as sensibly have played for sugar-plums."

"I have told myself so, but this Villary-Loguette is not like others. 'Tis a man who makes himself acquainted with the destiny of every seed he puts into his fields. We shall assume that he has no great yearnings to be marquis himself, but desires to prevent a certain other from becoming marquise. These russet gentlemen squelch so much in mud and clay with their thick boots that by degrees their souls acquire something of the same consistence. They cannot disengage themselves from an affair without an effort; to turn to a new face is like pulling up a footload of February mire. He has thought of this absurd revenge, he has risked five hundred thousand livres to deprive me of the title, and he has won. Is it in order to secrete the parchment in his cabinet?

We shall believe so when we see the cat return the mouse to its hole!"

Mailly rose to stretch his limbs, yawn, and gaze out of the window, which came nearly to the floor, and outside was but a few feet above the level of the gravel pathway. Ventailles, still dangling his legs over the edge of the table, continued more querulously:

"But do give me some advice, my dear friend! I no longer meet anyone, everything here is quiet as the inside of a box, and yet perhaps at this very moment they are running a mine under my feet, to waft me heavenwards. Mdlle. Aglaé has departed to Paris to seek direction. My wife sits at home with the old Hecate, revolving one knows not what schemes of malevolence. Villary-Loguette, for once, is not dreaming only of parsnips. 'Tis not in possibility that they will leave me in peace; yet no word reaches me. I am horribly nonplussed. Action of some sort is demanded, but what?"

Mailly went on looking out of doors.

"*Pardieu!* send out scouts!"

"The suggestion is not bad, but I cannot send flunkeys, and I have no more friends."

"If that is all, I shall go for you. I have nothing to do."

"You, Mailly?"

"That is, if you wish it. The affair is not one demanding special parts. 'Tis but to stir up all these people to speak, which I will wager they will be very ready to do."

"It is a notion. Whom, then, would you take first?"

Mailly came back to the table, shrugging his shoulders.

"Where is Ballieu, for example?"

"On the Paris road, a league or so past Auxerre."

"Villary-Loguette, where is he set?"

"He farms Sourthe, which is a great property lying towards Bourges, two leagues from this and three from the other. So you see that you will spend your horse, my dear fellow, and probably to no purpose, since what interest have they in relieving my suspense? Moreover, who sends out a courier to bring back ill news! I am trussed, and a miracle cannot save me."

"Then I shall stay here, and we will play. It grows late, in any case. I must set back before evening."

"To Paris?"

"Yes, to Paris."

"Let us send for cards, then. But you will eat with me?"

"On second thoughts, no, Ventailles."

"Why not?"

"I have just recollected business in Auxerre. So I shall do what I have to do, dine there, and return here for an hour or two in the afternoon. We will play then. I warn you, however, that my luck is in."

Ventailles, after staring at him with an incredulous smile for a few moments, descended slowly from the table to grip his arm.

"My dear Mailly, you have a way of conferring obligations which has to be experienced! Fortunately, I know you. Confess that this Auxerre transaction is mythical—you go on my affair?"

IX

The Black Dog

Mailly laughingly disengaged himself.

"And if so?"

"*Cordieu!* if so, considering that but an instant ago it was decided between us that you should stay here, some idea must have occurred to you, and I should very much like to know what it is, since it is too evident to me that the case is without remedy."

"If I tell you nothing, it is for a reason. The inspiration has sprung from the fumes of wine, so I cannot tell yet whether it is worth anything. I shall gallop off these fumes, then if the notion still appears not ridiculous, we shall see."

"Use no more rodomontade, but tell me, what is this famous conception?"

"Yes, that you may forbid my going! . . . Farewell! You will behold me again before evening."

"Come! what are you to effect?"

"You will be horrified."

"No, I swear it."

"Supposing, then, that we could change your wife for you!"

The Marquis turned pale, yet smiled.

"Ah! so they have started an exchange market for wives."

"No—but tell me, Ventailles, it is still Mdlle. Aglaé that attracts? This mischance has not created in you an aversion to the entire family? Were you free, you would not now wish to marry outside?"

"My dear Mailly, we are in the world!"

"Undoubtedly we are in the world, but that is not to say that we are therefore to shut our eyes to the hints of Heaven. *Peste!* I am not atheist, I; the world has not made itself, strangenesses do not come by accident, and 'tis impious to believe so. These sisters cannot have been cast from the same mould without a purpose. Manifestly, Providence has prepared beforehand for this very event. In a word, we shall juggle one for the other."

"Pshaw!"

"Though if the expression be uncivil as applied to ladies, I shall seek a better."

"But this is not an idea, it is a chimera!"

"And so I was wrong to tell you."

"However, you joke! Put off your hat, and I shall send for a pack."

"Faith! no. I have promised this monstrous conception a ride, and I shall give it one."

"Come, Mailly!"

"I am serious."

"You are serious in proposing that Mdlle. Aglaé shall take her sister's place in my establishment."

"Yes."

"I understand you! But there are two objections to your plan, my dear fellow. She is not that sort of lady, while, for me, I do not want to transform my life into a bad jest. I do not wish to bring a brood of bastards into the world. We will not speak of the religious side, though there is that side, too. Alas! this inspiration is decidedly of the grape!"

"I do not mean anything of all that."

"Then what do you mean?"

"Adieu!"

"Stay!—what are you about?"

"You have put me on my mettle, with your chimeras and inspirations of the grape!"

"Come, sit down! I forbid you to pass the door. *Mordieu!* you will end by landing both of us inside the Bastille! The times are grave, and if I see anything at all of your design, it is unlawful. I command you to sit down, Mailly!"

Mailly moved towards the door.

"Adieu!"

"Return, or I shall tell my people to shut the gates!"

"Adieu!"

"Well, go then, wretch! Hasten away to give this final impulse which is to precipitate my affairs to the bottom! But, before going, at least tell me what you are to do?"

"I shall propose the exchange to all these people."

"Your senses have quite departed from you!"

"Then they have departed."

"However, visit my wife first. I will engage that no more will be necessary!"

"Well, I will visit her first."

"To say—what?"

"To persuade her to this exchange."

"*Pardieu!* you will need all the resources of your diplomacy to persuade her to give up what she has worked so ardently for!"

"Diplomacy, yes."

"Come, Mailly!—to put it at the lowest, who the devil has set it in your head that you are a negotiator? What new fancy is this? You never were that way."

"I admit it is recent."

"Sit down, and open the mystery to me. Do not spare the bottle on such a fine morning."

"Yes, you would like it!" And Mailly laughingly approached the table again, but without offering to drink.

"Speak, what have you been doing with yourself lately?" proceeded the Marquis, with a disarming smile. "I do not think you have been at Court, or I should have seen you there. You say that you have quitted the Service?"

"Yes, Ventailles, I have discovered the theory of diplomacy, and you would be astonished at its simplicity."

"Ah, there is a formula!"

"Would you like to hear it?"

"Very much."

"Listen, then! Men and women are always to be moved by what they desire, but do not possess. One has therefore but to hold before their nose the object of their desire, and they will instantly follow one about with the utmost docility! That is the whole art. It flashed across me one day in remarking a cat remove a fish from the dinner-table. I perceived how the animal refused the wine, the bread, the fruit, and even the roasted joint, springing straight upon the fish as a steel filing springs upon a magnet. The entirety of politics was illuminated for me at a single stroke. I saw that passion effects all, and that, in order to get our cat on to the table, it is only necessary to place a fish there. There is no need to chase and hallo it around the room, we may take our ease in our chair, the animal will in a few moments ascend."

"*Diable!* a grand secret!" said Ventailles jeeringly.

"Yes, and, to translate all into human language, we have only to offer people what they greatly desire, and they will pay our price, even if the money must be borrowed. 'Tis of no avail to tickle, cajole, and flatter, 'tis of no use to promise this and that which the other is well assured we have not in our pocket, but we must produce our fish, when the transaction will immediately complete itself."

"And have you such a fish for my wife, for instance?"

"Assuredly, or it would be absurd to visit her."

"Then let us hear!"

Mailly resumed his seat.

"You do not pretend that she loves your person, Ventailles?"

"It is possible, my dear fellow, but at least she has never confessed as much."

"So that she has married your rank?"

"We shall suppose so."

"Villary-Loguette, however, has won your marquisate of you in play?"

"Yes."

"Then 'tis not you she will follow, but her fish. Do you take me?"

"In other words . . ."

"On the condition that she ceases to be your wife, we shall offer to her to be reconciled with him who has procured your title. That is to say, she shall marry her Villary-Loguette after all. Do I reason soundly?"

"Perhaps; but only if marriages are to be put on and off at will, like garments, which I have never heard to be the case."

"Do not make yourself ridiculous until you have heard all! That is for your wife. We next visit Villary-Loguette. What wants this one?"

"You would say that he wants back his bride, and, in truth, it is beautifully simple!"

"For you have not received her, Ventailles, and I dare swear you have not so much as soiled her with a kiss. His fish, therefore, will be Mdlle. Claire, whom he loves so passing well, even to forgiveness for a great treachery. Or do you think that he will not forgive her?"

"Faith! I have no ideas upon the subject."

"However, in case his resentment is paramount, we shall also apply to that. He desires to punish her—we shall oblige him. She will be very appropriately punished by marrying him, and losing the title after all. He shall divert himself sweetly and maliciously at her expense by secretly disposing of his new dignity—for which she marries him—before the ceremony, keeping from her the knowledge until afterwards. . . . But how say you, Ventailles?—could anything be more neatly balanced than all these conflicting motives? On her part, ambition; on his, love and revenge! Are not they all prime forces in the human soul, and do not we find them in these two persons in unmixed purity? Can you detect a flaw in my logic?"

"Bah! were it really possible to effect all this, I should affirm that you are in a fair way to bring about one more miserable union. One would cut the other's throat within a twelvemonth! . . . So I am to get back my marquisate?"

"Yes, for that is your price for restoring to Villary-Loguette his bride intact."

"And thus the road is clear for me to wed the other, and the circle will be completed. We shall end as we have started."

Mailly drank, and set down his glass.

"No."

"What then?"

"You will not wed her, for you have already wedded her. Do drink, Ventailles! You are exceedingly dull this morning. I thought that I had explained all that.”

“It is you whose ideas are strange, my dear fellow. I have married one sister, and you tell me that I have married the other!”

“Certainly.”

“Then what the devil are you talking about?”

Standing up, and thrusting forward his chest, Mailly struck it several times with his clenched fist, in order to relieve an indigestion which began to annoy him.

“It seems that you are not very well up in the customs of France, marquis.”

“Oh, you speak of a custom!”

“I do not say that it is a custom to marry one and live in matrimony with another. But there is a custom, in the provinces, at least, and among families of ancient tradition—or *peste*! if there is no such custom, then I have dreamt it. . . . I say the custom is for twin-sons or twin-daughters of a house to exchange their names in the cradle, whereby, for instance, Marie becomes Jeanne, and Jeanne, Marie—not in law, be it understood, but perhaps to perplex and mystify certain malign invisible potencies which do not love these twin births, and seek to summon by name one or the other from life. I affirm that if there is not, there ought to be this custom.”

“Come, Mailly, there is no such custom, and you romance!”

“So that the thing already fades from common memory, and, should we desire to confirm it, we must apply to our elders. The aged crone, the aunt—she will be the repository of this forgotten exchange, we cannot doubt it. Thus I shall visit her as well.”

“You are completely mad!”

“Not the least in the world! ’Tis impossible that these two demoiselles, while still mewing in long-clothes, should not have been made to obey this antique ritual of the countryside, perhaps passed down to us from the Gauls of Caesar and Germanicus. Have not the parents been of old establishment here? In short, the exchange was really effected. Then which have you married, Ventailles? . . . Do not answer, for I will answer for you. The contracts, the notaries, the witnesses, the priest, all unite in telling you that you have married Mdlle. Claire. Therefore, you have married Mdlle. Claire. But which of these sisters is Mdlle. Claire? All will depend upon that. I, for my part, affirm that it is she whom you have hitherto known as Mdlle. Aglaé. Then very well! You have after all married your betrothed. Heaven has intervened to save you from the unfortunate consequences of your ignorance, and but for this calamity, which is now proved no calamity, you would have by this been living in deadly sin with your wife's sister—that is to say, with the rightful Mdlle. Claire, your old affianced. For the marriage contracts would have been in the name of Mdlle. Aglaé."

"But *mordieu!* she with whom I have stood up in church is my wife."

"No. A hundred times, no! That one must be regarded as a proxy, a ceremonial figure, someone who could stand upon her legs in order to repeat certain words and perform certain actions which are necessary to be repeated and performed before you are entitled to come together with your wife without scandal. What though the proxy has not been declared at the time?—we shall declare it now . . . or, rather, there is no need to declare it, we shall allow it to continue to be thought that it was truly your bride who honoured you by attending for this celebration. *Peste!* the alikeness being so close, who is to guess that there has been a substitution? We shall not plague ourselves over the trifle of sin contained in the counterfeit. A deceit, injuring none and the salvation of four, must be very venial. You shall present S. Pierre with a few candles. There remains but the novelty of the name. For me, I find *Claire* less heathenish than *Aglaé*, besides having more of simplicity, less of preciousness. *Claire* is cold, haughty, stately, and decidedly of the best tone. A week will accustom you to its use, and then you will like it better than the other."

The Marquise poured himself out a glass. He looked round smilingly at Mailly.

"Have you quite finished, extraordinary man?"

"Laugh if you will, but is not the scheme feasible?"

"Come, my dear fellow! do you yourself honestly believe that one poor invention will ever stand the weight of so crushing a burden of consequences? I will admit its cleverness.”

“It will stand, for the reason that it cannot do otherwise than stand. We shall establish this change of names legally.”

“Proceed! Let us hear to the end!”

“We will have a notary to prepare an instrument, and we will have this instrument signed, sealed, and witnessed. The aunt shall declare before Heaven that the names of our demoiselles were transposed in infancy, and each shall forthwith accept her proper one.”

“Bah! I do not know a lawyer in France who would conduct such a transaction without insisting upon diving to its true signification. Do not forget that there is the question of date. Your instrument, to be of use to us, must bear a date prior to my marriage. It is a hundred to one that the lawyer will have heard of the marriage. He will therefore be knowingly circumventing the law. It is but one point.”

“I am acquainted with a man who will do our business for us. His curiosity is small, he knows nothing of what goes on in the world, while he has not been in his profession for forty years to remain ignorant of the safe and accurate employment of phrases and clauses; but he is avaricious; he will ask a thousand crowns, perhaps.”

“Of Auxerre?”

“No, of Paris. Fleurus, Rue du Mail.”

“But then, the old sibyl will not perjure her soul immediately before going aloft, even for a favourite niece.”

“You will grease her shrine.”

Ventailles reflected, then laughed.

“Then let us play with the devil a little! I have no more to lose.”

“I will be off at once.”

“Yes, go!—go, my dear Mailly, waste no time on the road, do all that you have undertaken, return swiftly to tell me that I am married to the right one, and I swear that I shall eternally regard you as my saviour, and the dearest and most faithful friend that I have ever had! You know how to address women?”

“I have a particular gift with them. I do not boast of it, but it is there. . . . Adieu, then!”

Ventailles wrung his friend’s hand with feeling.

“Depart, in Heaven’s name, and let us not doubt that Heaven will reward you! After six years of separation, you cannot have come to seek me out in my hour of darkest perplexity save by the direction of a higher Power. Visits of this kind are not accidental, they are the proof of an invisible interest in our destiny!”

“One must believe so. And upon my return we will play.”

“Ah, demon, you can still stay to drink! It must be that you desire to converse with those women by the light of candles. I release the bow-string, and the arrow does not budge!”

“I have done—I go. But tell me, Ventailles—that I may have something to think on as I ride forth—this ill-luck of yours, when did it commence? In the old times your fortune was phenomenal—you could do nothing wrong, as I remember it. To behold you in distress affects me as strangely as though I should witness a Paris cat fall from a roof on to its back! ’Tis to reverse nature.”

“My dear fellow, it is two years and more since I have got my shots on to the target. I do not know what it is. My blood is water, my brain is dulled, and I do stupid things. It is not ill-luck, it is some disease.”

“Farewell, Ventailles!”

“Yet do not forget one thing.”

“What is that?”

“My wife is beautiful, she will squeeze out tears for you, and you will soften. Do not pass to the side of the enemy.”

“I shall remember constantly that the sister she has wronged is of equal beauty. Have no fears! I am not a petticoat-maggot.”

The Marquis was standing with his back to the table, holding on to the edge negligently with both hands. Suddenly he straightened himself with a start, and glanced quickly down at his feet.

“Perdition! I thought that all those hounds were out of the

room!"

Mailly stared around him with surprise.

"What is the matter?"

"I could have sworn that a hound passed between my legs! Do you see anything?"

"No."

Ventailles bent to look beneath the chairs and tables. He contradicted the laws governing blood by getting up again with a face paler than before.

"Then no doubt it is my black dog!"

"Ah, you have a black dog!"

"'Tis a family presage of death. Put off your hat, Mailly! You need not go this journey."

"But . . ."

"Do not argue, my dear fellow, and do not banter! It is as I say. In the elder branch of my house such a token has ever been followed by a death. It needed this to fulfil my cup of misfortune, and it has been very absurd in me not to have suspected that something of the sort would happen. Sit down! I will send for stronger wine; we will spend the day in drinking. 'Tis the one profitable employment left to me."

"You cannot be serious!"

"I assure you, yes."

"Well then, someone is to die, we will allow it, but why must that one be you? There are others of your family. *Peste!* you are egotistical!"

"I am the head, the sign has appeared to me, and, if the truth must be told, it consorts well with my private feelings. No, you shall not leave me to-day, my dear Mailly!"

"Then we will grant as well that it is you who is to die, since you insist upon it, but is that to say that you will die to-day, to-morrow or the next day? At least, let us set our affairs in order before descending to the tomb. You do not desire your wife to inherit, for example?"

"Let us leave all that. I care not what happens when I am departed. For the few years of life, it is not worth the while of any to scramble after estates. Let them divide mine as they will.”

“Bah! you will end by making me angry. I do not laugh at these warnings, but there is great unreliability in them, of which I could give you a hundred instances. Sometimes the event hangs fire for a month, six months, or a year, and sometimes nothing follows at all. A man may easily go to the devil on his own account while they are preparing his death with so much fuss and ceremony on the other side. What is an omen? What good does it to us? It unsettles, without serving us—just the reverse, in fact! As an example, here you are to settle yourself in your seat to swill until you can hold no more. That is very well for to-day, but to-morrow you will still be to die, and you will have acquired an abominable head into the bargain. The devil! that is not at all the way to do it! Harness, rather, this excellent black dog to your affairs, and, since you have not long for the world, set to with all the more energy to undo the injury to your affianced, and to procure for yourself a son and heir to carry on your name. If Heaven refuses you time for such an act of repentance, we shall affirm that Heaven is greatly to blame.”

The Marquis smote the bell which stood upon the table.

“You have an astonishing fire of character, Mailly, and you are a capital fellow in every way, but, if there be a flaw in your nature, it is that you honour religion too little.”

The footman appeared.

“Remove all those bottles!” ordered Ventailles. “Bring, in their place, six of the ’76 Spanish red!”

The man bowed, gathered up the bottles, empty and full, and withdrew from the room. Ventailles resumed his seat on the table, again dangling his legs.

“You will drink alone, however, marquis,” said Mailly coldly. “I have had enough. I shall start for home.”

“So you desert me with the rest!”

“I have nothing more to do here. I cannot drink always.”

“Then let us play.”

“No, I thank you! I do not find it sufficiently amusing to play with the sick and dying. Send for a priest, if you must have company.”

“Come, you are offended!”

“Upon my honour, no!—I am exceedingly beholden to you for relieving me of a disagreeable mission, which, between ourselves, I dreaded. ‘Offended’ is rather good, I think! One souses himself over head and heels in a pool of green slime, I offer to bring him to the bank, and he declines. Does this refusal offend me? *Mordieu!* I am only too delighted to find that he is content with his situation!”

“Do not believe me ungrateful, Mailly, my dear friend.”

Mailly moved his shoulders impatiently, and made as if to go.

“After this sign, I dare not proceed,” continued the Marquis. “While I am in the very act of erecting one sin upon another, they address me. It is as though an angel stood across my path with folded arms.”

The handle of the door turned, and the door itself was pushed open from without. Both gentlemen turned their heads in expectation to behold the lackey return with the wine. No one entered, however. Instead, the croak sounded of the same porter who had previously announced Mailly himself.

“Mdlle. Aglaé de Dampierre waits in the Salon de Zodiaque to speak with M. le Marquis de Ventailles!”

The Marquis’s name swelled and died as before in a nasal wail. Mailly rammed down his hat on his head angrily.

“*Peste!* midnight strikes, the fiend has come, and Ventailles is a lost soul!” he said to himself. “The bottom falls from the pot!” And aloud he exclaimed:

“Don’t see her, marquis!”

Ventailles smiled, slid from the table, and straightened his coat. He raised his voice to address the invisible messenger outside the door, but without suffering the tranquillity of its tone to be disturbed:

“Beg Mdlle. de Dampierre to honour me by attending me here!”

Then, as the retreating porter’s footsteps shuffled on the tiled floor of the hall, the Marquis turned to his friend.

"Leave me, Mailly, but do not go far away."

"If I leave you, the affair finishes itself at a blow. Unforgivable things will be spoken on both sides, and . . ."

"I do not know that, but I know that I must be alone. Go quickly, my friend!"

"You will mortally anger each other, without having effected anything whatever. Let me see her, Ventailles."

"Go!—go, I say!"

"For what are you to tell her? *Pardieu!* that you exceedingly regret the mischance, and would that it were within your power to make adequate amends! She will at once be appeased, of course!"

"Do not persist, my dear fellow! I shall arrange nothing without you. Wait somewhere near at hand—perhaps I shall call you in."

The porter was heard returning, his steps accompanied by a lighter, sharper tread. Mailly still loitered.

"Well then, I will efface myself by the window yonder. I shall not be in the way."

"As you are a gentleman, leave me, Mailly!"

"Since you absolutely insist, I must, although I think it madness. You will present me first, however?"

The footsteps drew to the door, then ceased. The porter's voice sang hoarsely from without:

"Mdlle. Aglaé de Dampierre!"

Mailly whipped off his hat, and prepared to bow. A tall, stately, beautiful, and elegantly-dressed lady, still young, came with a rapid footfall across the threshold, and there stood undecided, to note swiftly whom the apartment might contain.

X

Aglaé de Dampierre

"Go, or by God I will put you out!" whispered the Marquis angrily to his friend.

"Present me, however," repeated Mailly in his natural voice.

At its pleasant and unusual *timbre*, Mdlle. de Dampierre vouchsafed him a single haughty flash from her cold blue eyes. Her pallid face bore an expression of settled sternness—the expression of one who has re-arrived at composure through anguish. A small gloved hand was held awkwardly underneath the floating end of the black lace scarf encircling her throat. She moved aside into the room to permit the strange gentleman to pass out.

Ventailles reddened.

"You can see that this is no time for civilities," he murmured rapidly. "Do not create a scene, for that is what will happen if you do not go away quickly. What are you thinking of?"

He advanced to receive his visitor, who remained near the door. She neither returned his bow, nor looked at him, and it was manifest that she waited for Mailly's departure before opening her business. The Marquis, turning his head to perceive his friend still motionless, strode swiftly back, to grasp his arm beneath the elbow with vice-like fingers.

"Have you no manners, my dear fellow?"

"*Peste!* I was about to ask you that very question. Since when have you left your guests to grope their own way out from the middle of your *salons?* I might be a shopkeeper come to present a bill."

"If that is all . . ."

They passed together to the door, and through it outside into the hall. Mailly drew his host a few paces further down it.

"What have you to say that cannot wait?" demanded Ventailles impatiently.

"She is a perfect Helen, marquis! I compliment you on your admirable taste. There is but one fault in her equipment, and it is a damnable one."

"What do you mean?"

"*Pardieu!* when you get back, remark how her right hand is decorated!"

"You would say that it bears a poniard. Very well!—I too have seen it. And what then?"

"The vagaries of feminine fashion are notorious, nevertheless Paris is still in advance of Auxerre, and Parisiennes do not yet affect these daggers. We must assume, therefore, that it is intended for use."

"We shall not doubt it."

"Then perhaps you are to be obliging enough to offer your throat?"

"These things are in God's hand, Mailly. However, I thank you. Mention what you have seen to none, and you will complete your service."

"Only guard yourself," replied Mailly disgustedly.

Without staying to witness his friend's retreat to the apartment, he turned on his heel, and started sombrely to walk down the hall, towards the entrance door.

The door of Ventailles's room banged behind him, just as he came face-to-face with the lackey returning with the commanded wine. The fellow had the tall, uncouth frame and the foolish face of a country lout. Mailly stopped him.

"You cannot go in. The Marquis is occupied."

"Then this wine, monsieur?"

"Set it down, and wait."

"Then I will wait outside the door."

"Do so, and your master will thank you! Proceed to cover a portion of the crack with your ear, that the breeze may not enter to annoy him! . . . Come, imbecile! take up your post opposite, across the hall. Should a lady issue from the room, or should you hear the Marquis call out, go to him at once."

"Very well, monsieur."

"So let me see you at your station!"

The footman bore his basket to the spot indicated by Mailly's
finger, set it on the ground, and, standing up again, started to gape
stupidly, uneasily conscious of his awkwardness under the
gentleman's critical glare. Satisfied that he would not stir from
where he was within a reasonable time, Mailly resumed his
passage down the hall.

The porter, having returned from announcing the lady, once
more filled his seat on the stone gallery overlooking the stairs and
the sunlit grounds before the *château*. The guest touched him on
the shoulder from behind.

"My horse!"

The other got up with an impudent leisureliness, turned round,
and took in the whole of Mailly's person, before sounding a
whistle attached to a cord round his neck. Another servant
appeared.

"Have M. de Mailly's horse brought round."

The footman bowed to his superior, and vanished. The porter
continued standing, humming beneath his breath, while looking
away. Mailly turned his back upon him, and stepped to the stone
balustrade above the intermediate landing, to inspect the yellow
closed carriage, with the single handsome grey between its shafts,
which stood drawn up before the house. It could only be Mdlle.
de Dampierre's. The broad, pimpled, impassive features of the
coachman in livery seemed familiar to him; it was a visage like a
hundred others, but he fancied that it recalled to him some old
association. He leant forward over the parapet to address the man,
who still did not look up.

"My friend, where have I seen you before?"

The coachman cocked an eye aloft from his seat, grinned, and
favoured Mailly with a military salute.

"I was in your troop, M. de Mailly. Jean Leroux."

"Ah, that was it! . . . And so you have left soldiering?"

"A dog's life, monsieur! Well enough for you young
gentlemen, who have only to be shot at, but a private's work
begins where yours leaves off, monsieur. If all served in the

ranks, there would be no more wars, I'll swear to that."

"So you have taken service with Mdlle. Aglaé de Dampierre?"

"Yes, monsieur."

"And you like it?"

"I make no complaints."

"Then see that you do not run off for higher wages. Money is not the only thing."

"Just what I say, M. de Mailly. If I cannot respect people, I will not wear their livery."

Mailly kept turning his ear towards the interior of the house, as though expecting a summons from the Marquis.

"It is not enough to respect others, though, Leroux," he went on, in a tone of benevolent admonition. "The principal thing is to be respected ourselves, and if we have not steadiness of purpose, we cannot be. Since Mdlle. de Dampierre behaves well to you, remain with her, and begin to build up a reputation for faithfulness."

"That is what I mean, monsieur. If a servant is not willing to allow himself to be cut into mincemeat for the benefit of those who employ him, he ought to try another line of business. In putting on a livery, it is not my master's clothes that I wear, but his honour. If I did not think like that, I should find service disgraceful, whereas . . ."

The faint and distant sound of a woman's shriek, coming from somewhere on the lower floor of the *château*, interrupted the speech of the coachman. Mailly started round abruptly, but not before a second shriek was heard. The porter had already rushed through the doorway. Other footmen appeared, hurrying up the hall. The shrieks discontinued.

Flinging down his hat and wig, Mailly ran forward, to overtake and pass the string of speeding house-servants. In doing so, he accidentally collided with the porter, who, after staggering sideways in a sort of drunken dance, finally lost his balance altogether, and sat down in purple wrath on the floor. Mailly flew faster, before all the rest, to the door of Ventailles's chamber. It stood open.

He hastened in alone, latched the door swiftly, and put the bar across.

A small group struggled, swayed, and panted in the centre of the room. A chair had been overturned. Mdlle. de Dampierre was being held as to both arms by a brace of footmen, one of whom was Mailly's acquaintance of the wine-basket. Her face was white, distorted, frightened, and furious, while the veins of her neck stood up like whipcord. Her dress was disordered. In her right hand was a dagger, which the wine-lackey, holding her wrist, was endeavouring to wrest from her.

Immediately afterwards, Mailly's eye fell upon Ventailles lying on the carpet beyond, nearer to the window, all bloody, and apparently writhing in agony, but still upraising his head to view the progress of the struggle. He ran to him, and fell on to his knees. There was a red hole in the Marquis's coat, over the right pap, and crimson spume was issuing from his mouth.

Mailly addressed him as one soldier another:

"Can we do anything for you, Ventailles?"

The wounded man shook his head with an effort which was convulsive, and pointed to his chest. The action exhausted his strength; his head fell back suddenly. Mailly believed that he was gone. A moment later, however, his eyes reopened, and he motioned feebly with his hand for his friend to bend lower still. Mailly set his ear almost against his mouth.

"*Save her!*" whispered Ventailles.

A shudder passed throughout his body, his limbs relaxed, and he was dead.

* * * * * *

Mailly rose, and for a few seconds stared gloomily at the swaying knot. Then he advanced to bring the affair to an end. Catching the forearm of the second footman with both hands, he gave it so sharp a twist that the victim cried out with pain, instantly to release his hold of Mdlle. de Dampierre. Next, he gripped the throat of the wine-lackey from behind, so that the surprise and the suffocation combined caused him to throw up his arms. Mdlle. de Dampierre, free, wildly brandished her poniard, as though fighting imaginary foes.

"Go to the window, mademoiselle!" said Mailly sternly.

She appeared not to hear him. The footman whose arm had been hurt approached him cautiously, but manifestly with no friendly intent. Mailly drew his sword.

"Attend to your master!" he directed.

The man stopped where he stood, as if weighing his chances with the new intruder, who was perhaps a confederate of the assassin. The wine-lackey seemed dazed and terrified, all the while opening and shutting his mouth like a fish. Mdlle. de Dampierre allowed the hand grasping the poniard to sink slowly to her side. Her eyes fastened themselves like blazing lamps on Mailly. Her bosom rose and fell painfully. With her disengaged hand she fumbled awkwardly at her bodice where it had been ripped open.

Mailly bowed to her stiffly.

"Mademoiselle, I have the honour to offer you my escort from this place! M. de Ventailles is dead, and you cannot stay here with any safety."

She was unable to reply.

"Therefore be pleased to adjust your dress, and to put away your weapon. Your carriage is in waiting. I shall accompany you for at least the first part of your way on horseback, but there is no time to lose."

The latch of the door having been vainly attempted from without, they appeared to be trying to force the bolt. Heavy thuds at regular intervals sounded. The porter's voice raised itself hoarsely above all the rest:

"M. le Marquis! M. le Marquis—open . . . open, if you please!"

The second footman began furtively to retreat backwards, with the obvious intention of admitting his fellow-servants. Mailly stamped his foot angrily, at the same time flashing his blade.

"Stop there, or I shall spit you, *mordieu!* About face, quick march, and to the window! What! do you hear me, or not?"

The lackey remained motionless, turning upon him an ugly and sullen countenance. Mailly strode towards him.

The porter's voice outside sounded:

"M. de Mailly, are you there? For the love of Heaven, what is going on within? Monsieur! Unbar the door, monsieur!"

Mailly swore beneath his breath. He called out:

"Nothing is happening at present, my friend, but you cannot yet enter. We shall not be long. Cease your bawling—you are doing no good by it. You shall be let in, in good time, never fear."

"M. le Marquis has been murdered!" cried the lackey with the evil face.

Mailly leapt upon him, seized him by the throat, and violently flung him to the ground, against which his head struck. He continued lying as senseless. His fellow of the wine-basket, stupefied by the spectacle, slowly crossed the room to the station before the open window which Mailly indicated to him with the point of his sword.

"Come, mademoiselle, right your attire, and quickly!"

XI

The Way Out

Mdlle. de Dampierre cast him an anguished look, turned her back, and busied herself with her apparel. When she faced him again, the poniard was once more concealed beneath her lace. The stuff of her gown was all smeared and splashed with the Marquis's blood.

Mailly viewed her appearance with dismay. Her association with the crime was too manifest. Outside the door was collected the whole establishment, and his was but a single arm, however determined, while also, the lady was near swooning. He must support her down the hall, perhaps, and thus he was not even one man against a mob.

Those without continued to batter at the door, but now it sounded as though they had brought up some sort of heavy ram. The panels must surrender. He eyed the window thoughtfully. The lackey had one leg across the sill, with the design of effecting his escape by dropping to the path outside, some six feet below the level of the window. Mailly darted forward, and in a trice had him by the collar. Still holding the man, he turned his head.

"Here, mademoiselle, swiftly!"

As she made a *détour* to avoid Ventailles's lifeless form she covered her eyes with her hand. Mailly pushed the lackey roughly into the room, caught hold of her while she was still unseeing, then swung her bodily in his arms on to the sill, so that her feet dangled towards the ground without.

"Drop, then!"

"I cannot!"

"Drop, I say! If I am to secure your retreat, we must have no timidities or obstinacies, if you please! I am doing the best, according to my poor judgment. They are about to break into the room."

Mdlle. de Dampierre slid forward until her feet were within a yard of the outside walk, then suffered herself to fall. She tumbled in a heap, and made no attempt to raise herself again.

Mailly turned sharply to the lackey, whose eyes by this time nearly started from his head.

"Now jump out, you!"

The door behind them cracked ominously with the weight of those bearing on it. The footman turned his head to glance that way. Mailly recovered his blade, which he had stood against the wall while lifting the lady, and promptly imbedded an inch of its point in the fellow's calf. He screamed.

"Booby!" cried Mailly. "I speak to you!" And he offered the point of the steel again.

The lackey shrank from it to the remote end of the window-frame, where, always keeping his face towards his persecutor, he hurriedly scrambled across the sill, to drop to the path. Mailly vaulted lightly out after him.

"Not so fast, my friend—we are not dismissed yet. Be so obliging as to conduct mademoiselle to her carriage! I shall be behind you."

The footman stared stupidly at the lady not yet risen to her feet, as though not understanding how to approach her. Mailly addressed her impatiently:

"Can you find nothing better to do than lie there, mademoiselle? I am endeavouring to save you, but I cannot perform impossibilities!"

He reached down his hand, and she permitted him to assist her to her feet. Then an ankle yielded beneath her weight, so that she was compelled to support herself against the house-wall.

"Now the foul fiend run away with it!" he muttered. "Her bones are paper, and she has lamed herself!"

He turned to the lackey.

"Take up mademoiselle!"

Mdlle. de Dampierre made a protesting gesture.

"Decline my arrangements if you desire, mademoiselle," said Mailly harshly, "but in that case a more disagreeable escort is preparing for you, I promise it! Have the great goodness to decide quickly what you wish to do.”

She closed her eyes, as if to shut out all thought of her situation. Mailly motioned to the footman.

“In your arms, fool!”

The fellow put out a hand like one warding off a blow. Watching Mailly’s face, he stooped, placed both arms underneath the lady, who no longer resisted, and lifted her completely aloft, as in a reclining chair. For a woman she was tall, so that he tottered beneath the burden, but he found no commiseration.

“Run, then, idiot! Do you think that I desire to inspect mademoiselle, that you hold her up to me? Hearken! Should they overtake us, I shall not spare to play with my sword, and you will be the very first, I shall make it my particular business. Come, set off like the devil! Do not stumble, for that will be an equal fault with the other.”

The footman showed a pair of fearful eyes above his charge.

“Monsieur, I have done you no wrong, and I cannot exceed my strength. Mademoiselle is very heavy.”

“What! are we to stay here to argue her weight? Run, beast, run!”

He made a bow of his blade between his hands, by way of additional encouragement. The lackey, already red-faced, started off, half-running, half-staggering, beneath the wall of the long side of the *château*, the extremity of which, fifty yards on, joined the front of the house. No one appeared at any of the windows under which they passed. Mailly, following close upon the heels of the man, with drawn sword, kept up an incessant fire of menace for his benefit. He also repeatedly glanced backwards to ascertain if the pursuit had yet commenced. Mdlle. de Dampierre lay with closed eyes and relaxed muscles in the bearer’s arms; her teeth chattered, while her head rolled miserably with the jerks and swayings of his clumsy motions.

“Halt!” commanded Mailly, in a low but cutting voice.

They had arrived at the corner of the house. The footman stopped, and Mailly crept round to reconnoitre. The carriage was still drawn up before the *château*, but a few paces from where he stood, but the coachman had quitted his box, and was gazing from the top of the upper flight of steps uneasily into the interior of the hall. The only other person within sight was the groom who had brought Mailly's horse round, and now lounged in charge of it.

His emergence having been unnoticed by either of these, Mailly returned to his companions. The footman had restored Mdlle. de Dampierre to the ground, and was wiping the moisture from his brow. The lady herself leant painfully against the wall with one hand for support.

"So now get off with you!" directed Mailly sternly to the man.

"Monsieur?"

"Return by the same way to the room we have come from, and admit your fellows."

The lackey needed no third bidding, but started to hurry back with awkward steps along the path bordering the side of the house. A dozen paces on he turned his head. Mailly's eyes still watched him. With his sword he made a wild pass in the air to accelerate the fellow's movements. The lackey took to his heels in earnest.

"Wait here, mademoiselle!" said Mailly, and, sheathing his blade, he walked tranquilly round the corner again.

He came up to the groom.

"The horse is mine. Here is for your trouble! You are required in the house."

The man accepted the coins, saluted, and passed round the other corner of the *façade*. Mailly called out up the stairs:

"Leroux!"

"Here, monsieur!" He hastened down. "Monsieur, what were those cries, and what has happened? Everyone has vanished, my mistress has not returned, I am in the dark, and yet I dare not quit my post to learn what is amiss. Is all well?"

"Your mistress is just coming. Up on to your box, Leroux! Ask no questions, but when she is in, drive like the devil."

"Home?"

"Auxerre and home."

Relieved, though mystified, Leroux ascended to his seat,

arranged the cloth about his knees, and gathered up the reins.

Mailly went back to Mdlle. de Dampierre.

"Your carriage is not a dozen yards distant, mademoiselle. Are you able to walk, with the assistance of my arm?"

At the same moment a confused uproar of voices sounded behind him. Turning his head quickly, Mailly beheld men running wildly down the pathway in their direction. Mdlle. de Dampierre grew white.

"Come! are you able to go on your feet, or not?" demanded Mailly, sharply.

She found no answer.

"So I must carry you!"

The pursuit drew nearer. He lifted her in his arms, turned the corner, and ran towards the carriage. Leroux recognised his mistress in a bewildered stare. He was about to descend from his box.

"Stay there, where you are!" commanded Mailly, in a voice which the other had learnt how to obey. "Mdlle. de Dampierre has injured her ankle, no more." He returned his charge to the ground, and swiftly opened for her the carriage door.

"Enter, mademoiselle!"

The coachman bent over anxiously. "Is all well, mademoiselle?"

She did not reply. Mailly arrested her, as she was exerting herself to climb in.

"Be so good, mademoiselle, as to order Leroux to take his instructions from me until we are further on our road!"

"Do so, Leroux," she brought out, faintly and with difficulty.

Mailly closed the door behind her. A breathless footman came rushing round the corner of the house, gesticulating to the coachman to stop.

"Off with you—do not pull up for the King himself!" cried Mailly. "I shall escort you. Your mistress is in danger. To Auxerre!"

Leroux whipped up his horse, and drove off cleverly. Mailly vaulted into his saddle. Simultaneously three more lackeys appeared round the corner, and four others from the house. They bawled to the driver to stop. The first man succeeded in reaching the step of the carriage and tried to raise himself. Leroux slashed at his face with the whip, but failed to dislodge him.

Mailly spurred up, to flash his sword. The lackey threw himself from the step. He lost his balance, tumbling shoulders first on to the gravel, where Mailly overrode him. His fellows hung back. Mailly trotted up alongside Leroux.

"Faster! faster!"

Down the straight avenue of chestnuts the carriage smoked and swayed. Mailly fell to the rear again. A quarter-mile farther on, after the *château* had vanished, the coachman bent his neck to come to speech with him.

"I cannot keep up this speed to Auxerre, M. de Mailly."

Once more Mailly advanced his horse.

"As far as the lodge only. After that we shall slacken."

"What is all this, monsieur?"

"It is a question of your mistress's life."

"Aha! her life. They must have two, however!"

"Forward!"

"There will be a pursuit, then?"

"Yes."

"Then we shall not cross Auxerre, for that would be folly."

"We do not go to Auxerre."

"Where to, then?"

"To the frontier."

Leroux, looking straight ahead, urged on his horse, and said nothing.

"Your mistress has wounded someone by mishap," explained Mailly, laconically. "She is to fly the country for a time."

"She will command."

The carriage continued to rush forward dangerously. "Which frontier, M. de Mailly?"

"The nearest. Germany."

"That is three days for wheels, monsieur."

"We shall go night and day. The carriage must be changed for another, and we shall also want relays. You know the roads? I have money, and they will send us more. Where is a town?"

"There is Tonnerre, some leagues on. Horses may be had there, at least."

"Take all the risks—it is no time for prudence. Here is the lodge!"

The gates were open, and Leroux smartly steered through without slackening his speed. Horses' hoofs sounded behind them.

"Forward!" cried Mailly. "I shall attend to the pursuit." And, falling back, he stopped his gelding broadside to the road.

A minute later three horses thundered up from the direction of the *château*, mounted by two grooms and the lackey whom Mailly had ridden over in the avenue. The face of the last was fouled by the dirt of the ground and bleeding from Leroux's whip-bite. He looked an ugly fellow. Mailly snatched a pistol from his holster, and pointed it.

"Halt! No passage!"

"Fall away there, in the King's name!" vociferated the lackey, in a jarring voice, constraining his horse on to its haunches.

"No passage!" repeated Mailly.

"I know you, and we shall return for you afterwards. Meanwhile, we want the woman. Back your horse!"

"No passage!"

"No passage, is it? Then by God, we'll make one!"—and the fellow drove his spurless heels into his horse's belly, causing it to rear.

Mailly fired. The shot took the footman's arm, and he tumbled into the road. One of the two grooms caught his horse as it prepared to bolt. The wounded man picked himself up, feeling his arm cautiously. Mailly restored the pistol to its holster, and drew his sword.

The lackey addressed his companions, over whom he had apparently assumed command:

"Take the other road, and you may cut her off that way. I shall go back to the house for help."

He seized his horse's bridle. The grooms turned their animals, to ride back past the lodge. The footman shook his fist at Mailly.

"Gentleman or not a gentleman, by God! you shall hang for this!"

Mailly walked his horse towards him.

"Verminous beast—what! do you dare insult me?"

The fellow gave him a malignant look. He attempted to mount, but the effort agonised his arm, and he turned the colour of chalk. Mailly drove his sword-point into the animal's hindquarters. The lackey was thrown to the ground again. The horse shied violently, and galloped riderless up the road, after the grooms.

Bestowing a glance of contempt upon the figure lying prostrate on the ground, Mailly returned his sword to its scabbard, and coaxed his own steed round, to follow the direction which the carriage had taken.

Eight minutes later he came up with it, as it was in the very act of stopping at a cross-roads.

"What's wrong, Leroux? Don't you know the way?"

"Perfectly, M. de Mailly."

"Then what is the matter?"

Fastening the reins to the pin, Leroux descended with deliberation from his box.

"It is here that the roads diverge, monsieur. Straight ahead will take us to Auxerre. To the right will bring us to Chablis and Tonnerre."

"Which is where we are to go. To your seat again!"

"Pardon, M. de Mailly, but since the proposed journey is to be a long one, I must receive a more particular instruction from Mademoiselle."

"*Peste!* you are quite right, and it is only your duty. Ask her, then. But make speed, for they are raising an army against us."

Leroux approached the window respectfully.

"Mademoiselle, may I beg a word of you, if you please?"

There was no response.

"Mademoiselle, will not you condescend to speak to me?"

Mdlle. de Dampierre did not answer.

Leroux appealed to Mailly, who still sat his horse.

"She does not reply, monsieur."

"Then reascend to your box, and continue to receive my orders. I will be answerable."

"Mademoiselle! . . . Mademoiselle!"

Everything inside the carriage was quiet. Mailly jumped off his horse, and slipped his arm through the reins.

"Name of Christ! what is that coming from under the door, Leroux?"

A thin stream of fluid, of the appearance of blood, trickled through the crack of the frame on to the carriage-step. Leroux, uttering a stifled cry, seized the door-handle suddenly, turned it, and thrust in his head.

Mdlle. de Dampierre lay huddled on the floor, motionless, where she had sunk, in a pool of her own blood. Her face was turned upwards. The eyes were glazed in death. The handle of her poniard still protruded from her left breast, above the heart.

"What has happened?" asked Mailly sharply, for the spectacle was hidden from him by the coachman's intervening person.

Leroux continued staring in horror.

"Speak—what do you see?"

The other came away from the door, which he closed softly behind him. He burst into tears.

"Hold my horse!" Mailly went across to obtain for himself the information which the man refused.

After standing in silent contemplation for a full minute, he too shut the door after him. Leroux touched him gently on the arm.

"Monsieur!"

"Well, you have seen! She is dead. She has killed herself."

"Monsieur, someone is responsible for this, doubtless!"

"What then?"

"His name?"

"He has no name. He too is dead."

"She has killed him?"

"Even so, Leroux."

Taking his pistol again from the holster, Mailly busied himself with repriming it. He passed the loaded weapon over to the other.

"What is this for, monsieur?"

"I leave you. On your way home you will perhaps fall in with the servants of the Marquis de Ventailles, who seek to detain Mademoiselle. Should they insult her remains, do your duty!"

"Thank you, M. de Mailly! But can you spare this weapon? Are not you in danger of arrest yourself?"

"I have my sword."

"I shall not pass on the information, monsieur, but where must one seek you, in case of trouble?"

"In Paris. Rue Carcassone, 1."

"You return there immediately?"

"This afternoon; but first I must go back to Jussault."

"You are not concerned in this bad business, then, monsieur?"

"Only in so far as I have assisted your mistress to escape."

Leroux shook his head.

"What have you to do in that house again? It is unwise."

"I cannot travel without hat and wig!" replied Mailly, shrugging his shoulders.

Neither smiled at the insignificance of the errand compared with its peril. Hastily wringing Leroux's hand, Mailly climbed into his saddle. He wheeled round his gelding to return slowly along the road by which he had come.

Leroux reopened the carriage door, pulled down both blinds, then, again closing the door after him, mounted to the box, and gathered the reins in his hand. He turned on to the Auxerre road. The afternoon sun shone brightly from a sky which resembled an immense ocean of blue, dotted with gleaming white islands of fantastic shapes. The breeze was mild and caressing upon his cheek, while all the air was odorous with the country scents of April. The birds kept up a melodious chorus.

XII

A Message From Monsieur De Pontchartrain

A fortnight passed. Mailly kept quietly to his rooms, showing himself abroad but little. The sensation caused throughout Paris and France by the assassination of M. le Marquis de Ventailles had by now spent its force, and so far he had received no summons to satisfy the interrogations of Justice regarding his part in that tragical affair, nevertheless he could not as yet feel at all easy in spirit as to the consequences of his loyal but illegal action in effecting the escape, if to no purpose, of his friend's murderess. Possibly much of significance worked behind the scenes, the discharge of which was still to descend like a thunderbolt upon his head.

It was eight o'clock on a fine and mild evening in May, as he sat at his open window overlooking the Rue Carcassone, digesting his supper and tranquilly contemplating the passers-by in the street immediately below, while puffing at the long clay pipe which he had procured from an itinerant vendor by the simple process of reaching down to his basket and substituting a coin there. Suddenly the door of the apartment was thrown open behind him, and a female voice sounded.

"A gentleman to see you, M. de Mailly!"

Mailly, expelling a cloud of smoke thoughtfully, turned his head.

"Let him enter."

A small, thin individual, with a bony face and gimlet eyes, dressed in a plum-coloured suit, without sword, and bearing his hat beneath his arm, at once slipped quietly into the room, as if from round a corner. Mailly did not know him.

"Bah! 'tis a lawyer, or some such beast," he pronounced privately. "I shall keep my seat for this one."

He carelessly motioned the stranger to a chair with the stem of his pipe. "Well, monsieur, what can I do for you?"

The other crossed the room to him, and bowed, but remained on his legs to watch the door.

"'Tis very well, Mdlle. Antoinette, you may go, and close the door after you!" said Mailly dryly. There was an inarticulate mutter, the toss of a turbaned head, and the door was shut sharply, followed by the deliberately emphasised noise of retreating footsteps.

Mailly yawned. The visitor waited a moment, then recrossed the room with swift silence, as in felt slippers, and suddenly flung the door open. The woman really had departed, and satisfied at last he closed the door again softly, to return to Mailly, before whom he remained standing.

"But sit down, monsieur!"

"There is no need, monsieur. My business is short. Before I state it, however, be so good as to let me have your name from your own lips, that there may be no mistake."

"It is de Mailly. What! have you come to announce a legacy?"

"No, monsieur, I have not." He lowered his voice. "I have come to announce that you are to accompany me at once to M. le Comte de Pontchartrain[13] who has a communication to make to you."

Mailly pulled hard at his pipe, and gazed out of the window. His brain reflected rapidly.

"It has arrived, I think!" he told himself. "This M. de Pontchartrain, let us see—he has the Marine, and he also has the Secret Service. 'Tis a twin-headed Minister. I have never served afloat, so it cannot be the Marine. It is therefore the Secret Service. Truth to tell, very unamiable stories are abroad concerning his custom of poking his nose quite superfluously into the private affairs of obscure persons, that he may have a hand in all that goes on in France. I will bet a hundred pistoles it is this miserable affair of Ventailles's! . . ."

He returned to the messenger.

"What does he want with me, monsieur?"

"I am not instructed to inform you, and I have nothing to add."

"But let us understand! Is this a command or a request which you bring me?"

"The request of a Minister is equivalent to a command, monsieur." He produced a snuff-box, and applied a pinch to his nostrils. "It is not supposed that you will see fit to ignore Monseigneur's wishes. It would scarcely be good sense in a man of your position."

"Come! what is my position?"

The plum-coloured stranger shrugged his shoulders.

"I have told you that I have nothing to add."

"You will not refuse a glass of wine?"

"I thank you, but I am on duty."

Mailly rubbed his chin in dubitation. "Then where is M. de Pontchartrain at this hour?"

"He is in Paris."

"And where in Paris?"

"I have a coach below, monsieur."

"*Peste!* this is nearly an arrest. It is not one?"

"No."

"Oh, well, since it is not an arrest, I shall come later. It is not convenient to me at this time."

"As to that, you must please yourself. I have only to remark that M. de Pontchartrain leaves for Versailles within an hour, and that he is too overwhelmed with affairs to bear your case in mind indefinitely."

"Since the fault will have been mine, I shall excuse him."

"Monsieur, it will be to your advantage to come with me, and to your disadvantage to refuse to do so—I can tell you so much. Only, make up your mind quickly."

Mailly laid down his pipe, and got up, stretching his arms with a gape.

"It is very hard that peaceable citizens are not to be allowed to rest quietly in their own homes, but must be dragged off like malefactors for interviews which they do not desire, with people whom they do not know! You are not setting an ambush for me, I hope? After this conversation with the Minister, I shall be suffered to return freely?"

"We do not set ambushes for persons whom we can take at any time. You will be permitted to return."

"What is your name, monsieur?"

"It is of no importance in the business. However, I am M. Passy."

"You are a devilishly plain-spoken man, M. Passy! . . . Well, I will come. I will just leave word with the woman here, in case I am inquired for during my absence."

"In my presence, if your please. And do not mention the Minister's name."

"The deuce! what mysteriousness! Come then, I am ready, and if they call for me they must wait for me, that is all." He clapped on his wig and hat, and seized his sword. "Go first, M. Passy!"

Passy preceded him out of the room, and down the stairs. They entered the vehicle which stood drawn up in the street outside. It was a shabby public cabriolet, drawn by a single wretched jade, and the man on the box wore no livery. Without giving any order, Passy closed the door upon them, sank back into the dirty cushions, and pulled out his snuff-box. The carriage started with a jerk.

Mailly for a time watched in silence the route they followed, then he turned to his companion, who continued to take snuff, while staring fixedly at the back of the seat opposite, as though to indicate that he was disinclined to conversation.

"Where do we go, then, M. Passy?"

"You will see, monsieur."

"What sort of a man is this M. de Pontchartrain in reality? Does one get on with him easily?"

Passy, without shifting his gaze, held his tongue for a few moments, and then grunted:

"His years are not many, but he is well able to maintain the dignity of his office, if that is what you are anxious about! You will find that two qualities will carry you through the best. The one is candour; the other is respect."

"*Peste!* are you trying to alarm me? Why should I study the singularities of a man of whom I want nothing? I shall behave to him as to any other gentleman."

"He is the representative of the King, monsieur, and you will comport yourself accordingly. As you bring the matter forward, I shall advise you from my experience. Venture upon no familiarities with him; confine yourself closely to the subject of the interview; reply with frankness and brevity to his inquiries; and do not attempt to combat decisions already arrived at. You will then have done all that you can."

"But is he the Cato[14] that he is said to be?"

"It is not necessary to be a Cato in order to be an honest man. M. de Pontchartrain serves the King. That is, he makes no concessions to private persons which must needs be concessions at the expense of His Majesty. I have repeated this a thousand times to gentlemen, and have thereby amazed and angered not a few. It appears generally to be believed that a Minister is a milch-cow."

"Come, M. Passy, if he is such a paragon of honesty, I shall keep my eyes open! But perhaps he is ballasted by other vices? Being young, he goes more for women? Diable! don't say I am wanted for an *escapade d'amour*."

Passy cleared his throat crossly. After a pause he took snuff, and then replied:

"Toys are for those who have time and inclination to play with them, monsieur, and M. de Pontchartrain has neither. If he were a private gentleman he would be austere; as it is, he is merely busy."

"This Phoenix sends for me, yet it is not an arrest," thought Mailly, as the coach continued to rattle and jolt over the rough paving-stones. They were now passing through back streets. "He has the Secret Service. My record is in his possession. I will wager that he is to propose to me some dirty piece of work in exchange for absolution."

They were in the vicinity of the Place des Victoires.

"M. Passy," he said aloud, "why, if we are going to the Rue d'Heudicourt, where is the residence of M. de Pontchartrain, do we drive there by way of the Rue Quiberon? It is to use three sides of a square, instead of the fourth side only."

"We do not go to the Rue d'Heudicourt," was the answer.

At that moment the carriage stopped. Passy alighted, and Mailly after him. The former paid off the driver.

"We return on our legs, then?" asked Mailly.

"You will return as you please, monsieur. . . . This is our way!"

They entered a narrow close, which ran as a passage between two of the houses on the north side of the Rue Quiberon, and plunged directly into one of those labyrinths of dilapidated dwellings where the unfortunate and criminal classes of Paris were accustomed to congregate. Mailly judged that behind this inhospitable territory should be the backs of the residences constituting the south boundary of the Rue d'Heudicourt, which was an important thoroughfare issuing from the Place des Victoires itself, being populated for the most part by men of the gown, tax-farmers, Government officials, and the like.

Suddenly the inspiration came to him that they were to introduce themselves to M. de Pontchartrain's abode privately from the rear. He glanced towards Passy, framed a question, then abandoned it.

The shades of evening fell. The close broadened into a gloomy court, the neglected pavement of which was littered with vegetable and animal filth, causing the air to reek. The sanitary arrangements of such a district would be of the most primitive, so, without consultation, they elected to hug the wooden planking of the houses, as they proceeded to the further end. The wisdom of the course was presently confirmed. Before twenty steps had been taken, something came flying from an upper window, accompanied by a warning which was an imprecation, that, had they remained in the concavity of the alley, must have caused their clothing to sustain a vexing damage.

Mailly dallied with the question which was in his head. He decided to approach the subject indirectly.

"M. de Pontchartrain is not at home, then?"

"He is in my house, monsieur," answered Passy shortly.

"So it is your house we are coming to?"

"That follows."

Mailly laughed. "*Peste!* we shall say that you choose an unsavoury neighbourhood to live in, M. Passy!"

"But I save rent by doing so, and I am sufficiently old-fashioned to be an economist."

"And doubtless from the love of being one, since the emoluments of your post must be considerable."

"Not so, monsieur. My salary is moderate, and I take no bribes."

"The devil! then if his name is Cato, yours is Favonius."[15]

"Fortunately, the race of upright men is not extinct," retorted Passy.

From its entrance the court had appeared as a cul-de-sac, but as they drew nearer to its other end narrow outlets to left and right presented themselves. Passy, when they had reached it, followed that to the left. The ancient houses on either side of the way leant towards each other, to meet overhead, thereby obscuring the remaining daylight, and Mailly's hand grasped the hilt of his sword in readiness for any sudden *contretemps*. No greater annoyance, however, was abroad than a troop of *gamins*, who divided to let them pass, immediately closing their ranks again to accompany them at a discreet distance with a running fire of jeers and gibes, prompted by an enthusiasm to impart to two absurdly-dressed gentlemen the consciousness of the folly of their existence as trespassers and aliens. Encouraged by toleration, they were proceeding to action, and a cabbage-stalk had already come hurtling past Mailly's ear, when Passy, quickening his pace, turned abruptly through a gap between two of the dwellings on the right hand. Mailly arrested the movement he had begun with a view to chastising the thrower of the vegetable, and at once followed.

The close was roofed by the sagging upper communication between the two houses and led directly into another court. It was the desolated centre of the world. All around them were decrepit buildings whose architecture went back to Charles VI[16] at least, when the English were in Paris. Daylight was nearly gone, not a window was as yet illuminated, the court was deserted, while the spirit of a May evening was prevented from descending upon the scene by a thousand odours of the gutter, which insisted upon the homage due to their sovereignty. At the further extremity of the thoroughfare, towering above the dwellings which formed its fourth side, and silhouetted against the pink and green of the upper twilight sky, a fantastic line of more distant gables and chimney-pots extended at right-angles to the direction they walked in. Mailly was assured that these gables and chimney-pots belonged to the houses of the Rue d'Heudicourt. The *gamins* remained clustered within the shadow of the close, doubtless deterred from venturing further in by the spectacle of the agile limbs, the athletic bearing, and the sword, of the more formidable of their two victims, in that light better visible.

Passy slowed his footsteps, grunted in his throat, and brought forth his snuff-box.

"Are you subjected to this impertinence on all your journeys to and fro?" asked Mailly dryly.

"No, monsieur."

"For I fancy there is a shorter and more convenient passage to your house from the Rue d'Heudicourt?"

"You know Paris well, it seems."

"Indifferently well, M. Passy. . . . But, if it is not a rude question, are you married?"

"I have the good fortune."

"Then you are happily married, which is better still! And your wife, does she like this quarter of the town?"

"You will see her, monsieur, and you will ask her yourself."

By this they had arrived at the top of the court. Passy now led the way sharply to the right along another dark and narrow passage, the continuation of which could not be seen, owing to an abrupt bending some thirty paces further on.

"So M. de Pontchartrain is for Versailles to-night!" said Mailly. "Do you accompany him?"

"I do."

"Then where do you pick up your carriage?"

"We shall join it where it is waiting, and that is evidently not here."

"What! have we arrived at your house?"

"It is this one, monsieur."

And Passy stopped before a wooden door-frame, warped with antiquity, which projected on to the left side of the gutter. Lifting the latch, he pushed the door back and stood aside to allow Mailly to pass in first. The interior was quite dark.

"Mademoiselle, a light, if you please!" he called out shrilly. The privilege of married women of quality to be distinguished by the title *madame* not yet having descended to the *bourgeoisie*, Mailly was unable to gather whether he addressed his wife or another female of the household.

The narrow, musty passage in which they stood began to be made visible by the rays of an approaching illuminant; the light grew stronger, and immediately afterwards a woman appeared, bearing a naked tallow dip in her hand. She was of a fragile aspect, tall and slight, carrying herself a little forward out of the perpendicular, which gave her an air of grace. Her age was about Mailly's own. She was dressed for her own society, but if her attire was the less fashionable on that account, it conformed better to the verities of nature, which is the final arbiter of what is becoming to its daughters. Her hair was black, thick, and coiled loosely around her head, without any sort of artificial dressing. The face was long, pale, pure, cold, simple even to vacancy—the veritable countenance of a nun; but of a nun who has mixed in the best society, and who sees no reason to add the sacrifice of exclusive manners to her other vows. She wore no jewels. After a single incurious, though feminine, glance at Mailly, her dark eyes at once hastened to veil themselves behind their long lashes. A small, delicate hand, of exquisite whiteness, continued to rest rather uneasily upon the wine-coloured skirt she had on.

"*Pardieu!*" thought Mailly, "if this is really Passy's wife, she is a good five-and-twenty years his junior, and her hands are suspiciously well-kept. I have also seen eyes like hers before, but never in a prude. He had better look out for himself! But the way to do it is not to lock her away in a lonely house. I will stake my fortune against Passy's that she already has a lover."

He bowed, and was about to say something civil, when the master of the household forestalled him by coldly taking the candle from the lady's hand.

"The Minister is still above, mademoiselle?" he demanded, with a severity unusual as between husband and wife.

"Yes," was the quiet reply.

Passy turned to Mailly. "Here is my wife, monsieur. I shall go up first to announce you. Be so good as to remain below with Mdlle. Passy until I shall have come again for you. . . . The parlour is lighted?" he asked his wife.

"Yes."

"I will conduct you along the passage. Wait! . . ." He bent down to slide the bar across the door, which had been shut behind them on their entrance. Then, rising again rather stiffly, he preceded the others through the house. A dozen paces brought them to a funereal little chamber, furnished in black oak, lighted by the rays of a single candle.

"Be seated, monsieur!" said Passy. "I shall not delay you long, and in the meantime my wife will entertain you."

He retreated down the passage, and almost at once his steps sounded on the uncarpeted boards of the staircase going up. The lady indicated a chair to her guest, then sat down herself. There was a moment of embarrassment.

"Your husband is a hero of the antique school, mademoiselle!" said Mailly. "He appears to believe that life has been given us for the purpose of politics, whereas no doubt there are other duties of a more agreeable kind."

Mdlle. Passy smiled coldly, and was silent.

"*Peste!* we are on the wrong track," thought Mailly. "Let us introduce a little of personal into our conversation, to give it warmth."

"For my part, I am not a politician," he went on, aloud. "I care nothing for this dry paper warfare where we fight at invisible range, and where the beaten enemy will come to life again next day. My trade is soldier. Therefore, it all the more surprises me that I have been summoned upon a political affair by M. de Pontchartrain, who, as a matter of fact, has not my acquaintance."

Mdlle. Passy regarded him from the corner of her eye.

"You are in great peril, monsieur."

"The devil!"

"It is unpleasant to me to see a brisk young gentleman brought to destruction through no crime of his own, so I wish to help you if I can. Yet, as I do not know you, it is possible that you may choose to decline a woman's assistance in your personal concerns!"

"Bah! mademoiselle, if I have ever possessed such sentiments, they have been buried these ten years. You alarm me seriously. You have been initiated into all this business, then?"

"Yes. Passy has no secrets from me."

"I see kindness in your eye. Enlighten me, I entreat!"

She fell to tracing imaginary circles on the floor with the pointed toe of her shoe.

"Now there is not time. Come to me afterwards."

"And when is afterwards?"

"They will detain you above for half-an-hour or an hour, perhaps. After that, you will depart from the house. A quarter of an hour later, come back to me. We shall then be alone."

"Then I will wait outside to see your husband and the Minister issue."

"They will not issue by this door."

"Ah, there is another!"

"The house communicates with that of M. de Pontchartrain in the Rue d'Heudicourt, and that is the way by which they will go out. But as they have no other business to transact after yours, you will be perfectly safe in returning at the end of a quarter of an hour. . . . If you set a value on your prosperity, monsieur, do not fail to do so."

Mailly rose to bow, then resumed his seat.

"But since you know all, mademoiselle, what are they to

propose to me upstairs?"

"They are to ask a service of you. . . . And that is another thing. However contrary to your code of honour this service may appear, do not return a flat refusal. Consent, even. The service will not be required of you. It is what we are to speak about on your second visit."

"I thank you."

"And so you will return?"

"Without fail."

"Say no more! I hear my husband coming."

She rose, and Mailly followed her example. Passy's tread was audible as he descended the stairs; a moment afterwards he appeared in the doorway.

He beckoned Mailly with his finger. "The Minister is ready for you."

"If mademoiselle permits!"

Mdlle. Passy smiled half-contemptuously, and turned away.

"Come monsieur, this excessive civility is ill-timed," said Passy rudely. "We have not brought you here to a reception. And you, mademoiselle! This monsieur and I are to be closeted above with M. de Pontchartrain, I do not know for how long. The house is closed. Should anyone knock for admittance, you will let that one go on knocking. You will remain in your own room, here below. When our conversation is concluded you will be informed, and you may then go about your business."

"I hear, monsieur."

The two men left the room. Bearing the lighted candle, Passy led the way along the passage and up the narrow staircase ascending from it, the steps of which slanted with age from one side to the other. Mailly rubbed his chin.

"That is to say, she is to baulk her husband and his employer!" he meditated. "This incredible solicitude on behalf of a total stranger does not satisfy. I have been right about the house being an annexe of Pontchartrain's; I am in the vein to-night. Let us see if I cannot produce more ideas equally happy. . . Come! Passy leaves her to talk to me; therefore, perhaps it has been so arranged. He orders her as a child, when she is not one; therefore, it is possible they are equals in the business. Her apparent treason may be to attach to the play, the first act of which is to commence immediately, a second, which will open on my return to the house. Where women are concerned, there is no certitude of anything, their wits strike at random like the lightning; nevertheless, I have no great faith in political wives, and, on the other hand, if she is lying to me, by pretending a danger which does not exist, it is possible that they have something on foot against the Minister, in which my cooperation is desired. To that I shall not say 'no' until I have heard what it is."

On the upper landing Passy stopped short before a closed door, and turned round.

"You must leave your sword, monsieur!"

"Ah, that is the rule, is it?"

"One admitting of no exception."

Mailly gave a light shrug, and, drawing the blade from its scabbard, passed it to the other, who stood it on end in a dark corner of the landing. Returning, Passy scratched gently upon a panel of the door, raised the latch, and entered. Mailly waited outside. The room was brightly lit, but the door being only half-open, he was unable to see into it.

"Here is de Mailly, monseigneur!" he heard Passy announce in curt but respectful tones.

No voice sounded in reply, but Passy came out again, and gestured to Mailly to follow him inside. He did so. Passy shut the door after them.

XIII

The Lettre-de-Cachet

The apartment was a small one, close-smelling with antiquity, and filled with black, death-like furniture. A high-set window, heavily leaded, faced the street. Passy glanced at it sharply, and at once crossed the floor to draw the belonging curtain of dingy brocade. A chandelier of eight lighted candles of pink wax was suspended from the low, blackened ceiling. The bare floor-boards had crumbled in places from rot.

The Minister sat facing the door, behind a small rosewood table at the far side of the room, which was the single modern intruder among the grisly chairs, coffers and tallboys of three centuries earlier, when ladies and gentlemen were more religious. It was strewn with miscellaneous papers, and on the top of all was M. de Pontchartrain's wig. His elbow was on the edge of the table, while the hand connected with it served partly to support his forehead, partly to shield his vision from the glare of the lights, as he perused a document, the contemplation of which Mailly's entrance failed to interrupt.

The latter remained on his feet, facing Pontchartrain across the table. The upper part of the Minister's countenance was hidden, but enough was visible to enable Mailly to condemn the whole as a work of beauty. The heavy blue-black jowl, the broad bones, the puffed cheeks, as deeply pitted by smallpox as his own, the energetic yet morose lines between nose and jaw, all this filled him with something like amazement, so that the conundrum sprang to his mind: This one of the six uncrowned monarchs of France is already an ogre when he is not yet thirty; what monster, then, will he be at fifty? And as Pontchartrain still did not look up, he continued:

"It is well for him, I think, that his father is Chancellor,[17] for decidedly such a face is not a key to open many doors! 'Tis a face to make gentlemen shudder, and ladies laugh. Where the devil can such a one come from? Not from the Franks, I swear! The bad blood of some forgotten field-serf ancestor has broken out in the Chancellor's stock, and has produced this bubble. He is a Gaul, a peasant; if his nature were fulfilled he would at this moment be chawing fat bacon in a hovel of dried mud, conversing with his Annette of the exploits of the morrow—that is to say, of the throat-cutting of pigs for market, and of the gathering of dung to enrich his three acres. Whereas, he sits perusing documents of State, while I, Gaston de Mailly, whose people were gentlemen six hundred years back, stand humbly before him, hat in hand, awaiting his good pleasure to vouchsafe me a glance! . . ."

Pontchartrain lowered his hand from his brow for the first time, to look upwards at Mailly with a surprised start, as though hitherto unaware of his presence. It could then be perceived that he had but one eye, the other being of glass.[18] Perhaps it was to retain the false organ in position that he continued to scowl while gazing down again at the paper he had left reading. Mailly bowed.

"*Peste!*" he reflected, until the other should begin his interrogations. "Here is a beauty which unveils itself by degrees, we are not shown everything at once! It is true that dragons have desired virgins in the past; nevertheless, I shall prefer to believe Passy's testimony—we are not on this occasion wanted for an amour. If physiognomies go for anything, I rather incline to the thought that he is to propose an assassination to me."

The Minister again looked up.

"You are M. de Mailly?" he demanded, in a harsh voice.

"That is my name."

"Yes. . . . Then to what branch of your family do you belong? Are you related to the Comte de Mailly who has recently died?"

"No, monseigneur. I am of the de Maillys of Rouen."

"I do not know them."

"No, for their time was before yours, my good monseigneur!" thought Mailly. "Yesterday you were feeding swill into the trough of swine." He remained silent.

"Your home is Rouen?" proceeded the Minister, toying with a

penholder on the table.

"No, but Paris."

"And your people?"

"Are in a better place, monseigneur. I am alone in the world, and until I make some more relations for myself I shall be without any. To the present I am unmarried."

"Your age?"

"Twenty-seven."

"You have the right to wear a sword, however? You are a gentleman?"

Mailly, who began to be annoyed by so many questions, delivered, as they were in a voice gruff, masterful, and rude, drew himself up with some haughtiness.

"I have that privilege."

"But it is one thing to bear a sword, and another to know how to use it. You understand fence?"

"So I think, monseigneur."

There was a pause, during which the Minister explored slowly and absently among his papers. Finding at last the one he sought, he laid it face downwards before him on the table.

"We shall now speak of your connections, monsieur. What intimacies have you in society?"

Mailly gave a shrug. "It depends upon what we are to call intimacies. I know good people. I do not go abroad much."

"You do not follow the Court, I think?"

"No. I find Paris more amusing."

"Then in what way or ways do you amuse yourself?"

"My amusements are simple, for I lead a quiet life. As long as women, wine, and cards are close at hand, I do not look much further."

Pontchartrain looked up with a deepened scowl.

"That is, you relinquish yourself to debauchery and have no serious employments! You are a *roué*. Do not attempt to qualify your statement. We have your record, and it tells us that you are this sort of man."

"Faith! if you have it written down, it must be so! I am not the first, and I shall not be the last, who has sought his pleasure in the passing hour rather than in the future. If you will show me, monseigneur, how many persons employed in serious pursuits are so for the sake of other people, I shall learn whether I am neglecting a duty or merely adopting a choice of enjoyments."

"The world will not go on in your way, monsieur! . . . Then I find that you are much given to intrigue and adventure, not always of an innocent kind. You have lately appeared on the outskirts of several cases reported to me and to M. d'Argenson, the Lieutenant of Police.[19] The State cannot tolerate bravoes and disturbers of the peace. However cleverly you may evade responsibility, if you are perpetually encountered in commotions we shall at last understand that you are an undesirable, a law-breaker; and we shall act accordingly. I do not go through the list, but you are found associated, for instance, with the assassin of M. de Ventailles. . . ."

Mailly interrupted him, with flashing eyes:

"Monseigneur, Ventailles was formerly my commanding officer. I admired him, I loved him, and we were the best of friends. By his death I had nothing to gain, and much to lose. I was not present at his wounding, but he died in my arms, and it was with his last breath that he entrusted to me the safety of the lady who procured his end. Until that moment I had not her acquaintance. The crime was horrible to me, but as a man of honour I had no alternative to placing her in sanctuary. In effect, she did not desire to go on living, she killed herself, so that I had but the satisfaction, on behalf of poor Ventailles, of sparing her some insults and indignities."

"All this is very magnanimous, monsieur, but we are not taking that case now. You will furnish your defence to those who shall interrogate you. I have only to remark, in passing, that you will need substantial evidence to support so improbable a story. . . . I say that it is your whole record which has recently been occupying the grave attention of those in authority."

"And I shall tell them that they might be better employed. I have committed follies, I admit it; but not crimes. Six follies do not make one crime, even in France, monseigneur!"

"Allow me to continue! It has been absolutely determined that licentious conduct of the sort on the part of irresponsible young men shall cease throughout the land, but especially in Paris. We are no longer in the days of the King's minority, and a capital which sees every hour distinguished strangers arrive from all the countries of the world must be made habitable and reputable. We do not desire forcible abductions of gentlemen from public hostelries. . . ."

"You have been badly informed, that is certain! If you refer to Jambac's case, I was not even there."

Pontchartrain, rising, thumped the table with his fist.

"No, monsieur, you were not there, and you never have been there! It is a singular circumstance connected with these transactions that it is always five minutes after they have occurred that you appear! You are exceedingly clever; which does not prevent you from having perhaps the worst record of any man of your age and station in France. You are gambler, drunkard, profligate, incendiary, and one knows not what besides. Without means of your own, you live as a parasite upon others, by persuading them to unlawful enterprises. You are hand and glove with a lawyer of dubious reputation. . . ."

"Ah, bah!" Mailly made a gesture of weary impatience, and turned away.

"However, now it is all to come to an end," said the Minister, lifting from the table the paper he had kept before him. "Do you recognise a *lettre-de-cachet*[20] when you are shown one, monsieur?"

"No, I have had no dealings with that class of animal!"

"Then you will start from to-day. Behold this, from where you stand! If your eyesight is not good, I will tell you its import. It is an instruction, signed by His Majesty the King and countersigned by me, to the effect that you, monsieur, are forthwith to be arrested and conveyed to the prison of the Conciergerie,[21] there to await His Majesty's further pleasure. The instruction is directed to M. d'Argenson, the Lieutenant of Police, who is prompt in such matters and will lose no time in executing it. If you return home upon leaving this house, you will sleep in prison to-night; but if you endeavour to effect your escape, you will be apprehended within forty-eight hours, such is the inevitableness of our system of justice. You may now see what you have brought upon yourself by your vicious courses. It is desired to make of you an example. The time has come when the young libertines of the capital are to be told that it is not through them that France flourishes; that they must give place to the sober, law-abiding, hardworking citizens through whose industry and virtue we find the country what it is."

"But, being lodged in prison, monseigneur, what is next to happen to me? That is a point you have passed over."

"I will acquaint you. You will receive a term of years in the Bastille, or Pignerol,[22] or another place, to be followed by permanent banishment from France. That is at the least. If you are found guilty in the case of M. le Marquis de Ventailles, you will be hanged. I shall not beat about the bush with a man of your temper."

"I thank you! Then you advise . . ."

Passy, who during all this conversation had stood aloof, with averted gaze, now came forward.

"Monseigneur advises this!" he said sharply. "He advises that you abandon your untimely insolence so thinly masked by an unnatural composure, and place yourself at the disposal of his mercy. I shall tell you at once, monsieur, that you will positively be hanged. If you desire a loophole of escape, there is one; but we must first of all hear this desire expressed by your own lips, and that in no impertinent accents!"

"I do not wish to go to prison, if you mean that," replied Mailly coolly. "I say nothing of hanging, which is absurd."

Apparently acquiescing in his subordinate's interposition, the Minister had sunk down again into his seat, where he leant back with folded arms, frowning abstractedly at the table before him. Passy proceeded in an exasperated tone:

"I shall request Monseigneur's permission to notify to you the service which will be required of you if you are to go free.

Volunteer this service, and your *lettre-de-cachet* will be in a good way to being suppressed; but decline it, the order for your arrest will be sent to M. d'Argenson within an hour. The Minister will confirm this."

Pontchartrain nodded, without looking up.

"*Peste!* we have arrived at the moment!" thought Mailly, and he said aloud:

"Speak, M. Passy!"

"You are doubtless wondering why you have been selected for the business, rather than another. In the first place, you are not indispensable to us, monsieur—do not think that! You have no special virtues for the affair which fifty or a hundred desperate gentlemen have not. You happen to be the first on our list, that is all. It will therefore in no way injure us that you refuse the service."

"So you will be the less annoyed with me."

"You are to fight a duel for Monseigneur."

"Oho! a duel."

"For State reasons, into which we need not enter. A certain individual is to be removed from the sphere of political activity, and we have decided upon this method."

Mailly smiled. "But is the individual in question a swordsman or not a swordsman?—for a great deal will depend on that. If he has received a proper education in his weapon, it is possible that he may object to allow others to pierce his jugular for him so conveniently. I do not profess to be a wizard, you must understand."

"When you have finished, monsieur, I shall tell you that we do not care if he comes off whole. We desire a duel with witnesses, but as to the result of the duel, on that point we are utterly indifferent. Get him but to stand up with you. The King's Marshals will see to the rest of our business for us."

"*Diable!* you are to take advantage of the edicts against single combat!"

"Exactly!—which, severe towards the challenged, are doubly severe towards the challenger, so that you will arrange that the affront comes from you. We do not wish a light confinement for our gentleman. Political needs demand a permanent exile, or, better still, a life-imprisonment in a fortress. Either of these will do; but nothing less than these will do, and if you fail to procure such a result for us, your commission will be deemed unexecuted, and your *lettre-de-cachet* will still go forward. . . . That is the sketch of the service required of you, monsieur. Acquaint Monseigneur with your disposition, if you please!"

"I know not what to say. . . . This must be a very dangerous malefactor, however, to deserve so rigorous a penalty!"

"Do not concern yourself with his crime! The responsibility will be ours. All your part is to do what I have said."

"You have omitted one difficulty, though. I shall be punished, too."

"No, for Monseigneur will throw his protection over you. I do not think you will dispute his influence. You will gain honour and reputation at a cheap rate, monsieur; you will have fought with a Peer of France, yet you will have no untoward consequences to fear for your share of the offence. Make his acquaintance upon equal terms, take an early opportunity to insult him, meet him before witnesses, and the Minister will see to all the rest."

"But the deuce! a Peer of France!"

"Yes, a Peer of France. Be assured, in the case of a private gentleman we should go to work in very different fashion! . . . However, if you are frightened, you will say so, monsieur."

"Launch one of your charming *lettres-de-cachet*, M. Passy."

"Come, your decision."

"But how must I introduce myself to this *seigneur*? He will not know me."

"That is your affair."

"I do not like it."

"That also is your affair. If you will not undertake the business, another will. You have but to say yes or no!"

"Yet be reasonable, M. Passy! It is a question of honour. To fight a man without an honest quarrel is little better than an attempted assassination. Could I be well angered with him, the case would be altered."

"That is to say, you refuse?"

"I do not refuse in so many words, but if my arm is to be engaged, my enthusiasm must be so, too."

"Take care, monsieur!"

"It is for the good of the State," said Pontchartrain in a sepulchral voice, still leaning back in his seat.

Mailly at once turned to him respectfully.

"But it is not the State that employs me, monseigneur. I do not attend here as an executioner or sergeant, blindly accepting certain orders from a recognised superior. I see in you only an individual—a distinguished one, I agree, but still without authority to command me to crimes. My reason must be convinced that the affair is good, before I can undertake it."

The Minister sat up slowly. "It is a treasonable conspiracy, monsieur."

"Poh! there are treasons and treasons, monseigneur, just as there are conspiracies and conspiracies."

The Minister exchanged glances with his subordinate.

"There is a plot to assassinate Monseigneur," said Passy, irritably. "Now you know everything."

"Show me this plot!"

"Do we keep it in our pocket, do you think? I tell you that his death is planned. His Majesty's representative is to be destroyed. It so happens, however, that he who meditates this detestable treason is of consequence in the realm. We cannot bring him to justice in the common way; and, on the other hand, he is an over-heavy fish for our net. We are therefore compelled to resort to policy. . . . For my part, I do not think there is need to go into all this with you. Monseigneur is very obliging. Pray let us know on which side of the wall you are to come down!"

"Who is your nobleman?"

"That will be told you when you have decided."

Mailly shrugged his shoulders helplessly.

"Over and above the revocation of your *lettre-de-cachet*, you will receive a sum of money," added Passy. "We owe you none, but fear is a cold counsellor, and Monseigneur prefers that you shall set to work with vivacity. The matter being brought to a successful end, he will give you five thousand livres—which no doubt is very much for you."

"I thank you, but it is sufficient to entrap a strange gentleman without taking money for it."

"It will wait for you, and we have seen a romantic philosophy exchanged for a practical before this! . . . Thus you have accorded to you liberty, protection, and gold—three very excellent things; you will be a fool if you stand out longer."

"I am in Monseigneur's hands."

"The name of the *seigneur* in question is the Duc de Chastelnoir."

"He is in Paris?"

"Yes. Do you know him?"

"Not the least in the world."

"He is a man of some thirty or thirty-five; much of your build. The face pale and resolute, profoundly scarred from eye to mouth across the right cheek. Of medium height, broad in the shoulders, and deep-chested, with quick movements. So much will serve you to identify him."

Pontchartrain got up.

"That is the man," he said, rapping the table with his knuckles, "and it only remains to speak a word as to his habits. Paris is his element; he is always here. His circle is disreputable. He maintains half-a-dozen seraglios. He has no office or any sort of employment, unless to preside at a gaming-table may be called such. When not abroad, which is generally, he is to be found at the Hôtel Chastelnoir, which is seldom. His evenings commence with the Opera, and then proceed through drunken feastings with his kind, and street brawls, to unnameable orgies, which are the scandal of the capital. He is married."

"*Peste!* he is complete, at least! But why does he assassinate you, monseigneur? for there is little of political in all this picture, so admirably drawn."

"He formerly served in the marine, monsieur!" replied

Pontchartrain shortly.

"I understand you. He has a service grudge of some sort against you, which increases, instead of diminishing, perhaps owing to his manner of life. The worst side of his nature rises to the top. Formerly he has framed an image of you, which has now become to his hazed and sodden wits a grinning demon, needing to be exorcised."

The Minister moved round the table.

"You are going, monseigneur?" inquired Passy.

"Yes. Bring everything away."

He turned round at the door. "You have tact and discretion, I hope, monsieur?"

"I have sense, at all events, monseigneur."

"It is of course understood that I do not appear."

"Until after the duel, when you will appear to cast over me the veil of your protection, like Venus in the case of a gentleman at the Siege of Troy, whose name I have forgotten.[23] I rely upon that, monseigneur."

"And, above all, do not set your intelligence against ours! Our agents are everywhere. Betray your commission, and we shall not make this an affair of policy, I promise you. You are not a Duke, you!"

He wound up with a disagreeable laugh, and immediately left the room.

While Mailly still stared after him, Passy lightly nudged him with his elbow. "Hasten, monsieur! I must light you to the street, and Monseigneur waits."

"Then you leave for Versailles at once?"

"Yes. So be quick!"

"'Tis a delightful night, and the drive will be a pleasant one."

"Come, monsieur, follow me out! Do not forget to take up your sword as you pass."

"The devil! that is odd," thought Mailly. "Why this solicitude about my sword? 'Tis a beast that says nothing without a reason; who weighs all his words as upon scales. Is it that he wishes me not to return to the house to recover it? Is he terrified for his wife?

I shall test him a little, for I still think they are in partnership in desiring my return."

Passy had already quitted the chamber, bearing the dip. He closed the door behind them both, thus effectually shutting out the light of the room. While Mailly was groping for his weapon, he began the descent of the stairs.

"Halt, M. Passy!" exclaimed Mailly, putting out his hand towards the corner where the blade should be. "This is foreign territory to me. I do not want to bark my shins. . . ."

With great presence of mind he arrested the expression of astonishment which flew to his lips. The hilt gripped by his hand was strange to him, yet no second sword was visible on the landing.

"*Pardieu!* an exchange," he thought rapidly. "They have taken mine, and given me another. Nevertheless mine was by no means of Damascus steel, that it should be so desirable. Then Passy has been with me throughout. That leaves, to the best of my knowledge, but his wife in the house. And yet, since the days of Lycomedes's daughters,[24] women have never greatly interested themselves in arms."

Passy looked up impatiently from the foot of the stairs, but it was only his head that he turned, the light was still before his body, so that Mailly remained nearly in darkness. He passed his hand along the blade, shrugged his shoulders, then thrust it into the sheath by his side. The steel was too long by an inch.

He joined Passy in the passage downstairs.

"You are in an infernal hurry, my friend! I could scarcely see. . . . Then I shall start prospecting the field to-morrow, and as soon as I have something to report. . . ."

"You will let me know at once, here."

Mailly grasped his arm familiarly. "Does not one say good-night to your wife? . . . *Peste!* 'tis the arm of a skeleton!" he added to himself. "A sword is not to toast cheese with, and they have not borrowed mine for nothing; I smell a crime; but I cannot believe that this one has ever had much to do with steel, or will begin now. I shall rather suspect the woman."

Passy replied snappishly to his question:

"She is employed, monsieur, and I am in a hurry." He shook off Mailly's hand.

"What disappointment! I hoped for this adieu, to efface the impression of your Cyclops upstairs, of whom I shall now dream!"

"Come! I cannot stand here talking."

"Yes, I am keeping you. But you are a bold man, M. Passy."

"In what respect?"

"To travel to Versailles, leaving such treasure unguarded."

"Monsieur, my wife is not for you, so you will have the civility to let her alone. Upon my departure the door will be barred, as it is every night, and nothing short of violence will cause it to be reopened before daylight. I have not rented the house to use it as a trysting-place for licentious gallants. The remark does not relate to you unless you choose it to do so. Good-night, monsieur!"

He opened the street-door.

"But when do you return?" asked Mailly, laughing.

"It is not your concern, but I return to-morrow."

"So a good journey to you!"

Hardly had he crossed the threshold when the door was shut upon him with an impatient bang, and the rasping sound of the inside bolt being drawn struck his ear. He raised his wig to scratch his head.

"Bah! it is to show me that they do not co-operate. As soon as I have moved away, the bar will be withdrawn. To the investigation of a mystery nothing more is needed than common-sense; the track which one mind has made, another can follow. I have a quarter of an hour to kill—let us explore what all this means!"

He started to promenade the alley, not that he might come anywhere but that the motion of his legs might assist thought.

"Let us take only facts," he reflected. "Passy's wife has stolen my sword. It is Passy who has rendered possible the theft, by disarming me; and who has concealed it, by hastening me away in the dark. Therefore there is collusion between husband and wife. . . . Next, it is not any sword they want, but my sword, for they have given me another in its place. That points to a desire to associate my property with a certain action to take place. What is this action? A wounding, since that is the use of a sword. A wounding—that is to say, a death; an assassination! . . . . *Mordieu!* 'tis a great step forward in our logic, yet the only one possible. This amiable couple are to assassinate someone, and the crime is to be fathered upon me, through my sword, which will be identified. . . . And next still? A crime without motive carries no weight. Whom could I wish to murder in this house? The Duc de Chastelnoir? He is not here. Moreover, they cannot prove the connection without condemning themselves at the same time. Ah, the devil! the *lettre-de-cachet!* I am to re-enter the house to possess myself of it. But it is not enough to suppress it, for a duplicate can always take its place. I must also prevent such re-issue. Pontchartrain must be put away! 'Tis he who is to be assassinated. They are to do the thing with my blade; then entice me back to the house for arrest. . . . Here, then, we have the grand mystery of this evening's work! While that demure mademoiselle, with her overflowing charity, is imparting to me her famous secret in the lower apartment, while her bosom continues to heave and her cheeks to suffuse, my own sword is treacherously acquiring evidence against me, in the shape of ministerial blood-gouts, in the upper. The police arrive. I hear the commotion of their entry, I endeavour to escape, since I have no business in the house; my flight is intercepted; and my crime is manifest. I shall be broken on the wheel, while this charming pair will consolidate their spoils, supposing that robbery is their object."

He paced forward in increasing agitation.

"I am in the devil of a hole, that is certain!" he continued. "I cannot remember to have been so dangerously circumstanced in my life, for, whichever way I turn, I am equally bogged. If I go home quietly, relying on my innocence, this innocence will not save me. Pontchartrain will, none the less, be killed with my weapon, and that accursed *lettre-de-cachet* will hang me six times over. If I fetch the police, it will be either too soon or too late. If too soon, no crime has been intended; while Passy will revenge the fright I have given him by causing Pontchartrain to send me to prison out of hand. If too late, my bringing in the police will at once be rejected as the audacious device of a cunning assassin, and I shall still hang, on the evidence of the sword and the *lettre-de-cachet*. As the third alternative, let me return to the house for that pleasant little interview with Mademoiselle; then perhaps, before I have well set foot inside the door, the signal will have been given for the murder of the Minister, and I have by this very action precipitated my destruction!"

He turned to go back. Not a soul was abroad as he dragged his feet dejectedly along the alley, bordered by black houses like cliffs, above which appeared a roof of paler sky, already sprinkled with faint stars.

"Come! energy, that is what is required!" he told himself, throwing out his chest and squaring his shoulders. "Action must kill action, and cunning must undermine cunning! There is a plot. Good! Then there are plotters. By preventing their designs merely, I permit them to take cover, and from this cover they will ruin me. By allowing the murder, in order afterwards to accuse them of it, I shall with open eyes walk into the trap they have set for me. Therefore, I must discover them in the act. The assassination will not take place outside, here in the street, but in Pontchartrain's house, of which Passy's is a part. Therefore, it is there that I must take up my station. The woman expects me. Therefore, I must contrive something unexpected, to serve my plan, without at the same time serving hers. I judge that my quarter-hour has elapsed, and I shall put my logic to the proof while it is still hot from the oven!"

At the very moment that he arrived back at Passy's street-door, a neighbouring carillon played ten o'clock very sweetly. He pressed his hat firmly on his head, loosened the sword he wore in its scabbard, pushed back his cuffs, and silently lifted the latch, to discover the door unbolted.

XIV

The Thread Of Divine Logic

Leaving the door ajar, Mailly crept on tiptoe along the passage, towards the room where he had sat with Mdlle. Passy. Suddenly the blackness became permeated by a dull ruddy glow as of firelight from an interior apartment out of sight, and the silhouette of the lady herself loomed up before him. Arresting herself with a start at the vision of the intruder, she laughed lightly, at the same time continuing to place a stray lock in position at the back of her head.

"How you alarmed me, monsieur! I believed it to be a thief."

Mailly swept off his hat.

"Let us see if there is nothing that we can steal, mademoiselle! I am delighted to see you again. But first of all, you are required outside, I fancy."

"Outside!"

"Faith! yes. 'Tis some acquaintance of yours, I think. He has been waiting without for some time, not desiring to knock, and, seeing me about to enter, has begged my good offices to notify you of the fact, although I do not know the individual. It seems he has something of importance for your ear. Still, if you prefer not to accede to so strange a request, *pardieu!* he must go away, that is all; and I shall tell him so with the greatest pleasure in the world."

Passy's wife became pensive. "Believe me, monsieur, I do not know who could wish to speak to me at this hour. What is his name?"

"As to that, I had not the impertinence to ask."

"What appearance has he?"

"The street is dark, and I could not well distinguish. Let us say, he is tall and thin."

"Oh, well, I will see him. Remain here, monsieur."

"Permit me to stand within the door, that I may be at hand in case an insult is intended."

"I thank you, but I am well used to take care of myself. Go through to the fire, rather, and sit down at your ease."

"I obey. But first suffer me to bring you to this person, as it is exceedingly dark outside."

To this Mdlle. Passy made no demur. With lifted brows and a hurried swish of her skirts, she passed by Mailly to go to the door, on the threshold of which she remained for a moment standing, peering out in perplexity to left and right.

"Which way is it, then, monsieur? I can see no one."

"It is that way, mademoiselle!" And quietly raising both hands to her back, which was towards him, he impelled her with such suddenness and violence into the roadway, that, taken completely by surprise, she had extreme difficulty in preserving her balance. Mailly jumped backwards into the house, and hastened to close and bolt the door.

"Now let us see if you will make a fuss, Mademoiselle Delilah!" he laughed to himself. "Let us see if it is desired to arouse the quarter, or whether this is not rather a night for quietness."

The muffled sound of a voice in itself low came faintly through the door:

"Let me in—let me in, monsieur! What have you done!"

Mailly, applying his ear to the crack, smiled sarcastically, and said nothing.

"Open at once, monsieur, or I shall bring assistance!"

He returned no answer. Mdlle. Passy attempted the latch, but desisted at once. There ensued a long pause: after which the slow and hesitating click of her high heels sounded, as she seemed to retreat in bewilderment down the alley. Mailly stood up, then made his way softly to the room from which the fire-glow came.

"Bah!" he soliloquised. "That is not the step of one who goes for assistance. In five minutes she will return, to ascertain if in the meantime the door has miraculously reopened itself. But it will not have, mademoiselle! Neither do I think that you will seek to enter by way of Pontchartrain's house, to advertise these strange doings. Your goose is cooked, and we are now at liberty to turn our attention to the next."

The apartment he now went into was both kitchen and living-room. Summer approached on wings, but a blazing fire of ship-timber was burning merrily in the ancient grate—doubtless by virtue of Passy's office in the Marine. Arm-chairs were drawn up on either side of the hearth. A long table covered with green baize occupied the centre of the room; on it were a bowl of roses, some women's needlework, and an opened flask of green elixir, with two glasses on stalks. From the rafters were suspended hams and sausages. Long ropes were swung from wall to wall, for the purpose of drying clothes, but at present they were unoccupied except by one of Mdlle. Passy's under-garments, which evidently she had overlooked in preparing the room for her guest. The wall opposite to the fireplace was entirely taken up by a massive dresser of stained pine; its shelves glittered with glazed blue-and-white Dutch crockery, everything was spotless and meticulously neat. A scullery was disclosed through another half-opened door.

Mailly took up the flask, unstoppered it, and sniffed cautiously at its contents. After setting it down again, with a disapproving shake of the head, he next cast his eyes aloft, to behold the hams and the drying-ropes. He stood in thought for a moment, then went to the dresser-drawer for a knife. All the house-cutlery was there, sorted into kinds. He found what he wanted, and shut the drawer again. Jumping agilely on to a chair, he reached up to the clothes-lines, severed the one end of both of them, and then, repeating the action across the room, picked up the fallen ropes from the floor, to lay them on the table ready to his hand. The woman's shift caught his eye. It had fallen with the ropes. Without regard to propriety or possession, he caught it up, slit a side of it with his knife from end to end, and folded the whole into a bandage, which he kept in his fist. Six or eight minutes had passed in these various operations, when at last he took his stand by the door, to listen for noises in the upper part of the house. Everything was quiet.

"'Tis truly astonishing what a load logic will bear when

compelled!" he meditated while waiting and hearkening. "On the pedestal of a substituted sword, it has erected for me the statue of an assassination so lifelike in its hideousness that it has caused me already to eject a lady from her own domicile, and now persuades me to await in a deserted house the appearance of a man who should by this be on his road to Versailles! It is to follow a thread through chaos, and is the most audacious feat of pure reason that I have yet encountered. There is even beauty in it. To the divine sciences of astronomy, music, poetry, and philosophy, we must assuredly add logic as a fifth. 'Tis a picture of the soul struggling through the gross appetites and passions of the world. Pulled down on all sides by material considerations, she is ignorant of her destination, which is heavenly; but she deduces it from her own resources, and this deduction possesses more of certitude than all the flesh, blood, and gold of the visible cosmos!

"*Peste!* why do I continue to stand here? 'Tis not to honour logic to confine its extent; it has not brought me so far to leave me with a gaping mouth. We shall proceed with the inquiry. Mdlle. Passy has not been expelled, let us suppose, and I am in her society. Then what is to happen next. Her husband is upstairs, we assume. Thus he awaits my arrival before starting the wheels of this murder; and therefore he must know of my arrival. But he is upstairs. Perhaps he works with Pontchartrain in the other house. It is unlikely that he will be able to hear my entrance. From time to time he absents himself from the Minister, that he may listen over the stair-rail. But the kitchen-door is shut, we will say, or there is a silence between our voices; and if he creeps downstairs to ascertain more closely, there is the chance of detection. Or if it has been arranged that his wife shall go up to inform him, he may at that time be with Pontchartrain, and she will not dare to linger, for fear I shall escape from the house. . . . Therefore, a signal! . . . And what kind of signal? Since the house is dark, a light! A lighted candle. And where must this candle be set, in order to be seen? He is upstairs, she down; therefore it must be somewhere in the passage visible from the stair-head. . . .

Let us discover if there is an unlighted candle there, ready to transmit such a signal."

He stepped noiselessly outside. The passage was feebly illuminated by the glow of the fire, so that he was enabled to distinguish on a wall-bracket opposite to the foot of the staircase two whole candles as yet unignited, in copper stands. After a brief hesitation, he possessed himself of one of the candlesticks, and returned to the room.

"*Pardieu!* my brain enjoys a halcyon calm to-night, and insight succeeds to insight! If there are two, it is because one alone will not serve. First one is to be lit, then both. Two separate signals; therefore, for two separate stages of the affair. The first shall be lit when I arrive, the second . . . bah! the second, when I am drugged and disarmed! Then may the assassination safely proceed. . . . 'Tis as Satanic a business as one will hear of in twenty years!"

When he had paced up and down the room before the fire a few times, he made an abrupt gesture of decision. Stuffing the rolled-up shift into a side-pocket, he next made the ropes into coils, through which he thrust his arm. He lighted the candle from a blazing splinter, returned to the door with it in his hand, and again stood to listen. All was as still as a church at midnight.

Gliding along the passage to the bracket, he lighted the second candle, then placed the other beside it, so that two lights burned together. The old, warped stairs creaked beneath his feet as he went up them. On the upper landing he turned to behold the candles below, piercing the darkness like twin spearheads of flame. The door of the room in which his interview with the Minister had taken place was ajar, and all was black inside. He entered. Swinging back the door to a mere crack, he set his eye to the aperture, and waited.

Minutes passed.

Just as he became restive and anxious, the door of the chamber opposite to his own, on the other side of the landing, seemed to open an inch or two, but he could not be sure, since the only light afforded was that of the candles in the passage downstairs. After a considerable pause the gap really widened a little, then suddenly the door was swung open to its full extent. The shadow of a smallish man stole out without sound, to stand for a few moments on the landing, just outside the apartment he had quitted.

Presently, evidently at once attracted by the burning candles and disquieted by the utter stillness of the house, he moved a couple of steps nearer to the stairs, when at last the direct light caught his face. It was Passy. In their drawn sharpness and concentrated energy, his features resembled, to Mailly's thinking, those of a weasel or a polecat whose nose has struck some scent not altogether satisfactory.

Lightening his weight by the hand-rail, and treading as if in velvet shoes, the little man began to descend the staircase, halting at each second step to listen for sounds below. Everything in his appearance indicated great perplexity and uneasiness.

"Bah! I see what is wrong, and this evening my very mistakes are helping me!" thought Mailly. "It was absurd in me not to have closed the door of the kitchen to shut out the fire-light, since it is the flicker of this fire-light, coupled with the absence of voices, which nonplusses him. Nevertheless, he will now be compelled to go all the way down to ascertain what is the matter, and that will afford me my opportunity to intercept his retreat. He will find no one under, he will plague his head for five minutes, then it will occur to him that his wife is upstairs, where he will reascend to seek her. As soon as he has vanished along the passage below, I shall slip across to the room he has just vacated, to lie in waiting for him on his way back to Pontchartrain; for, whatever goes on in this part of the house, he will not be able to exceed his leave."

After many pauses, Passy finally reached the foot of the stairs, and moved towards the kitchen. At the precise moment of his disappearance, the carillon in the neighbourhood startled the silence of the house by the commencement of the shorter tune belonging to the half-hour. Mailly stole across the landing, to secrete himself in the apartment from which the master of the establishment had issued.

By the dim rays of a nightlight on a table in the far corner of the room, he ascertained that it was small, rather elegantly furnished, and possessed two other doors, besides a window on his left-hand, above the street. One of these doors, which was on the right, facing the window, was shut; the other, opposite to himself, across the floor, was partly open. A closer inspection showed him that it was not a door at all, but a sliding panel, of the height of a man, which had been drawn back just sufficiently to permit one to squeeze through.

"Thus it is the communicating way between the two houses," he told himself, "and that which resembles a bare corridor beyond is doubtless an aerial gallery spanning some back yard."

Simultaneously the shut door on his right opened itself, and a woman's head and shoulders came through, shadowed by the illumination of a lighted chamber behind her.

Mailly started round. He saw a fashionable headdress, the outline of a shapely and voluptuous throat, which was that of a lady still young, and one small, plump hand and wrist raised above the level of her head against the door-frame, but the face itself was indistinct by reason of the circumstance that the stronger light was at her back. The perfume of her person, however, was so exquisite that he had no doubt that she was beautiful. She was low in stature, with rather broad shoulders.

He said not a word. Bowing very slightly to the mysterious demoiselle, who was evidently greatly astonished by what she beheld, he set his fingers to his lips as an invitation to a similar discretion on her part. She made no response, but almost immediately withdrew into the room from which she had only partly emerged, closing the door behind her softly and silently.

Mailly gazed at the panels for full ten seconds.

"What the devil is this one, then?" he reflected in amazement. "The Passys cannot receive to-night. A mademoiselle in hoops is of no use for an assassination. So 'tis a little visitor of the Minister's. *Peste!* we shall only think one thing of an attractive woman who waits upon a distinguished personage at ten in the evening. That does not concern me, but what does concern me is that if she has issued from her chamber once, she may do so twice, and I do not care to have two on my hands at the same moment. I think that we must be uncivil enough to secure the door of the cage."

He glanced around him with a restless eye, then, picking up the most fragile of the chairs, broke off a leg. It needed but a minute to wedge its narrow end into the free space of the latch of the door, in such a manner that it could not be lifted from within. The chair he deposited in a dark corner.

After that, he took up his post behind the door open to the landing, drew the folded linen bandage from his pocket, adjusted the coils of rope on his left arm, and waited.

The stairs creaked twice.

Passy entered the room, looking pale, evil, careworn, and anxious. Inside the door, he clapped his hand to his forehead, and stood thinking. Without wholly arousing himself, he started mechanically to walk across the floor, apparently with the intention of repossessing himself of the nightlight, for the purpose of his return journey to Pontchartrain.

Mailly stole from his retreat, and approached him from behind. Suddenly his arms shot forward. Before Passy had time to comprehend what had overtaken him, his mouth was tightly gagged with the bandage, which his assailant proceeded deftly to knot at the back.

Mailly drew his sword.

"Put down your hands, Passy, and listen quietly, or you are as good as dead! 'Tis I, de Mailly, and I care not if I go to extremities. I am to bind you. Struggle, and this sword skewers you, but keep quiet, and you will sustain no harm as at present. . . . Ah, demon! . . ."

Passy, by a sudden movement as of a wild-cat, had attempted to snatch off his gag. Mailly sprang back a half-pace, and pricked him in the thigh. A well of blood began to spread over the leg of his breeches.

"On your knees, wretch!" commanded Mailly sternly, but in low tones, in order not to alarm the lady beyond the door. . . . "Come, I am earnest! We cannot both of us have our way, and I am resolute to have mine. Do not delay for assistance; none is coming."

Passy knelt sullenly. He tried to stanch the blood from his wound by pressing upon it the cloth of his breeches.

"Ah, *corbleu!* the bleeding will do you good!" said Mailly, as he thrust his sword-point into the flooring, to free his hands. "Your blood demands this purification; it is foul—or, rather, one cannot think that it is blood at all. It is snake's venom, it is poison, and that is why you desire to murder people. A few ounces let off will never hurt you; I even advise you to rid yourself of as much as possible. Your hands behind your back, if you please! Quickly, now!"

Passy obeyed. Forming a slipknot with the rope, Mailly first tied his wrists together, then made both arms fast to the body.

"On to your legs!"

The victim attempted the feat, but fell over. Mailly raised him unceremoniously. He bound his ankles and legs. Afterwards, he adjusted and tightened the gag, and stood back to inspect his work.

"So you are trimmed, beast!" he whispered. "You see! It has not benefited you so largely that you have visited my rooms this evening. Because with no birth, you have the cleverness of twenty fiends, that is not to say that every gentleman in France is a fool. For the future—supposing that you have a future, which is what we do not know—however, if there is to be one for you, let this adventure serve you as a lesson to select only those for dupes who are inexperienced in affairs; who go through the world in the imagination that innocence in itself has greater force than villainy, which is to asseverate that the lamb has nought to fear from the wolf. Of such there is store, therefore, it has been all the more stupid in you to fasten your fangs upon a man who has had dealings with all sorts. . . . I leave you temporarily, to explore this passage before me, so interesting and so strange. Yet since, if I mistake not, we find ourselves in the house's highway, while M. de Pontchartrain appears to entertain to-night, it will be more polite if I first deposit you in another place."

He recovered his sword, and restored it to its scabbard, Passy in the meantime continuing to glare at him unflinchingly. Next, Mailly lifted the trussed man bodily in his arms, and so bore him through the doorway, across the landing, into the room of his conference with the Minister; where, finally, he laid him on the table, face upwards, like a body for dissection.

"Listen, Passy! Do not try to liberate yourself. I have tied you skilfully, the table is narrow, and 'tis an ascertained fact that pinioned men fall heavily. I will return for you shortly; or if not I, another. I would search your pockets, but cannot see to do so. Also, time runs on. We think that you have desired to expedite Monseigneur's passage to Heaven. Should it clearly manifest itself that you have not possessed this intention, we shall apologise, and the affair shall be as if it had never been. I now depart. While I am gone from you, think profitably upon your sins."

He quitted the room, to re-enter that across the landing, in which the nightlight still burned. Sinking into a chair, he consulted his chin with his hand, and stared with wide-open eyes at the light, while reflecting swiftly.

"Now I have done too much or too little!" he informed himself. "I have stopped a crime, perhaps, but I have not discovered one. In five minutes more we shall see Pontchartrain come this way, in search of Passy. I advance towards him with a respectful bow. 'Monseigneur, there is to-night a conspiracy against your life, and I have had the honour to eject one assassin from the house, and secure the other. It is the Passys.'—'The proof, monsieur?'—I abbreviate the interview—'For proof, they have stolen my sword.'—'Bah!'—He summons his lackeys, and sets me under arrest pending my transference to prison. . . . *Peste!* we must contrive something quickly. He will be here at once. Where are my wits! . . . Come! shall I interrogate the lady? Ka! that would be a famous thing to do! 'Madame, do you know anything of a plot to kill the Minister?' Whereupon, she will tell me all in a breath, without a doubt! Still, something must be done. . . . Why the devil does he employ a feeble nightlight, instead of a candle, to guide him through these upper apartments?—this man who does nothing without a reason. Have we a clue here? Let us investigate methodically. What is the advantage of a nightlight over a candle? It sheds less light; it does not reveal so much. Thus perhaps there is a thing to be concealed. What thing? and from whom? To take the second question first: who is here, upstairs? I am here, but 'tis not in the programme; I was to have remained below with his wife; therefore, the nightlight is not for me. Passy is here. Our mysterious madame is here. Bah! what can there be to hide from her?—unless Pontchartrain's face! Who else remains? The Minister himself. And so the nightlight is on his account. He is not to see something. Where? His own room, where he is, must be thought lighted; he is, therefore, to make the passage of the upper part of the two houses, in company with Passy, bearing the nightlight. That is to say, hitherwards, to his tryst with the lady. And what is he not to see? . . . *Pardieu!* a certain sword, perhaps. 'Tis *en route*, away from assistance, that Passy is to assault him. But let us see—let us see! How is this to be managed? Who bears the light? Pontchartrain, going first. Then, when he falls wounded, the light falls with him, and is extinguished. All is blackness, Passy has no means of ascertaining if the wound is mortal, or not mortal. So Passy himself must bear the light. Does he walk in front? Then Pontchartrain will see him bear a sword, which is neither his habit nor his privilege. So he must walk behind, and pick up the sword somewhere on his passage. And thus the Minister, going first, must walk in darkness. Moreover, one cannot make sword-thrusts without violence, so that, in dealing his blow, Passy will all the same extinguish his light. . . . *Peste!* an assistant is necessary! There is an accomplice! . . . His wife? No, for she is below, and dares not leave me. Then this madame here? Bah! . . ."

Mailly stood up.

"That is, somewhere lurking in these upper chambers, and between me and Pontchartrain, is another, a bravo, hired to the purpose, and possessed of my sword. 'Tis well. This other shall be my proof and my salvation. By his presence in the house, the plot to assassinate shall be exposed, the Passys shall be brought to ruin, while, for me, I shall have earned the minister's substantial and eternal gratitude, which will bear me at last to fortune."

He pondered for a moment longer, then blew out the nightlight, and groped his way through the sliding panel.

XV

Through The Panel

For a half-dozen paces the boards sounded hollow beneath his feet, then the flooring became dead again, and Mailly guessed that he had passed from Passy's residence to Pontchartrain's. He came up against a wall which compelled him again to the right. Then he encountered an open door, through which he entered cautiously into a carpeted chamber. He went straight forward, halting every little while to listen for faint sounds of human presence. All was still.

A hand caught his arm.

"Is it you, Passy?"

The voice was low and brutal, but Mailly believed that he detected in it the drawl of good society. Startled though he was, he retained *sang froid*, not only replying to the question with the punctuality of an echo, but mechanically reducing his tone to a whisper, that the mistake might proceed.

"Yes."

"What in the name of all the Furies has delayed you? I suppose I have been kicking my heels here for half-an-hour, since you left me. I was going home. Is all well?"

"All is well."

"Is it Passy?"

"Who else should it be?"

"You answer back in a cursedly funny way. Where is your light?"

"It went out."

"Oh, it went out! . . . Well, has your gentleman returned?"

"*Peste!* this establishes my faith, and I am really in the piece," thought Mailly, wrinkling his brow in the darkness. "But who is this well-spoken individual who sells his soul to a Passy. 'Tis no common cut-throat. Is it some needy, well-born adventurer come hither to improve his fortune, or can it be an affair of private vengeance, in which the Passys are but the instruments? Whoever it is, it is certainly a man of quality, so if I am to keep up the deceit I had better start to 'monsieur' him."

"You do not seem very sure," interrupted the strange gentleman, in a tone of ominous dryness.

"He has returned, monsieur."

"You are positive?"

"Yes."

"Then your wife plies him?"

"Yes, monsieur."

"And he will remain? There is no doubt about it?"

"He will very assuredly remain," replied Mailly in his toneless whisper.

"Then do we stop at the bottom of this pestilential pool all night? I think I have been waiting here throughout eternity. If it were a campaign, I should have you hanged. Pontchartrain has probably left by this. You take things devilishly easy, my friend!"

"I could not come before, monsieur, but we shall now proceed," returned Mailly at a hazard.

"Then plague take it, do so! Go and fetch madame. I shall get back behind the curtain. Be off with you!"

"*Parbleu!* so she serves as decoy, and that is her function," meditated the counterfeit Passy. "First she is to be brought here, then the Minister, to meet her, while all the time the assassin continues concealed behind his hangings. 'Tis crystal-clear at last. I have but to effect my retreat, and seek Pontchartrain, and we shall have bagged this brigand without a blow struck, just as his jackal already has been bagged. It is my night of destiny. It is at this precise moment that I cast the ill-luck of a life-time, to come into my rightful own. Monsieur, whose face I cannot see, trust me, I am sincerely and entirely grateful to you for the honour you pay me in having borrowed my sword from among a thousand possible others! 'Tis evident that you were not led thereto by your intelligence, therefore was it so ordained by Fate. Nothing remains but to extract my reward from Polyphemus. It must, however, be suddenly, as a spark struck out of flint, for I think that his nature is to sink back very readily into sluggishness. A multitude of men, besides, pass constantly before his table, and by tomorrow the first lively recollection of my features will have started to become obscure. . . ."

"What is it now?" demanded the unseen, in a voice like a whip, though always low. "Is there something else we have not heard about? What is wrong?"

"Nothing is wrong, monsieur, and I was but rehearsing the business in my mind. I go at once."

Setting off in the blackness in what he judged to be the direction of Pontchartrain's apartments, Mailly immediately came into contact with a table, and swept a porcelain bowl to the floor, against which it was shattered into fragments. The other leapt after him, to grip his arm a second time.

"What are you doing?"

"It is that I am always lost in the dark. Put me in the way, monsieur."

"Yes, I will put you in the way! But this arm belongs to a bigger man than Passy, I fancy. Whom the devil have I caught?"

Shaking himself free, Mailly drew his sword.

"You have caught someone, monsieur, be very sure of that."

"Death of God! you are not that hired bully of Pontchartrain's, by chance?"

"At least, I do not belong to the party of murder. Draw, monsieur!—whosoever you may be. 'Tis not the best light in the world, but doubtless one will find the other. On guard!"

"That is, you are eager to earn your money. Good! I am ready. But wait!—where is Passy?"

"There is to be no assassination to-night, monsieur. Defend yourself!"

"I shall try, for I do not love people who know more than they are intended to know. But are you really de Mailly?"

"Perhaps."

"So much the worse for you, if not."

"Your own name, monsieur?"

"I am the Emperor of China. On guard!"

A light shone. The combatants lowered their blades, to look round. At the end of a short passage showing through an open door, which was opposite to that by which Mailly had arrived, appeared Pontchartrain, bearing in his hand a candle. When he saw what was going on inside the room, he stopped.

Mailly glanced around him. The apartment was small but well furnished. It was curtained off at one end. Portraits in oil hung on the walls, and there was a pair of cushioned divans, in place of chairs. The carpet was strewn with the splinters of the broken bowl. He looked across to his antagonist. It was a broad-shouldered young man, of his own height, carrying two swords— a drawn one in his fist, and a second in its sheath by his side. His face was strong-featured, pale, sullen and scarred. Mailly bowed, with an ironical smile.

"If I mistake not, M. le Duc de Chastelnoir?"

"And then?"

"'Tis a great honour for me to arrest a Peer of France."

"Too great. There will be no arrest, monsieur. Guard yourself!"

The blades crossed. Mailly found himself pressed by a hard adversary. He gave ground. The Duke's face grew crueller and still paler, as he continued to force him round the narrow circuit of the chamber. Pontchartrain came forward slowly.

Mailly skilfully parried a pass.

"I think, though, that is my blade that you use, Duke!"

"Taste it, and see!" He lunged again.

Mailly turned aside the thrust, and immediately riposted. The Duke's weapon flew from his hand, struck the further wall of the room, and clattered to the floor. Mailly laughed.

"Your first life, Duke! Fortunately, you go well-provided with steel this evening. Draw, and fall to!"

Scowling and breathless, the other drew his own blade from its scabbard, to place himself on guard. At the same moment, the Minister came up to the door of the apartment. His face wore a blacker frown than the Duke's as he stood, candle in hand, silently regarding the armed intruders.

The young men sank their weapons under his glare.

"What is this, then, messieurs?"

Neither replied.

"How come you to be here?" demanded Pontchartrain, finding fresh courage and energy in the sound of his own uninterrupted voice. "What are you about? Put up your weapons instantly, and answer!"

"Monseigneur! . . ." began Mailly, advancing a foot, with an ingratiating smile. But the Minister waved him to silence angrily.

"M. le Duc, it is you to whom I address my question. What means this intrusion? What scuffle goes forward?"

The Duke eyed him gloomily, but said nothing.

After a pause Pontchartrain went on, with still greater harshness:

"M. le Duc, your rank entitles you to certain privileges which no one wishes to refuse to you. But I have yet to learn that, among these privileges, is that of entering a gentleman's house at dead of night, without invitation! Satisfy, therefore, a not unreasonable request for information!"

The Duke returned no answer. He glanced down at his sword.

"M. le Duc," said Pontchartrain, "since you appear to desire not to speak, I cannot compel you to do so; but at least I can insist upon your immediate withdrawal from my residence, and this I do. To-morrow, at Fontainebleau,[25] I shall complain to His Majesty. Your whole conduct of late has become insufferable. My patience is great, but it is not inexhaustible; and even were it so as a private individual, I still have my office to consider. I am a Minister, M. le Duc. That may not be much in your eyes; still, I am one. There are insolences of a nature impossible to pass over. I say nothing of your audacity in fighting here, contrary to the edicts—though rest assured this also shall be brought before the King in Council. . . ."

"Phélypeaux, I am come here to kill you!" said the Duke, in a hollow voice.

Pontchartrain shrank back beyond the door.

"I do not know how mad you may be, monsieur, but I advise

you to attempt nothing desperate! I am armed with this poniard, and ample aid is within call. Put up your sword!"

"Yes, I shall first kill you, Phélypeaux, and then your bully! That is the order."

"*Peste!* you arrange things very much to your liking!" said Mailly, between his teeth. He quickly stepped to the fallen sword, picked it up, and bestowed upon it a hasty scrutiny. It was his own. Taking it in his right hand, in place of the one already there, he set the latter obliquely against the floor and snapped it into two pieces with his foot. The fragment remaining with him he cast down.

Pontchartrain signed to him.

"M. de Mailly, I invite you in the King's name to arrest M. le Duc de Chastelnoir! I go to summon a guard."

"No, it is too late, wretch!" returned the Duke, with a strange quietening of his voice, as in a kettle of water at the instant before boiling.

Suddenly depressing his head, and directing forward his blade, at the level of his own breast, he charged the Minister. For a single instant the latter gazed at him with a fascinated horror, then, casting his dignity to the winds, he turned his back, to run grotesquely down the passage in the direction of his occupied apartments. The rapidity of his flight caused the candle he held to become extinguished. All was abruptly plunged into night. Mailly heard scurrying footsteps, the Duke's bellow of rage, and, a moment or two afterwards, the slamming of a door. He gave chase.

Round the second corner, light began to shine again. It came through the ventilator above a closed door. He rushed forward across a little antechamber, seized the latch, and let himself into a long, rather narrow room, illuminated by a hanging chandelier, which bore perhaps a dozen lighted candles, a quarter burnt down. The side-wall on the right contained a great fireplace, without a fire. The end wall held another door, which was shut. On the side of the room opposite to the grate, three or four wooden steps led up to a recess, about a third the size of the main apartment. The recess had a window, and could be entirely curtained off, but at present was not so. A table strewn with papers occupied nearly its whole space. There was a single chair beyond, with its back to the window.

The lower room was lighted by day from above. Heavy eastern rugs decorated the polished flooring. A circular table, and two chairs, were all the furniture. Mailly guessed that the recess was Pontchartrain's working chamber, while the greater inferior apartment was for the reception of his official visitors.

Pontchartrain stood by one end of the table on the upper platform the broad side of which was towards the steps, covering the Duke, whose foot was on the lowest of these steps, with the muzzle of a heavy cavalry pistol. He had thrown down his poniard on the top of the papers, ready to his hand. His face was bilious and exasperated. The Duke grinned with anger at his check, as he continued gazing upwards, prepared at the least wavering on the part of the Minister to be at his throat. It was at this instant that Mailly ran across the room, caught him violently by the shoulder from behind, and dragged him round.

"What are you doing, Duke! Do you want to get blown into the next world?"

The other stared at him for an instant with a smile. Then, suddenly clenching and raising his left fist, he gave him such a buffet on the jaw that he reeled again.

"That is for interest, de Mailly! You will receive the principal in a minute."

He darted up the stairs. Pontchartrain fired, and missed. He threw the pistol at the Duke's head, caught up the poniard, and retreated behind the table. They started to dodge each other round it. Mailly, nursing his face, was compelled to laugh. At last the Duke leapt on to the table.

"Now, Phélypeaux, I think! . . . ." And he thrust downwards with his sword at Pontchartrain, who cowered against the window-frame behind him, just out of range.

The victim appealed to Mailly, in a voice agitated and constrained:

"Monsieur! monsieur!—cannot you see it is an assassination?"

At the same moment, the door at the further end of the room below opened noisily, and a number of men burst in. The leader was a middle-aged gentleman of heavy habit, with large and terrible features, and a complexion as of burnt clay. The three who supported him had the appearance of indoor lackeys.

"Holá! what is going on here?" Sweeping back his associates with an extended arm, the newcomer stopped just within the door to survey the scene.

The Duke jumped down from the table beside Pontchartrain.

"No, you shall not escape!" He wrested the poniard from him, and raised it aloft to strike home.

Mailly leapt up the stairs, just in time to catch the uplifted arm. He twisted it sharply, and the poniard fell to the table. The Duke again shifted his sword to his right hand. Pontchartrain seized the opportunity to slip out, and rush down the steps.

He gesticulated wildly to the group at the door.

"M. d'Argenson, quickly! quickly! Murder is being done!"

The person addressed strode heavily across the room with the gait of authority. The servants followed uncomfortably. Simultaneously, the Duke lunged savagely at Mailly, who warded off the pass with difficulty. They separated to a better fighting distance.

"Return swords there, in the King's name!" commanded Argenson in a voice of thunder, from the foot of the stairs, while Pontchartrain hastened to place himself under his protection. "He who disobeys shall be tried for his life. It is the Lieutenant of Police who says so!"

"M. d'Argenson," replied Mailly, without looking round, and with his speech liberally punctuated by the offensive of his adversary, "I have a wolf by the ears! If you will show me a way to come off without a bite, I shall be delighted to comply with your command. Otherwise, I must continue to do what I can!"

Argenson, drawing his own sword, mounted the steps to part the combatants.

"Go down, d'Argenson!" said the Duke, rather breathlessly.

His face was white, and his eyes were blazing, but he, also, did not turn his head. "We have not crossed swords in order to be separated. You will have all the rest of the night in which to convey the survivor to prison. I think it will be I!"

He concluded the gibe by a lightning thrust directed towards Mailly's midriff, which it seemed as if nothing could stop. The heart of the Lieutenant of Police leapt to his mouth.

"He has it! . . . No, by St. Denis![26] . . ."

His admiration quickly turned to dismay. The Duke's blade had slithered aside along Mailly's. The latter tried to disengage. The Duke pressed him again, this time not so strongly. Mailly parried with ease, but then his foot slipped. Overbalancing himself, his sword went forward without design, and before he could recover his equipoise, six inches of steel stood in the Duke's left breast. Mailly withdrew his weapon. The Duke's dropped from his hand, and he turned to lean with both arms on the table. From there he slipped on to the floor.

Argenson pushed Mailly roughly out of the way, and bent for the best part of a minute over the wounded man. At last he stood up. In the meantime Pontchartrain had reascended.

"Is it a bad case?"

"He is dead meat," replied Argenson. He put his hand on Mailly's shoulder. "You are arrested, monsieur. Your sword!"

Mailly passed it to him, with a shrug.

XVI

The Estate Of Royale

The Lieutenant of Police herded the others downstairs, and, in following them, drew the curtain completely across the recess. He laid Mailly's blade on the table of the lower apartment, sheathed his own, then went to the door by which he had come in, and put his head through the gap.

"Marbois!"

A heavily-built young officer, with an open countenance and flashing, pale-blue eyes, came to the salute just inside the door.

"Take these three footmen, and set them in a room by themselves under guard from without."

"Monsieur!"

"Who is surgeon to the Hôtel Chastelnoir?"

"Chignet."

"Where is he?"

"Doubtless at his own house, monsieur."

"Let him be fetched. No excuses. It is the Lieutenant of Police who sends for him."

Marbois marshalled the three lackeys before him out of the room, saluted again, and went out, closing the door behind him.

Argenson turned to the Minister with a stiff bow.

"Monseigneur, we have here a conspiracy. It is my office to investigate it, and I purpose to do so on the spot. You do not interpose a claim of privilege?"

"No. But I do not understand what you do in this house."

"I have been summoned by one who has given information. The threads of the affair appear to be intricate, so that it will be necessary for me to examine a number of persons—in your presence, if you so desire!"

"Persons of my establishment, monsieur?"

"We shall see that! . . . However, if you elect to remain, it must be on the condition that the conduct of the examination shall be mine. Only those questions shall be put which I authorise.”

“Very well. Since I know nothing of all this, and cannot imagine what it is, I shall not interfere. I will just send for my secretary Passy, and then I shall be ready. It is singular where he can have got to!” And he glanced in perplexity towards the door through which he had entered in fleeing from the Duke.

“You will soon hear, monseigneur. He will be swept up with the rest. My men that way have their orders to apprehend everyone without distinction of person. It is a liberty I have taken for the King’s service.”

Pontchartrain’s face darkened.

“I also serve His Majesty, it seems to me! Your authority for so strong a measure?”

“An assassination has just missed fire—that is my authority! If I have exceeded my functions, you shall judge me afterwards. When you have heard all, I do not think that you will make this a quarrel.”

“But who has told you that my house harbours criminals?”

“’Tis not what we have been told, monseigneur, but what we are to discover. Pray be seated!”

Pontchartrain dragged a chair towards him, and sat down.

“And you?”

“I will stand. I shall see faces the better.”

He snatched off his hat and wig, and threw them carelessly on the table, beside Mailly’s sword.

“We shall reduce things as much as possible. Yourself, for instance, monseigneur—I have but one immediate question to put to you.”

“Ask it.”

“I arrive to find you murderously assailed by the Duc de Chastelnoir. Very well! But why has he desired to slay you? That is my question. Has he received an injury, real or imagined, at your hands?”

The Minister hesitated.

“He formerly had a command afloat, monsieur, and thus served under my Department. Well, I have had the misfortune to disoblige him in an application, that is all. I know of nothing else."

"It is a sufficient insult for a sensitive *seigneur*. We shall say that it explains his action, and we will not look behind it at present. . . . I will next interrogate the prisoner under arrest. Your name, monsieur?"

Mailly bowed, and informed him.

Argenson bent a pair of shaggy brows. "The de Mailly who was concerned in the affair of the Marquis de Ventailles?"

"The same."

"You are a fatal person, it seems! However, we have only to talk about the combat which has just ended so badly. Did you come here to-night intending to kill the Duc de Chastelnoir?"

"No, monsieur; and for two very good reasons. Firstly, I do not know M. le Duc, and have no quarrel with him; and secondly, when I entered the house I had no idea that he was in it."

"These are your assertions. Still, you have killed him!"

"If so, it has been in self-defence—or, rather, in defending Monseigneur, who was attacked, as you saw."

"Describe what prefaced this attack on Monseigneur."

Mailly pointed towards the door communicating with Passy's house.

"The Duke and I were having a slight debate with swords in another room, when Monseigneur unexpectedly entered. The Duke at once transferred his animosity from myself to Monseigneur. The scene shifted, and we all found ourselves together here. The rest you have witnessed."

"Thus you were already fighting!"

"I do not deny it."

"Then why were you fighting?"

"For me, I joined swords to prevent Monseigneur's assassination. For the Duke, presumably, that this assassination should not be prevented."

"So that the Duke announced to you such an intention?"

"M. d'Argenson, I shall be quite frank. He announced nothing in so many words. We encountered in the dark, and he mistook his man. He said enough to confirm to me that something was afoot, so I took a risk, and drew.”

“Who was the other for whom he mistook you?”

“Passy.”

Pontchartrain jumped up wrathfully. Argenson signalled to him with his eyebrows. The Minister coloured, made a gesture of impatient unconcern, and resumed his seat.

“So he addressed you by the name Passy?” demanded the Lieutenant of Police of Mailly.

“Yes.”

“And although he did not announce an assassination, he led you to infer one?”

“That is not quite how it was, M. d’Argenson. I had already . . .”

“Be careful, de Mailly! How came you to suppose that this individual whom you met by chance in the dark in a strange house was anything but amicably disposed towards Monseigneur?”

“*Peste!* it is not in itself a very friendly thing to do to lie in waiting in another’s house towards midnight! . . . It will be best that I begin at the beginning. Earlier in the evening I was called hither for an interview with Monseigneur. . . .”

Pontchartrain regarded Mailly thunderously from his chair, but the latter continued to study the brim of the hat he had removed, pulling it this way and that between his fingers. He proceeded:

“Of the interview itself I do not speak. Monseigneur, it seems, has contemplated my record, of which he does not approve. He desired to exhort me to a better mode of life; which, accordingly, he did, and I was presently dismissed. In introducing me to Monseigneur’s presence, however, Passy—for he it was that brought me—he, I say, obliged me to leave my sword without, for the better security of the Minister. Conceive my astonishment, then, when upon coming forth again I discovered that the sword I picked up was not my own!”

“That is to say, you picked up the wrong one?”

“M. d’Argenson, I picked up the only one there was to pick

up."

"This sword on the table here?"

"No, that is my own. The Duke used it against me, and I had the good fortune to send it flying from his hand. The other lies broken in the room we fought in. You may see it there."

"So the Duke effected the transfer?"

"Perhaps; or perhaps it was Mdlle. Passy who did so. Passy himself was with me throughout."

Argenson turned away to pass a huge hand over his forehead.

"But why do you fasten upon the woman for this?" he demanded.

"Because it is she who invited me back to the house, after her husband and Monseigneur should have departed to Versailles, which was to be within fifteen minutes after the conclusion of my interview."

"You deduced from all this—what?"

"That a crime of violence was to be committed, and that such crime was to be placed on my shoulders."

"By Passy?"

"Aided by his wife."

"But you kept your counsel?"

"M. d'Argenson, I am not a fool exactly! I went away."

"In order to return!"

"Assuredly. Someone was perhaps to be murdered. Should I have done nothing?"

"So, having returned, what happened? Whom did you first see?"

"First, Mdlle. Passy, whom I put out of doors."

"Why so?"

"That I might investigate at leisure. After that, I encountered Passy, whom I gagged and tied up."

"*Corbleu!* there is Passy for you, monseigneur!"

Pontchartrain clenched his fist, and began to strike with it his knee.

"I hear! . . . But let this monsieur, so nimble and so ready-handed, take care to know what he is about, for it is possible that, before all is concluded, the affair may bear a different colour from that he desires to give it! The Duc de Chastelnoir must have accomplices. Very well! But who is to affirm that this man is not one? He is an intruder here. He fences with the Duke for awhile, not very seriously. He maltreats Passy and his wife, that they may not appear upon the scene. He interposes himself between the Duke and a defenceless man precisely when other assistance arrives. These facts, added together, form a curious sum, in my opinion! And then, when all has failed, and interrogations must be expected to begin, he runs through, without the smallest necessity, the one person whose evidence would have accused him! . . . The indictment is sufficiently close. Consider, in addition, that there is a *lettre-de-cachet* in readiness to be executed against him. It is a clear case for trial!"

Mailly snapped his fingers impatiently.

"On account of what crime is the *lettre-de-cachet*, monseigneur?" asked Argenson thoughtfully.

"Whatever it is, monsieur, it is one concerning which His Majesty has satisfied himself! You will continue to confine your examination to the affair in hand, if you please."

The face of the Lieutenant of Police acquired an additional shade of red, as he turned again to Mailly.

"Let us go forward. After binding Passy . . ."

"After binding Passy, I passed through the house, to encounter the Duke, as I have described. But it should be mentioned, and I do not know how I have forgotten to place it in its right order, that before binding him I had another adventure in Passy's apartments, though a trifling one. A pretty madame peeped out of her door for an instant, only to withdraw immediately. That is the whole concerning her, and it is of no use to ask me further questions. I am ignorant whether she is inmate or goddess descended from the skies!" And he stole a malicious glance at the Minister, who bit his lip and looked down.

"So, after all this, you came upon the Duke, who expected Passy?" interrogated Argenson rather hurriedly.

"Yes."

"You say, he expected him. Had Passy left him, or was this to be the first meeting?"

"He had left him."

"To go where?"

"To ascertain if I had returned to the house."

"Thus nothing was to be done until you had returned?"

"Exactly."

"You know this, or merely hazard the conjecture?"

"The Duke stated it explicitly."

"That is to say, the crime was to be placed to your account?"

"I have said so."

"And why did they select you for the purpose, rather than another?"

"I suppose because a man who has a *lettre-de-cachet* hanging over his head may be considered desperate; and Passy knew of this order."

"What further passed between you and the Duke?"

"He commanded me, believing that I was Passy, to bring madame to the room in which he was. In the meantime he was to re-conceal himself behind some curtain."

"Why was madame to come there?"

"He did not say."

"And thus his intrusion in the house may simply have been for the purposes of an amour!"

"Yes, with my sword in his hand!" said Mailly ironically.

"You think, then, that the lady had some legitimate appointment with the Minister, that Passy was to conduct her to that apartment in order to meet Monseigneur there, and that the Duke was to conceal himself behind the hangings, to choose his moment for dealing the blow?"

"That is my theory, M. d'Argenson; and until someone can find a better, I shall hold by it."

Argenson addressed Pontchartrain:

"This lady, monseigneur!—I do not wish to cause annoyances to people unconcerned in our affair."

The Minister frowned.

"I was, in fact, to have granted an interview to a certain individual of the other sex this evening—on what business I do not precisely know."

"I understand. But may she be examined?"

"It will be better that I examine her myself in private."

"That is enough. Rest assured I have no wish to meddle with your official arrangements, monseigneur! . . . For you, de Mailly, you will stand back for the present. We shall test your story by those of the other witnesses."

An interval succeeded, during which Pontchartrain remained crouched in his chair, biting indifferently his lip and his finger-nails, Mailly stood, arms behind back, whistling softly between his teeth, and Argenson strode up and down the length of the room, occasionally throwing out a hand, as a new idea bearing upon the case under investigation struck him. At the end of two minutes a knock sounded at the door communicating with the front of the house. Marbois entered, and saluted.

"Chignet is here, monsieur!"

"Let him come in!" said Argenson.

Marbois returned to the door, and flung it open.

* * * * * *

"Ah, good evening, Chignet," exclaimed the Lieutenant of Police almost jovially, moving towards the short, rotund, rosy-cheeked individual who came forward with an air of solemnity, bearing with him a case of surgical appliances. Marbois saluted, left the room, and closed the door after him.

"I see you come prepared!" proceeded Argenson, taking the other's arm. "There has been an accident."

"I guessed as much when your name was given me, monsieur. A wounding, for five pistoles!"

"Worse! We have only had you here for form's sake, Chignet. The damage is done. The affair is political; interests are involved, and so we shall have to swear you to secrecy."

The surgeon bowed in acquiescence, then turned to salute still more profoundly Pontchartrain, who grunted in response. Argenson took a lighted candle from the chandelier, and, stepping across the room, drew aside the curtain of the recess.

"Come up, Chignet!"

The two disappeared behind the curtain, which fell into place behind them.

Pontchartrain immediately beckoned to Mailly, and rose.

"A word, monsieur! Your business will be quite safe. If I have not shown myself your friend, it has been for the sake of appearances. Passy will be examined. He will certainly speak of your interview. . . . Do not slip the rope round your own neck, that is all I have to say to you! Nothing has been intended against the Duke."

Mailly bowed. The curtain became agitated, and the Minister hastily resumed his seat. Argenson and the surgeon reappeared, the latter looking still graver than before.

"Well, M. Chignet?" demanded Pontchartrain.

"There has been nothing for me to do, monseigneur."

"I do not know many in France who will shed tears!" said Argenson. "Still, 'tis a man of a thousand connections, and we cannot afford a scandal. Can you remain here in the house till I have concluded my examinations of witnesses, Chignet?"

"I must, if you wish it."

"Then go outside, and ask them to find you a private room, and refreshment. Monseigneur will not grudge it."

The surgeon made a comprehensive bow to all present, and retired.

Scarcely had he done so, when the door communicating with Passy's house was thrown back, and a tall, lean, muscular individual, with lank black hair and swarthy skin, in full military equipment, entered the apartment, and halted in the doorway to regard its occupants, a naked sword in one hand, a lantern in the other. At once perceiving Argenson, he saluted with his blade.

"Very well, Savary!" said his superior. "Come forward, and make your report."

The officer strode into the room, halted again, and once more saluted.

"Monsieur," he said, in a cool, audacious, intelligent bass voice, "the door of the house at the rear of this being securely fastened, I forced a window. I have been through all the rooms that way, and have taken two persons, who remain under guard in separate apartments. They are a man, said to belong to the establishment, whom I found tied up, and have released, and who gives his name as Passy; and a woman, well-dressed, who refuses information."

Argenson turned to the Minister.

"What commands have you concerning the lady, monseigneur?"

"I shall see her to-morrow."

The Lieutenant of Police addressed his subordinate: "Detach a man to conduct Madame to her carriage, or where she will. Express my official apologies for the unpleasantness caused her, which occurred, however, in the ordinary course of duty, and notify to her that Monseigneur will have the honour of communicating with her in the morning. Bring in Passy."

Savary saluted, and turned on his heel.

Two minutes later he came back escorting Passy. The latter, whose dress was disordered, and whose eyes were cast down, perhaps to hide the concentrated venom which stood in them, barely responded to his employer's inquiring glance by an inclination of the head. A frown quickly settled on Pontchartrain's features.

He stood up.

"Passy," he said, in a choked voice, "certain incidents have occurred here to-night which demand investigation. The Lieutenant of Police will investigate them. I not only authorise you to reply freely to all his interrogations; I command it. But it has been agreed between us that no reference shall be made to the lady whom I was to have seen, and who is still in the house. Your responses, therefore, will not include her name. This being well understood, proceed, M. d'Argenson, and let us get the matter finished."

"Retire to the door, but hold yourself ready!" said the Lieutenant of Police to Savary.

He took the post indicated.

Argenson scratched his rough cheek, as he continued to regard Passy reflectively.

"How came you to be bound?"

"I was surprised and mastered by the person standing here, whose name is de Mailly."

"What was his intention in so attacking you?"

"I do not know," replied Passy.

"Was he alone?"

"Yes."

"Where did the assault occur?"

"In a room immediately above the stairs in my own house, which is at the back of this."

"Then were you stationary in the room, or passing through it?"

"I was passing through it."

Passy's face, as he answered these questions, grew ever paler, as though he apprehended that a trap was set for him the mechanism of which did not yet appear.

"Where were you going to?" demanded Argenson, screwing his eyes thoughtfully.

"I was returning to Monseigneur, with whom I worked."

"So that you had come away from him?"

"Yes, monsieur."

"And why had you come away?"

"I sought my wife."

"Who was—where?"

"I sought her in her own room on the lower floor of my house."

"You were at work with Monseigneur. What were you to do with your wife?"

Passy bit his lip, and remained silent. Argenson viewed him for a few moments with an alarming grin.

"Did you perhaps desire to leave instructions concerning your supper?”

“No, monsieur. And without Monseigneur’s permission I cannot answer your question.”

The Lieutenant of Police looked inquiringly at Pontchartrain, who reddened.

“It is true,” said the latter. “Passy left me to ascertain if the lady had come whom you have just dismissed.”

“That is different! Since you say so, monseigneur, we shall leave it. . . . Well then, Passy—did you find your wife?”

Passy hesitated.

“You have only to tell the truth!” said Argenson, in a bullying voice. “I shall draw all the consequences which are necessary. Did you exchange words with your wife?”

“No.”

“And, why not?—since you descended for the purpose.”

“She was not there.”

“Then where was she?”

“I thought that she would be upstairs, I mounted to seek her there, and then this assault occurred.”

“You have told us that you were returning to Monseigneur when the assault occurred!”

“That is to say, I was coming towards Monseigneur while continuing to seek my wife.”

Argenson, covering his eyes with a hand, remained silent for a space. Suddenly he looked up, to point a thick forefinger at Passy’s breast.

“Are you acquainted with the Duc de Chastelnoir?”

“I have formerly seen and spoken to him on occasion, in Monseigneur’s presence.”

“No more? You have not met him to-night, for example? Think what you are to say!”

“I have very assuredly not met him to-night.”

“Nevertheless, he is here!”

Passy cast an involuntary glance round the room, but the curtain was drawn across the upper recess.

“I have not seen him.”

"Have you contrived this visit for him?"

"On the contrary, I know nothing about it."

"Could he have passed through your house?"

"I do not think it possible."

"The outer door is kept barred?"

"Not always; but the communication between the two houses is through an aperture closed by a panel, which, when closed, a stranger would not suspect to be what it is."

"Therefore, since M. le Duc is here, he must have come by another way?"

"Yes."

"We shall see!" He signed to Savary, who came smartly forward.

"Ascertain without fuss if the Duc de Chastelnoir has been observed to enter from the Rue d'Heudicourt since four o'clock this afternoon, when I myself saw him abroad. Do not be put off by loose general assurances, but have the matter set beyond doubt."

As Savary went out, the Lieutenant of Police returned to Passy.

"Attend! Do you take bribes?"

"No."

"Commissions? Gifts of an innocent character from people requiring introductions or posts, whom you have been able to oblige without detriment to His Majesty's Service?"

"My hands are clean."

"So that you absolutely have nothing but your salary, paid to you directly by Monseigneur?"

"I have only my salary."

"Confess that such a squeamishness exceeds human nature, and that there are exceptions to your rule! Monseigneur will not think the worse of you, provided these rewards have been legitimate."

"I repeat, monsieur, that I accept gifts from none."

"Your father was *maître des requêtes*[27] in Bordeaux?"

"Yes."

"Did he die leaving you much?"

"No. He was not rich himself, and his estate was greatly divided."

"Your wife is daughter of the late notary Barbesson of Caen, who also was not rich. You do not pretend that she brought you anything considerable?"

"No; and, to cut the tail from the argument, I am a poor man. Yet this poverty does not say I am dishonest."

"You are without expectations?"

"Yes."

"So you are poor! But what is your notion of poverty? On how much could you lay your hands, supposing that you were obliged suddenly to realise your estate. A hundred thousand livres?"

"I do not know what you are aiming at, monsieur, but I shall tell you how it stands with me. When I say I am poor, I do not mean as compared with the rich, but absolutely. If I am worth ten thousand livres, it is as much as I am."

Savary came back, and Argenson beckoned him forward.

"What is your report?"

"The Duc de Chastelnoir has not been seen to enter from the Rue d'Heudicourt at any time to-day."

"It is certain?"

"Yes, he has not come in by that way."

"Then post yourself as before!"

Savary obeyed. The Lieutenant of Police placed his hands behind his back, narrowed his eyes to slits, and addressed Passy, with a portentous smile:

"I find you negotiating the purchase of the estate of Royale, in the independent Duchy of Savoy. Be so good as to explain to me this transaction!"

Passy paled. "Monsieur. . . ."

"I listen!"

"Without disrespect to you, monsieur, if you have obtained this information, it has been by treachery! The affair is innocent, but no one concerned has had the right to speak of it without the consent of all the rest."

"What is to be the purchase price?"

"It is still debated."

"No, it has been fixed. The sum of four hundred thousand livres is to be paid. The amount is vast. Who is to find it?"

"Monsieur, I am the agent of another. I am not allowed to talk of a business which is not yet concluded."

"Why does your principal withhold his name?"

"It is his whim."

"Is it with Monseigneur's sanction that you have entered upon this negotiation?" He raised his brows at Pontchartrain.

"I know nothing whatever about it!" said the latter, with an angry laugh.

"Well, then, now you have heard! Passy is buying an estate out of France. His principal's name is withheld, but the preliminary draft of the instrument, which I have seen, is in the name of one Jacques Berthold. That is very well. But it is for the Lieutenant of Police of Paris to be acquainted with the destination of all great sums of money that leave the country mysteriously, so I have been at pains to ascertain who Berthold really is. It is a man of straw, monseigneur. To be exact, it is a petty official residing in Dijon, the second cousin of a maternal aunt of Passy's wife, who, I suppose, is worth not four thousand livres, to say nothing of four hundred thousand! . . ."

"Monsieur," broke in Passy, in a voice tremulous with indignation, "you have found out half a story, perhaps, but you have assuredly not discovered the whole! Berthold's name appears in the draft. In the contract itself the name of the actual finder of the money will appear, and he will be the real principal."

"You repeat my words. Who, then, is this real principal?"

"I may not say."

"Come, that is no answer! I do not put the question as a private man, but as the representative of the King and of the Parliament of Paris. They desire to know. . . . . I will take you across the room, and you shall whisper his name in my ear!"

"It is impossible, monsieur. I cannot betray my trust."

Argenson signed to Savary, who came up.

"Monseigneur, this appears to be a case for the Conciergerie! I shall definitely arrest Passy."

"On what grounds?" asked Pontchartrain.

"His explanations are unsatisfactory. Without a closer examination I cannot incur the responsibility of dismissing him. . . . Savary, take your prisoner!"

Passy, bestowing upon him a glance of spite, retreated towards the Minister.

"Monseigneur, I protest! This arrest is illegal. I have not been formally accused, and I am ignorant of any offence or misdemeanour. Also, it is a violation of your privilege. We are a Ministry here. The Lieutenant of Police has no right of official entry here. A Department which has for head the King is responsible to the King, and not to the Paris Parliament, or its servants. I do not take thought for myself. A detention of a few hours in the prison of the Conciergerie will certainly not bring about my death; but it is the precedent. The other Ministers will not thank you, monseigneur, for having permitted the end of this new wedge to be driven in!"

Pontchartrain sank moodily into his seat.

"You claim the arrest as your right, M. d'Argenson?"

"We can reserve the point for future debate, monseigneur. In the meantime I will ask your consent to the thing."

Passy made a vehement gesture. "It is that I have foolishly suffered myself to be attacked, gagged, and bound by a night-intruder, whose motive in entering the house is sufficiently manifest, since a *lettre-de-cachet* is upon the point of execution against him! This must constitute my crime! I see no other in the field."

Instead of replying to him, Argenson again addressed the Minister:

"For the present, it is but to remove him to another room, monseigneur. We shall not transfer him to the Conciergerie until the whole preliminary examination has been concluded."

"If that is all, take him."

"But, monseigneur. . . ." began Passy angrily. Argenson cut

him short.

"Arrest the man," he commanded.

Savary laid a hand on Passy's arm. The latter tried to free himself to approach the Minister.

"Take care, monseigneur, that in sacrificing your servants you do not at the same time forfeit their gratitude!"

Pontchartrain jumped up, while a blotch flew to his cheek.

"What! you threaten?"

"Silence!" roared Argenson to Passy, with the full force of his lungs, stamping heavily with his foot on the floor. "Savary, remove the prisoner to the place he has come from! Let him be closely guarded by two men, without liberty of speech. Search his person for papers and weapons. Any papers bring to me here. Report quickly!"

Savary saluted with his eyes, and, gripping Passy firmly by the arm, impelled him from the room. The door closed behind them.

XVII

Mademoiselle Passy's Examination

Pontchartrain strode up and down agitatedly. He came to a stop before the Lieutenant of Police, to glare at him with his single eye.

"Then what is this affair of the estate?"

"We shall see, monseigneur, if the principal's name is not Passy, and if the four hundred thousand livres were not to have come out of your exchequer."

"Is it mere supposition, or have you proof?"

"The proof will depend upon the disposition of the next witness."

"Who is that, monsieur?"

"Passy's wife."

"Was it she who summoned you here?"

"Yes."

"Because she had been put out of doors?"

"And to stay a crime, it seems. Let us not anticipate her story, monseigneur."

"She accuses her own husband?"

"Stranger things have been."

"She has a lover, you would say?"

"It is imaginable, but I know not where to look for him, monseigneur. Let us not anticipate. I am waiting for Savary's report, then we will have her in."

Pontchartrain fell sullenly to twisting his pouting under-lip with his fingers. He sat down again.

Savary reappeared.

"The prisoner is guarded, monsieur. I have searched his person, and there are neither papers nor weapons."

"Very well," said Argenson. "Now bring in Mdlle. Passy, who is with Marbois. Ascertain first that she has overheard no conversations, and, upon entering with her, inform me of this by a nod only."

Savary went out by the other door, while Argenson brought up another chair for the use of the witness, a proceeding which Pontchartrain regarded sourly, although he did not comment upon it in words. Instead he said:

"You continue to retain de Mailly, monsieur, which appears to me to be irregular. He is a party."

"I may want him, monseigneur."

"Nevertheless it is irregular."

"Monseigneur, the conduct of the inquiry is mine, it is not my first case, and I know perfectly well what I do. Suffer me to act in the manner which my intelligence suggests."

Pontchartrain threw himself impatiently back in his chair, and folded his arms.

Mdlle. Passy came into the room, escorted by Savary, who, privately interrogated by a glance from Argenson, returned him the required nod. Meanwhile the lady, having for an instant lifted her pale, chaste, tranquil countenance to perceive whom the apartment contained, at once dropped her gaze again coldly to the floor. Argenson and Mailly bowed. The Minister closed his eyes, frowning.

"Be seated, mademoiselle!" said the Lieutenant of Police with blunt courtesy, pushing forward the unoccupied chair.

She sat down. Argenson cleared his throat.

"Well, mademoiselle," he began, "the business develops, and now Monseigneur wishes to hear your story, as you have told it to me. Do not permit yourself to be intimidated by his office. Above M. le Comte is the King, and above the King is the Law. Justice demands your assistance in elucidating to-night's occurrences. Speak freely and candidly, conceal nothing, and add nothing of your own. Come, then!"

"I shall conceal nothing, and am not intimidated, M. d'Argenson, but before I speak I must know what has happened here to-night during my absence. I have been told nothing. You have arrested this gentleman, I see, if such he is to be called, but where is M. le Duc?"

"He has departed."

Mdlle. Passy directed a glance of sharp and doubtful inquiry at the features of the Lieutenant of Police, who added hastily:

"Your husband, again, is elsewhere in the house. At present nothing is going on, so that you need not fear that you are wasting precious time by your recital, which, on the contrary, is very necessary to our complete information. Proceed, mademoiselle!"

She hesitated for a moment, then calmly faced the Minister, whose chair was set obliquely to her own.

"I trust that all is well, monseigneur, so I shall now repeat to you what I have already affirmed to M. d'Argenson, and afterwards you will tell me what has really taken place. I find it very difficult to commence, however. . . ."

"Come! I shall have to assist you," said Argenson bluffly. "A raid on your treasury has been planned, monseigneur. And the name of the thief, mademoiselle?"

"I know not whether I should give it."

"For it is her husband, monseigneur. The scruple is pardonable. In effect, he was to have stolen a parcel of securities from your vaults, and covered the robbery in a fashion doubtless suggested by the Devil. Such is your statement, mademoiselle?"

"Yes," replied Mdlle. Passy quietly.

"Now tell Monseigneur; had your husband accomplices in this theft?"

"None. He has intended the whole prize for himself."

"Has he taken the money, or only planned to take it?"

"He has taken it."

"Then where is it?"

"In a cavity of the wall in a room in his own house, concealed behind false wainscoting."

"Where you could lay your hands on it?"

"Surely—unless someone has already removed it."

"And the sum?"

"It is a parcel of seven hundred and twenty thousand livres."

Pontchartrain started up, only to sit down again. Argenson, deliberately producing a snuff-box, applied a liberal pinch to each nostril in turn. After blowing his nose vigorously with a trumpet-like blast, he turned towards the Minister.

"That would have bought our estate for us, monseigneur, and still left something in hand. . . . I believe that before we go further with the interrogation of this witness, you will desire to repossess yourself of the money. It is much to lie unguarded. If it pleases you to accompany Mademoiselle to the hiding-place, Savary shall escort you."

"At once. And supposing it to be there, Passy shall hang."

"I have no objection. Go with Monseigneur, then, mademoiselle, and when you come back we will hear the rest of your story."

He signed to Savary, who picked up his lantern. The Minister, frowning thoughtfully, with bent head led the way out of the room, followed by the tall, slight form of Mdlle. Passy, whose face expressed nothing except weariness. The officer closed the rear, with drawn sword. The door shut upon them.

Argenson laid a rough but friendly hand on Mailly's shoulder.

"I have contrived this opportunity for a private word with you, de Mailly. I suppose we have five minutes. I will speak, and you will listen. The business is a bad one."

"You saw how it happened, M. d'Argenson. You will give your testimony for me?"

"I will do what I can, but you, in turn, must obey my directions. You are a man of the world?"

"Yes."

"No folly, no indiscretion, then. Add nothing to what you have already said. Should Pontchartrain question you, wait before answering until I shall have recast the interrogation in the form in which I wish it replied to, and, above all, do not let the Passy woman surprise you out of taciturnity by her accusations and defences. You are to use your intelligence. It is not a case of hanging one, two or three villains, but of smothering a scandal—you understand? The honour and good fame of great houses are involved. As Lieutenant of Police in Paris it is my duty to expose all crimes, but as man of sense and heart it is even more my duty to discriminate, where discrimination is called for, so I shall take a broad view of my office and let go a few rogues, rather than bring disgrace to two distinguished families. Between ourselves, de Mailly, I care for Pontchartrain no more than for the last bite on a cold shoulder of mutton, but I esteem greatly his father, the Chancellor. . . . Have you yet guessed the name of our little visitor this evening, whose secret everyone is so solicitous to preserve?"

"No."

"It is Madame la Duchesse de Chastelnoir, the wife of the man you have just slain."

"That is very bad, M. d'Argenson."

"Sufficiently so, I think. You are not personally acquainted with her?"

"No."

"You are not to suppose that she has been here to-night to be made love to by Pontchartrain—that is, by the man of perhaps the nastiest physiognomy in France. Far from it, she has come to try at last to arrange the notorious differences between her husband and the Minister, for she is very good-natured, and it was also to her interest. Pontchartrain contrived the Duke's disgrace and ruin, and, had the thing succeeded, she would have been forbidden the Court, at least. Nevertheless, her husband was not to know the purpose of her visit; neither, perhaps, was Pontchartrain. This devil's spawn, Passy, has persuaded the one with the other, I have no doubt, that a pretty woman can be made to surrender to a monster. In a word, he fancied that, in the greater turmoil created by the tour of inspection of a jealous spouse and its consequences, namely the Minister's departure to another world, his robbery of public funds would pass unnoticed. To-morrow then, Madame's reputation becomes torn to shreds, and she is a really virtuous woman; while the Chancellor, a venerable and respectable monument of another generation, will mourn in retirement the official degradation of a son for whom he has done so much. For Peers of France are not assassinated with impunity even by Ministers, de Mailly. I say nothing of you, and yet you will be hanged, of a surety. So that is why we are to let the Passys go, and give the Duke a natural death. Do you find my reasons sufficient?"

"Yes, M. d'Argenson, if you can get over so many witnesses."

"We shall take our obstacles one by one. It will entail a busy night, but that is preferable to an unprepared morning."

"Will Monseigneur consent?"

"He will propose it. . . . So, that is what I had to say to you. I think our time is nearly up. Remain at home to-morrow afternoon, and I will try to get to you. Your address?"

"Rue Carcassone, 1."

"I shall then inform you how the business has gone, and whether you are to pack your portmanteau for a journey. Meanwhile follow your routine quietly, but be careful not to approach the vicinity of this house, drawn by curiosity; and neither visit me, nor send to me. If the news is bad, you will hear it fast enough. Provide yourself with ready money in case of need."

"And if you fail to come?"

"I will come or send."

A minute later the door was thrown open, and Pontchartrain strode into the room with heavy energy, holding in his hand a bulky packet, his face darkly flushed with a sort of grim triumph. Mdlle. Passy and Savary followed.

"You have it, then, monseigneur?" inquired Argenson.

"Yes."

He came up to the table, snapped in two the tape which bound the package, and, laying down the pile of bills within, bent over to examine them, contriving in so doing to turn his back so as to exclude from the others present all view of the operation. After a few moments he stood up straight again, evened the edges of the bills against the surface of the table, retied the bundle, and put it into a side-pocket of his coat.

"Well, monseigneur?" asked Argenson.

"It is Naval money, but whether it is all that has been stolen I cannot say without a scrutiny."

"But the amount corresponds with that stated by Mademoiselle?"

"Yes."

"Then we shall give her a clean discharge."

Pontchartrain seated himself.

"I do not know about a clean discharge. Events have occurred which she has not yet explained."

"Sit, mademoiselle! Monseigneur wishes still to interrogate you."

"I will stand."

In the meantime Savary had taken his former post by the door.

Pontchartrain scowled, and cast his eye on the floor. "Why have you denounced your husband?"

"Because I am an honest woman, monseigneur."

"A good reply. But why have you waited until now to do so?"

"As long as the crime was in preparation only, I was as one in a dream, and could not think him serious, but when money and life were at last to be taken, my conscience struggled free."

"What life was to be taken?"

"Not yours, monseigneur."

"Then whose?"

"M. le Duc's."

The minister coloured.

"Who was to take his life? What did he in this house?"

"In obedience to my husband, I admitted him at shortly after nine o'clock, while you interviewed M. de Mailly."

"Who was to kill him, and to what end?"

"M. de Mailly was to be brought to the deed, in the belief that it was for your service."

"You tell us a curious story, I think. How could the Duke's death advantage Passy?"

"It would have occurred in your house, monseigneur, at the hands of a man who had been coerced to it half-an-hour before, by means of a suspended *lettre-de-cachet*. Passy thus believed to force you to silence regarding the theft of money."

"Thus I was to receive the credit for this atrocious

assassination?"

"No, monseigneur; but only if my husband were brought to justice for the theft. Otherwise it would have been put about that M. le Duc had been slain while feloniously attacking you in your own house."

"So how was he enticed hither?"

"He came to seek Madame la Duchesse, his wife, monseigneur."

Pontchartrain started up.

"She has not been here."

"Yes, she has been here."

"It is well, mademoiselle, and at last your lying and malice appear. You desire to exculpate M. le Duc, and why? Because he is your lover. . . . Ha! you think I do not know it. Then I shall tell you that I have not the Secret Service for nothing, and that I have in my pigeon-holes the names of the lovers of every woman in France with pretensions to position and beauty. You are intimate with a Mdlle. Taranne, who is in the household of Madame la Duchesse, you have frequently seen M. le Duc in that house, and he has afterwards visited you in your husband's. There is, therefore, nothing absurd, in my opinion, in conceiving a plot between the three of you to assassinate me and thereby secure vast wealth for yourselves. The plot breaks down, and you are to save your lover—that is the history of your evidence! However, you will be disappointed. . . ."

He strode angrily across the room, and jerked aside the curtain of the recess.

"Here, mademoiselle, this way. Here you will see something interesting."

Mdlle. Passy's face turned paler. She walked hesitatingly to the foot of the stairs. On the upper table the candle still burned which had lighted Chignet during his examination. Behind it, on the floor, half-hidden by the legs of the table and its hanging cloth, lay outstretched the dead body of the Duke, whose limbs had been decently composed by the surgeon before his withdrawal. From the lower apartment the face could not be distinguished.

She set her foot on the lowest step, caught at the curtain for support, and stared upwards, while those grouped behind her watched her movements in silence.

She turned round, to meet Argenson's eye.

"Who is dead?" she whispered.

Pontchartrain laughed harshly. "Go up and see. It will not hurt you for once to behold the final state of all of us, and I engage that he will not jump up to contradict your statements. Ascend, mademoiselle!"

"It is M. le Duc, then!" Suddenly her body began to tremble from head to foot.

"Yes, M. le Duc de Chastelnoir. He who was your lover, and whom you admitted to your house in order that he might enter mine to kill me. But why do you quake? He has been spared this crime—I am still alive. Conquer your delicacy, and go up."

Casting the speaker a glance of exquisite scorn, she ascended the few stairs. She passed behind the table, and stood looking down upon the dead man. For a minute she remained thus, motionless, having her face hidden from those below.

When she came down again, she gazed with a smile into Mailly's eyes.

"The worse man has killed the better, but was it in fair fight?"

"Why do you fasten upon me, mademoiselle?"

"I do not think that Monseigneur is accustomed to weapons. But did you do it?"

Mailly bowed coldly.

"In fight?"

"I am not an assassin, mademoiselle."

"To win your pardon, was it not?"

"No; I was attacked, and defended myself."

She turned from him. "We have all been unfortunate to-night—I certainly not the least so. However, where is my husband?"

"He is in another room, under arrest," said Argenson. "Do you wish to put more interrogations to the witness, monseigneur?"

"Since she has admitted that the Duke was her lover . . ."

"I have not admitted it," interrupted Mdlle. Passy quietly, with a curl of her lip, and shrugging her shoulders.

"Then on what account are you especially unfortunate to-night, mademoiselle?"

"In that I loved him, perhaps, but that concerns not you, monseigneur."

"So that you were already his mistress in imagination, if not yet in fact, which is the same thing for our purpose."

"No, he was not my lover."

"These refinements will not serve you, mademoiselle. There has been a bond of some sort between you—we shall not inquire whether of airy admiration or of positive sin—a bond, that is to say, a union, a connection, and this connection has swelled into a conspiracy for the taking of life and treasure. . . ."

Argenson interposed.

"Monseigneur, we shall get nowhere by this road. If Mdlle. Passy is still to be examined, it must be regularly. Perhaps she has loved the Duke from afar, and perhaps he has not loved her—there is nothing incredible, nor even singular, in such a situation. If the conspiracy existed, then she has denounced the Duke equally with her husband, which I do not believe you want. I have little doubt that we have heard her whole story, but, with your permission, this is what I shall do. It is past midnight, and the Conciergerie does not like late visitors. I shall have the Passys removed to my office, where they will be as secure as in prison. Thus, between now and daybreak, we can decide together the course that is to be taken with them."

"Very well, then do so."

"Savary!"

The officer sprang to attention, and saluted.

"Remove Mademoiselle to another apartment. Let two coaches be fetched. Detail two men to escort Passy; one, Mademoiselle. Upon arrival at the office, they will be lodged apart, and let this lady be treated with the consideration due to her sex and station. The escort need not afterwards report here, save in case of accident. Dismiss all your men that way, bar the street door, and return to me."

Savary, having again saluted, motioned to Mdlle. Passy to precede him from the room. She twitched her shoulders contemptuously, kept down her eyes, and complied.

The door closed behind them.

XVIII

The Second Report of Monsieur Chignet

The Lieutenant of Police brought forth his snuff-box, while Pontchartrain, without explaining his intention, mounted to the recess behind the curtain, which he drew across after him. After a few moments he reappeared, with a paper in his hand. He once more drew the hangings completely across the top of the steps, and descended to the others.

"Here is your *lettre-de-cachet*, monsieur!" he said to Mailly. "Destroy it yourself. Passy drew up your record for me, and, in the light of what has passed, I have no doubt that he has falsified its facts. You have my permission to burn it here, at once."

"Thanks, monseigneur!"

"As far as I can penetrate the matter, you are in no way implicated in the crime planned for this evening. Nevertheless I advise you to change your manner of living. It will do you small good to have your name constantly mentioned in connection with scandalous affairs—the better sort of people will speedily come to shun you, and you will be thrown back of necessity into the society of rogues and malcontents. I tell you this for your advantage. Behave soberly and discreetly, and the probability is that the proceedings against you for your part in the Ventailles business will be quietly dropped. Meanwhile you will be pleased to wait here until M. d'Argenson and I have framed a counsel concerning the events of to-night. We shall then instruct you what story you are to tell, if you are to avoid detention upon the capital charge."

Mailly bowed. He handed the *lettre-de-cachet* to Argenson.

"Do me the favour to read and burn it, M. d'Argenson. Thus there will be no doubt in the mind of any that it has been really cancelled."

"Here is prudence! So much the better for all of us, however, if you can see two steps ahead." He glanced his eye over the order, then, setting light to it from the flame of a candle, suffered it to burn in his hand until all was consumed save an inch of one corner. The sparks of this corner he trod out underfoot.

"There has gone your interview with Monseigneur, de Mailly. Forget that there has been one."

"Now your proposals, M. d'Argenson!" said Pontchartrain, rather grimly.

"Regard me as benevolent, monseigneur. You are Minister to His Majesty. If political reasons demand the suppression of a part of to-night's evidence, I am at your disposal. If you desire that the Passys shall be brought to open trial, it is all one to me. I wish to do what is right."

"I do not say that political interests are involved. Neither do I in the least care though Passy and his wife be tried and hanged. But since the Duke has come to this house to-night with intent to assassinate me—and we can show it—we must consider how we can explain his death without bringing disgrace upon a rich and honourable house. The money having been recovered, and I unhurt, I should perhaps even be willing to let the Passys go unpunished, if the other end could thereby be attained. Let me have your view. I, too, wish to do what is right."

"*Peste!* we are in a disinterested atmosphere!" thought Mailly. "If that is all, I also wish to do what is right, so long as I am not hanged for it. I have caught it from this pair, and I shall begin to think that public life is a school for magnanimity!"

Argenson looked at the Minister shrewdly.

"You know as well as I do that there is only one way of accomplishing the feat, monseigneur. It will be necessary to establish that the Duke has died naturally. I do not pronounce it impossible, but it will be risky, and it will cost money."

"Yet if it is to spare some, and injure none, it appears to be a duty, though disagreeable. Let me hear how you would set about it."

"I was the nearest witness of his death, therefore my story will carry most weight. As chance would have it, I watched the skirmish pretty closely. What happened was this. Attend you, de

Mailly. As you delivered your final thrust, the Duke's foot caught against some unevenness of the floor, and he staggered. Your point took his clothing, but not his flesh. In fact, the accident would have saved him, but for the circumstance that he was already dead. My opinion is that the shock of overbalancing at so critical a moment, coupled with the violent effort to recover himself in time, precipitated a death which the disordered condition of his heart might have brought about at any minute. I was tolerably familiar with his personal appearance in life, monseigneur, and I have noticed a certain sharpness of the nose, a pinched character of the nostrils, a blueness of the lips, which one frequently finds associated with this type of infirmity. We will have Chignet in again. If he confirms the thing, I do not know that we need seek any further."

His speech was succeeded by silence.

"Lackeys were present," objected Pontchartrain gloomily.

"I shall deal with them after Chignet."

"What of you, M. de Mailly?"

"Monseigneur, I shall be only too happy to believe that I have not slain this unfortunate *seigneur*. My sword, however, lies on the table, so that it seems that I am in arrest for something."

"You are a quick fellow," said Argenson, with a twinkle. "The arrest is removed—take your blade."

Mailly did so, and restored it to its scabbard.

"And Madame la Duchesse?" inquired Pontchartrain, gnawing his nails.

"I shall break the intelligence to her, monseigneur. The Duke shall be conveyed to the Hôtel Chastelnoir to-night, and since there has been no particular love between them, I have no doubt that she will not search for wounds with a candle. Chignet shall accompany me, so that by daylight all will be prepared for burial."

"But still there are the Passys."

The Lieutenant of Police took snuff. After he had resettled himself, he replied:

"The Passys will not constitute for us a difficulty, but only an expense. That is what I refer to when I say that the affair will cost money. You cannot send them for trial, you cannot let them go free to perpetrate new crimes, you cannot well knock them on the head; you can only send them from the country. There is Spain, for instance. Spain is a very good place. 'Tis the remotest of our neighbours, and persons do not return thence too easily. There is also the Inquisition there. *Pardieu!* we know that in case of trouble the holy officers are most intelligent and accommodating fellows! However, we always come back to the same point. Spain is a long way off from Paris. A carriage, post-horses, an armed guard, subsistence on the road, a maintenance in a foreign country—all these cost money; while I myself have not a pistole to spare for such an object."

"When could they set off?"

"At daybreak. 'Tis but a question of funds."

"And such a journey would procure their permanent silence?"

"Assuming that they set a value on their necks, monseigneur! We could have them spied upon in Spain as well. That would entail additional charges."

"Including these additional charges, what is your estimate of the total amount?"

"Fifty thousand livres."

"What!"

"It sounds much in itself, but is not excessive when we have regard to our escape from an awkward situation. However, good or bad, fifty thousand is the sum."

"But to transport two wretches of no quality a few hundreds of miles! You make haste to be rich, I think, monsieur?"

"Just the reverse. I shall not touch a sou of it, and may even be out of pocket. . . . Still, you do not wish to go into it further! That is enough. To-morrow, then, I shall transfer the arrested to the Conciergerie, and as soon as the official day has commenced the First President[28] shall be notified in form that the Duc de Chastelnoir has died from a sword-thrust in your house overnight."

"Wait! I fancy you forget that this fifty thousand must be from my own purse. Well, I am a poor man."

"And therefore you cannot afford the sum! So it is of no use to go on debating the subject. I shall withdraw my party, and say good night, monseigneur!"

Pontchartrain's face darkened.

"You shall have it."

"At once, if you please!"

"I have passed my word."

"The business will not wait for the honouring of your word, monseigneur, while I have no money of my own to advance."

The Minister drew from his pocket the tied-up parcel, undid it, and counted out bills to the nominal value of fifty thousand. The rest he returned to his pocket.

"Here, then!"

Savary returned, and stood inside the doorway.

"What is it?" demanded Argenson impatiently.

"I have sent for coaches, monsieur. The woman prisoner now requests leave to take with her certain personal effects."

"Articles of clothing, no more! Stand by, to see that she does not put up papers, weapons, or valuables."

The officer saluted, turned on his heel, and went out. Argenson finished counting the bills, then put them in a pocket of his coat. He went to the other door.

"Marbois!"

Marbois appeared.

"Bring in Chignet!"

Two minutes afterwards, the little surgeon re-entered the room, pink-cheeked and sleepy-eyed. Marbois retired.

"Accept my regrets at having kept you, Chignet!" said Argenson. "We can now go on. The affair has taken a new turn, and I wish you to examine the deceased a second time. Pray come up! Monseigneur, I shall leave you below for a moment."

He pushed the little man before him up the steps, and both vanished behind the curtain.

The Minister turned to Mailly.

"As soon as the house is cleared, monsieur, I will see you

alone. Stay after the rest."

Mailly bowed.

A low, intermittent drone of voices sounded from the recess. Presently it ceased, to be succeeded by the shuffling of feet; then the hangings parted again, to pass Chignet, steered by Argenson behind. The surgeon seemed annoyed.

"At last we can finish up all this, monseigneur," said the Lieutenant of Police, producing the snuff-coloured handkerchief to wipe his brow. "It has been as I thought. Chignet will give you his report."

"Has death been natural?"

The surgeon replied in carefully picked words, addressing them to his boots:

"Monseigneur, I have viewed the body twice. On the former occasion it was in order to confirm death; now it has been to establish the cause of death. M. d'Argenson claims the case as political; I do not know political cases, and I must do my duty, which is to relate the truth. There is a wound—perhaps a rapier-wound—in the region of the heart. This wound might have sufficed to produce death. I cannot say certainly, since I am denied an autopsy. M. d'Argenson, on the contrary, assures me on his personal testimony that M. le Duc staggered and fell against the table before receiving the wound. Such a dizziness in a sober, well-nourished young man would assuredly point towards a temporary failure of the action of the heart; but if the failure has been temporary, it is always possible that it might pass into permanence. I am therefore prepared to furnish a certificate, on M. d'Argenson's testimony alone, that death has occurred naturally. It seems that M. le Duc had leapt upon a table but a minute previously. Such a violent feat might well exaggerate a concealed vice of the heart, and effect a sudden lesion of the fibres of that muscle. In simple language, monseigneur, M. le Duc has probably imposed too severe a strain upon a diseased organ, and has dropped dead from that cause. It is as far as I can go for you."

"Only, since the wound was dealt after death, there can be no need to allude to it in your certificate, Chignet," said Argenson. "We have merely to satisfy people concerning the actual cause of death; the rest is a purely personal concern. Also, it will be good sense not to bring my evidence into it before it is wanted. Your professional opinion will be enough."

The surgeon bowed.

Argenson proceeded: "I will ask you to extend your complaisance by accompanying me to the Hôtel Chastelnoir, there to acquaint Mme. la Duchesse with the disagreeable intelligence, and to prepare for the reception of the body, which I shall get my fellows to remove thither forthwith. You can then stay on the spot to perform the necessary offices yourself, with safe assistance."

"As you will, monsieur."

"Monseigneur will settle your fee at once."

"One hundred gold *louis*, monseigneur!"

Pontchartrain scowled, and turned his back. After a moment or two, apparently of reflection, he walked across to the steps leading to the upper chamber, to disappear behind the curtain. He came back jingling in his hand a small leather jug-bag.

"Here is the money!"

Chignet widened the neck to glance inside, but did not count the coins. He slipped the bag into his pocket.

"I thank you!"

Savary re-entered the room.

"Well?" asked the Lieutenant of Police.

"The prisoners have set off, monsieur. I have dismissed the rest of the men. The house is clear as far as this, and the street-door fastened."

"Take a man from Marbois, this way, and go in search of a hand-bier. No trappings. But do not bring it back before twenty minutes. Send in Marbois as you go past."

Savary went out by the other door, and almost simultaneously Marbois entered.

"Now bring those three lackeys!" directed Argenson.

A moment later they shuffled into the apartment, while

Marbois, having closed the door, mounted guard before it.

"Attention, fellows!" exclaimed the Lieutenant of Police loudly. As they halted in a ragged line, he inspected them with a wrathful eye.

"Your names?"

"Thibaud, monsieur."

"Baltz, monsieur."

"Chappelin."

Argenson turned his head. "They have spoken to none, Marbois?"

"To none, monsieur."

Pontchartrain sat down.

Thibaud was a tall, bony fellow, with large, loose, and eager features. Baltz was short, slight, saturnine, and monkish; swarthy-skinned, and very neatly dressed. Chappelin, with a nondescript person, had a vulgar, insolent eye, and the ugly mouth of a mongrel.

Argenson interrogated the Minister:

"What sort of men are these, monseigneur?"

"You find them in my service, monsieur."

"Then hearken, fellows. I am M. d'Argenson, the Lieutenant of Police of Paris, and people do not play with me. You have seen a gentleman fall. Is he known to you?"

They glanced at each other. Chappelin stepped forward.

"I suppose it is no crime to tell the truth, so we do know him."

"Do not roll that word 'crime' on your tongue until you are accused of one! . . . Very well! It is M. le Duc de Chastelnoir. You know that, but perhaps you do not know how he has come to die. I shall tell you, and then you will no longer be ignorant. He has succumbed to a sudden stroke. M. le Duc's heart has been unsound, so that his life has, as it were, been suspended by a single hair during weeks and months. Here is M. Chignet, the surgeon, who leads his profession. He will tell you the same thing."

Chignet appeared vexed and embarrassed.

"What M. d'Argenson has said is true. M. le Duc has died

naturally.”

“You hear, fellows?”

“Certainly, monsieur!” said Thibaud quickly.

“And you, Baltz?”

“It is no business of mine, monsieur, and if you say he has died thus, I am perfectly agreeable.”

Chappelin remained silent.

“The third man there—you, Chappelin—cannot you find a word to spare?”

“My eyes and my understanding have always been very good friends to the present, monsieur. Do not seek to divide them!”

“It is well! Monseigneur, I request Chappelin’s discharge from your service!”

“He is discharged!”

“Marbois!”

Marbois stepped forward.

“Arrest this man!”

The officer laid hold of the footman’s collar. The latter turned rather pale, but offered no resistance.

“You are for His Majesty’s Army!” said Argenson. “You have too long been warming your breeches and growing fat in Monseigneur’s antechambers. You will now go for a soldier.”

“I cannot be taken in a time of peace.”

“All that you shall explain to your commanding officer! There is to be a bloody war, tall fellows are being everywhere sought, and we shall send you from Paris. . . . Have him removed to the office, Marbois!”

“Wait!—wait, monsieur!” cried Chappelin, with an appealing gesture. “You do not go about your business in the best way. I will do whatever you require of me!”

“I shall not waste time with you, Chappelin. How has M. le Duc died?”

“As you have said, monsieur.”

“Not as I have said, but as you have seen with your own eyes! Well, what have your eyes seen?”

“They have seen M. le Duc drop suddenly, without a

wound. . . ."

"What wound?—what is this? How should he come by a wound?"

"No, no, I speak by way of illustration, monsieur! You take me up too quickly. He was talking quietly with Monseigneur, when suddenly he sank to the floor, without warning. Was not it so, Baltz?"

Baltz shrank from his appeal. "M. d'Argenson has already done me the honour to accept my witness."

"Mine also!" said Thibaud hurriedly.

Argenson continued to glare at all three.

"Besides Monseigneur, myself, and you men, who else was spectator of M. le Duc's death?"

They hesitated, with uneasy glances between themselves.

"No one else was in attendance, monsieur," hazarded Chappelin.

"You are positive?"

Satisfied by his tone of the response required of them, all three hastened to assent in chorus.

"Then pay attention!" said the Lieutenant of Police, bending his brows. "Should any foolish fable become circulated that M. le Duc has perished otherwise than by an act of God, it must needs be one of you three who has propagated it. We shall not spend time in discovering which, but you will all go for soldiers. And if so, be sure you will be received as marked men. Double fatigues and treble kicks will be yours, all the dangerous posts will know you; you will be the first dish of the meal for the enemy's cannon! I do not mean this to hold good only for as long as you remain in Monseigneur's service, but altogether. You will not find sanctuary with a new master. . . . Monseigneur now dismisses you for the night. Do not hang about, but go to bed quickly!"

Chappelin lingered anxiously.

"I shall request Monseigneur to restore you to your post on probation," replied Argenson to his unspoken inquiry. "Report in the morning, when he will notify to you his decision."

The lackeys departed.

The Lieutenant of Police yawned. "We have to get the body downstairs, monseigneur. It would be as well to dismiss the rest of your people."

"Yes," said Pontchartrain. He rose, and went out to give the necessary order.

A clock in the house struck one just as he came back. Savary had not yet returned. An embarrassed silence descended upon the room, and all stood about restlessly, avoiding the eyes of the others.

"Monseigneur," said Chignet, so abruptly that everyone started, "I have a nephew who is sub-lieutenant in the Brest Coastguard. He is clever at his trade, brave, sober, honest, and zealous; but he does not advance very fast. There appears to be some obstruction in the way. Pray give the matter your consideration! . . . The name is Dumont."

"You pick your occasion skilfully, M. Chignet!" grunted the Minister. "We shall go into it some other time."

"I do not seek to extort a favour, monseigneur, but you are a public man, with many calls, and one can rarely get to see you. Have this young officer to Paris. I have no doubt you will discover that he really merits promotion. His name is Dumont."

"May I interpose in an affair which is not mine, monseigneur?" asked Argenson, with a twinkling eye. "Rather send an emissary down to Bretagne to behold this mythological youth at his work! It is no sort of test to get a youngster to stand up straight and answer questions. Instruct your messenger that a careful, not a quick, report is what is wanted, and let him take a month over the transaction if necessary. . . . Such an expedition would suit you, I fancy, de Mailly!"

"I could undertake it," replied Mailly, intelligently.

The Minister pulled his under-lip.

"It is not only Dumont, but twenty others as well. To the journey itself I do not object. You understand that I can bind myself to nothing, M. Chignet?"

"I shall be your eternally grateful servant, monseigneur!"

"When could you start, M. de Mailly?"

“In thirty hours.”

“Then let it be so settled. Only, since it is M. Chignet’s affair, it is to him that you must look for travelling expenses.”

The surgeon bowed. At Savary’s re-entrance a few minutes later, he seized the opportunity to draw Mailly apart.

“Your address, if you please, monsieur!”

“Rue Carcassone, 1.”

“I shall be with you at noon precisely.”

Mailly nodded. They rejoined the others.

“Who was in the house as you came through?” Argenson was asking Savary.

“Our own men only.”

“So your people have retired, monseigneur. We can do the business at once. You have four archers, Marbois, including the one who came back with Savary?”

“Yes.”

“Post them outside in the street, then come back here. While they are waiting, let them disperse any loiterers, drunken night-birds, and the like.”

Marbois saluted, and went out.

“Fetch in the bier, Savary!”

Savary, too, went out, leaving the door wide open. A moment afterwards he staggered in again with the unwieldy frame, which apparently had been deposited in the adjoining chamber. The Lieutenant of Police directed him to set it ready on the floor, at the foot of the steps, and he did so.

“De Mailly, you have earned the duty! Help M. Savary with the body on to the bier.”

Mailly bowed. He followed the officer upstairs to the recess, and between them they shifted the table against a wall, to leave an unobstructed road. Then, with a strength disproportioned to his lean habit, Savary stooped to lift without obvious effort the head and shoulders of the dead Duke, while Mailly took up the legs. They descended with uncertain steps to the bier, on which they set their burden.

“A cloth of some sort will be needed, monseigneur,” said

Argenson. He took out his snuff-box.

Pontchartrain left the room, to return quickly with what looked like a table-cover, of heavy blue taffetas. At his heels was Marbois, who had executed his commission. Argenson, with Savary's aid, spread the cloth over the bier.

"We shall carry him down ourselves, and our men can take hold in the street. That is to say, I, Savary, Marbois, and you, de Mailly. . . . Chignet, no doubt you will be obliging enough to take up M. Savary's lantern, and light us downstairs. . . . Monseigneur, you had better stay here, and I shall say good-night, or good-morning, whichever we are to call it! I shall report to you at an early hour of the day."

"After this, you have finished with M. de Mailly?"

"Yes, I shall send him off home to bed."

"I wish a single word with him, concerning that journey to Brest."

Argenson stroked his nose doubtfully, but said nothing. Mailly bowed. Then, while the surgeon picked up the lantern, the four men bent as one to their allotted handles.

The procession moved slowly out of the room, through the house, and downstairs. Chignet, going first, unfastened the double doors opening on to the Rue d'Heudicourt. The street was in pitch blackness, and no one was abroad, except the waiting archers. The bier was transferred to them without being set down.

Argenson then issued his final orders:

"Savary, you will command the party. Go before with the light. Marbois will close the rear. If any stare, do nothing, but go quietly on. If any question, rebuff them. If any attempt to follow, first warn them, then draw. Your destination is the Hôtel Chastelnoir. I go straight there, and shall receive you."

The two officers saluted sharply, then ran to place themselves at their respective stations, three paces before and after the bearers. After a military pause, Savary briefly spoke the word of command, and the party set off into the darkness.

Argenson stayed to whisper in Mailly's ear:

"You are going back to Pontchartrain. Guard yourself in the

presence of the most treacherous beast in France! Undertake what you please, but do nothing till you have seen me. Adieu!"

With a last friendly grip of his shoulder, he left him, to overtake Chignet, who had gone discreetly ahead.

XIX

A Visitor

Mailly returned to the house thoughtfully. He barred the door from within, then, taking a lighted candle from the hall, made his way up through the house again to the room of the tragedy.

The Minister was still there, pacing up and down, with arms folded across his chest. He raised his head as Mailly entered.

"Well, they are off?"

"Yes, monseigneur."

"I shall not detain you five minutes. What do you see on the table?"

Mailly shot thither a quick but cautious look, to perceive five crimson-wrapped *rouleaux*,[29] apparently of coin.

"I see what looks like money."

"It is good gold, monsieur. Each roll contains one hundred newly-minted *louis*—that is, five hundred in all."

"Speak, monseigneur!"

"It is yours if you can guess the service for which it is intended—otherwise you may go home. I know you no better than the first gentleman I may meet in the street, monsieur, and that is why the test is necessary. If you are a shrewd man you are good for me, but if you are only a lucky fool my money will be better bestowed. Come! then."

"It cannot be to stop my tongue, monseigneur, for that is effectively stopped in any case. . . . It is possible that you already regret an arrangement arrived at with Monsieur the Lieutenant of Police against the law and your more considered judgment, but I do not think that you would find it necessary to offer me so much money for my consent to a readjustment of the affair, since you have but to clap me into prison as an accomplice of the Passys, to render my story of the *lettre-de-cachet* malicious and pre-concerted with them, whereas M. d'Argenson would not dare to confirm it, lest his attempted concealment of the whole business should appear. I believe, then, that you desire a more complete information concerting to-night's transactions, but that you do not wish the thing to go through your regular channels. In a word, I am here, I have witnessed everything and listened to all the evidence, so that I am the one whom you have naturally thought of to dive to the bottom for you. You think there is more to come."

"Proceed, monsieur!"

"You are delivered from the Duke, who is dead, and from the Passy couple, who are for Spain. Who, then, remains, monseigneur, but M. d'Argenson himself? I bet that it is his case you are meditating."

"And what part of the night's proceedings has struck you as peculiar in connection with that individual?"

"He has been in a devil of a hurry to throw sand on the fire—I have noticed that, monseigneur."

"His whole examination has been a comedy. He has made no search of Passy's house for incriminating evidence. He has questioned Passy as though it were an affair of simple theft. He has not questioned the woman at all, and, had not I intervened, would have dismissed her. One might swear that he has come here prepared beforehand to smother the case. You are not his man?"

"No."

"Has he made you proposals while I have been absent from the room?"

"No, monseigneur."

"But he has certainly arranged to see you again?"

"I don't deny it. This afternoon."

"To arrange what?"

"To report to me my situation, monseigneur."

"Be simple if it pleases you, but I shall tell you—it is the most slippery rascal in France. For instance—and hearken well—that Mdlle. Taranne whose name you heard to-night, she is on terms of excellent friendship with Mdlle. Passy, she is also in the Duchess's—that is, the Duke's household. Passy is his wife's husband. All these persons are intimately connected, and there has been a conspiracy directed against my life. Well then, do you know what Mdlle. Taranne is besides?"

"No."

"She is d'Argenson's creature. She is a paid spy of his."

"The devil she is!"

"If I did not know that, I should be ill served. And what conclusion do you draw from the circumstance, monsieur?"

"The conclusion that he is perhaps very wise to act as he is doing."

"Exactly."

"And that the affair becomes political, though I am not well up in politics, and, therefore, cannot pretend to fathom the motives of the Lieutenant of Police in participating in a conspiracy directed against the person of a Minister."

"So I shall enlighten you by a hint, monsieur. You will observe the closest secrecy. Understand that M. d'Argenson would at any time sell his soul to obtain for himself my Ministry, which would at once render him a man ten times as important, and which, for example, joined to his present office of Police Lieutenant, would enable him to realise his ambition of tyrannising over one and all in France through their misdeeds, actual or pretended. I think we need not seek further for a motive."

"That is . . ."

"I speak plainly in the belief that you are a man of honour. It is always in the head of that person to play me some devil's trick, in order to achieve my political destruction. It is not the first occasion. Should I fall, the pear will drop into his lap. Let us suppose that he divulges, after all, that the Duke has been slain. To whose detriment will that be?"

Mailly moved towards the table.

"Monseigneur, I shall take the five hundred *louis*. I shall report to you as soon as may be."

"Should you demonstrate to me that he really cares for nothing save to get out of the business with a whole skin, you will receive five hundred more. Should you discover treachery, and put it within my power to prevent it, you shall be given thrice as much. Take up the money, monsieur."

"When and where must I wait upon you, monseigneur, to deliver my budget?" And without a second bidding, he stuffed the *rouleaux* into his pockets.

"You will enter by the door of Passy's house, which I shall cause to be left unfastened, at ten o'clock in the night to come."

Mailly bowed, then scratched his head. The allowance of time was small, but, on the other hand, money is a wonderful quickener. His expostulation remained unspoken.

Each continued to regard the other in silence as though waiting for more to be said. At the end of a minute Pontchartrain likewise bowed, thereby intimating that the interview was closed. Mailly set on his hat, while the Minister took up a candle, to light him to the street.

They went out by way of Passy's apartments, through the aperture formed by the sliding panel. Descending the staircase, they passed to the door, and Pontchartrain stooped to draw back the bolt.

"There is one thing, monsieur," he said suddenly, standing up again. "I do not desire that you should approach the Hôtel Chastelnoir for the purpose of conducting inquiries there. The most discreet advances might perhaps awaken the suspicions of Madame la Duchesse that things have not occurred to-night precisely as they have been represented to her. She is to rest undisturbed in the thought that her husband has died naturally. Do not believe that, because she is a woman, you may hoodwink her; she has all her life moved in the highest circles—that is, she is as sharp-witted as a Jesuit and as keen of nose as an officer of excise. A single question in that household will somehow reach her ears, it is always so; and from that question will spring up in her mind a mystery, and from that mystery an assassination. You will avoid the house altogether, monsieur."

"*Pardieu!* monseigneur, if I am to discover all, and question none, it seems to me that the five hundred *louis* will have been well earned."

“Nevertheless, it must be as I say.”

“Well, I shall see what can be done without going there. I shall sleep on it. Good-night, monseigneur—lest other forbidden approaches occur to you, and I find myself standing upon the head of a pin, entirely surrounded by territory which it is unlawful to enter. Ripe or unripe, you will receive my report this evening.”

Pontchartrain smiled unpleasantly.

“Let it not be unripe, monsieur, for if we are taken by colic, you will be the first to leave the table, I promise you. Understand well, that, should it become a public case—as it may still easily do, despite all that has passed—absolutely the earliest interrogation of the judges will be, who the actual slayer of M. le Duc de Chastelnoir has been? In that event, you must make up your mind to a handsome hanging. It will not advantage you that there has stood one behind you, even could you establish it. I advise you to think less of bed than of a full and circumstantial delivery of the activities of the personage with whom we are to deal. It is very improbable that that one will seek his sheets to-night. First of all, comprehend your situation, monsieur.”

Mailly bowed, without replying.

The Minister, whose face still bore a sickly smile, raised the latch for him, and he passed out, the door being immediately closed and barred behind him.

He looked aloft at the stars shining through the gaps left by the house-roofs, filled his lungs to the full with the night air, so sweet by comparison with the dust-laden atmosphere of the apartments he had quitted, then started off along the narrow alley for the Rue Quiberon, and home. It was nearly two o’clock, and not a soul was encountered.

* * * * * *

Stumbling into his room heedlessly, all dull, weary and yawning, as he was, a brace of surprises arrested him upon the threshold like twin shocks of lightning, the one following instantly upon the heels of the other.

The window curtains were drawn, on the table a solitary candle burned low towards its socket, and in his accustomed arm-chair at the further end of the chamber sat, with reclined head, closed eyes, and half-parted lips, a strange lady, who apparently awaited his return, despite the unseemliness of the hour. The soft, youthful curves of her face pictured an innocence confirmed by the lovely bloom of her cheeks in repose, and Mailly could not put her age at more than twenty, yet her dress was modish, and that of a woman of the world, while her bosom was high. A white throat appeared above the poetically mysterious silken folds of her bodice; her shoulders were covered by an unfastened dark cloak, its hood thrown back. Her hair was pale yellow—that is, she was a blonde. A valise was beside her on the floor.

Even as he stared at her in amazement, rooted by the door, he experienced his second stroke. This demoiselle, who opened her eyes immediately, but wonderingly, and as if imperfectly awake, was not so entirely strange to him. He must have seen her before—recently. *Corbleu!* it was his apparition of Passy's house—she whose shadowed head had emerged during the fraction of a minute from the doorway of that upper room, whom he had shut up in it, and who had afterwards been liberated, unexamined, by d'Argenson's orders, with the Minister's willing consent. . . . In a word, Mme. la Duchesse de Chastelnoir—the wife of him he had killed! It was she in person, and she had come to seek him. Bah! he was not mistaken; his eyes had been given him for the purpose of distinguishing between one individual and another. He closed the door behind him, pulled off his hat, and bowed, then advanced a little way towards her.

"Her eyes are blue and beautiful, and she could not well be younger," he told himself. "Seeing that her marriage has preserved all this for her, she cannot have been so unhappy with the Duke, therefore I am very sorry to have dispatched him— which cannot now be helped, however; and she will survive the blow, to find a second husband, worthier of her. The singularity is, who can have directed her to my apartment? What pressing matter has she to speak of, which necessitates a visit to a male at close on three in the morning? That valise, again—does it portend that she proposes to take up her abode with me? *Diable!* my bed seems farther off than ever. . . ."

The visitor rose, and then it was put beyond question that she was the same. She was shorter than himself, but full of grace and fashionable ease. Mailly came still closer, bowing a second time.

"To what circumstance do I owe the honour of a visit so late, madame, and in what way can I serve you?" he asked gravely.

She bit her lip.

"You know me, at least, monsieur, if you do not know my name. We have met already during these hours of darkness."

"Her voice is tuneful, virginal, yet companionable," thought Mailly, regarding her with ever-increasing interest. "It reminds me of someone, but I cannot think of whom. How the deuce came such a child to intermeddle with the affairs of that misbegotten Pontchartrain? 'Tis not in nature." And he said aloud:

"Madame, I recognise you very easily, and did so at the first; neither is your name so utterly unknown to me as you deceive yourself. It is your business which I cannot imagine."

She smiled impatiently. "If you do, in fact, know my name, my sister must have told it you."

"Your *sister*, madame! We are at cross-purposes. I was even unaware that you had a sister, and certainly have not her acquaintance."

"You are M. de Mailly?"

"Why, yes."

"Then you should have met Mdlle. Passy, and she is my sister."

"We shall believe that, madame, when we see the sun at midnight." But although he understood that this young Duchesse for evident reasons desired to remain *incognito,* the baffling resemblance of her voice to another's which he had remarked already began to whisper of Passy's wife. He wiped his brow, and stood irresolute.

"However," he added, "if it pleases you to pass in this poor house for the sister of the lady you have mentioned, far be it from me to cross your whim. It is agreed, then, that you are that one. Let us proceed."

"But in the name of Heaven, monsieur! for whom do you mistake me?"

"Oh, it is not I, madame. It is Monsieur This, and Monseigneur That, and a round half-dozen others. All these have joined to give you one name, while you choose to call yourself by another. Well, I accept your version, that is all. This being settled, be pleased to say how I can serve you, for it is very late."

"But there is my valise for proof. My initials are branded into the leather, as you perceive. The I represents Isabelle, which is my baptismal name; the B, Barbesson, which is my surname. I am accordingly Isabelle Barbesson, and my sister, before her marriage, was Rachel Barbesson, just as now she is Rachel Passy, her husband's name being Passy. Do you believe me now?"

Mailly was shaken.

"What is this valise, however, mademoiselle? since I am to call you so. Why have you brought it here, for instance?"

"It contains my changes. I passed through Paris to-day—or yesterday, I think—and had intended to spend one night with my sister, before proceeding to Caen, where my home is. She could not receive me at once, so sent me here to you; or rather, to your apartments, for your return to them was to be the signal to me that the house of my brother-in-law was again clear of visitors."

"*Parbleu!* I am exceedingly grateful to your sister for her expression of friendship—all the more so, as we have known each other but these few hours. Nevertheless, without my being so impolite as to question your veracity, Mademoiselle, a certain small difficulty presents itself to me. I myself encountered you in that place at half-past ten, or thereabouts, since when, to my positive knowledge, you have not conversed with Mdlle. Passy, nor even seen her, while we are now towards three o'clock. If she really invited you to visit me, it must have been much earlier, it seems, and you did not immediately adopt her counsel."

"We spoke together at eight. She said there was to be political company, so that she could not receive me as yet. I was indignant, as a girl would be, straight from a tiring journey as I was. I demanded where I was to go, then. I am not a man, to take shelter in a strange inn. She reflected, then offered that, as M. Passy was even then bringing you from your apartment, to participate in the political discussions of which I speak, and as your return hither would be the sign that these discussions were concluded, I might with complete propriety and great convenience seek you here on the pretence of business, in the knowledge that you would be absent. She was impatient and annoyed, and clearly desirous of ridding herself of me, so I took up my valise and came away."

"But not to arrive here, for two hours later we again find you in that house."

The visitor flushed.

"You have the right to be suspicious, monsieur, therefore I shall continue to answer your inquiries until you are satisfied, although I, too, have questions to put. Well then, you must understand that I was displeased with her explanations, for surely the smallest and most employed residence is large enough to afford an obscure corner for one's own sister. Also, her bearing puzzled me. . . ."

Mailly interrupted her, which showed that he was at least as much occupied by his private thoughts as by her words.

"But are you indeed Mdlle. Barbesson?"

"I have said so, monsieur."

"It is very strange that all should build upon your being another. I cannot disbelieve you, however, since you positively assert it; and, in truth, you are over-young for marriage, and to that individual in particular."

"What individual, monsieur?" asked the girl, wrinkling her brow.

"It does not matter. So you are really Mdlle. Barbesson? I am very glad to hear it, for I confess that my conscience troubled me so long as I confounded you with this other lady—who, now that I remember to remark the circumstance, would scarcely be likely to attend a *rendezvous* carrying a valise. So you are surnamed

Barbesson. I have heard the name before to-night, and, therefore, it is the more probable."

"Nevertheless," he went on to himself, "it does not improve matters that so youthful, pretty and interesting a person should belong to the conspiracy of those others, which is what her simulation of the Duchesse's identity signifies. Perhaps all have been in possession of the secret, including d'Argenson—which would explain his great haste to dismiss her—but with the exception of the Minister, with his single exception, who desired the departure of the Duchesse for another reason. Light dawns on me. It may be that I shall earn my money. But I am exceedingly sorry for it, for she is far too agreeable a girl that I should wish to see her entangled in the snares of filthy justice. 'Tis a case for discretion."

She stole a quiet glance at him, which descended imperceptibly from his eyes to his shoes, as though he, also, had started to acquire a certain individuality for her.

"Then you are at last convinced, and my intrusion here in your lodging is sufficiently accounted for?"

"Nearly so, mademoiselle. But let us resume at the point at which we broke off. You accordingly went back to your sister, upon second thoughts, still bearing your valise?"

She smiled for the first time, and Mailly discovered her face to be thrice as fascinating in consequence.

"Poh!" he declared inwardly. "She is a young maiden, as ignorant of crime and plotting as the blessed saints. I have wronged her."

"The valise appears to excite your curiosity, monsieur, yet you perceive it exists, I had it with me, and could not well throw it away. However, no; I did not take it back there. Listen! I had already stopped a public carriage, intending to come to you, as my sister recommended, when something of a sudden entered my mind suggesting new doubts, and I determined to investigate the affair a little yet. But as it would look absurd to inform the coachman that I had stayed him to speak of the weather, for example, I bade him convey the valise hither in advance of me, with the message to the woman of the house that its owner would follow presently. This he faithfully performed, since I found it here, awaiting me, on my arrival at midnight."

"Which done, you returned to your sister?"

"Monsieur, I am not old, but I am not a fool. If I returned, it was in order to become initiated into a mystery, not to dispute to no purpose, and be driven forth again with ignominy. I resolved to enter the house privately, and conceal myself somewhere, to learn, if possible, the sort of politics which demand an entire dwelling-house for their debate."

Mailly admired her, with a smiling stare of approbation.

"It is what I would have done myself. Then the geography of Passy's abode was familiar to you? You have been there often before?"

"Not often, but still I have been there."

"Proceed, mademoiselle! I begin to feel a great sympathy with you in this adventure."

"The rest is quickly told. It was already dark within. I opened the street-door without sound, entered, and shut it again. Then I stole softly up the stairs. When near the top, however, I was arrested by the whispered voice of my sister, addressing me from the passage below. I admit that I turned pale, and that my heart hurried."

"It was a predicament for a tested soldier, mademoiselle. You must have been well startled. So she discovered you!"

"No, she was incautious, for all her cleverness. She mistook me for an expected visitor—she could not distinguish me in the dusk, you understand, save that I wore petticoats, and was thus a woman. She whispered . . ."

"Yes, let us hear that. 'Tis important."

"'Is it you, Uranie?'"

"Ah!"

"I replied 'Yes,' in a voice as low as her own—for I had gone too far to draw back, monsieur. I was committed to the enterprise, for good or ill."

"Do not excuse yourself; you acted very sensibly. You are

sure, though, that the name was Uranie?"

"Yes, but have no notion to whom she referred. She then went on to say: 'Be quick to conceal yourself—he will be here immediately. It is the room on the left, and then that on the right. It is lighted. Do not enter by mistake the first room on the right; the Minister is there awaiting de Mailly. When within, make sure to draw the bolt, and obey no summons to open, however imperative, save on the agreed signal.' She then added the single word, 'Hasten,' and glided out of sight into the interior of the lower house. I performed punctually everything that I was commanded. Afterwards I sat down with a fast-beating heart, to think what next to do."

"The 'he' who was to be there immediately—you believed this person to be the same with the de Mailly whom the Minister awaited?"

"I thought so then, monsieur, but it appears I was in error, for, half an hour later, perhaps, mingled footsteps approached and passed the door of the chamber in which I remained secured, and a man's voice growled. '. . . if he fails?'—to which my sister's whisper responded, 'Oh, his alarm will assure Mailly's return. That is the last thing I fear.' In short, their conversation was of you, and, therefore, he that spoke to my sister was not you, but someone else; thus nearly certainly the one who was expected, and had now arrived."

"And then?"

"I waited for above an hour more, I suppose, nothing happening. I looked forth from the room some half-dozen times, but all was darkness and silence. On the last occasion you confronted me—to fasten me in, so that I was now secured both within and without. Much later still, a number of police archers— as they gave themselves out to be—broke into the apartment, and I was set under a kind of arrest, which did not last long, however, for I was presently dismissed, with polite professions of regret, and conducted by a single archer to the first coach abroad at that hour in the street."

"To come straightway here?"

"Yes."

"But why did not you inform these archers that you belonged to the house?"

"Because I saw that they mistook me for another woman, and I desired my liberty."

Mailly threw his hat on the table. He glanced at Mdlle. Barbesson's large blue eyes, and her exquisitely-modelled lips, set in the suspended tranquillity of a female angel's; then passed his hand over his brow, to turn away.

"Your story is flawless, mademoiselle, and I shall believe it; but 'tis very late, I am very tired, so we must bring all this to a short end. Since you have come from that house, you cannot wish to return to it. You doubtless have it in mind to sup, and then to bed. I shall arouse my landlady, who will provide you with suitable accommodation; then in the morning we shall renew our discussion over breakfast, and discover what is best to be done.— Be seated, I beg, while I depart on my errand."

"Monsieur, I have answered many questions of yours, now reply to one of mine. I have sat here a great time, you also are returned, things may, therefore, by this be quiet in my brother-in-law's house; the intruders may have departed. Is it at all possible for me to go back there now, that I may spend the remainder of the night with my sister?"

"Briefly, no," responded Mailly. "I shall be quite frank with you. There has been trouble, and the house remains under observation; you must not dream of returning thither before daylight, at the least. In fact, too little of the night is left, the streets are unsuitable to you at this hour, and not a coachman is abroad, so we must make the arrangement I speak of. It will be a trifling inconvenience for you, but better that than an arrest."

The girl's face paled. "But an arrest indicates a crime, monsieur!"

"A crime, yes—or one attempted. For your comfort, however, Mdlle. Passy is very well, and in no danger of anything worse than a short and honourable exile from Paris. No doubt they will permit you to see her before she leaves."

"Be pleased to tell me very quickly what has happened. Is my sister in prison?"

"Assuredly not; but she is detained. She is in good hands, and nothing evil will happen to her. We shall try to arrange an interview for you after breakfast."

"Where is she lodged, monsieur?"

"With her husband, at the private residence of M. d'Argenson, the Lieutenant of Police; but, however it may be with Passy, in her case the detention is purely nominal. She has been removed from her house, merely because that house is the seat of an attempted misdemeanour."

Mdlle. Barbesson clasped her small hands eloquently.

"Ah, what a disgrace! How would my poor father have regarded this—he who was the soul of honour and uprightness. With what offence is M. Passy charged, monsieur?"

"With embezzlement; and I give you leave to be as indignant with him as you wish, for your sister's sake."

"Is the sum great?"

"Yes, we will give him credit for that. He has not aimed at small things."

"But has Rachel—has my sister been privy to this crime?"

"On the contrary, mademoiselle, it was she who summoned the police."

"Then who was that man?"

"An accomplice, I have no doubt. She entered into her husband's plans, in order to render them abortive."

"And the woman for whom she mistook me?"

"A decoy."

"And your part in all this, monsieur."

"I was to be Passy's scapegoat, I think, but God has been merciful enough to deliver me."

"The theft was to have been fastened on you, monsieur?"

"I should indubitably have hanged."

"Thank God indeed! . . . So that it was my sister who saved you?"

"She would have done so, mademoiselle, she would have done

so, I don't question, but I escaped by other means."

The girl thought quietly for a moment or two.

"It appears to be a singular reward, however, for her information, that they have detained her, and are to send her from Paris. You are keeping something back, I fear."

"It is very simple, though very unjust. One cannot be married to a criminal without bearing a degree of his disgrace. You have not been upon affectionate terms with the man, mademoiselle?"

"I have always feared him. When he has spoken to me, I have frequently been at a loss for a reply. He has seemed to me like the emissary of a cleverer and darker world. . . . Well, Rachel has paid for her folly. What will they do to him, monsieur?"

"'Tis a political affair, and it is probable that he will merely be thrust out of France. There will be no open scandal, I gather, for neighbours to rejoice over. All will be arranged privately."

She sought his eyes with hers. "You are being very kind to me, and I do not wish to appear ungracious, but only one person can truly reassure me of my sister's safety, and that is the Police Lieutenant himself. Were you to conduct me to his residence now, would he receive me?"

"No, no—great men want sleep just as much as others, and at this hour all Paris is in bed, except ourselves. There is nothing to be done till daylight."

"Well, then, I shall visit him immediately upon waking."

"And they will detain you too, to swell the number. Your acquaintance with your sister's place of lodging will convict you of complicity out of hand, mademoiselle. The lamb will call upon the wolf to inquire concerning her sister. That is a good joke."

Mdlle. Barbesson coloured with confusion. "This is ungenerous, monsieur. Did not you promise me but now that you would contrive for me an interview after breakfast?"

"Yes, but not with M. d'Argenson. We must approach the business more cleverly than that. You shall see Mdlle. Passy, and you will accept her assurances regarding her safety from her own mouth, but with the Lieutenant you have nothing to do. Come! I have thought of a plan for you. It seems that your sister has a friend of her own sex, who knows M. d'Argenson, and is indulged by him. A Mdlle. Taranne—and now that I remember it, she is resident in the Hôtel Chastelnoir, which is situated in the Rue St. Honoré. . . ."

"Stay!" cried the young girl. "That is our Uranie."

"*Diable!* You know her, then?"

"No, I do not; but there is a Mdlle. Uranie Taranne, of whom my sister has sometimes spoken. I had forgotten the circumstance together with the name. It must be she."

Mailly sank into a chair, to gaze towards the ceiling.

"So, then, this spy of d'Argenson's was to personate the Duchesse, and we advance another step towards simplification," he meditated uneasily. "In the light of such a discovery, I will now wager that there never has been an affair between the latter and Pontchartrain, but that her responses have been forged. No one has expected her to-night but the Minister himself, and the Duke her husband, both of whom have been fooled. 'Tis a veritable plot, in which d'Argenson begins to appear prime mover. Hence the speed wherewith the supposed Taranne was bundled by him out of the house, before the counterfeit should be exposed. But, by a chance in a million, this young girl slipped into her place in the gloom. Then what has befallen the other, that she failed her duty? Bah! some accident prevented her; or she was not intended to come, and d'Argenson was grievously taken aback when he learnt from the Passy woman that she had done so. Whichever way it is, the error by now has been disclosed. The Lieutenant, with Mesdemoiselles Passy and Taranne, they all will be at their wits' end to conceive the identity of this Duchesse at the third degree. *Peste!* until they have found that out they cannot move against Pontchartrain, and there will still have been no midnight duel—that is to say, my neck remains unbroken on its shoulders; though how to turn the business to still greater advantage, I cannot yet see. Therefore, they must not find out. So it will constitute a piece of imbecility for mademoiselle here to pay the visit to that woman which we have contemplated. They will immediately connect her."

"You appear disturbed by my information, monsieur."

"No, I am not disturbed, mademoiselle, but I am thoughtful. I have been ruminating, and I believe that it will after all be unwise in you to attempt to meet your sister for the present. You will have opportunities hereafter. Justice is suspicious, your brother-in-law is to be charged with a crime, and you were, very awkwardly, in his house at the hour of its commission. You had better leave Paris. I shall procure you a post-chaise and horses at daybreak."

"But I am innocent."

"I know it; but public examinations are disagreeable, and not always safe, even for the innocent. Be advised by a man of more experience than your own."

"But if I swear that I shall not as much as mention your name . . ."

Mailly rose again. "I thank you. Others are involved, however. It will do your sister no good to appear to have introduced you to that room in the guise of a different woman. There are many considerations, and I must have my way."

"I don't understand you, monsieur," said the girl almost angrily. "Have you not just promised me that I should see her?"

"Let us not be pedantic. There are promises and promises. There are the cold and deliberate promises which set a man beneath a definite obligation, but there are also the promises which merely express a provisional judgment; and this sort it would be worse than folly to keep, as soon as the judgment is reversed. I am so wearied, that my brain arrives at its final judgments more slowly than usual, that is my excuse for disappointing you."

"She is my sister, she is in distress, she is without friends or counsel, and I must go to her."

"You cannot at least go to-night. Over breakfast, we shall ask ourselves afresh what is best to be done."

"But you are not my guardian," exclaimed Mdlle. Barbesson, with sudden fire in her eyes. "It will, after all, not be necessary that I obtain your permission to wait upon this lady. You will hardly dare to attempt to detain me forcibly in your lodging."

"Mademoiselle, you will sleep on it, and then your good sense will come to my assistance."

"So that if your sister . . ."

"I have not the happiness to possess one."

"But if you had a sister—if I were she, for instance. . . ."

"Do not trouble to conclude, for I know what you would say. You are grieved and anxious—very rightly. It is not, however, a question of assuaging your grief and anxiety, but of behaving circumspectly. Mdlle. Passy has only a journey before her, she will be treated honourably, and at the end of it she will be suffered to regain her liberty. On the other hand, if you seek to visit her at M. d'Argenson's house, you will be closely interrogated by those who have made an art of it, the truth will come out, there will be the devil to pay. Be patient now, that you may rejoin her in a week, since you love her so well."

"And how do I know that you do not say all this to quiet me! How do I know that she is not in equal peril with her husband. Can I depart tranquilly, without having ascertained anything whatsoever of how matters stand with her? Listen to me! . . ." She stamped her foot forward, at the same time making an energetic gesture with her clenched fist. "You bid me return to Caen, to my mother, who is the only other one I have in the world. . . ."

"So she has not a lover," thought Mailly, with a strange and unaccountable lightening of his heart.

"Well then, my mother will greet me. 'And how have you left Rachel?'—my sister's name, I have told you already. 'She is in prison.'—'Merciful Virgin! what has she done? What has happened?—quickly, for the love of God!'—'I cannot say; I have not inquired.' 'What, wretched girl! have not you been to seek her out?—your own sister, in prison.'—'No.' 'Why not?'—'I was counselled against it by a stranger gentleman.'—'Who is this gentleman?'—'I do not know. . . .' Ah, it would be laughable, were it not so terrible! But it is because you are a man. Men are made of iron, I think."

"No, mademoiselle, I have a heart. Believe that I understand your cruel situation, and feel for you. I advise for your good."

"I could not endure the suspense."

Mailly was silent.

"You have not told me everything, monsieur. I am certain that there is more behind, and that she is in a bad way. Either you must let me go to her, or you must reveal the whole story—I insist on the one or the other. . . . Besides which, she will herself speak of my arrival at her house from a journey at the beginning of the night."

"No, for she is clever."

"And wicked, do not you wish to add? I have noticed that not one good word have you uttered regarding her, during all our talk. You refuse me this meeting because you are throughout aware that she is equally concerned with her husband in the business for which both are arrested. She . . ."

"Mademoiselle, I am unacquainted with the secrets of your sister's inmost soul, so cannot say whether there is much guilt upon it, or a little, or none at all. I merely affirm that she is at present under high protection, but that such protection will be immediately withdrawn so soon as it is learnt who that woman is who has usurped the rôle of Mdlle. Uranie in your brother-in-law's house. In brief, it is to spare Mdlle. Uranie and those who stand with her that Passy is not to go for trial. When it is shown that she was elsewhere at the time, when another lady can be produced, whose presence in the house establishes itself, yet does not matter in the least to those solicitous for the welfare of Mdlle. Uranie, *pardieu!* then things will be altered, and Passy must face his judges in spite of all, there is no doubt of it. If so, however, your sister must perhaps stand by his side. Am I explicit, mademoiselle?"

"Such fearful precautions would not be taken for a simple robbery. Something bad has happened, I am sure. There has been violence, monsieur. . . ."

"It is very true. Someone has been injured. But since Mdlle. Passy is neither the injured nor the injurer, you have no need to tremble for her additionally on that account. You must go to bed.

In the morning you shall quietly leave Paris, you shall furnish me with your address, and I will send you news of your sister as soon as there is any. I beg you to be seated, while I summon Mdlle. Antoinette."

The girl sat down, trembling. Her face was white, and she urged no further objection to Mailly's proposed course.

He quitted the room, to return five minutes later.

"She is coming, mademoiselle. I shall speak for both, so refrain, if you please, from volunteering unnecessary explanations."

"I thank you for being so very good to me," was the almost inaudible response.

Mailly bowed. Mdlle. Antoinette entered, in her night attire, partly hidden by a *négligé* which had once been white; her expression was disagreeable, and she was also very sleepy.

"M. de Mailly, mine is a respectable house," she began at once.

"Or I should not inhabit it. I am sorry to disturb you in the best of your slumbers, mademoiselle, but I have been abroad late, I have returned but within these few minutes, and I find here, waiting for me, my cousin, Mdlle. Barbesson, whose home is not in Paris. It seems that her coach has sustained an accident in travelling from the country, or she would have arrived here at a more reasonable hour than midnight, but it cannot be helped; we must do the best that we can. To-day, immediately after breakfast, she will resume her journey to Normandy. For the hour or two of darkness which remain to us, she will seek some essential repose. You have a room?"

Mdlle. Antoinette grumbled to herself, while the girl blushed scarlet, not knowing where to look.

"You shall receive five pistoles for your trouble," proceeded Mailly masterfully, "in addition to ten pistoles more for your reticence in the matter; but the ten will not be paid you until the end of the week. That is to say, if it is not earned, it will not be given. Are you agreeable to such an arrangement?"

"How is one to know that she is your cousin, M. de Mailly?

Moreover, it is not customary to demand lodging for young women at a time of night when all good Christians are fast asleep in their beds; and I do not understand what you mean about the five pistoles and the ten."

"That, then, is your case—you have expressed it very well. You will take a little glass of wine with me; then your comprehension will be quickened regarding the money. Apropos, Mademoiselle my cousin must be famishing; could not you discover the end of a sausage, or some such matter, and a morsel of bread, with which to stay her?"

"I could not eat, monsieur."

"You may freely call me Gaston before this good friend. But, at least, if you will not eat, you will drink."

He unlocked a cupboard, and drew forth a bottle three-parts full of wine, together with a trio of glasses, which he proceeded to supply.

"Here is for you, cousin!—toss it off like a trooper, for one sees that you are exceedingly tired. And here for you, Mdlle. Antoinette! I wish you health and prosperity. *Peste!* I am thirsty; I have not drunk these six hours. There is still a glass, Mdlle. Antoinette." And he filled it. "So the money is not enough. Very well, you shall have ten pistoles now—stay! here they are; take them. That is for having you out of bed, and for Mademoiselle's accommodation. Then, at the conclusion of a week, provided people have not gossiped concerning this visit—for there is nothing wrong in it, but they are not to know that—provided, then, that no foolish tales have got abroad, there will be twenty pistoles more for you. Thus thirty pistoles altogether, which is a sum not often so easily won. State your decision, if you please!"

"I have an excellent empty room, M. de Mailly. The sheets of the bed in it are aired, and everything is ready. Follow me, mademoiselle!"

"Do so, cousin Isabelle." Mdlle. Barbesson smiled faintly, with a heightened colour, but averted her eyes. "And believe that we are both excessively grateful to you for your kindness, Mdlle. Antoinette. I shall remember the service in other ways."

"I do it particularly to oblige you, M. de Mailly. I would not do it for everyone. But if people speak, in spite of me, I cannot help it."

"They will not. At eight I go to order Mademoiselle's post-chaise, at half-past eight we breakfast here, in this apartment, and at nine my cousin shall be smuggled forth.—I regard the reputation of your house as my own," he added, as a whisper, in Mdlle. Antoinette's ear.

He picked up the valise, and handed it to her, then lit a second candle from that which was burning, to pass it to the girl.

"Wait at the door, Mdlle. Antoinette. My cousin has still a private word for me—we have not met for a great while."

"It is only this, monsieur," murmured Mdlle. Barbesson, when they were apart. "I do not know you in the least, and am certainly not acquainted with your business in my sister's house to-night, but at all events I am sure that you are not an enemy, for your generosity proves it. I wish simply to assure you, on my honour, that you shall come to no manner of harm on account of any speech of mine. When we shall have parted, we shall thenceforth be total strangers to each other. Does this content you?"

Mailly bowed.

"While thanking you for the thought, mademoiselle, I do not like the form in which it is put. For me, I am as confident that we shall meet again, and frequently, as if the thing had been announced to me by authority."

She held out her hand. "I, too, wish to be friends, but do not take this unless you will promise to serve my sister. She is not wicked."

"That you are her nearest demonstrates to me that she is not. I shall do what I can towards liberating her swiftly for you. But then, I am to have my reward?"

"What reward?"

"The reward of sometimes seeing you."

"I have said, I also wish it, monsieur."

Mailly grasped her hand warmly, then bowed again, and released her. She hurried to the door, where Mdlle. Antoinette awaited her, yawning constantly. From there, she looked back with a quick smile.

After her disappearance, the owner of the apartment remained standing, as if stunned, for a whole minute. The increased flare from the candle, expiring in splendour, aroused him from his reverie, and while there should still be light to see by, he made haste to deposit in his chest the *rouleaux* of gold which continued to embarrass his pockets. That done, he blew out the candle, entered his inner chamber, fastened its door, and rapidly undressed in the dark, flinging his clothes, as they were discarded, haphazard upon the floor.

"This Mdlle. Passy," he thought, as he mounted to his bed, "she receives Dukes and masqueraders by night, she denies admittance to her own sister, she steals my sword and is in readiness to drug me with wine, she has very white hands, she grieves for the death of a strange nobleman, she is cognisant of her husband's villainy, and, to a point, furthers it. With all this, I am desired to believe that she is not wicked. *Cordieu!* I don't say that she is the wickedest to-night, but she is doubtless wicked enough. Nevertheless, a promise is a promise, and I have engaged to serve her; which will offend my conscience the less, as she interests me. All that family are uncommon, it seems. Both sisters, otherwise so unlike, possess that breath of pedigree which never deceives, in whatever rank or fortune; and I shall inquire in Caen—for I shall make it my affair to pass through Caen, on my road to Brest, supposing that I go to Brest—I shall inquire there whether the deceased lawyer Barbesson did not marry above his station. A woman's wickedness, besides, is never so atrocious as a man's, since it is invariably founded upon something soft and forgivable in her nature, whereas a man will kill, rob, and betray from pure debasement. Thus, could I summon up the ancient dead, I would not wish to behold the lineaments of a Nero, a Caligula, or a Commodus,[30] stamped with vileness and madness as they were, but I should be extremely curious to view the mortal likeness of Messalina,[31] who was as evil as they, yet in another fashion. Mdlle. Passy, then, interests me within herself, but, above all, through her sister. The younger has the calmness, dignity and intelligence of the elder; all the sourness of the stock, however, has been drawn off in the person of the latter, so that the junior daughter has been enabled to come into the world equipped only with virtues. *Peste!* it is right that she should love the other, for having relieved her of so much nastiness, and I shall play the part of a man of limited discernment if I distinguish between the identities of the two in my willing service. In addition, it appears that I owe the married one some reparation for the loss of an individual who might have become her lover, if he were not in fact so. . . ."

But his thoughts already commenced no longer to know themselves, and within two minutes more he was soundly sleeping.

XX

The Expedition To Brest

After some four hours of a loglike unconsciousness, Mailly awoke, with the punctuality of a campaigner, to discover the room flooded with sunshine, and to hear the clocks of the neighbourhood in the act of sounding the chorus of seven. He leapt from bed, seized the water-jug, and started his ablutions.

In the parlour, when he entered it, fully-dressed and with his hat on, Mdlle. Antoinette was engaged in preparing to set the table. He saluted her genially.

"For how many am I to lay, then, M. de Mailly?" she demanded, scratching her cheek with the handle of a fork, and appearing bewildered.

"Come! have you ever known me to entertain for breakfast? There will be but the two of us—my cousin and myself. I am going out, but will return shortly."

"So she will return, too?"

Mailly's countenance fell suddenly.

"How do you mean?"

"She has left the house, with her valise, this half-hour."

"Oh, the devil! . . . With her valise. With what intention?"

"How am I to know, monsieur? She said 'Good-morning!' and remarked upon the beautiful sunshine, then passed me to go out. So that I do not know whether to lay for one or for two."

He remained silent for a moment, following the pause by an unpleasant laugh.

"For one, Mdlle. Antoinette, for one—since persons who take early morning promenades in search of appetites do not customarily encumber themselves with baggage. But had I been aware of this intended departure, I promise you I would have risen much later. Things being as they are, let breakfast be served immediately. There is no longer anything for me to do outside." And he flung his hat down.

The meal was consumed in solitude, slowly and methodically, with a twelve hours' hunger which was unimpaired by the disappointment of his roseate hopes of a charming companion, on a morning which seemed especially created for dalliance; yet, throughout its length, it might be asserted that he scarcely knew what food he conveyed to his mouth. He meditated ceaselessly upon the action of Mdlle. Barbesson in decamping so suddenly, without even the politeness of a farewell.

"*Peste!* there I do her injustice," he corrected himself. "She promised nothing overnight, her mind is fully set on that visit to Mdlle. Uranie, and she was confident that the morning would bring forth a renewed crop of dissuasions from me, the prospect of which has disconcerted her. But she could have left her valise, and returned for it. If she has not done so, it is in the fulfilment of her contract—she is to deny my acquaintance, and has not been here. That is to say, she is an excellent girl, with noble feelings. But now let us see what will happen. She goes to Mdlle. Taranne, to solicit her aid towards an official permission to visit her sister, in detention at d'Argenson's. At this very moment, while I am breakfasting, they are speaking together, perhaps. La Taranne quickly understands everything, for the Lieutenant of Police does not select imbeciles for his instruments; she feigns compassion and tenderness, assents to the request, as to a thing of difficulty which she will attempt out of the milk of her womanhood, and, without the loss of an instant, makes ready to conduct to d'Argenson the individual whose presence in Passy's house has nonplussed him for six hours past—for it is six hours since he has learnt that Mdlle. Taranne herself was not in that house. . . .

"She will be for Spain with the others, then. Unless, indeed, the case is reopened, which I hold very probable. In either event, a pure, sensitive, refined young demoiselle is to be caught up in the sordid machinery of authority—it is abominable to the imagination. There is no one to say to d'Argenson: 'No, you shall not!' except I, so I shall say it. He will visit me this afternoon, when I shall feel my way, and see what sort of a bargain can be struck. But I have now to be cunning for two—I must borrow from the devil. In the first place, should they attempt to arrest me also during the day, I shall appeal to Pontchartrain, for whose ears I already have something. And in the second place, it is very essential that I should know more of the person of Mdlle. Taranne—but I have been forbidden that hotel, and moreover, it is indubitable that she accompanies Mdlle. Barbesson out-of-doors this morning; and seeing that we are at war, we must use the stratagems of war, of which surprise is the chief and head—in short, she is not to guess that I am acquainted with the turn of her face and shape, which some other shall furnish me with.

"Chignet waits upon me at twelve, to press home the business of his nephew, whose name is Dumont, that miserable youth who refuses to get on in the world. He must be familiar with all the principal individuals of the Duke's household, for he is surgeon there, and has been there on a melancholy errand as late as this morning; he will tell me what I wish to learn. Until his arrival, therefore, and that of d'Argenson, there is absolutely nothing for me to do, so I shall seek some rest in my chair."

He emptied the last glass of Bordeaux from the bottle which had flanked his meal, then removed to his favourite coign of vantage by the window looking out on to the Rue Carcassone, where he resumed the pipe which had been interrupted by Passy's visit on the preceding evening. It was not long before his eyes closed, his head nodded, and the long clay dropped from his nerveless fingers, to break to pieces on the floor.

When, presently, he awoke again, the sunlight had shifted along the walls, and Chignet was standing before him, the door of the apartment being closed.

He jumped up, to bow.

"A thousand apologies, my dear M. Chignet!—but have you been here thus long?"

"No, monsieur, I have just entered, and was about to arouse you."

"I hope so. Well then, how has our affair gone off? Is all well?"

"As well as possible. Everything has been arranged, and there will be no more trouble."

"I am delighted to hear it. Sit down, M. Chignet! What wine are you accustomed to drink at this hour of the day? It is noon, is it not?"

Chignet seated himself.

"Almost precisely, monsieur. Since you ask me, I shall take a little Burgundy by preference."

Mailly went from the room, to return a minute afterwards with a brace of bottles. He uncorked one, and poured out for both.

"To the good success of our Brest expedition M. Chignet!"

"Certainly; seeing that it is of that journey, and of nothing besides, that I have come here to speak."

"I shall set out to-morrow morning."

"If you please. And with regard to your expenses . . ."

"We shall not quarrel over them. But before going into all that, do let us conclude this sad affair of last night. The bottle is at your elbow. So you were received without difficulty at the house we know of?"

"Yes. This is an excellent wine for body. The room has a good light. What apartments compose the suite, and what might you pay for them?"

"There are but the two rooms, for I am a bachelor. The reasonableness of the rent would surprise you. So whom did you see?"

"We were received by Mdlle. Taranne. The Duchesse had retired, and it was thought advisable not to arouse her until matters were advanced."

"The other, doubtless, was shocked and horrified beyond measure by your errand?"

"Not so much so. In such emergencies, I have remarked that females are wont to flutter and to lose their heads to a greater degree than men, but the thing does not go very deep down with them, and I conclude that their emotional sensibility is less. Then, the worthy Lieutenant of Police is a veritable tower of strength in crises of the sort. He has a bearing which women seem to find irresistible."

“Two glasses or two bottles of this wine, it is all the same, M. Chignet, ’tis so light and innocuous. Don’t spare it. You would say, then, that Mdlle. Taranne is of a type easily influenced by masculine roughness and vigour? She has thus, in all probability, the female opposites of delicacy and timidity? I don’t know her.”

“She is a very delightful creature, monsieur.”

“I believe you,” replied Mailly, winking. “She is d’Argenson’s mistress, is she not?”

The surgeon averted his gaze, laughed with reserve, and went on sipping his wine.

“I don’t know where you have heard that tale. It may be so. At least, we shall say that she is quite worthy of the honour.”

“Describe her for me, M. Chignet, I am something of a connoisseur.”

“She is tall and slender, after the manner of a sylph, with a skin of pale olive, softly-piercing black eyes, of the narrowest, high-boned cheeks, a perfectly-cast rounded chin, inclined to a voluptuous fullness, hair of jet; and all this supported, and commonly thrust back by a neck like a pillar of alabaster. Her age twenty-six, or so. You may thus pick her out from any company.”

“I do not like them dark, however. When is to be the funeral, M. Chignet?”

“To-morrow.”

“*Peste!* you lose no time. Has the Duchesse so ordained it?”

“Yes, monsieur; upon the counsel of M. d’Argenson.”

“What reason has he urged for this haste?”

“None, that I can remember. It appears that Mme. la Duchesse has agreed at once. The affair interferes with her removal to Fontainebleau, whither the Court goes to-day. She does not wish to be left behind, and, therefore, M. le Duc is to be interred without delay.”

“What! will there be no period of mourning?”

Chignet stared at him with marble eyes.

“You are either very innocent or very malicious, monsieur. Since when, I should like to hear, have bereavements in high circles been permitted to obstruct the pleasures of His Majesty?—

and it is always his pleasure to have his nobility around him. It is not fashionable to mourn. No one has accused Mme. la Duchesse of being unfashionable, that I am aware."

"Replenish, M. Chignet!" And Mailly pushed the nearly-depleted first bottle towards him, following the action by preparing to draw the cork of the second. The surgeon continued to take all that was offered.

"The court seems a bad sort of place, then. But is she also pretty, your Duchesse?"

"Passably so, but not so markedly so as the other. She also is tall and slim, of much the same age, but brown instead of black, less perfect in feature, less clever, more vivacious. Both are handsome women in their way. Let us talk of my nephew, if you please."

"Yes, let us do so. She inherits, of course, and will marry again?"

"And these are two excellent arguments against excessive grief, supposing that she has felt the inclination towards any, which I doubt. At all events, I have seen no tears."

"I may have met her in some assembly or other. Describe her a little more minutely, I beg."

"She has a mole beside the left-hand corner of her mouth, so that you could not mistake her, having once encountered her. My nephew, monsieur . . ."

"Yes, yes, your nephew. Let us have done with these women, and come to him."

"You have invited me to four glasses, so I shall invite myself to a fifth."

"The bottle is for you, M. Chignet. Empty it."

"We are to talk of that journey."

"I am agreeable."

"You are one man of the world, and I am another. Putting two and two together, I judge that the mission will suit your convenience admirably. We shall, therefore, name but a nominal figure for your expenses."

"Fifty *louis*," replied Mailly lightly, shrugging his shoulders.

Chignet shed a sickly smile.

"You will not come to ruin by reason of your modesty, monsieur!"

"Nor you, *pardieu!*"

"I?"

"Since fifty is but the half of one hundred, which is the sum you extorted from M. de Pontchartrain last night."

The surgeon rose with dignity.

"I extorted nothing. One hundred *louis* was my fee for a dangerous service which I did not desire."

"While fifty is mine for a disagreeable one, which I desire as little. And be very sure that I shall not put on black though Dumont on this occasion fails to break his crust."

"The promotion is promised. It will not depend upon your journey, which I understand is but to get you away from Paris for a time."

Mailly made a movement of incredulity.

"You think it is not promised?" demanded Chignet sharply.

"I think that the pot also promised to boil, so long as fire was beneath its belly. To-day is not last night, M. Chignet, and to-morrow will not be to-day."

"That may be—but if so, I have no security that your departure to Brest will transform the affair."

"And, therefore, if you will condescend to accept advice from a younger man, I should leave it altogether. In five years, or ten, Dumont will become lieutenant in the ordinary course. You will at least have saved fifty *louis*."

"Come! what is the least that you will take?"

"I am not a Jew, monsieur," responded Mailly haughtily. "If I say fifty, it is because I mean fifty."

Chignet, looking very much annoyed, produced the identical jug-bag of leather which he had received from Pontchartrain the night before. He counted out on to the table the fifty *louis*.

"Apropos, what is your nephew's station?" inquired Mailly, leaving the gold untouched.

"It is the second company of the first battalion, in the Brest

Coastguard, quartered in the town itself."

"Then I shall review his abilities, and report accordingly. A last glass, M. Chignet!"

"I thank you, but my thirst has disappeared." He brought from a pocket-case a card. "That is where I am always to be found."

"I shall see you upon my return."

The surgeon buttoned his coat angrily, and turned to go.

"I am commanded to inform you that M. d'Argenson will give himself the pleasure of waiting upon you at four o'clock this afternoon, or a little later."

"Good. I will remain in."

"But I shall recommend you from my own intelligence not to build extravagantly on this foundation. One may guess what is going forward. He is a gentleman who does not care though others render him services for nothing, and you must not expect to find everyone sufficiently accommodating to fill your pockets with gold for the mere asking."

Mailly returned his bow, smiling, accompanied him to the head of the stairs, then came back to the room, to gather up his harvest.

"In other words, our little friend has tried to turn the case to still greater advantage," he mused, "but has failed to touch the sensibilities of the Lieutenant of Police, who loves money equally with himself. So much the better, for greed at all times is abominable. Yet he reminds me of a thing I had near forgotten. The devil, no!—have I endured all that upset of last night, with its dangers and discomforts, merely to escape with a whole skin and be so far worse off than I was before, seeing that the strain of anxiety must have robbed me of some months, at least, of life? I do not count the release of innocents into the bargain—that is, of Mdlle. Isabelle, and Mdlle. Passy, by courtesy—for it is the natural right of innocence to go scatheless, and d'Argenson cannot in justice set it against the other. Then he, as originator and prime chief of so much mischief, decidedly owes me a relief in money; and I shall be very remiss if modesty withholds me from making known to him this conclusion. I shall calculate the mean between what may be regarded as a fair recompense to me for my sufferings and the extreme point to which his purse might be made to stretch by one of less reasonableness than myself."

He opened his money-chest, in order to add to the five hundred *louis* already deposited there the fifty which he held in his hand. The operation was scarcely concluded when Mdlle. Antoinette, who had been watching below for the departure of the visitor, entered the room to announce the immediate serving of dinner.

XXI

Riposte!

Five o'clock approached, and the golden afternoon sunshine flooded the room with light, while Mailly reclined in his low chair by the open window, smoking tobacco in a new pipe and moodily watching the incidents of the street below, when the arrival of the Lieutenant of Police was heralded by a heavy creaking of the boards of the outside passage.

An instant afterwards the latch was raised, and he entered unannounced. He closed the door solidly behind him, removed and cast on the floor his hat and wig, wiped his scarlet forehead with a huge handkerchief of vivid green and gold, walked ponderously across the intervening space to the seat in the window opposite to Mailly's own, into which he flung his weight without ceremony, stretched forth a hand to draw the curtain further along, so that his person might be hidden from the street, and finally, producing the familiar snuff-box, applied a liberal dose to each nostril by the medium of the ball of his thumb. After a squinting grimace and a clearing of his nose, he again began to wipe the moisture from his brow. Mailly, having bowed without rising, went on smoking and watching his formidable visitor.

"Well, my young monsieur, so we are still alive, and none the worse for our adventure over-night!" chuckled Argenson, with a sort of grim amiability, but casting him he addressed a sharp look from beneath the tail of the gaudy handkerchief.

"But why should we be otherwise, M. d'Argenson?" was the dry counter-question.

"*Cordieu!* many a man I know would have taken to his bed from sheer fright after such happenings—but you, it appears, are of tougher stuff. How have you passed your day?"

"I have followed your advice, and have taken things quietly. I have not been out."

"That is the best. So you have not heard the news? Passy is

dead.”

Mailly was genuinely shocked.

“What!”

“He expired this morning, from poison self-administered. It seems that he dreaded the ‘Question’; and I shall not say that he was wrong. Without nonsense, it is a very good thing.”

“But did he carry this poison?”

“If he did not beg or purchase it from his guard, which is unlikely. However, his departure clears the air, and we can now afford to stretch a point with his widow. She will not be for Spain, but for Brussels, where she affirms she has connections. A lady of the Duchesse’s establishment, who is a good friend of hers, has interceded for her, and since, after all, she is not guilty, though better out of the way, I have agreed to what they want. That is for her; let us now come to your case.”

“I thank you.”

“I shall address myself to you without circumlocution, de Mailly. The woman you encountered last evening in Passy’s house, as we all now know, was really not Mme. la Duchesse, but a young girl, the sister of Passy’s wife, who is arrived from the country. No doubt she happened in that room more by chance than by design; still, it was she. I do not seek your confirmation. We have taken her up, and her sister has told us all that we wish to learn.”

“Well guessed!” thought Mailly. “Nevertheless, it may be no more than a guess—I shall await the conclusion before supplying the gaps of their information. It appears already that Mdlle. Isabelle has not confessed.” And the Lieutenant of Police having paused, to watch him shrewdly, he replied, in a meditative tone:

“I can neither confirm nor deny, M. d’Argenson. I saw her only a moment, and in deep shadow, and since I am unacquainted with either . . .”

“Do not go on. It cannot be positively asserted that you saw her then at sufficient leisure to mark her features, but you had more than ample opportunity afterwards. You will find that it will not pay you to pretend otherwise. I say that she has spent the night here with you, in these apartments—Well?"

"Mdlle. Passy's sister?"

"The same. Her name is Barbesson."

Mailly made a smiling gesture. "M. d'Argenson, I am a man of virtue—believe it."

"I am not concerned with your virtue, but with your testimony. Or rather, the fact is established, and I do not even want your testimony. Now listen!—for what I am about to say is grave. If last night I consented to relax my office and shelter criminals from the law, rather than cause a scandal in high places, it was principally from regard for Mme. la Duchesse de Chastelnoir. I tell you so, and it is the truth. But now that it is known that she was not in that house at all, the case is different. I shall still, perhaps, smother the affair, seeing that steps have been taken which it would not be easy to retrace: it is almost equally dangerous to go forward as back, however, so that I inform you without reservation that my determination in the matter remains suspended, though inclined towards a hushing. A feather's weight will depress the scale the other way, when all who deserve it will yet be brought to trial. I wish you to understand the instability of your situation."

"*Peste!* I understand it very well."

"So what do you propose for yourself?"

"In what respect?"

"You have seen Chignet, and are to take that journey for him?"

"Yes."

Argenson held up a stout cautionary finger.

"Then do not hurry back. You understand the significance of a hint, coming from the right quarter?"

"Certainly, and I thank you."

"I undertook to try to get you out of your scrape, and I am a man of my word. Things sleep for the moment, but that is not to say the devil is dead. You saw how I contrived this mission for you—you are better out of sight. Now attend again, de Mailly. I shall use a little authority here; for your own good, be it comprehended. You will arrange to absent yourself from Paris for twelve months. For a year by the calendar I do not want you back here. And when I say Paris, I mean within thirty leagues of Paris. You are unencumbered—go to London, Madrid, Italy, or where you will. Travel is wholesome for a youngster.”

“Your reason for so extreme a measure, M. d’Argenson?”

“Some of those who saw the Duke fall will perhaps point you out, and that may lead to undesirable conversations. Hearken still! I do not assume to be the man in France of the greatest power under the King, but within my limits I am able to enforce my will, and my will is what I have just said. You shall leave the city to-day before dark; I shall know if you do not. If my agents report to me to-night or to-morrow morning that you still linger, it will be a defiance of my order, and I shall so regard it. The initial consequence will be that I shall withdraw my protection.” He stopped to glare at Mailly, who barely removed the pipe from his mouth, to nod, with slightly lifted brows.

“That is to say,” went on Argenson, clenching a massive fist in the air, “upon the least hint thereafter of recalcitration on your part, I will change all my plans, and I will have you hanged. You hear me?”

“Yes, for you speak even louder than is necessary.”

The Lieutenant glanced mechanically at the door, only at once to return to Mailly.

“So you will pack up now, in order to make a clear start before evening.”

The younger man blew out tobacco-smoke composedly, without offering to reply.

“There is something singular about all this,” he meditated. “Perhaps it is as he says, and he is only frightened; but on the other hand, Passy is dead—we don’t know how—his widow may be bought with money, Chignet the same, the three lackeys again coerced, a story fabricated to account for the delay in declaring the Duke’s true death, I sent after as a fugitive from justice, and the Parliament of Paris assembled, to initiate the proceedings for the ruin of Pontchartrain and my own appearance upon the scaffold. It is at least possible, therefore I shall prefer not to depart in too great a hurry. Also, I owe a duty to the Minister for those five hundred *louis*; and further, Argenson himself has not yet paid me a doit. There is Mdlle. Isabelle, besides, to see after. We have not yet heard what is to become of her. *Tudieu!* it is high time I showed that I also have cards in my hand."

"Well, de Mailly, how is it to be?"

"I cannot do things so quickly as that, M. d'Argenson."

"You cannot, forsooth! And why cannot you?"

"I have an appointment in Paris for to-night."

"*Morbleu!* what care I for your appointments! What appointment?—with whom is it?"

"With M. de Pontchartrain."

"Hey!"

"So, as it is out of the question for me to fail so great a personage, I must, at the earliest, defer my journey until tomorrow."

Argenson maintained a displeased silence for a few moments.

"What is your business with the Minister?" he demanded, in a sulkier tone.

"It is merely a report which I have to furnish."

"A report. Take care, de Mailly! What report?"

"Bah! it is evident enough what such a report must be. They have tried to murder him, and he wishes to know all about it. No agent was more convenient to his hand than I, that is why I am picked. However, you will agree that my quitting Paris to-day is an impossibility!"

"We shall see that. Thus your report is ready to be presented?"

"Yes, I could show it at once. The time named for my reception, however, is ten o'clock this evening."

"You pretend that you have sounded to the bottom of the affair?"

"*Peste!* no. It is too deep for me. I have discovered all that I can."

"From whom, for example? You have not stirred abroad to-day."

Mailly shrugged his shoulders.

"It is a question that I ask," said Argenson.

"Since you insist, monsieur! The woman, then, whom you have mentioned—I have truly not been abroad to-day, and I have not discussed her with any, nevertheless I find it difficult to believe that she was really Mdlle. Passy's sister."

"She who was in Passy's house, you mean?"

"Yes," replied Mailly, setting down his pipe. "I mean that one. I have been thinking, M. d'Argenson, and it appears to me that she was more probably some female of the Duchesse's household, counterfeiting her mistress. I reason thus. A deceit was to be practised upon M. de Pontchartrain, I shall not say with what design; but, in two words, he was to imagine that he beheld Mme. la Duchesse de Chastelnoir, when in fact it was to be some other person in her stead. Well, then who would be selected for such a rôle? Would not it be, above all, a woman nearly resembling her in shape and colour? For me, if I managed the business, I should unquestionably make this my first care; and so, I think, would anyone but a demented. Now, I am not satisfied that your young demoiselle from the country resembles the least in the world her whom the Minister expected. You will tell me. Is she tall, slender, brown—this Mdlle. Barbesson? since you give her that name. Has she, while travelling in her chaise, painted upon her cheek an easily distinguishable mole, such as Mme. la Duchesse notoriously possesses?"

"I do not say that she was there by intention: I say merely that she was there."

"It is equal. If she but happened there, she occupied the place of another, who was prevented. It is this other with whom Monseigneur is concerned, so I shall impart to him my conclusion. There is a plot. The Duchesse, I will swear, has never even known the Minister, though he will ascertain that for himself; yet he has been made to believe that she was in that house, for the purpose of an interview. He was to go to this interview—perhaps to his destruction. Then there must be a woman to be produced, at least distantly assimilating to the Duchesse. It would be absurd, I mean, for such an one to be low, fair and blue-eyed, when the other is just the reverse; for not M. de Pontchartrain himself would fall into so palpable a trap. Thus we shall assume that the rôle was reserved for a lady who has not yet appeared upon the scene—a lady possessed of three qualifications. That is, she must be of equal height, slimness and colour with the Duchesse, she must be intimate with her, in order successfully to simulate her voice and bearing and she must enjoy a previous acquaintance with Mdlle. Passy, to be introduced to that house at all. Everything points, therefore, to this same good friend of Passy's wife, belonging to the Duchesse's establishment, whom you have mentioned as interesting herself upon her behalf in the matter of the Spanish journey. *Mordieu!* it seems to me that such an interest is very natural, when another knows certain circumstances and is to be kept amiable."

"De Mailly, I have listened to you. Now explain to me: on what ground do you presuppose that the Duchesse herself has not really arranged this meeting? We know that she has not attended it, but who has told you that she has not been prevented from attending it?"

Mailly ordered his thoughts.

"I shall reply by an interrogation and an anecdote, M. d'Argenson. Here is the interrogation. Great ladies of title, equally with their lesser fellow-mortals possess baptismal names, is it not so? Then what is that or those of Mme. la Duchesse de Chastelnoir?"

"Her names are Marie Louise. Why do you ask?"

"You will see by the anecdote, which is to follow. At some time after eight o'clock last evening, a certain female entered quietly a house that we know of, as it grew rapidly dusk, and ascended the staircase, unperceived, as she believed. Before she had succeeded in reaching the upper storey, however, the voice of another female accosted her from below. A name was pronounced. 'Is that you, thus-and-thus?' Well, M. d'Argenson, the name so uttered was neither Marie nor Louise. It was Uranie."

The Lieutenant of Police eyed him with an ominous fixity.

"And what was replied?"

"An affirmative reply was returned, and the error was permitted to proceed. For it was an error. A lady bearing the name Uranie was expected, it appears, since her continued progress upstairs went unchallenged after the interrogatory; but this was not she. The one below was Mdlle. Passy, the other, perhaps, the sister whose presence in the house you have related."

"So this Uranie. . . ."

"*Diable!* there are not six women in Paris of the name, whereas it chances to be that of Mdlle. Taranne, the friend of Mdlle. Passy and the companion, or what you will, of Mme. la Duchesse."

"It is not a likely story. You have concocted it between you, I dare say—and, therefore, you can no longer deny that she has been with you here overnight."

"But there is an additional detail which has certainly not been concocted between us, M. d'Argenson, seeing that I had it last night, or rather this morning, from the lips of M. le Comte de Pontchartrain himself. It is that Mdlle. Taranne is your agent, and in your pay."

Argenson jumped up, crimson with wrath, his eyes protruding from their orbits.

"Malediction! You dare to address these words to a man who holds you in his hand—so! puppy? Then you have lost your senses."

Mailly lay back in his chair, without in any way offering to appease the sudden storm he had brought upon himself. The Lieutenant of Police strode across to him, in front of the window, to shake his fist before his very nose.

"You wish, then, to go for trial? I will oblige you. . . . Consider yourself under arrest!" he added abruptly.

Mailly smiled coldly.

"Your sword."

"It stands yonder in the corner."

"Rise you!"

"On the contrary, I advise you to sit down, M. d'Argenson. If you continue to dance before the window, you will assemble a crowd. It will be time enough to rise when my escort appears."

Argenson glanced at the street, uttered a spluttering growl, put a hand to his throat to loosen his cravat, and, with one more menacing glare at Mailly, resumed his seat, angrily producing his snuff-box as he did so. A silence ensued.

"So what is your game, rascal?" demanded the Lieutenant at last, bending forward in the chair, with both hands on his substantial thighs.

"M. d'Argenson, let us restore to the conversation its original simplicity. I have arrived at certain conclusions, which I am to lay before M. de Pontchartrain, according to my engagement. I shall do so. But, in doing so, I shall not be actuated by malice towards any. I shall exaggerate nothing, I shall add nothing of my own, Monseigneur will draw his own inferences and furnish his own counsels. If such conduct be in any respect at fault, correct me, I beg it."

"Let me warn you, however, that I have known cooler ruffians than you to grow warm enough at the end."

"For instance, I very much doubt if M. de Pontchartrain has acted sensibly in hushing up the business at all, for what has he had to fear? The Duke has entered his house by night like a thief, without invitation. He has murderously attacked the Minister, and I, in defending the latter, have slain him. The lackeys were there to see it. Why, then, should Monseigneur choose to make of the thing so fearful a secret? But he is a gentleman, we shall say; he desires to preserve the good name of Mme. la Duchesse. Well, she was not within the house, you have told me so. Then it seems to me that, in acceding so inconsiderately to your plan of concealment, he has actually lent himself to a conspiracy against his own life and fortune, for though one is killed, and two were to be sent from France, there still remains . . ." And Mailly concluded with a shrug.

"You play a dangerous game, de Mailly."

"I play no game at all, and the proof is that, on my visit to the Minister this evening, I shall maintain silence upon all these considerations, merely relating to him what I have found out—

namely, that Mme. la Duchesse is probably unacquainted with his advances, and that the negotiations have passed through the hands of Mdlle. Taranne, who belongs to you, and who was to have personated the Duchesse last night, had not some accident prevented her. If this relation is a defiance and an insolence, M. d'Argenson, I am very sorry for it, but cannot help it. Should you arrest me before my interview with the Minister, I shall tell my tale to the judges instead; it is all the same. And mark me well!"—he sat up, and hammered the arm of his chair with his fist, by way of emphasis—"Let others be frightened by the name of justice who have cause to be, I have nothing to fear, I, from an open trial before men of probity and experience, who will know easily how to distinguish between a wicked conspiracy and its accidental fruits. I shall not allow myself to be browbeaten by a Lieutenant of Police who causes corpses to be carried through the streets at two o'clock in the morning."

"Have you quite finished, de Mailly?"

"Yes, I bear you no animosity, but I shall not suffer others to assure me that my interest lies behind my back, when I see it very distinctly in front of my nose. If M. de Pontchartrain is sufficiently obliging to do so for his part, that is his affair."

"Have you now finished? Then let me say a word, and do you pay attention. You doubtless rely upon Pontchartrain's protection. He can do nothing for you. He bears the name, but I possess the substantial power—I have more agents in Paris alone than he in all France. You will do prudently not to attach yourself to the wrong personage."

"M. d'Argenson, since you provoke me to speak my private mind, I honestly do not believe that you will retain your office long enough to work me a serious injury, whereas Monseigneur, in all probability, will remain Minister for many years, and will be able to do me much good. I have gone into it pretty closely with myself."

"I am to lose my office, hey?"

"For M. de Pontchartrain, from the little that I have seen of him has impressed me as being a grim and sinister individual, with an iron tenacity; and he has always the ear of the King. I do not pretend to like the man, but that appears to be his character. I do not believe that he will allow one to whom he has entrusted a commission to languish in prison on account of that commission. I am a fair physiognomist, and that is what his face has told me."

Argenson wriggled uneasily.

"A commission signifies a payment, de Mailly."

"Perhaps."

"Let me hear the sum."

"I have no authority to disclose the bargain—supposing that there is one."

"He aims specifically at me, however?"

Mailly smiled contemptuously, and gazed out-of-doors. The Lieutenant of Police mopped his brow.

"Let us make the conversation practical," he said after a moment, in a new voice of complaisance. "You understand me—I am a busy man, have much to do, and cannot stay here all the day. A youngster is always in need of money. See if we can reach a reasonable accommodation."

"I have no objection."

"What is your price for the service you are able to render me?"

"It is always equal shares, monsieur. M. de Pontchartrain gave you fifty thousand livres, so I shall require twenty-five thousand."

"Bah!"

"In return for which sum I shall inform Monseigneur this evening that I have failed to penetrate further into the affair, at the same time handing back to him his money—assuming that he has paid me some; since it will not have been earned, and I am honest. From your twenty-five thousand, therefore, this sum must be deducted in arriving at my profits, so that it will not amount to so much as it seems."

"But you must also warn him that the Duchesse has privately expressed a desire to be no more molested by him, in view of the hand of God upon her husband."

"Agreed."

After a new pause, Argenson said:

"But I must first be sure that you have kept your side of the contract. Wait upon me for the money before your departure to-morrow."

Mailly returned no reply, but rose, yawned and stretched himself. He then crossed the room, and, collecting from a bureau the materials for writing, brought them back with him to the still seated Lieutenant of Police.

"What are these to do?" asked the latter dubiously.

"The order for the gold, monsieur. Be pleased to step to the table."

"We do not employ formalities of that sort for an irregular transaction."

"M. d'Argenson, when I shall have broken with the Minister, twenty-five thousand may begin to appear to you an excessive sum, so that you will perhaps discover that your memory has been at fault."

Argenson grunted angrily, and started up. He strode to the table in the centre of the room, which he cleared by the simple process of sweeping with his arm what was on it to the floor. Dragging a chair forward, he sat down autocratically, while Mailly set before him the ink-pot, pen and paper.

"Your whole name?"

"Gaston de Mailly, gentleman."

The Lieutenant hammered in thought against the interior bottom of the ink-well with the point of the quill. After a moment he began to write, in hair-like characters strangely out of keeping with the mighty fist which traced them. He completed three lines, and was about to add his signature. Mailly, who stood behind him, bent over to arrest his hand.

"What now?"

"There must still be witnesses of your signing."

"And why? Shall I contest my own handwriting within twenty-four hours, do you think?"

"It is at least possible, M. d'Argenson, and I am unacquainted with your sign-manual, but your person is tolerably well known to all classes, so we will get one or two respectable people to witness."

"Do you keep such in your pocket?—for I do not."

"I am thinking who there is. There is my landlady, but she is imbecile. . . . Be quiet for a moment, if you please. . . ." He gazed out of the window in puzzled meditation.

Argenson got up, and took snuff.

"Listen, de Mailly! You are without present employment. You are a shrewd youngster. Enter my service altogether, and the need for this stupidity will disappear. You shall still have your twenty-five thousand."

"I thank you. I would consider a special case for you occasionally, but I do not care to enrol myself regularly. You can always find me. I am not sufficiently in love with malefactors to become a Savary. It is the work of negotiation which principally appeals to me. However, we shall see afterwards."

"Then I retract my judgment, and you are not so shrewd, since you refuse an offer which I should not make to everyone."

Suddenly Mailly ran across the room to the window, clutched the sill with both hands, and thrust out his head and shoulders.

"Ho there, Mimizan!—Holá! Halt!"

XXII

The Safeguard

Mimizan, who was in the act of passing by the opposite corner of the street, accompanied by another gentleman, wheeled sharply round, and stared straight up in the direction of the voice. His bold, swarthy face flashed into recognition. He forcibly escorted his companion across the roadway.

"What signs and wonders do we see! What do you aloft there, Gaston?"

"I am delighted to behold you. This is my new abode, you must know. Come up! There is a door at your elbow."

"What! have you women with you?"

"Nothing of the sort. But come up."

"I cannot. Here is Bartolmy. We are just off to Fontainebleau."

Mailly remarked a slight, pale gentleman, of woebegone aspect, seeming as though he had dropped from a strange planet.

"But listen, Pierre!" he called down. "I will not detain you a minute. I need two witnesses to a paper. Bring Monsieur with you."

Mimizan waved an acknowledgment, and pushed his friend before him through the doorway. Mailly came back to the table, beside which Argenson was still standing.

"We don't want these good messieurs to read what is written above your signature, so I will fold the sheet neatly in two, and you shall sign on the blank half."

He was yet engaged in the operation when Mimizan's tall, military form appeared on the threshold of the apartment, supported from the rear by the less imposing one of Bartolmy, who seemed embarrassed and uneasy. Argenson moved his back on Mailly, to return their bows stiffly.

"You have a nice place here, Gaston," said Mimizan. "Where is your paper?"

"There, on the table. You know M. d'Argenson messieurs?"

"The terror of the evilly-disposed. But what the devil are you doing here, Lieutenant?"

Argenson shrugged his shoulders.

"It is he who is to sign the paper," explained Mailly. "That is why I have raised the point of identity."

"Bah! he who knows not M. d'Argenson is ripe for heaven. He is perhaps the one man in Paris who cannot be counterfeited."

"But do you know the reason?" asked Bartolmy diffidently. "He is a fairy."

Mimizan gave a bellow.

"That is good. How is he a fairy?"

"I do not know how, but I am sure that he is one. He impresses me in that way. When I see M. d'Argenson, I wish to sing and dance."

"Dance! dance!" exclaimed Mimizan, shouting with laughter.

"I am enchanted to amuse you, gentlemen!" growled Argenson.

Mailly smiled politely.

"Will you drink, Pierre?—and you, monsieur?"

"No, I thank you, on behalf of both," replied Mimizan. "We are travelling with ladies. Apropos, they await us."

Mailly dipped the quill in the ink, and offered it to Argenson.

"Sign, monsieur, and these friends will witness."

"The business is severely confidential, gentleman," said the Lieutenant of Police, bending his brows on the two.

"The signing is not to become common knowledge, Pierre, that is all. You understand."

"My dear fellow, it is no affair of mine—why the devil should I speak of it? Only get done." He turned to his companion. "Come! make the declaration in form. Those dear creatures will be furious."

"I am convinced that if I annoy M. d'Argenson, he will translate me to one of his fairy palaces, there to languish for a hundred years, so rest well assured I shall know better than to allude to magic bargains defended by his potent spells."

This time Mimizan did not guffaw, but merely chuckled.

"Sign, M. d'Argenson!" said Mailly. "I shall vouch for M. de Mimizan's discretion, and he for that of Monsieur. We are all gentlemen here."

Argenson re-dipped the pen in the ink-pot, then signed his name at the top of the blank half of the sheet, where it was folded, the other half, which bore the written order itself, being turned face-downwards to the table. Mimizan and Bartolmy afterwards attached their signatures as witnesses of the prime signing.

Bows were exchanged. The Lieutenant of Police stooped to repossess himself of his hat and wig. The two companions moved towards the door. Mailly lingered behind just long enough to pick up from the table the signed paper, which he continued to wave to and fro in the air, to dry the ink.

"I will join you at the bottom, Bartolmy," said Mimizan, upon reaching the head of the stairs, giving the other a friendly shove from behind to start him on his descent. He gripped Mailly tightly by the arm and whispered:

"I am rejoining. There is to be certain war, and I have the refusal of a regiment of foot. Can I be of service to you?"

Mailly wrung his friend's hand. "You are the best of fellows, I have always said it. On this occasion, no. I also see the distant possibility of a regiment."

"*Diable!* So you have followed up that little *coup* of Versailles?"

"Yes."

"Then that is as it should be, and I rejoice. Adieu, Gaston!"

Mailly watched him downstairs, afterwards returning to the room, where he carelessly threw on the table the order in his hand. Argenson was waiting to depart.

"On second thoughts, monsieur, I do not find this document very suitably expressed to our purpose, so I shall suggest another," said the younger man, with a tranquillity which completely took the other aback. "Permit me, therefore, to sit down before the table, to draft a new. I regret to detain you, but shall not occupy above three minutes more of your time."

"I care not if there is none at all. But so you have had your witty friends up here for nothing?"

"*Peste!* do we wish to put things upon a solid base, or not, M. d'Argenson? I tell you that the reflection has just occurred to me."

"Then what is wrong with what I have written?"

"As it is merely to read what I shall set down. . . ."

"You will do what you please, but be quick about it."

And, crushing the order into his pocket, Argenson went back to the chair by the window, into which he flung himself with an air of chagrin. He continued to beat a devil's tattoo with his thick fingers on the padded arm-rest for as long as Mailly sat writing. The latter's quill flowed smoothly on without intermission.

In five minutes he got up, holding the paper still wet in his hand.

"Here is the composition, M. d'Argenson. The ink is not completely dry yet, so I will read it aloud."

In his resonant tenor, moderated that it might nor carry beyond the confines of the room, he proceeded to recite the writing:

> *"I engage to pay to Gaston de Mailly, gentleman, for services which have been or shall be rendered by him, the sum of Five Hundred Thousand Livres upon his demand; but, should he die within five years of the signing of this engagement, the like sum to his legal heirs. And should the said Gaston de Mailly be cast into prison without a public trial, or should he otherwise disappear from the knowledge of his friends, then after the space of sixty days he shall be considered as dead for the purpose of this engagement, and upon a clear showing his legal heirs shall recover the said Five Hundred Thousand Livres in the same manner as if his death were proved. And this instrument shall have effect for five years, as from this 14 May 1700."*

Argenson, retaining his seat, smiled ferociously.

"Well, my young monsieur, and having amused yourself by

writing this pretty paper, to what use do you now intend to put
it?"

Mailly drew the curtain completely across the window. The
Lieutenant's face became suddenly purple.

"You are not to have the madness to attempt to force a
signing?"

"No, monsieur, but I wish you not to give private signals to
your people, who are perhaps waiting in the street below.
Nevertheless, it would not greatly matter, for while they should
be coming in at one door, I would be departing by another. M. de
Pontchartrain would harbour me."

"I have constrained more nimble gallants than you."

"Bah! you are all fat and grossness, M. d'Argenson. Do not go
on dreaming of twenty years ago, but rather read again the paper
which you have thrust into your pocket."

"What new language is this, villain?"

He dived his hand into his pocket, and pulled forth the
crumpled sheet.

"It is in order. What is amiss?"

"Turn it over."

Argenson stumbled to his feet. "The signature is wanting.
Here is some trick."

"In short, it is waste paper. Your signature, and those of its
witnesses, stand here, on the instrument which I hold in my hand.
Remark them!" And Mailly opened the sheet to its full extent,
revealing on the upper half his own writing, as yet barely dry, and
on the lower the names of Argenson, Mimizan and Bartolmy.

The Lieutenant of Police uttered a sound of choking, and
snatched at the paper. Fending him off with one hand, Mailly
slipped it into his pocket.

"These are the sleights we amuse children with, M.
d'Argenson. You have been very absurd. If you do not violently
control yourself, you will have a stroke, I think. Sit down, and let
us discuss the matter quietly."

With a meekness which would have been amazing had not it
obviously proceeded from fear of the overstraining of a vessel,

Argenson obeyed. He sat recovering himself for a few moments.

"Thus it is established that you are nothing but a common rogue and trickster, de Mailly!"

"Fair words, Lieutenant! The paper is not to make my fortune, but only to secure me against your malice. I have not asked to become acquainted with you. I have not desired to be threatened with arrest, trial, hanging, exile, and what not. I am a gentleman, I have sensibilities, and you have exasperated these sensibilities. Not being a malefactor, I do not love to be treated as one. Now, if you are resolute to carry into execution your threats, it shall at least cost you five hundred thousand livres—I shall have had the satisfaction of making a hole in your fortune. And be sure my heirs will exact from you the uttermost *denier*."

"A writing so obtained cannot stand."

"*Peste!* it will stand like an animal with four legs."

"You do not know, perhaps, that for this class of fraud the law has provided?"

"M. d'Argenson, I am not a fool. The instrument is good and valid in law, and cannot be proved otherwise. Moreover, you are exceedingly dull, with your threatenings. You give me twenty-five thousand because you are in the devil of a hole,—if you successfully contest the payment of this larger sum, will you therefore be extricated? I say I do not wish this money. I do not wish money from you at all; I wish only to go to bed at night, knowing that I shall awake there in the morning. Well then, this paper will secure me. I shall not present it for payment. I shall leave my heirs to do so—and note that they become my heirs within sixty days from the date of my disappearance, although I can be proved not dead."

Argenson tugged at his neck-band.

"Then what of Pontchartrain?"

"Offer me peace, and I shall declare to him that the affair is killed. Refuse it, and I shall perhaps show him what I have procured from you. *Corbleu!* I will bet that he will conceive my services to be very valuable to you, to have drawn so much from your coffers. 'Tis the price of an assassination."

"And how will that advantage you, de Mailly?"

"If he is induced by the perusal of this document to break with you, suddenly reopen everything, and throw all into the public crucible, why then, I have no doubt you will be ruined, monsieur, and so I shall have one powerful ill-wisher the less."

"Enough, monsieur! You skate on thin ice."

Mailly met his gaze sternly.

"Let us recapitulate. I want nothing of you save security—I do not want a pistole of your money. I shall return to Paris from my Brest journey, and I shall remain in Paris. Mdlle. Passy and her sister you shall let go free, sending the former to Brussels, if you will, but forwarding the latter to her home in Caen. You will, further, work nothing to the detriment of M. de Pontchartrain regarding all this business. That is on your part. On mine, I shall persuade Monseigneur that the conspiracy has really failed, and that he has no more to fear, provided that he permits it to remain a closed affair. I shall likewise assure him of the quick cooling of the affection for his person of Mme. la Duchesse. Doubtless, he himself is cool enough by this, with a dead husband upon his conscience. There will be no more interchanges, I will swear it. That is the truce which I have to offer you, M. d'Argenson. It is for you to judge whether you can do better by still blustering."

Argenson rose, and bowed stiffly. He passed Mailly, to move towards the door.

"I have to add," said the latter after him, "that this paper is to be lodged where it cannot be come at. It will not be left here, in my apartments, so it will be useless to send your people to search for it here. But are we to have war or peace, M. d'Argenson?"

The Lieutenant of Police faced round.

"As far as I am concerned, it will be peace. I do not recognise the validity of a signature fraudulently obtained, I shall pay you not a pistole at any time, and you will receive no special consideration at my hands; but as long as you remain quiet, you will not be harassed or molested. On the contrary, should you attempt to turn this false paper to use, or should you endeavour in any other way to procure new concessions from me, then I shall set those upon your track whose dealings with you will not be of the pleasantest. That is my last word. The women will be discharged to-morrow. I wish you a good day!"

Mailly bowed, and conducted him as far as the stairs.

XXIII

The Ambuscade

He came back into the room, looking rather pale, shut the door behind him, and at once went across to his coffer. His feelings were suddenly solemn and exalted, as those of one who should challenge a god to single combat.

"In short," he mused, "I am the rabbit, and d'Argenson is the kite. He has all the sky from which to swoop, while I have only my hole to creep into. *Mordieu!* let us find this hole without delay. Within ten minutes the house will be surrounded."

Meanwhile he was stuffing the more valuable of the contents of the chest into different pockets of his coat. These consisted of Pontchartrain's five hundred *louis*, Chignet's fifty, two hundred pistoles of his old money, and the residue in securities of his Versailles spoil, namely, Hôtel de Ville stock to the worth of eighteen thousand livres, and the receipt for his deposit with Fleurus, amounting to ten thousand more. Altogether, his hoard to the present represented upwards of forty thousand livres. He was to adventure the whole upon his person in a considerable promenade through streets certainly infested by a hundred dangerous agents of the malignant and potent individual who had just departed from him in wrath, and the thought gave him pause. He took from a drawer a short poniard, putting it into an inside pocket. Then, hastily assuming his hat and sword, and glancing rapidly round the chamber to assure himself that nothing essential had been forgotten, he left it, to pass along the passage to the second staircase descending to the Rue Martel. Upon reaching the bottom of this staircase, however, instead of directly quitting the house, he turned back for the purpose of entering the kitchen. Mdlle. Antoinette was scrubbing the table.

Mailly saluted her.

"I am come to inform you that I go out, mademoiselle, and I shall perhaps not return until midnight. Have you red pepper?"

"Monsieur!"

"I say, have you red pepper? That with which one conceals the insipidity of certain foods. Have you store?"

"Assuredly I have pepper, M. de Mailly, but for what do you require it?"

"That is not in the contract. If I ask for red pepper, it is because I have a use for red pepper. In few words, I need a half-pocketful."

"Behold the canister, monsieur—take all that is in it, and I will buy more, and charge it to you. But I do not know what red pepper is good for, unless to season soups and suchlike."

"In fact, it is for a soup that I desire it. Your excellent bouillons have rendered me fastidious, I sup abroad, I shall perhaps discover the *consommé* not to my palate, and I shall surreptitiously add at my discretion, which is why it is into my pocket that I empty your receptacle."

Ignoring the expression of amazement created by his words upon the face of his landlady, who had even yet not accustomed herself to the oddities of an otherwise admirable and well-behaved young gentleman lodger, he followed the speech by its conformable action, restored the canister to the shelf, and passed out, with a hearty laugh of good-humoured mystification, which succeeded only in elevating the extreme corners of Mdlle. Antoinette's open mouth.

Lounging against a projection immediately outside the house, a man of nondescript appearance, with big shoulders, crafty eyes and a long upper lip, who was dressed plainly, as a clerk or tradesman taking the air, permitted his gaze to rest incuriously on Mailly's person, as he entered the street, before turning it away, to yawn and straighten his body. Mailly looked back suddenly, in time to behold this individual signing to another across the roadway. The visage of the second man was as bare of flesh as that of skeleton, while his attire was ragged. Both put themselves in motion at a discreet distance behind him, although he could not detect that further signals were made.

Twenty yards on, still another person on the opposite side of the thoroughfare abruptly manifested his inclination to exchange a stationary posture for the movements of perambulation. He was the worst clad of all, and had but half a nose. Mailly scratched his own in sympathy, as he proceeded ahead.

"*Peste!* it is not so much that I conduct a procession as that I am an octoped, having two pairs of legs on either pavement which obey my volition as accurately as the single pair I was born with. If they are to accompany me as far as my destination, which is the *Trois Fontaines*, I shall feel myself to resemble some monster escaped from a fair. I have no ambition to be the captain of such a tatterdemalion troop—people will stare at me. So that it will be necessary to throw them off. But then, it seems, I must go through back ways, for in the open street they can attempt nothing, and I shall still have them on my hands."

A minute later, accordingly, he plunged into a friendly maze of squalid courts, alleys and archways, which could be constituted a circuitous route to Midard's inn, and the clue to which was as securely in his head as that to most other parts of Paris. He turned about once more, to discover himself always followed by those three men of one mind, who yet appeared to claim no further acquaintance among themselves, since they walked apart, each concerned with meditating upon his own affairs.

Half-way down the length of a dark and noisome passage, flanked by the bulging sides of wooden houses which showed neither doors nor windows, the first individual, he of the great shoulders and respectable clothes, of a sudden came running up towards him. Mailly pressed against the house-wall to suffer him to pass, when the fellow, raising his hat in rushing past with a muttered apology, halted at no more than three paces beyond him, and faced about, as though all at once he had not a solicitude in the world. His sinister associates, who were still some thirty steps to the rear, slackened their approach, in the manner of men whose part was not to join the main affair, but only to guard the avenue of flight.

Mailly stopped short before the single ruffian.

"Permit me to remark that you intercept me, monsieur."

"You think so?" was the thick response. "Then how shall we manage it? for I feel devilishly indisposed to move, even for a sprightly little dancing-master like you."

"You are in the employment of M. d'Argenson, I fancy?"

"I am in my own employment, my little cock-sparrow. Do you desire to dispute it?" He swiftly whipped out a butcher's knife, while bringing down his brows and the corner of his mouth.

Mailly, whose hand was already in his pocket, drew it forth, closed, with the rapidity of a flash of lightning, and neatly blinded the man with its freight of red pepper. As he yet howled, he knocked the knife out of his nerveless fingers, then caught him catapult-wise behind the ear with his clenched knuckles. The wretch went down to the gutter, where he remained lying like a log.

The pair in the background ran forward. Mailly leapt with agility over the victim, and took to his heels. Without in any degree doubting his fitness to cope with such miserables, having treasure upon him he felt that he could not indulge such a luxury. Past the first corner, however, he arrested himself, to seek sudden refuge in an obscure doorway, trusting to the unintelligence of the physiognomies of his pursuers that they would continue as they had started. The calculation proved just, and from his retreat he watched them pant by, down the alley. He turned back, to follow another route.

It was upon the stroke of seven that he arrived at Midard's.

The *Trois Fontaines*, as usual at that hour of the day, was empty of clients. The host welcomed him with a sleepy amiability. Mailly produced his purse.

"I have a few hours to live through, Midard. Behold five pistoles! Give me the blue *salon*, and send me up a good supper, with a bottle. If any inquire for me, by name or description, I am not here."

Midard bowed in silence.

"Then I shall go up," said Mailly. "When you have issued your orders, I should like a private word with you."

"I will be with you immediately, monsieur."

Mailly ascended the stairs, and entered the chamber he had selected. He disposed the window hangings to afford a good light, with the minimum of observation from without. The action was scarcely performed to his satisfaction when Midard appeared.

Mailly faced him, hand on hip, and smiled.

"The house is quiet as ever?"

"The devil has run away with the trade, monsieur."

"Yet you keep open."

Midard yawned. "In fact, the establishment does not pay me, but it does what is nearly as good—it amuses me. I see an occasional new face, I can be as idle as I desire without reproach from any, and it serves as an excuse for maintaining an excellent cellar for myself. I possess just money enough of my own to afford these fancies, and still pay my way."

"Thus you agree with Epicurus. Over and above, you hear retailed all the news of Paris at first hand, which is a fine advantage. What is said of Chastelnoir's demise, for instance? I knew him. Has he died naturally?"

"Some say that he was stabbed in a midnight affray with drunken fishwives on the Quays," replied the host, with a wink, "others assert that the blood rushed to his head during an altercation with a watchman concerning his privileges as Peer of France; but I, M. de Mailly, know that both these reports are fictitious, and that the genuine and only truth of the matter is that the Duke broke his neck while attempting to jump the moon, in quest of a pretty woman whom he believed he beheld there."

"That is, you are discreet; and I do not blame you. But come!—my business. . . . Tell me, Midard. I am not a police spy—I do not wish to poke into your secrets, but could not you lay your hand at short notice on a desperate fellow or so, for an action lasting not an hour?"

Midard opened his mouth, rubbed his chin, and looked away, without saying a word.

"I will acquaint you with what I have in mind," went on Mailly. "I am compelled to visit a certain house to-night, and my way takes me through a dangerous part of the city. I have, therefore, thought of an escort. No one is to be assailed, but if any molest me I shall protect myself.”

“You carry money with you, then?”

“Something which I do not wish to lose, at least. But your fellows need not know that. The play will commence at half-past nine, if commence it does; and terminate at ten or thereabouts. It only remains that I shall pay liberally.”

“I don’t say it cannot be arranged, M. de Mailly, but has this attack on you been actually planned, or do you merely take precautions?”

“A skirmish is probable.”

“Can you conjecture the approximate odds?”

“I suppose that there will be six or twelve in waiting.”

“But what men will they be?—for that is important. If it is the police, I cannot touch it for you.”

“It will be the police, but. . . .”

“I cannot touch it.”

“Will you listen, however? It will be the police, but I hold d’Argenson’s signed immunity. There is no need to explain how that can be; the case is political, and he shows two faces, that is all. Therefore, your people may wound one, two or three, but so long as they are sensible enough not to permit themselves to be taken, nothing more will come of it. You have my word for the thing.”

“Show me this immunity, monsieur.”

Mailly brought from his pocket the paper signed by the Lieutenant of Police, and passed it over carelessly. The host started to read it with pondering, sleepy eyes. Upon arriving at the sum written down, however, his expression changed sharply to one almost of dismay. He finished the perusal in silence, and Mailly returned the contract to his pocket.

“Political with a vengeance!” pronounced Midard, looking down at his feet. “It seems that the services you render are valuable ones, monsieur.”

“It is not for all the world, you understand—what I have shown you.”

"I am not a dolt."

"Then your decision, Midard?"

The other slowly scratched his head.

"As long as you retain that paper, M. de Mailly, you appear to be sufficiently secured, but it is very possible that they may take it from you. . . ."

"*Mordieu!* for what then, do I engage an escort?"

"And in any case, I do not see that my men will be secured at all."

"Yes, for I shall constitute myself their protector. Be certain that a few damaged archers will not weigh in the scale as against my insistence, with a man who has promised me a half-million livres."

"You are a gentleman, and I, for my part, trust your word, yet. . . ."

"See, Midard!" Mailly began to turn out his pockets. "Here are five hundred and fifty gold *louis*. Here is paper to the tune of eighteen thousand livres. Here is the receipt for a deposit of ten thousand more. Well then, hold all that for me, and if your fellows get into difficulties on my behalf, and I fail to restore them to you, keep it for yourself. Is it a handsome proffer, or not?"

Midard took up the money.

"Since there will be twelve against you, you will need six."

"Yes, if it is sheep that you intend to provide me with. What are you thinking of? The street will be dark, and I shall arrange a surprise. *Peste!* two will be ample. I shall account for the half myself."

"Then for payment?"

"Ten pistoles apiece for earnest-money. Should there really be an affair, a solid gratuity afterwards, according to its warmth. You may see I have the wherewithal."

"Where lies the house, monsieur?"

"Near the Rue Quiberon."

Midard reflected for a minute.

"I could find you two, perhaps. There is M. Laharpe, whose trade is master of fence, and who is very deadly with rapier and poniard: and there is Bolli the Swede, who knows scarce twenty words of French, but is able, nevertheless, to fell an ox with his bare fist. However, they will demand twenty pistoles apiece, not ten, for earnest, besides the later consideration; while I shall ask a third twenty for my share."

Mailly brought forth his bag of pistoles.

"Here is the forty, Midard! For you I had intended forty more, so here it is! Let those fellows be presented to me after supper. Apropos, where is my supper?"

"They await my descent to set the table, M. de Mailly."

* * * * * *

At half-past eight, Midard knocked at the door to announce the attendance of Laharpe and Bolli the Swede. Mailly gave the word for them to come up.

Laharpe proved to be an individual neither young nor old, shaped after the fashion of a tall, straight post of steel, at the upper end of which was a smallish head. He had a pale moon-face, lightly fringed with whiskers, his mouth perpetually smiled, his eyebrows were melancholic, while the eyes beneath them were quick and shifty—the eyes of a regular duellist. His hair, worn naturally, was short, thick and bristling. He bore a sword, and was otherwise dressed as a gentleman, yet manifestly was not one. Bolli was a big raw-jointed fellow, of a peasant type, having huge bones, but little flesh upon them. The red knuckles of his hands stood up like mountain-ridges. His face was young, but already he was half-bald. His sulky, light blue eyes followed Mailly's every movement with a somnolent suspiciousness. A leather-sheathed knife was stuck through his belt, but he carried no other weapon.

Mailly reviewed them quietly for a minute.

"Messieurs," he said at last, "we need not use many words about this business. M. Midard has told you my requirements, and my terms. Are you agreeable?"

"Why not?" responded Laharpe, smiling more than ever.

"That is well! But you know whom you will have to meet?"

"The police. What of it? I have no great friends among the police. They may go to the devil for me!"

"What weapons do you bear, besides your sword, M. Laharpe?"

"Poniard."

"And your companion?"

"Bah! he has knife, fist, knees, feet, and teeth!"

"What a savage! However, there is to be no firing—that is what I want to impress upon you. For the rest, you may fight as you please. Now then!—we leave for the Rue Quiberon at half-past nine, M. Laharpe. Have you received your advance of pay?"

Laharpe slapped his pocket.

"Respecting the plan of campaign," proceeded Mailly, "which you can translate downstairs for the benefit of M. Bolli, when you leave me in a minute. . . but first, are you a cool fighter?"

"It is my trade."

"What as to M. Bolli?"

"No. He is worth three others in a *mêlée*, but he does not understand how to come off."

"Then listen, M. Laharpe! I wish to arrive at a house, but it is probable that I shall be stopped by a party. Therefore, at the Rue Quiberon we separate. I will go ahead, you and your friend will shadow me. The street being dark, at the moment that I am halted by any, you shall creep up unremarked to join yourself, with M. Bolli, inconspicuously to the arresting force. If they evince suspicion, you must say that you have been sent as a reinforcement by M. d'Argenson. Then, when the scuffle begins, the pair of you will cry 'Treason! treason!' and strike out on all sides. In this way they will not know who is their friend, and who their enemy. Is my meaning clear!"

"Yes, and the manoeuvre is cleverly designed, and simple to execute."

"So leave me, and wait downstairs till I shall come for you. Here is a last pistole to drink with! . . . Stay!—regard me well!

We do not want mistakes in the dark."

"Have no fear!"

"And above all, do not let yourself be taken."

"On the other hand," interposed Midard, yawning, "do not show your faces here again without M. de Mailly. I shall take no excuses."

Laharpe expostulated warmly. "M. Midard, have you ever known me to desert a comrade? Well, then!"

"What wants Midard?" demanded Bolli, in a thick voice, looking from one to another. It was the first time that he had opened his mouth, and everybody laughed. Midard shepherded his men from the chamber, leaving Mailly to drink alone in the gathering dusk.

At five-and-twenty minutes after nine he went downstairs.

Bolli the Swede dozed with drooping head over a pewter tankard of Flemish ale. Laharpe leant back gracefully in a straight-backed chair tilted on its rear legs, his feet crossed, while holding a wine-glass lightly in his hand, conversing at his ease with Midard, who stood before him, gaping, inattentive, and saying little.

"Gentlemen!" said Mailly.

Laharpe rose, and stretched himself. He drank off his glass, set his hat on at an angle, then roused his companion with a hearty kick. Bolli uttered a guttural shriek, jumping high from his seat. Again all roared with laughter.

"O my mother! what is the time?" demanded the bemused man, and suddenly he peered suspiciously into the tankard, to assure himself that he had not been robbed of liquor during his slumber.

The room rang with hilarious shoutings. Mailly tapped sharply on the table.

"Gentlemen!"

Bolli scowled, and finished his ale at a gulp. Laharpe recovered his hat for him, then laughingly dragged him by the arm to the door. The three went out.

Within fifteen minutes they were at the entrance to the court on the north side of the Rue Quiberon which was the way to Passy's house. Mailly halted to give his final directions:

"Here is where we separate, M. Laharpe. Keep me in sight, but make the distance between us as great as possible. Continue well under the houses. I shall take the middle, to be seen the better. If I am attacked, come up at once."

"Forward, Captain!"

Mailly drew his blade and passed into the court. Night had already descended. His eyes searched the shadows on left and right for hostile shapes, but no one was abroad; the court was deserted. Pausing at its further extremity to discover if he were still being followed by his guard, and to indicate to them the new direction, he was startled by a voice which seemed but six inches from his ear:

"Where now?"

"To left, then right!" whispered back Mailly. He went on again.

Five minutes later, at the very top of the second court, and within hailing distance of Passy's house, not more than a few steps along the passage to the right, though invisible in the gloom, a black form stepped out of the surrounding night.

A low whistle sounded, and a second shape emerged.

"Who goes there?" demanded a cool bass voice.

Mailly pulled out his poniard. "Ah, good evening, M. Savary! I hope it is not Passy's abode you are guarding? I have an errand there."

"Our man!" said Savary to his companion. "Give the signal!"

The whistle blew shrilly twice. A third and a fourth figure detached themselves from the blackness. Mailly slowly backed, until his shoulder-blades touched the wall behind him.

"But what is all this, M. Savary?" he asked, as if astonished. "Does not one pass here?"

Two more men became substantial shapes. There were six in all. Mailly put himself on guard, with both weapons. Savary advanced cautiously.

"You see the odds, de Mailly! I advise you to give yourself

up."

"And why should I do that?"

"My orders are to take you; not to argue with you!"

"Do not come too close, that is all!"

"Listen! Have you a certain paper on you? If you have, produce it, and turn back home. I shall then not trouble you further."

"I do not like inquisitions in the King's highway, M. Savary. To ascertain what I carry upon my person, you must first disable me. I promise you I shall fight!"

"Go in, men!" ordered Savary, stepping aside.

Three came forward at a rush. There was barely light to see by. Mailly nimbly wheeled, so as to face but one adversary. Under the guard of this one he ducked, plunging with his left hand six inches of the steel of his poniard between his ribs. The fellow lurched and sank with a groan. At the same moment a huge shadow sprang forth with arm upraised, to thrust a knife into the chest of the second assailant. He also tumbled.

From Savary's rear, Laharpe's voice suddenly thundered, "Treason! treason! We are betrayed!"

Men passed like phantoms to and fro, in and out of the darkness. Bolli leapt upon Mailly's third attacker, who had half-turned to retreat. He gripped his throat with a bunch of bony fingers, bent him backwards, and stabbed him twice from behind. The archer fell across the body of his comrade.

"Where is Barthe?" cried Savary angrily.

"Here, Lieutenant!"

"Bring off the party in the Rue d'Heudicourt! Something has gone wrong."

Laharpe's voice sounded in Mailly's ear:

"Eight in all, and six more to come! I shall intercept the order."

He vanished at once. Simultaneously, Savary ran at Mailly with a sword. The latter parried the thrust, almost by good fortune, then riposted like lightning. Savary's blade clashed on to the pavement, while he clutched with an oath at his wounded arm.

A strange bellowing behind caused both to look round. Bolli the Swede was leaping and gesticulating like a madman, in pursuit of an archer, who doubtless thought that he had to do with the devil, since he had cast away whatever weapon he had come provided with, and was fleeing with bare hands uplifted in terror. The bellowing proceeded from Bolli's mouth, and perhaps resembled the insane yells of one of his own Berserk ancestors. . . . Suddenly Savary threw himself on Mailly with arms extended, with the apparent design to take him unwounded. Mailly jumped sideways. A dark form slid forward, to pass a rapier under Savary's exposed arm-pit. He cried out, writhed for an instant like an eel, then sank to the ground. The weight of his body snapped off the point of the sword, which his assailant had been unable to disengage.

"Thanks, Laharpe!" said Mailly. "This concludes the business, I believe."

"The man Barthe is accounted for."

"How many are left, besides that one of Bolli's?"

"Two."

"Let them go!"

"To bring up reinforcements! We don't commit stupidities like that, Captain. . . . Wait!"

"Stop, I tell you!—this is not a massacre. . . ."

But Laharpe had already disappeared. At the same instant Bolli straightened himself from stooping over his latest victim. He caught sight of Mailly, and turned with a whoop upon him.

"Not so fast, M. Bolli the Swede!" laughed the latter, retiring. "For me, I wish to sleep between sheets to-night."

"Yes, you will sleep well when I have finished with you! Come you here to me, pig! I will give you a bloody crown."

The smile faded from Mailly's lips, as he continued to fall back.

"Multiplied ass! Don't you know your friends?" The clash of blades near-by sounded. "Go and help Laharpe!"

"Laharpe!" . . . Bolli stopped to stare at Mailly.

Almost simultaneously the metallic hissing ceased, and next

moment Laharpe's shape emerged. He appeared rather crestfallen.

"Well?"

"I have settled one, but the other has been discreet."

"Was not your blade broken?"

"There are plenty of blades."

"So seven are down, and one has got away?"

"I could not be everywhere. You should have seconded me, Captain!"

"It does not matter, for I am arrived. However, he will fetch the other party in a minute. Retreat swiftly, with your madman!"

"And you?"

"My house is yonder! Be off with you!"

"You have arrived here, then; but you have still to get back. Midard will want to know how you have managed."

"I shall return by another way."

"So we are dismissed?"

"*Peste!* I keep saying so! Get back to Midard's and tell him I follow."

"If you are agreeable, I am," replied Laharpe coolly.

He saluted Mailly with a grin, and, grasping the stupefied Bolli by the arm, pulled him round, to vanish with him quickly in the darkness by the way they had come.

Mailly stepped alertly to the door of Passy's house. Having glanced to right and left, to assure himself that he was not followed, he lifted the latch.

XXIV

Precipitation

The interior was illuminated, and even before he had completely entered he was confronted by Pontchartrain, bearing a lighted candle.

"Ah, good evening, monseigneur!"

"What has been going on outside?" demanded the Minister quickly, drawing down his brows.

Mailly bent to bar the door before answering.

"*Ma foi!* a pitched battle, by the casualties. I myself tripped over three."

"You saw nothing of it, then?"

"All was quiet as I came in."

"Nevertheless, you have a drawn sword in your hand."

"And what should I have?—a walking-cane? Had I known what I was coming to, you would see me brandishing a cocked pistol as well. You should keep your back-yard in better order, monseigneur."

"So you have no information concerning this *fracas*?"

"Bah! the police will arrive directly, and then you will hear all about it. Let us get to business."

"Put up your sword, monsieur, and come with me."

He conducted Mailly through the two houses as far as the apartment with the upper recess, in which the Duke had fallen on the preceding evening. The recess itself, however, was curtained off. Pontchartrain remained standing by the table.

"Before we begin," he said, "you are going that journey to-morrow?"

"To Brest! Yes, monseigneur."

The Minister brought out a paper from his pocket.

"Here is Dumont's new commission as captain. Take it, and give it to him in person—that is, unless you find the promotion ridiculous, in which case we shall think of something else."

Mailly put the commission into his own pocket.

"And now declare what you have found out," said Pontchartrain.

"Passy is dead, by poison self-administered, monseigneur; and his wife, in consequence, will go to Brussels, not Spain. The conspiracy is finished. You have no more to fear."

"All this I know. What else?"

"That is the whole."

"My own people have told me as much already."

"Then you are well served. Yet as I have discovered all that was to be discovered, I believe that I have earned my recompense."

"What of a certain personage?"

Mailly shrugged his shoulders in silence.

"You will get no further sum from me, monsieur," said the Minister harshly.

"I do not say the fifteen hundred *louis*, but the five hundred."

"It is not my notion of investigating an affair to bring me back the story that one has died, and one is to go to Brussels—plain matters of fact that will presently be known to all the world. You must do better than that if you are to make your fortune in this trade."

"So be it, monseigneur. If you will not pay me, another may. Adieu!"

"Wait! What does this mean?"

"I say that if you were the only man in France with money, I should in all probability die poor; but there are others."

"M. d'Argenson?"

"Perhaps he."

"So he has tampered with you. Well then, let us hear what he wants, and what he offers for it. For me, I cannot see that your value is so exceptional that he should make you any very great proposals."

"'Tis all comparative. To one a half-million of livres will not appear so vast a sum; to another, yes."

Pontchartrain stared at him with open mouth.

“What half-million?”

“That is the figure.”

“It is not a likely story. For what should he pay you half-a-million?”

By way of answer, Mailly produced and unfolded the promise written by himself, and signed by Argenson, Mimizan, and Bartolmy. He passed it quizzically to the Minister.

“But what can this mean, monsieur?” demanded the latter, after a bewildered perusal.

Mailly repossessed himself of the paper from his yielding fingers. “*Pardieu!* I suppose that it means what it says. Five hundred thousand livres await me, when I shall send for them. It is plainly enough set down.”

“But the provision in case of your disappearance?”

“Conceive a dangerous service, monseigneur.”

“What service?”

“No fly-service, it is evident,” was the laughing reply.

Pontchartrain started to pace the room, with arms crossed behind his back. He stopped again before Mailly.

“You are right, monsieur. There can be but one service of so much worth to M. d’Argenson. That is my ruin. It is clear. . . . That you have brought this criminal engagement to me proves that you are an honest gentleman; and such is the sort that will always find favour in my eyes. You shall indeed have your fifteen hundred *louis*. I will retain the paper for safe keeping.”

“I thank you. But let us reckon. Fifteen hundred *louis*—that is thirty thousand livres. This, however, is a half-million.”

“It is what you have just demanded—or rather, you have demanded but the five hundred pieces. I am to give you fifteen.”

“That was for the discovery, monseigneur. This is another branch and concerns a contract. We are discussing the paper I have returned to my pocket.”

“Then you are not so honest, monsieur. Still, let us hear. What is your price?”

“Change the expression, if you please, monseigneur. It is distasteful.”

"Come, Monsieur Hypocrite, you are here to sell yourself, it seems, and I shall perhaps buy you, supposing that the figure named is not too inordinate. Let me hear it."

"*Peste!* I do not sell myself the least in the world. My honour is nearly all that I have. If I sell anything it is the paper you have seen."

"It is all one. Your price for it?"

"First let me understand your wishes, monseigneur. You require, for instance . . ."

"I require from you an absolute silence regarding your earliest interview with me in yonder room—that in which you were induced to engage yourself to a certain action."

"I shall promise it."

"I further require that henceforward you shall belong to me and not to the other."

"That is, I shall not belong to him. If hereafter you have offers to make to me relating to your service, I shall consider them."

"Then you shall refuse all moneys from M. d'Argenson."

"Save such alone, monseigneur, the refusal of which would awaken his suspicions."

"To that end only. Furthermore, I must hear in detail what this contrivance is, for your co-operation in which he is to pay you so prodigious a subsidy."

"No, monseigneur," replied Mailly firmly. "I have said that my honour is not included in the bargain. I have a right, perhaps, to repudiate a contract, but, having repudiated it, I have very certainly no right to impart to another the information which has gone towards its making. When M. d'Argenson shall freely present me with his secrets for no service at all in exchange, it may be that I shall consider myself at liberty to sell them—at present they are merely mine conditionally on my purchasing them with my assistance. 'Tis a point of honesty."

"So I am to buy in the dark, monsieur?"

"I have a thing to sell, but you need not buy it."

"I need not, assuredly. . . . However, I confide in the circumstance that this man is the most notorious trader in Paris, and that all his purchases are known close ones. Pass me simply your word, therefore, that the half-million connects itself with no other business than this of the Duke.”

“It is for nothing else.”

“I was sure of it. I say that he is the most dangerous villain in the realm. . . . Nevertheless, whoever may come to grief, you will do very well from the affair.”

Mailly set his hat on more firmly.

“Attend to me, monseigneur. Some twenty-six hours have passed since first I was summoned to you by Passy. During this period”—he counted with his fingers—“I have narrowly escaped death twice—if not thrice. I have been made to exert myself disagreeably three or four times more. I have been menaced by sundry with hanging, imprisonment, disgrace, exile, and the permanent displeasure of those greater than myself. I have been arrested, browbeaten, and insulted. I have lived constantly in suspense and trepidation; I have been compelled to unworthy tricks and expedients, unbecoming in a gentleman, merely in order to preserve my life and liberty. I have even been forced to expend money of my own. Now, all these annoyances have directly arisen from your summons to me of yesterday, which was, in fact, an arrest. Had not you sent for me, I should have spent this twenty-six hours like any other, and you may conceive that I should have preferred it. So that when you say that I shall do very well from the affair—why, *pardieu!* either you are joking, or you must be smoothing the way to a ridiculous offer; as to which, however, I shall inform you I have already arrived at a definition in my mind.”

Pontchartrain picked gloomily at his chin. “I have no doubt that you have been hardly used, monsieur, but the blame for that attaches to Passy, who is dead. He it was who persuaded me that you were this sort of man, and seemed to prove it. I am very sorry for it. However, you are still alive, and in a fair road to establish the beginnings of a fortune you might otherwise have missed. You assure me, upon your oath, that the business cannot go forward without you?”

"Upon my oath, monseigneur."

"Then where is your paper again? I shall retain it."

"There is no bargain struck yet."

"What do you demand? Understand, however, that I for my part have no half-millions to play with for hypothetical stakes."

"It is not money that I ask."

"What then?"

"A regiment, monseigneur."

"A *what?*"

"A regiment. As Minister, you have commands and offices at disposal. I do not know that it will cost you anything; but supposing that it does so, remember what it is that I have renounced in order to come to you."

"In order, monsieur, to serve the party of uprightness, in place of that of vicious intrigue and crime."

"Bah! I have no trick of reading hearts. I do not know in this world who is honest and who is not. If I have chosen you, it is because I am a soldier. I desire a command; and you can procure me one—whereas M. d'Argenson, I think, cannot."

Pontchartrain grumbled to himself for a space.

"You have served, then?"

"In six campaigns."

"Is your record fair?"

"Yes, and I will engage that few will object to the appointment."

"Nevertheless, there is great competition for these vacancies as they occur, monsieur."

"You have the King's ear. Whisper in it but thrice that my promotion has been too long delayed, and the thing is done. *Corbleu!* of what use is it to be Minister, if one cannot oblige friends?"

"His Majesty is suspicious of unknown men. You do not show yourself at Court, monsieur. That is enough to damn anyone."

"Just the reverse! 'Tis but a few weeks since I had the honour of a personal reception at Versailles. On that occasion His Majesty manifested marked favour to me. You will find that your recommendation will delight him."

"Then I will feel my way, monsieur, but I cannot promise."

Mailly yawned.

"As you please!"

"In fact, there are no regiments going at present."

"It is for you to decide."

The Minister resumed his pacing up and down. He stopped again.

"I will try to find something for you within six months."

"So let us get to work with pen and paper, monseigneur! The business will be shaped best while it is hot."

Pontchartrain rather reluctantly led the way to the curtained recess.

"Permit me to write!" offered Mailly, and, to the other's surprise, he slipped past him to occupy the single chair. He took up a freshly-cut quill, and a sheet of clean paper.

"I begin to acquire practice in the drawing of agreements, monseigneur! Without offence to anybody, the essential thing is to stop all holes by which our fox may escape!"

He dipped the quill in ink, and wrote, without pausing:

> *"I engage to purchase at my own charge for Gaston de Mailly, gentleman, Rue Carcassone 1, Paris, the command of a Regiment in the Armies of His Majesty the King of France, within six months of this 14th May, 1700. Failing which I engage to pay to the said Gaston de Mailly upon demand the sum of five hundred thousand livres. But this contract shall continue good only for as long as I shall retain my office of Secretary of State to His Majesty."*

"Sign, monseigneur!"

Pontchartrain read, started, scowled, arrested the exclamation which descended to his lips, and hesitated.

"The half-million alarms you!" said Mailly negligently, leaning back in the chair, and stretching his legs. "It is but a quickener. You will give me my regiment, and thus the money provision will fall to the ground.”

“You are an exceedingly clever gentleman, M. de Mailly!”

“Come, monseigneur! recollect that it is only owing to me that you are able to sign anything. They would have assassinated you.”

“That is true. Yet it is a bad business!”

“However, if you do not wish to sign, I shall not force you.”

Pontchartrain’s brow grew black. “Guard your language better, monsieur!”

“Only be quick to decide!”

“Well, I will sign.”

“And since there are to be no witnesses of your signature, monseigneur, it will be as well to affix your official seal to the paper, lest there be any dispute hereafter.”

The Minister said nothing, but reached behind him to take from a cupboard the implements of his authority. Mailly vacated the chair for him, and he seated himself. He signed, waxed, and sealed the agreement.

Still retaining it in his hand, he descended to the lower apartment, followed by Mailly.

“Give me the other, then, monsieur, and receive this.”

“What of the fifteen hundred *louis*, monseigneur?”

“That payment is superseded by your command.”

“*Mordieu!* a colonel without money for equipment and table— your *protégé* will cut a fine appearance. You cannot mean it.”

“You are unconscionable.”

“No, but needy.”

“You will take my money and my signature, and, for aught I know, you will desert to M. d’Argenson after all.”

“I repeat that M. d’Argenson cannot give me a regiment.”

Shrugging his shoulders, Pontchartrain again ascended to the recess. He returned, bearing a leather bag in either hand.

“Here is the money, then. It is very heavy, and I do not know how you will get it home.”

“Eh, I have a strong pair of shoulders for this sort of

commodity.”

Taking the bags from the Minister’s hands and reposing them on the table, he once more brought forth Argenson’s signed undertaking.

“Give it to me, then!” said Pontchartrain impatiently, seeing that Mailly hesitated. “Or have you thought of something else still which it is possible to demand?”

“No, I have finished, monseigneur; but I am anxious regarding the destination of this paper. You have said that you will retain it.”

“Certainly, since I have bought it.”

“On the contrary, you must burn it—here, in my presence.”

The Minister coloured, cast down his eye to the floor, and scowled.

“You believe that, by its aid, I shall play you false, monsieur?”

“I do not say so, but the peril which threatened you being now past, no one is to trouble you any more, and the case is better closed. M. d’Argenson is not to know that you have burnt it, so it will still hang over his head as a deterrent, supposing that he should wish to punish me for my failure to move with him. Let it be so, monseigneur.”

“I do not care.”

Mailly passed the agreement to the Minister for identification. He re-perused it, frowning; then, without a word, held it in the flame of a candle. Together they watched it consume. Afterwards, Mailly folded and put away the new engagement.

“One matter more, and I have done, monseigneur. Mme. la Duchesse. . . .”

“What of her?”

“I do not seek to penetrate your secrets, but it will be prudent not to pursue that affair. Chignet has seen her this morning. She wishes that all shall be brought suddenly to a close. Do not claim the acquaintance.”

“I am so little interested, that I do not even know that it was she who came here last night.”

Mailly winked significantly. “Be sure it was not she. It was any other lady in Paris whom you choose to settle upon, but it was not she. Let that be established."

Again Pontchartrain flushed.

"I thank you, and I will take the hint."

Mailly lifted the bags, stuffing one into each of his side-pockets. The Minister then seized a lighted candle, and they moved to leave the room.

"By the Rue d'Heudicourt, if you please, monseigneur."

"My people are on duty that way."

"I do not care for the stares of your lackeys, whereas, with this wealth, I desire no more fields of battle. It seems that assassins are abroad to-night."

Pontchartrain signed to him to wait, then went out by the door leading to the front of the house. In a few minutes he came back.

"The coast is clear. You may go."

They walked through the house, downstairs to the street entrance. The Minister opened the door. He returned Mailly's bow none too civilly.

The latter stepped out into the night, and the door was closed behind him immediately.

A few persons were still abroad, but all appeared occupied with their own destinations. His anticipation that he would be molested was in a fair way of becoming falsified, when he grew aware, to his surprised vexation, that a pair of dark forms really followed him noiselessly on the same side of the roadway. To afford the two the opportunity of manifesting their honesty, he halted. They also stopped. He went on again, and they resumed their motion.

He turned back to meet them.

"I believe that you do me the honour to accompany me, gentlemen? Do not protest to the contrary, for I am assured it is so. However, you may spare yourself the trouble. My business is concluded, I have done what I had to do, and I do not carry upon my person the thing which you want. Under these circumstances, you will oblige me the most by retreating. I am in a devilishly misanthropic humour. I wish to be alone. Let me see your backs, gentlemen, then, and instantly. Otherwise, I swear that I will draw upon the spot."

"Monsieur," replied one, "to prove to you that you are mistaken, we will go to where we wish to go by another road, although it will put us to inconvenience."

He raised his hat in the imperfect darkness, his companion followed suit, and a moment later the couple had become merged in the night, to be no more seen.

At Midard's, Mailly divided one hundred *louis* among the host himself, Laharpe, and Bolli the Swede.

XXV

The Last Actor

Dawn broke before he ventured to recross Paris to his own dwelling. He passed an hour or two in bed, then rose to breakfast. The sun shone brightly.

At eight, while he was still upon his meal, a gentleman was announced. Marbois was shown in. His appearance was amiable, but his eyes were more than ever like those of an eagle. They flashed, and took in all the apartment at once.

"My dear M. Marbois!" exclaimed Mailly cordially, having risen from the table. "What a delightful surprise! The day augurs well for me, when you are my first visitor. Have you breakfasted, or will you do so with me?"

"I have eaten, I thank you."

"You bring me intelligence from headquarters? Sit down. I am preparing for an expedition."

"There is no need for me to sit down, monsieur. I am simply instructed to give you this bag, which contains five hundred double-pistoles. M. d'Argenson begs you to accept them for the journey you speak of."

"Set it down, and let us talk."

"Then you do accept?"

"We shall see."

"He desires, in short, to be assured that last night's adventure has changed nothing."

"*Corbleu!* it was only amusing. Between ourselves," he added, lowering his voice, "what are the casualties?"

Marbois regarded him with a certain respectfulness.

"Between ourselves, monsieur, it was an exploit—on the wrong side, but still, it was one. Savary is badly hurt, but will recover. Of seven with him, one is dead, two have dangerous wounds, the neck of another is dislocated, two are lightly pricked, one only has come off unscratched. How many were with you?"

“Two.”

“Then their names are known.”

“Let them not be known, monsieur—that is my advice to M. d’Argenson. They are particular friends of mine.”

“I shall pass on the information. So you permit me to reassure the Lieutenant?”

“It will depend. What, for instance, is he doing on his side? Two women have been detained. Are they yet liberated?”

“Not yet.”

“You see. M. d’Argenson still hangs upon events, and so shall I.”

“But supposing that they are discharged?”

“You will then return to me, M. Marbois, and we will resume the conversation where it is now broken off.”

“And meanwhile this money . . .”

“Take it with you.”

Marbois placed a reluctant hand upon the bag.

“Stay!” said Mailly thoughtfully. “There is a better way still. I am for Brest, and it is possible to arrive at Brest through Normandy. Well, it seems that the home of the younger of the arrested ladies is in Caen. An excellent contrivance will be that I shall escort her there in person—thus I shall know that she is truly dismissed.”

“I will forward the suggestion to the proper quarter,” responded the other, with a concealed smile. “And what do you propose concerning her companion?”

“That she be enlarged, that is all. She is of an age to travel alone, supposing that it is still Brussels she desires.”

“You will remain in, however?”

“During a reasonable time, monsieur.”

Marbois saluted lightly, and made for the door, the bag in his hand.

“But where were you yourself last night, M. Marbois?” called out Mailly after him.

“I commanded the party of the Rue d’Heudicourt.”

“I congratulate myself upon my good fortune. Farewell,

monsieur!”

The officer departed, while Mailly sat down again to conclude his interrupted meal.

At half-past nine a knock sounded at the door, and, opening it, he found himself face-to-face with a man who appeared to be of the valet sort, though not wearing a livery. He held out a sealed letter.

Mailly, instead of at once breaking the seal, asked curiously:

“From whom, my friend?”

“You will perhaps ascertain from the interior, monsieur, but, if not, I am not directed to inform you. You are M. de Mailly?”

“Yes.”

“Then the letter is for you.”

He went away. Mailly tore open the fastening, to discover a fragrant perfume, and the following words, penned in a delicate writing, which could only be a woman’s:

> *“He who receives this is desired to ascend to the first room of the second floor of No. 26, Rue Taitbout, at a quarter past ten this morning, when it is possible that certain of his desires will be fulfilled and a measure of his inquisitiveness gratified.”*

Nothing was added, and there was no signature. For a foolish instant he permitted himself to believe that it was from Mdlle. Isabelle, but logic speedily showed him the absurdity of such a fancy.

“Bah! she is hardly yet free; and supposing that d’Argenson has provided her with this house for the purpose of an assignation, where is the need, when she already knows her way to these apartments? It is no letter for a young girl to write, fresh from the shocking death of a brother-in-law. It has an airiness, a sprightliness, a gaiety about it which comes from a more practised nature. It is not even from her sister, who, I will bet, feels small disposition to joke with me. No, but it is from that one whom I have not yet seen, and should extremely like to see, and who now offers of her own accord to satisfy this longing. It is Mdlle. Uranie Taranne who writes to me. She does so at the bidding of her employer M. d'Argenson. In short, he is dissatisfied with Marbois for his failure, and will not send him a second time. This time it shall be a clever woman's head that shall conclude the truce he suddenly desires. I have no objection. They cannot now harm me, and I own freely that the reports of her beauty and intelligence, coupled with the circumstance that she is, in a manner, the link of connection between all concerned in the case, have awakened within me a distinct enthusiasm for the making of her acquaintance. I shall retire at once to prepare for the visit."

He put on richer clothes, as for a call of ceremony, took his hat and sword, and by ten o'clock was outside the house, to start on foot for the *rendezvous*. At a quarter past the hour he was climbing the uncarpeted stairs of a residence whose dust, echoes and silence spoke of utter desertion; and yet the door had been left unbarred. The second flight brought him to a door which corresponded to the direction in his missive. He rapped sharply on its panel.

A female voice, tuned to sweetness, desired him to enter. Upon his doing so, he beheld reclining in a decrepit chair in an ancient room, a young and graceful lady, attired wholly in black, who smilingly held out her hand to him without rising. She was tall, slender, black-eyed and pale of skin, her neck was long, bare and beautiful, and she wore a deep veil, merely thrust off her eyes, so that she might have sat for an allegorical personification of tragic grief, but for the damning fault that there was no grief in her countenance at all, but only a gay, though discreetly-restrained mischievousness. Mailly bowed low, thinking her very handsome.

"I am M. de Mailly, mademoiselle, and I am here at your bidding."

"Will not you sit, monsieur? I do not rise, because I am very sure there need be no forms between us. You know me?"

He seated himself at a distance.

"That is, I am nearly positive that I have the honour at last to be received by Mdlle. Taranne."

"We should meet, for we are a pair. Have you guessed that I have been admiring your conduct exceedingly, monsieur? You alone, commencing in the dark, have ended by triumphing over us all. Not once have you suffered yourself to be tripped. M. d'Argenson says as much. I am as clever as you, perhaps, but then I have no courage—I am a coward, I am of no use at the moment of action."

"It is not required nor expected in a woman, mademoiselle. . . . Is it for the Duke that you wear mourning?"

"I do not affirm that he deserves it, but the unfortunate is dead, and all too few will hoist these colours for him."

"What do you desire of me, mademoiselle?"

"I am ambassador from M. d'Argenson. It appears that you scorn his money, and he is distressed in consequence."

"It is not that, but I say to you what I said to M. Marbois—first liberate Mdlle. Passy and her sister, then we will speak of money."

"They are liberated."

"I am glad to hear it."

"Mdlle. Passy is already upon her road to Brussels. You did not wish to meet her?"

"No, no—she is well departed. But the sister?"

"Your solicitude for the sister is perhaps greater than that for the other."

"For she is young, innocent and honest, all of which I do not know that we can say for the elder, mademoiselle. Where is she, then?"

"She is in this house, and you shall be brought to her when we have finished. You plan to carry her to Caen, it seems?"

"Yes, that is the best."

Mdlle. Taranne uttered a silver laugh, like a cascade of spring water.

"You propose to marry her, then?"

"Ah, mademoiselle, do not joke on this subject, I beg!" said Mailly, colouring violently. "Her brother-in-law lies dead, her sister is disgraced, and we must not talk of such matters in her connection."

"I do not joke in the least. In how many stages will you reach Caen?"

"I have not thought. In three or four."

"Then you travel with this young girl as her—brother?"

Mailly jumped up hastily, to make a gesture of self-reproach.

"Ah, imbecile that I am! . . . So it is impossible. . . ."

"No, it is still not impossible, monsieur. Listen. Mme. la Duchesse is for Fontainebleau to-morrow. I do not care greatly to accompany her thither, and she can well spare me for this one day. If you could accommodate your mind to a third in your chaise, I am a good friend to Mdlle. Passy, and, therefore, to her sister. It is also desirable that someone should relate to the mother what has really happened, for Mdlle. Barbesson knows nothing at all, while you, it may be, know too much."

"*Pardieu!* I know less than she, I fancy. I am completely unaware what Mdlle. Passy has attempted, and what she has not attempted."

The lady looked at Mailly strangely for a moment.

"Then I had better tell you that, lest you carry away with you a mistaken impression. It is no great while since M. le Comte de Pontchartrain caused to be conveyed to her, through her own husband, an infamous suggestion."

"That is very bad, mademoiselle!—And through her own husband. He begins to acquire for me the shape of one not belonging to our common humanity. . . . So she was to be revenged upon both?"

"But unequally; and the weapon was put in her hand; it was not of her seeking. It was Passy alone who conceived the robbery, and M. de Pontchartrain's death, to cover it. He alone determined upon the Duke to execute this assassination, as upon you to bear the brunt. . . ."

"There is another point I cannot understand. The Duke was

inveigled to the house in order to discover M. de Pontchartrain with his wife, as he believed, and then to slay him. But that was a crime in anger. To use for the purpose a sword which he knew to be mine, in order to father this assassination upon me—that was a murder in cold blood and by premeditation. I cannot reconcile the two."

"The Duke was informed that you were introduced to that house as bodyguard to the Minister for the purposes of his intrigue, and it rendered him furious against you."

"That is understandable. But why needed Passy two persons for the shouldering of one crime? He already had the Duke—wherefore was I brought in?"

"The Duke would have slipped out, and left him stranded. He was too great an individual. Being without conscience, he would not only have suffered Passy to hang, he would cheerfully have assisted in the process. Such was M. le Duc de Chastelnoir, monsieur, for whom the world tells me that I must clothe myself in black."

"You interest me amazingly, and I am very glad I came here this morning. But to return to Mdlle. Passy. . . ."

"She was intimate with all these designs, for her husband could not have managed without her. I am her friend, and I am resident in the Hôtel Chastelnoir. She fell in with them, therefore, but only to betray them. Everything, piece by piece, as it happened, was imparted by her to me, and by me to M. d'Argenson."

"She is really his mistress!" thought Mailly.

"In brief, she meant to ruin her husband, mademoiselle?"

"Her affection was dead, so her duty was to the law."

"But I do not yet see how she was to obtain her revenge upon M. de Pontchartrain, whom the law would protect."

"He would be sufficiently punished by being exhibited to all the world in his true shape—not as the upright and chaste Minister, for whom the flesh was merely a thing to be ignored, or subdued when troublesome; but as an obscene monster of iniquity, pursuing his horrid amours under cover of the dark, when men should think him at work. A seducer of the young wives of the nobility. All this must have been established by the presence of the Duke, who could only be there in quest of Mme. la Duchesse."

"Whereas, the Duchesse was ignorant of everything?"

"Yes," replied Mdlle. Taranne, smiling slyly and sweetly.

"And you mademoiselle, were to have occupied her post?"

"But my fortitude deserted me at the last—for less faults than which men have been shot in the field before this. I stayed at home, nor even attempted a message."

"It falls together with marvellous precision and clearness. Mdlle. Passy really was to have saved me, then, and I treated her very cavalierly. There remains only one whom I cannot as yet fit into the picture. M. d'Argenson himself—what have you to say of him?"

"He, too, is innocent, monsieur. He would have appeared to prevent the assassination. His greatest offence—I shall be quite frank with you—was to plan the throwing of everything into the utmost confusion, so that the King might observe how the Lieutenant of Police knew better what went on in the house of M. de Pontchartrain than did the Minister of the Secret Service himself. That would have been very disgraceful for a man whose office it is to be acquainted with all impending disorders. He might have fallen."

"Yet there was confusion enough, and he has done nothing."

"Can it really be that you are not able to distinguish the difference? To arrive in time to prevent an outrage, the design of which was unguessed by M. de Pontchartrain—that would have been triumphant; but to appear too late. . . ."

"And wherefore was he too late? . . . Let us hear what was actually to have happened, mademoiselle. Let us start from ten o'clock, when Mdlle. Passy had already stolen my sword, I had re-arrived upon the scene, and drugged wine stood prepared for me in the room which was to receive me. . . ."

"But Passy set the wine there, and you would have been dismissed unharmed."

"I do not now inquire about Mdlle. Passy or her husband, but about the Lieutenant. Or rather, I shall offer you my surmises, and you shall inform me if they are correct. I think, then, that M. d'Argenson has travelled a stage beyond your good friend, and that if he did not appear at the appointed place of meeting with her—for indubitably such a place must have been appointed—in time to receive her signal that all was ready for his entrance in force into the Minister's house, it was because he had found, doubtless to his extreme annoyance, a more pressing business elsewhither demanding his attendance. In fact, why should he care whether it were M. le Duc who slew the Minister, or the Minister who caused M. le Duc to be slain? In either he would have found his account. He discreetly held himself at a distance, therefore. But Mdlle. Passy, having discovered his retreat at last, and having—a little breathlessly, we shall suppose—communicated to him, with the rest of her intelligence, the news that a certain lady was secreted in that house whom he had designed not to be there; why, then he flew to arms at the devil's own speed, as we have witnessed."

Mdlle. Taranne reddened.

"But this is accusation without proof or probability, monsieur."

"You must understand that I have no great faith in your cowardice. I fancy that you are as resolute as another, and would not quietly stay at home when the motion of so many wheels depended upon your presence in the affair."

"So don't let us discuss it, monsieur. My absence has wrought you, at least, no injury."

"You are right, and we will jump to another tree. Tell me this, if you can, mademoiselle. M. de Pontchartrain feared the Duke sufficiently to wish to put him away. On what account?"

"Passy has worked upon both. The pretended intrigue between M. de Pontchartrain and the Duchesse has been faithfully reported to the Duke, and he has said terrifying things in consequence. The Minister is perhaps unused to threats."

Mailly said nothing more immediately, but walked to the

window, and remained looking out. He examined his thoughts, to find but one more question to be asked for the complete elucidation of the case.

"In her examination, Mdlle. Passy gave false testimony, mademoiselle, manifestly to shield the Duke from the charges to be brought against him. He was, then, really her lover?"

Mdlle. Taranne studied her finger-nails.

"Does this concern you, monsieur?"

"I am answered! . . . Come, then, where is your bag of double-pistoles that M. d'Argenson has sent? On the assurance that he will attempt no more against me, I shall now accept them."

"It is in the next room, with Mdlle. Barbesson."

"*Diable!* we have talked and talked, while she has all the time sat there neglected, and is doubtless upon the point of tears. Let us instantly go to her."

The other glanced at him, and laughed.

"You have met her but once, monsieur, and that by night?"

"But once to remark her, though twice in actuality. Wherefore the question?"

"She is adorable. Then am I, or not, to companion her to Caen?"

"If you please, mademoiselle!" And Mailly bowed, blushing a fine rose.

"You will discover that I am very enamoured of landscapes."

She got up from her chair with a singular grace of body, but he regarded only her remark.

"If we are to go to her, however," he responded. "I shall request you to disencumber your mind of any foolish notions which would but serve to prejudice me in Mademoiselle's judgment."

"So you are ignorant?"

"Of what?"

"Of her name. She is Mademoiselle Andromeda, and you are Monsieur Perseus. I assure you. It is you, and no other, that has rescued from captivity her sister and herself. At this moment, monsieur, she rehearses to herself the first warm speeches she is to address to you.”

“Then I shall undeceive her, that is all.”

“Do not do so in this house, I entreat, or we shall be here during the entire morning. She knows nothing. That is, she knows that Passy is dead, but not that the Duke is slain, and little of the rest. Her sister has so ordered it. On some other occasion, when you are better acquainted, you will relate to her the whole story; but not to-day.”

“As you will; but I do not like these constant innuendoes.”

“There is a remedy. Abandon your journey to Caen.”

“Pray cease this profitless talk, and let us go in to her,” said Mailly, with a rapid blinking of the eyes, which was in him a sign of excessive vexation.

Mdlle. Taranne preceded him laughingly to the door.

* * * * * *

In a second chamber, no bigger than the one they had quitted, they found Mdlle. Barbesson, gazing disconsolately through the closed window, her arms folded upon the high ledge. She turned about quickly at their entry.

“Oh, M. de Mailly!—it is really you, then.”

“Yes, mademoiselle; but what is of larger importance, it is you who ask it. I am glad to see you free.”

“Rachel and I will be grateful to you all our lives long, monsieur. I was absurd to go against your counsel. However, you see!—I have been with my sister, and all has turned out well. Are not you looking pale, monsieur?”

“It is possible. I have had but little sleep these two nights. The sea breezes will restore my colour. We are to travel all three in company, mademoiselle, unless you forbid.”

“I, forbid?—oh, heavens! I shall never forbid, be sure of that. Never again shall I dispute your judgement. Then you come with us, Mdlle. Taranne?”

“It is better so. Rachel desires me to speak with your mother.”

"Poor Rachel! I begged her to return home with me, but she is ashamed. Yet she has done nothing wrong, monsieur."

"I am convinced."

"I think that she will return to us later, when the first grief shall be worn. Is not my duty rather with her in Brussels, monsieur?"

"No, but with your mother. When we have brought you to her, it is she who will advise you your course. So your sister has started?"

"She is but now on the road."

"Then what subsistence has she?"

"M. d'Argenson, persuaded of her innocence by your facts, which you have set before him, monsieur, has been very liberal. He has furnished her forth with fifty thousand livres."

Mailly raised his brows, then stole a glance at Mdlle. Taranne, and smiled to himself. A shade of confusion appeared upon the latter's countenance.

"*Pardieu!* it is a fine thing to be the bosom friend of the mistress of a Lieutenant of Police, who has a Ministerial fifty thousand lying idle on his hands," he reflected. "I cannot explain as much to Mdlle. Isabelle, so must, it seems, continue to bask in her gratitude, which, in any case, provides an excellent foundation for a closer intimacy."

"I am very glad." he said aloud to Mdlle. Barbesson, in his simplest manner. Then turning immediately to the other:

"We forget the funds for our own journey, mademoiselle."

Mdlle. Taranne smiled, and pointed to the table, where lay the same bag of coin which he had obliged Marbois to carry back with him that morning.

"There is the money, monsieur."

"That is well. I shall annex it. And since we have concluded here, and the day wears on, we had better separate, to meet again. I go first to order the chaise and horses. At what hour will it be convenient to you to be ready for a start, mesdemoiselles?"

"At noon," replied Mdlle. Taranne. "Give yourself no concern for the preparations, however, for M. d'Argenson has seen to all.

The chaise, with Mdlle. Barbesson in it, will wait upon your lodging at midday. I myself will join you outside the gate, seeing that it will be undesirable that we are remarked in company together through Paris. The coachman will receive his instructions to that end. So now be off, M. de Mailly, and do what you have to do."

"*Au revoir!* monsieur," said her companion. "Do not forget to ask Mdlle. Antoinette to provide you with the end of a sausage, or some such matter, before setting forth, for it is ill-faring upon an empty stomach."

For perhaps the first time in his career, Mailly was without repartee.

"You overwhelm me, mademoiselle," he replied, flushing like a silly schoolboy. Then, angry at his own want of address, he bowed stiffly to the pair, and, taking up the bag of coin, left the room, to descend to the outer air.

"*Peste!* she already laughs at me, and I understand now why she refused to take bite in my apartments. The fare was too low. It is no matter,"—and he jingled his bag, as palpable proof of the ability of his parts, despite all ridicule—"I bear her no grudge, and she shall, during this journey at least, feast like a queen, for here is that which shall pay for it. Apropos, I visit in the first place Fleurus, to place all the rest under seal. Upon my return to Paris, I shall cogitate what may be done with such a beginning of wealth. I have no doubt that it can be made to breed more."

He arrived at the street-door, and passed outside. The morning was sweet, soft, perfumed, and dazzling with sunlight, causing him to look forward in exultant anticipation to the first stage of his excursion to the sea. Gazing upwards at the window of the room he had just quitted, which during his descent had been thrown up, he perceived two lovely laughing faces, framed in curls, bending over to exchange salutations with him in the silent language of the eyes. A moment afterwards, Mdlle. Taranne withdrew into the interior, and the girl with the hair of pale gold and he saw each other perhaps for the first time.

A Note on Money

Mailly handles several types of coin throughout his adventures, sometimes in large, sometimes in small quantities. The relative worth of the *louis* could change, but, as a general rule:

> 1 **double-pistole** = 2 **pistoles**
> 1 **louis** = (about) 20 **livres**
> 1 **pistole** = 10 **livres**
> 1 **livre** = 20 **sous**
> 1 **sous** = 12 **deniers**

As a rough guide, a day's food might cost around 10 sous. A soldier might earn 5 sous a day (though would be provided with food and drink in addition). A lackey — i.e., a liveried servant — might earn 100 livres a year.

A Note on Swearing

Mailly and his peers pepper their conversations with exclamations. The particular words used matter less than the fact that they're exclaiming/swearing, but if you want to know exactly what they're saying, here's a guide.

Broadly, there are two main categories of exclamation. The more blasphemous end in *-dieu,* and of course refer to God:

Pardieu! — By God!

Mordieu! — Death of God!

Cordieu! — Shortened form of "Body of God!" or "God's body!"

Tudieu! — Shortened form of "Par la vertu de Dieu", meaning "By the virtue of God!"

Mon Dieu! — My God!

Those that end in -bleu are less blasphemous variants on the -dieu words, replacing "God" with the meaningless-but-less-offensive "blue":

Parbleu! — By Blue!

Corbleu! — Body of Blue!

Morbleu! — Death of Blue!

And, to mop up the miscellaneous exclamations:

Certes! — Assuredly, certainly!

Diable! — Devil!

Peste! — Plague!

Deuce! — Less profane replacement for "Devil!"

Ma foi! — My faith!

("Prutsch!" seems to be a sound rather than a word.)

Explanatory Notes

1. For this, and other exclamations, see the Note on Swearing, p. 306.

2. For this, and other coins, see the Note on Money, p. 305.

3. Charles II of Spain, last of the Habsburg line, would in fact die on 1st November 1700, after naming Louis XIV's second-eldest grandson, Philip, Duke of Anjou, his heir. A "Grand Alliance" of England, Austria, the Dutch Republic, and the Holy Roman Empire opposed this by supporting Charles, the Archduke of Austria (later to become Holy Roman Emperor Charles VI), and the subsequent War of the Spanish Succession spanned the years 1702 to 1714.

4. The Palace of Versailles. It became the official seat of political power in France from 1682.

5. Relaxed, unconstrained

6. Lacedaemon was the region of Ancient Greece ruled by the city of Sparta. Also known as Laconia, it gives us the word "laconic", which is what madame is saying Mailly is.

7. Alexandre Bontemps (1626–1701) was the most senior of the four Premier *Valets-de-chambre* to Louis XIV. As a man who could control access to the King, he had a great deal of power in the Court of Versailles.

8. Marie Adélaïde of Savoy, the Duchess of Burgundy, was Louis XIV's granddaughter-in-law and a great favourite of his at court. She would have been 15 years old at the time of this novel. She would later give birth to Louis XIV's successor, Louis XV.

9. A signal, of drum or trumpet, from one warring side to another requesting talks, for instance to discuss terms of capitulation.

10. No doubt as part of the Nine Years War (1688–1697), fought between Louis XIV and a coalition of European nations, including Austria, the Dutch Republic, Spain, England, and the Holy Roman Empire. Mailly would have been 15 years old in 1688.

11. *Lives and Opinions of Eminent Philosophers* by Diogenes Laertius, written in the early third century.

12. He was playing (and losing badly at) piquet, a 2-player card game devised in the 16th century. Pique, repique and capot are bonus points earned when one player is winning all the tricks.

13. Jérôme Phélypeaux (1674–1747), Comte de Pontchartrain, Secretary of State for the Navy (1699–1715) and Secretary of State of the Maison du Roi from 1699 to 1715, whose duties included overseeing the policing and general administration of Paris and the provinces.

14. Cato the Younger (95–46 BCE), a Roman politician, had a reputation for scrupulous honesty.

15. Marcus Favonius (90–42 BCE), a Roman politician, was known for imitating his contemporary Cato the Younger in straightforwardness and honesty.

16. Charles VI of France lived from 1368 to 1422. Paris was the headquarters of a Lancastrian government from 1420 to 1436, following Henry V's campaigns in Northern France.

17. Louis Phélypeaux (1643–1727), Comte de Pontchartrain, Chancellor of France from 1699 to 1714. Jérôme Phélypeaux was his only son.

18. "Jérôme was physically unattractive, badly scarred from childhood smallpox, and blind in one eye…" — *Private Ambition and Political Alliances: The Phélypeaux de Pontchartrain Family and Louis XIV's Government, 1650-1715*, by Sara E Chapman (University Rochester Press, 2004), p. 27.

19. Marc-René de Voyer de Paulmy d'Argenson (1652–1721) was lieutenant-general of police from 1697 to 1718. From *The Memoirs of Louis XIV and His Court and of the Regency During by the Duke of Saint-Simon*, chapter LXXXIV: "I have already shown in these memoirs, that the late King had made of the lieutenant of police a species of secret and confidential minister; a sort of inquisitor, with important powers that brought him in constant relation with the King." He was widely feared. He was married to a kinswoman of de Pontchartrain.

20. An official letter, signed by the King and sealed with the

royal seal (*cachet*), invested with absolute authority.

21. Originally part of the Palais de la Cité (the Palace of the Kings of France), from the 14th century onwards, the Conciergerie housed the treasury and the Parlement of Paris (not a political body, but a court of appeals), as well as the judiciary. Part of it was used as a prison.

22. The Bastille was a famous fortress and prison in Paris. It, and the Fortress of Pignerol (now Pinerolo, in Italy), both held the famed Man in the Iron Mask, an unidentified prisoner held during Louis XIV's reign, who also features in the last of Alexandre Dumas's novels about his *Three Musketeers* hero, d'Artagnan.

23. The "gentleman" is Paris. After he shoots Achilles with a poisoned arrow, Venus (Aphrodite) transports Paris to safety back inside the walls of Troy. Mailly is, perhaps, hoping to win Pontchartrain's loyalty by likening himself to the namesake of the city the Comte has responsibility over.

24. With the Greeks preparing to attack Troy, Thetis disguised her son Achilles as a woman and hid him among the daughters of King Lycomedes, to prevent his taking part. Learning of this, Odysseus entered Lycomedes's court disguised as a pedlar, and among the wares he set before the King's daughters were weapons. At this moment, one of Odysseus's companions blew a horn, as though an attack were under way, and Achilles revealed his true identity by taking up a weapon.

25. The Palace of Fontainebleau was a residence and hunting lodge for the Kings of France. Louis XIV (and his court) went there every autumn.

26. Saint Denis is the patron saint of Paris.

27. Masters of Requests were officials who judged petitions to be laid before the King by commoners. In France at the time of Louis XIV, there would have been about eighty such.

28. First President of the Parlement of Paris (the court of appeal at the Conciergerie) was a high magistrate appointed by the King, part of whose role was to moderate between the King and the Parlement. Interestingly, considering how often Achilles has appeared in these footnotes, in 1700 the First President was

one Achille III de Harlay.

29. Cylindrical packets, most often of coin.

30. The three most infamous Emperors of Rome in terms of wanton cruelty, tyranny, and depravity. Caligula ruled from 37–41 CE; Nero from 54 to 68 CE; Commodus at first co-ruled with his father, Marcus Aurelius, from 177 CE, then alone from 180 to 192 CE.

31. Valeria Messalina, the wife of the Roman Emperor Claudius (who ruled from 41 to 54 CE), had a historical reputation for political intrigue, taking many lovers, and having her enemies killed.

About David Lindsay

David Lindsay (1876–1945) is best known for his first novel, *A Voyage to Arcturus*. Published in 1920, it has been called "the greatest imaginative work of the twentieth century" (Colin Wilson), "a stupendous ontological fable" (E H Visiak), "a masterpiece... an extraordinary work" (Clive Barker), "that shattering, intolerable, and irresistible work" (C S Lewis), and "less a novel than it is private kabbalah" (Alan Moore). John Grant, in *The Encyclopedia of Fantasy*, called it "a masterpiece of allegorical fantasy".

Lindsay himself said that as long as publishing existed he would have readers, however few, and has been proved right. *A Voyage to Arcturus*, and his subsequent novels *The Haunted Woman* (1922), *Sphinx* (1923), *The Adventures of Monsieur de Mailly* (1926) and *Devil's Tor* (1932), have found a growing audience of devotees, enabling his unpublished novels (*The Violet Apple* and the unfinished *The Witch*) to be brought out in the 1970s. He has been translated into French, German, Spanish, Dutch, Bulgarian, Russian, Japanese, Catalan, Romanian and Turkish.